Looking For Trouble

K'Barthan Series: Part 4

Here are some things readers have said about the M T McGuire's writing.

Looking For Trouble, K'Barthan Series: Part 4

"It's oozing with charm but it's not a sweet, chintzy charm. It's charm with a side order of sarcasm and drizzled with attitude. You can't help but be drawn in. I loved every moment... "
– Ignite (Amazon top 500 reviewer).

"A nice light read and it has the irony and funny bits just right. Similar in overall tone to Terry Pratchett. Good Read." – Reader review on Amazon.

K'Barthan Series: Part 1

"The UK has another excellent SF/ Fantasy Comedy Author, if you enjoyed the work of Adams and Pratchett – then get this book, you will love it. – Reader review on Amazon.

K'Barthan Series: Part 2

"The K'Barthan series is the kind of writing that gets me excited about reading and inspires me to write!" – Kate Policani, Awesome Indies reviewer.

The K'Barthan Series, Generally

"This whole series is absolutely amazing. I got the first one just to kill time, and I bought the other three right away. I could not put them down. I read them in every spare moment. They have a wonderful story and very relatable characters. – Reader review on Google Books.

"I was quite unexpectedly delighted to find a story brimming with the sort of whimsy and character that Sir Terry Pratchett himself would give approval to ... The happiest accident I've had in some time." – Reader review on Amazon.

Looking For Trouble

K'Barthan Series: Part 4

M T McGuire

HAMGEE UNIVERSITY PRESS

First published in 2014 by
Hamgee University Press,
www.Hamgee.co.uk
This version February, 2021

ISBN 978-1-907809-22-4

This book is written in British English, with a bit of light swearing
UK film rating of this book: PG (parental guidance)

Written by M T McGuire
Designed and set by M T McGuire
Published by Hamgee University Press
Edited by Kate Jackson and Mike Rose-Steel
Cover design by A Trouble Halved
This copy printed by Lightning Source UK Ltd, Milton Keynes

For
Mum and Dad and my family for all their support.

M T McGuire is around 50 years old but still checks inside unfamiliar wardrobes for a gateway to Narnia.

Thank you for buying this book.
If you enjoyed it you can keep up with news of the author online by visiting www.hamgee.co.uk

You can also sign up for the M T McGuire mailing list by visiting www.hamgee.co.uk/freebook
or bling your life with K'Barthan merchandise at http://bit.ly/UHSUshop

Thank you to:-
The Editors – Kate Jackson and Mike Rose-Steel for help, advice and support over and above the call of duty.
Press Officer and Ninja Sister In-Law – Emily Bell; ditto
The Beta Readers – Emily Bell, Kel Crist, Geoff Hughes, Hayley Humphrey, Claire McGahan, Kath (Ignite) Middleton, Kate Policani, David Staniforth and Dr R J Westwell.
Gerard, at ATH for understanding exactly what I wanted for the cover ... as usual.

And thanks to my husband, son and family, for their support and understanding.

Chapter 1

The Pan headed for the old Palace and Doctor Dot at a half jog. It would take a good forty minutes to walk there, and he wasn't sure he had them. He quickened his pace. How long would he take to blag his way in to see Doctor Dot? He didn't think Trev could afford for him to take long. When he reached the marketplace at the end of Turnadot Street, he stopped for a moment – wondering if he could save some time by going over the roofs and whether he dared with a duff arm. How he wished he had the SE2, yearned for it even, but Captain Snow had the keys and …

Hang on. Captain Snow had one set of keys but he didn't have the spares. The Pan had left those with Snurd when the SE2 had gone in for the deluxe rebuild Sir Robin and the Underground had paid for: The Pan's reward for persuading the Mervinettes to carry out a robbery at the Bank of Grongolia. Breathlessly, he pulled the envelope from his pocket and tore it open.

Sure enough, there were two sets of spare keys to his snurd, and a compliments slip upon which, someone had written, *'spare keys plus an extra set for emergencies, I know what you're like – cheers, Gerry'*. The Pan chuckled. Gerry was one of the best mechanics at Snurd and he had rebuilt the SE2 for his apprenticeship piece. Clearly his ability to read his customers matched his skill in the workshop. Captain Snow may have taken one set of keys to the SE2 but he was using a plastic facsimile of The Pan's fingerprint. Snurd had just returned the other set, plus a spare and, obviously, The Pan had his fingerprints with him.

"I wonder …" said The Pan quietly. "Worth a try …"

Smiling to himself, he pressed the homing button. He'd give it five minutes. He couldn't afford any longer. And he wasn't certain the SE2 would come. And he'd better hide, too, just in case it did, and arrived with Captain Snow in situ.

Too late. Before he'd even moved, the SE2 was parked next to him.

Uncanny.

"Have you been following me?" he asked it.

For Arnold's sake, what was he doing? Of course it hadn't, it was a machine.

Cluck, said a voice.

"No, I meant the SE2, here. But thank you for letting me get on with it for the last few hours."

Cluck. Brrrrugh. Cluck. The Pan had the distinct impression that the first two clucks meant something like, 'some of us have to sleep' and the third was along the lines of 'nice wheels'. The snurd revved its engine a tiny bit faster for a second and if he hadn't known it was inanimate, and a machine, The Pan would have sworn that it too, had heard the chicken and was acting a little bit smug.

For a moment he hesitated. The SE2 had arrived suspiciously fast. Might this be a trap? Was Captain Snow about to pop up, the minute The Pan got in, and accuse him of 'stealing' his own wheels? No. He trusted the snurd. He ran his hand affectionately along the door, opened it and got in. The seat was as far back as it would go. Only natural, Captain Snow was a lot taller than he was. He adjusted it to his normal driving position and the snurd's doors locked with a click.

"Ah," said The Pan. "That's not normal."

Cluck?

"No." A red light began to flash on the dash. "Neither is that."

Cluck?

"This is a safety message," the SE2's sexy voice intoned, "a security anomaly has been detected which is ..." there was a pause and a different robotic voice said, "error number PF16: ident mismatch." The SE2's normal voice resumed, "An attempted theft of this vehicle is suspected. Fingerprint ident confirmed, initiating retinal scan. Please remain calm, assume normal driving position and face forward, with your head still, until the scan is complete."

Cluck?

The Pan shrugged.

"Please remain still," said the snurd. "Re-initialising retinal scan."

"Sorry," said The Pan.

Cluck?

"Search me. I didn't know it had ever scanned my retina. Now I'm wondering what else it looks at."

"Retinal scan complete. You are cleared to drive."

"Very strange." Never mind, at least The Pan would get to Doctor Dot. He pulled out into the traffic.

"Initialising scan of position and technique. Please continue driving," said the SE2.

"Arnold," said The Pan anxiously, but he did as he was told.

"Positional check and sub-check complete, loading for nervousness applied and checked. Vehicle ownership confirmed."

Cluck?

"I hope so," said The Pan.

"Welcome back, Pan of Hamgee."

The light on the dashboard stopped flashing and the doors unlocked. Good.

The Pan felt very strange driving up to the allotted parking section for non-Grongles in the square in front of the Security HQ. It was small because the idea of K'Barthans driving snurds was frowned upon even if it was an accepted reality that many did. Self-park was not allowed in this area, all snurds had to be left in plain view. Typical. Then again, after the mischief the SE2 had done to Lord Vernon's window The Pan did understand the reasoning behind this policy.

The Pan cruised round the parking area a couple of times searching for a space and then put the SE2 into a handbrake turn, sliding it, sideways, into the only spot, a very tight one with less than a couple of inches each end. He killed the engine and got out with the slight swagger of a man who knows he's just done something pretty cool. Sideways parking was alright for a lorry, but it wasn't as if anyone who could drive needed that sort of gimmick.

Cluck?

Ah yes. Thinking about it, sideways unpark … The Pan hoped one of the other snurds either side of his would be gone by the time he left or getting out of the space might take several minutes of seriously uncool backwards and forwards manoeuvring.

Cluck, said the chicken.

He strolled up to the checkpoint, trying to appear confident but not cocky, and stopped in front of the red and white pole which blocked the route into the old Palace. The Pan had hoped it might be staffed by a member of the Imperial Guard but unfortunately it was manned – or at least, Grongled – by a member of the army. He was the epitome of the jobsworth selected for this type of duty; his red and black uniform was pristine and his brass buttons blindingly shiny. The Pan suspected his intellect was of a slightly less blinding type that applied rules with officious zeal and no room for argument.

"What do you want?" he said.

"Good morning," said The Pan. "I'm here to see Doctor Dot, she's the Imperial Guard's MO."

"I know who she is, you piece of K'Barthan rubbish. Why d'you think she'd want to see you?"

"She treated me and she said if I had any questions I should come back. So, I do have a rather urgent—"

"Yeh yeh," the guard interrupted him. "Now sling yer hook."

"Wait. Please, I'm telling the truth. She set my collarbone."

The guard looked him up and down.

"And I'm your fairy godmother. I've got better things to do with my time than listen to a load of cobblers from some posy chancer who just turned up in a hairdresser's snurd. I tell you what though, K'Barthan nothing, I'm looking forward to seeing how you get your wheels out of that spot."

"I'm sure you are." The Pan tried to summon up some semblance of natural authority. "Listen," he said calmly. "I happen to be a close friend of Lord Vernon. You can check it on GNN Local. He gave me a pub to run for dobbing in the last of the Underground. I'm guessing if I told my mate Vern that you'd ticked me off he might be annoyed."

The guard sighed. The Pan hoped it was a good sign and that calling Lord Vernon 'Vern' hadn't been laying it on too thick. But the TV vans had been there, outside the Parrot, and they'd filmed Lord Vernon announcing his candidature – as well as The Pan playing his own shameful part. He had no idea if all the footage had been broadcast or not. The upcoming installation was big news, but they might not have shown any more than Lord Vernon making the actual announcement.

"Wait here," said the guard. He walked back to a sentry post and rapped on the window, which was opened by a huge and surly Grongle. After a brief conversation, one of them got out a standard army issue mobile phone and dialled. There was a brief conversation and then he put the phone back in a pouch on his belt. Then the other one got out a standard issue organiser and they conferred for a minute, examining the screen. The Pan waited nervously, trying to look calm and at ease. Eventually the guard came back. "Looks like you're right. What with you parking like a joyrider I thought you was some chancer yanking my chain but blow me down if you aren't telling the truth. Don't get ideas though, it was only GNN Local and not even the whole city, just your little scum-laden patch." He shook his head, "Unbelievable. Follow me." He didn't raise the barrier so, being careful to use his good arm, The Pan vaulted over it and followed him into the building.

The guard showed him into an anonymous room.

"She'll be down in a minute." He went out and locked the door.

Chapter 2

Gladys sat quietly on the filthy straw mattress in her prison. After several bouts of 'training', Humbert had returned, although she didn't take much notice of what he was carrying until Ada jumped up.

"Bingo!" she cried. "Gladys, dear, have a look at this. I knew he would remember in the end."

"Yer, I has to hand it to you Ada, Humbert has done you proud," she said, although thinking about it … "is you thinking that key is the key?"

"There's only one way to find out," said Ada, with a twinkle.

The two of them made their way over to the door and listened. Slop and porridge had been finished some time ago, now all was quiet. Gladys nudged Ada.

"Go on then."

As Ada put the key in the lock, even Humbert was silent. Slowly, carefully she turned it; there was a grinding noise and a click.

"Ooo," squeaked Ada.

"Yer," whispered Gladys. She stopped to consider. Their part of the plan was to stay in the Palace, but nobody said anything about moving from room to room, especially if they could do so without being noticed. "I reckons we oughter go and explore."

"It might be fun," said Ada, "although, what if they notice it's missing?"

"Putty in a box," said Humbert, "Polly put it in."

Gladys sucked the air in through her teeth. Surely Humbert hadn't remembered that much of his training?

"You sayin' that you is giving us a copy, Humbert?" she asked.

"Buff my knobs!" said Humbert, sidling towards her.

"What does you reckon, Ada?" asked Gladys. The key was certainly shiny, with the gleam of one newly forged.

"Humbert is a highly intelligent, highly trained espionage tool."

More of the tool than espionage, Gladys thought, and chided herself for being uncharitable.

"Winkle my trussocks!" said Humbert, enigmatically. He went over to one of the beds and began to jump up and down, shouting, "Futtocks away!"

"I reckons he wants ter stay here," said Gladys.

"Yes, Gladys dear, but what about us? Should we stay here?"

Gladys thought about it some more.

"Alright. If we goes, what is the Grongles going ter do if they catches us?"

"Well, we know that Gladys, dear, they'll try us and behead us."

OK, that was quite bad but since Gladys suspected she and Ada were going to be tried and beheaded quite soon anyway, it was all relative. There was a brief silence as the pair of them thought this through.

"Humph," said Gladys with a smile, "I reckons we oughter go an' cause some trouble."

"Oh yes!" Ada beamed, clapping her hands together gleefully, "Come along Humbert."

"Snack time for big boy!" squawked the parrot, jumping up and down on Ada's mattress.

"Yer …" said Gladys slowly.

"Hmm, perhaps it's for the best if we leave him to it."

"Yer, we is only makin' an early foray."

"Exactly, we won't be long, will we?" said Ada.

"Nah," said Gladys.

Slowly, stealthily, or at least, as stealthily as two slightly arthritic septuagenarians could, they swung the door open. Like many elderly ladies, Ada and Gladys could both mouth conversations at one another without actually making any noise.

"Shall I lock it again?" mouthed Ada.

"Just put it to, in case we is in a hurry when we comes back."

Ada carefully closed the door, without locking it, and then the two old ladies made their way along the hall. At the closed door of the guardroom, they stopped to listen.

They tiptoed past and moved on. Gladys and Ada walked the length of a corridor, rounded a corner and descended a set of stairs. Now that she judged them to be far enough away, Gladys started looking around for somewhere where they could take stock unobserved. This corridor seemed to be disused.

"Tsk, will you look at them skirtings. 'S disgusting."

"I quite agree, dear, so much dust and yet the paintwork is all brand new. I'm almost tempted to clean the place up."

Gladys put her finger up in the air excitedly.

"Ada, you is a gen-gen- you is a very clever lady. I has an idea." She backtracked to an 'invisible' door in the wall they'd just passed and tried it. It was unlocked. Once opened, the old ladies discovered it belonged to the cleaners. There was a trolley full of equipment: brooms, dusters, mops and buckets and even better, two nylon gingham pinnies hung behind the door, one pink and one green.

"I reckons this is goin' ter do us. The only thing more invisible than two old ladies, is two old ladies what is disguised as cleaners."

"Absolutely, dear," said Ada as she took the pink pinny from the hanger and held the green one out to Gladys. "It's a clean pinny too."

They backed the trolley out of the cupboard, making sure they shut the door behind them, and pushed it down the hall.

"Oh look, what a lovely view onto the quadrangle," said Ada and they stopped by one of the windows.

"Yer, they done the bedding nice this year."

Gladys squinted over at the clock tower.

"I reckons we has an hour. Could be longer but we has to be careful."

"Yes dear. A quick trip this time, to get our bearings. Isn't it wonderful that Humbert remembered so much of his training?"

"Yer," said Gladys. Humbert had proved uncharacteristically well schooled this time and she was on the lookout for a snag.

"Well, we have the whole Palace, where shall we go?"

Gladys sniffed.

"Staff bathhouse, judging by the smell of us," she said. "We isn't going ter blend in if we smells like a muck heap. We has got the trolley. We can tell 'em we has got soiled in the line of duty."

Chapter 3

The Pan was just beginning to panic when the door was unlocked and a member of the Imperial Guard arrived.

"Good morning, sir," he said.

"Hello," said The Pan.

"If you'd like to follow me, I will take you to Doctor Dot."

The Pan nervously followed the guard further into the building, along a maze of corridors. Were it not for the artworks, he would have suspected he was being led in circles. As it was, each identical corridor was marked out with a different piece of historic K'Barthan art. The Pan reckoned most of the things he saw were looted from other parts of the country. The Palace had been the seat of government for 2,000 years, so it would be stuffed with antiques and works of art before the Grongles even started on it. Yeh, and the best stuff would have been shipped to private homes in Grongolia by this time. Eventually the guard brought him to a door labelled 'Medical Officer' and knocked.

"Come in."

"Patient to see you, ma'am," said The Pan's escort and then ushered him into the room and left.

The Pan found himself in a standard doctor's consulting room. There was an examination table, partly obscured by a curtain in one corner. Near to it was a cupboard and shelves full of salves, lubricants, syringes, rubber gloves and those flat wooden lolly stick type things they poke in your throat when they want you to say 'Ah'. Next to them was a basin and above it a locked cupboard – the drugs cupboard, presumably. Abutting the basin was another few feet of workbench and at a right angle, sticking out into the room, was a desk. Behind the desk, sitting on a swivel chair, was Doctor Dot. She was working at a laptop computer when The Pan arrived. Without her hat, her curls tumbled around her face with random abandon. She stood up and walked round to greet him.

"Hello young man."

She smiled and the laughter lines around her eyes crinkled as the two of them shook hands.

"Hi," said The Pan. Now he was here, he wasn't quite sure what to say.

"I was worried the guy outside wasn't going to let me in."

"Yes well, the sentries are all army." She smiled. "We're not that fussy about who we recruit into the Imperial Guard but we do at least require folk with an IQ that's into double figures."

The Pan laughed before he could stop himself.

"Are you supposed to say stuff like that to people like me?"

"No. But I'm a doctor first and a Guard second."

That sounded hopeful.

"Does General Moteurs know that?"

She smiled.

"I'd say he does or I wouldn't be here and neither would you. So. What's the problem? You look in very good shape."

"I am, thank you. You've fixed me up pretty well. The thing is, I … I probably shouldn't be here but I need your help." She looked straight into his eyes. Confident, perhaps a dash intrigued and totally unperturbed. It was unsettling.

"Why?" she asked

"Can I talk to you in confidence?"

"I'm a doctor and we're having a consultation. In this situation, everyone talks to me in confidence."

"Right."

"So, young man, I'm thinking this might not be about your shoulder."

"It isn't."

"How did I guess? OK. Carry on."

"Are we still consulting?"

"Yes."

"And this office isn't bugged?"

"No."

"OK. I have a friend who is seriously ill."

"Then I suggest you take him to a doctor."

"Well now, there's the thing, you see … I can't."

"Why not?"

"He isn't registered. He moved here recently and he's informed his old doctor but he hasn't found a new one."

"That doesn't matter. Until they know where to send them to, the old practice will have to keep his notes."

"They haven't."

"They will have. Don't worry, I'll look him up." She went back round behind the desk and jiggled the mouse to wake her laptop. "Do you have his K'Barthan health service number?"

"Not with me. The thing is, it doesn't really help, though, because …" How much should he tell her? He trusted her to help Trev because he was sick but he didn't want to put her in a difficult position. OK, as little information as possible then. "Alright, look, he's dead."

"Then I suggest you bury him."

"No, not actually dead. I meant more, officially dead."

"That's not one I've heard before."

"He is unregistered because the authorities believe he died this morning."

"Then take him to his doctor, the paperwork won't have come through yet."

"Well, I think he's rather too conspicuously dead for that."

Again Doctor Dot looked The Pan in the eye. Her expression was still unfazed, serene even, but now there was a hint of stern.

"What does that mean?"

"He 'died' rather publicly."

"What?" She stood behind the desk, glaring at him. She was definitely stern, or worse, angry.

"He was in the wrong place at the wrong time, that's all," said The Pan. "Alright, look, thinking about this, I shouldn't have come here, but last time we met, you said that you'd sworn an oath to heal and I guess I just hoped that …" While he paused to compose himself she watched him intently. He doubted she was missing much. "I'm sorry I shouldn't have put you in this position. I—"

"Never mind that, how sick is he?" she demanded. Suddenly there was an urgency to her tone that hadn't been there before. It made The Pan nervous.

"He has a broken leg. There's …" The Pan could feel himself going pale at the thought of Trev's wound. "The bone has broken the skin and—"

"How did it happen?"

"He was beaten up." He didn't want to give her many details. "They put his leg over a step, held him there and jumped on it."

"Animals! How do people do this to one another? OK. How does he look?"

"Ill—"

"Gods man! I realise that. I mean the wound."

"Smeck. Sorry. It's bruised, red, angry – and it smells. There are these marks: red lines, running along his leg. My friend has some basic first-aid training. She thought that was bad."

"It is." Doctor Dot hefted her rucksack onto the table. "Is he running a temperature?"

"Yes. I think so."

She started moving around the room opening drawers and cupboards collecting bottles, bandages, dressings and other strange-looking pieces of equipment, which she lined up on her desk.

"Is he conscious?"

"No."

Doctor Dot paused to run her eye over the stuff she'd collected thus far and sighed.

She looked The Pan up and down, although with her being Grongolian it was mostly down.

"I want to bring the right kit. If I don't then, from what you're telling me, your friend may die. You should also understand that treating the natives is one thing but if I'm caught dispensing treatment to an illegal, I'll be shot. So, if I'm to cover my actions adequately, I need something from you."

"Alright."

"Good. While I pack, I need you to drop the secret squirrel cobblers you're spouting and tell me the truth: everything you know about what happened and who's involved."

The Pan weighed up the pros and cons. Arguments against telling her everything? Nearly all of them except for the big one: that she'd asked him and if he didn't she might not help.

Tight-lipped, she went back to her packing, searching the cupboard behind her desk.

"Are we still consulting?" he asked.

"Yes," she said over her shoulder.

"I …" he stopped, unsure.

"If it helps you to relax," she said, as she went to rummage through a chest of drawers on the other side of the room, "after I treated you down in the cells, General Moteurs showed me your file." She removed some vacuum-packed surgical instruments, putting them on the desk with the rest of the things. "He thought I might see you again."

"Did he?"

"Yes."

"Alright. My friend is blacklisted. He was here, in custody, when Captain Snow and his goons broke his leg for him. He was in a lot of pain and he lost consciousness. He thinks they tipped the slop bucket over it and rubbed it in while he was out. It certainly smells like it. We've washed it, disinfected it as best we could and put it in a splint. When I left he was out cold but he needs some serious expertise. And drugs. Stuff I can't get."

"OK. Now we're getting somewhere. Not a good place but somewhere," said Doctor Dot. She was shoving things into the bag with a great deal of vehemence.

"You did ask," said The Pan.

"Yes. I did." The bag was getting a proper pasting. "Thank you for your honesty." Nothing was left to pack now except for five bottles. "Wait here," she said and disappeared into the corridor. For a few fearful moments The Pan wondered if she'd gone to report him. He was relieved when she returned, in moments, with a big bag of cotton wool and some socks. She put each one of the bottles into one of the socks. "Here, you can help me with this," she said as she packed the first sock with cotton wool, "it'll stop them breaking."

The Pan did as he was told.

"There," she said as she put them into the bag. "That should do it. I will need an assistant on this one, someone who's not going to faint at the sight of blood. Is your first-aider contact up to that or will I need to bring my own?"

The last thing The Pan wanted was to risk letting some random Grongle into the Parrot. Not even a Grongle who worked for Doctor Dot.

"I think my friend can provide the help you need," said The Pan, hoping he wasn't putting Lucy on the spot.

"Good. OK, I'm ready. Lead on."

He hesitated.

"My snurd's outside. But I think I may need your help leaving the building."

"What? My army colleagues? Tell me you didn't break in here?"

"No-no. I'm talking about finding the exit."

Chapter 4

Sitting in an internet café in Ning Dang Po, Simon took a bite of the bun he'd ordered as a celebratory breakfast and took a slug of coffee.

He, Nar and the Professor had set themselves up as users on a forum. They were now conducting any conversation about the portal they hoped to build by private message. By using the cloaked tablet at the Professor's and Nar's end and an anonymous internet café terminal at Simon's, they had managed a reasonable degree of privacy. He signed into his account and sent a private message to the Professor and Nar.

The Professor's account replied to Simon's message at once. It could equally have been Nar. Simon's department back at HQ was under surveillance so Nar and the Professor had separate accounts but they only had one unmonitored internet terminal between them. Whichever account was replying to him, Simon knew they would both be there. He typed again:

'I have found the pub.'

'Marvellous. That was quick.' The Professor – it had to be the Professor because Nar didn't use the word 'marvellous' – typed back.

'I drank there as a student.'

'Have you been in?'

'Not open yet.'

Simon smiled, recalling his salad days. He had spent a lot of time in the Parrot and Screwdriver as a student and he was looking forward to revisiting it. That beer, and those fantastic cheese sandwiches. Home-made bread and the pickle, ah … he closed his eyes and sighed ecstatically. Hotter than the fires of hell but it tasted like heaven.

There was a short silence while Swamp Thing, Galorsh and Spiffle, at their separate ends of the connection, paused for reflection.

'Go and meet him, fast,' replied Professor N'Aversion, *'before IR does.'*

'What if he disappears on me?'

'He won't if you're polite.'

'What if he won't help?'

'Ask him nicely.'

'What if he still won't?'

'Beg.'

'Then what?'

'Beg harder! See how he reacts and go from there. Whatever happens you must get him onside.'

'Righto.'

Simon glanced at his watch.

'Time to go.'

'Good luck.'

'Thnx.'

Simon signed out and purged the browser history. Then he sat for a minute, finishing his bun and coffee and looking out of the window over the lake and the Botanical Gardens. Opposite him, far away, stood the old Palace, the Security Headquarters. Black and forbidding, it loomed against the sandy-coloured buildings around it like a patch of anti-colour, deadening the atmosphere, sucking in the light. Not to mention the hope, he thought as he recalled the bungled rescue attempt there a few hours earlier.

Another execution. They were becoming an everyday occurrence. Lord Vernon was tightening his hold, it would take a miracle to get rid of him now. With a sigh, Simon hopped down from his chair. He mustn't get maudlin. He had a few hours before the pubs opened and some stolen electrical components to collect from a drop point across the road in the Botanical Gardens.

He trotted to the door and opened it, returning the proprietor's friendly wave before he adjusted his hat – a Spiffle could never be too careful of his hat, it would be terrible if a sudden cheeky breeze caught it and blew it away.

Chapter 5

At the Resistance HQ, the park was quiet. It was outside statutory breaktime hours for the Resistance's 'civilian workforce'. Colonel Ischzue and Lieutenant Wright sat in plastic chairs while Professor N'Aversion stood and briefed them on his findings. When he was done they stood to leave.

"Professor, before you go, I have one last question," said Colonel Ischzue. "What if Denarghi's standpoint does not alter?"

"I'm sorry?"

"He may consider the building of a portal a treasonable offence, regardless of where the information is sourced."

"I appreciate that, but for the sake of all the beings here, I have to give him the chance."

"And if he refuses and denounces you, what then?" asked Ischzue.

"I-I suppose I will be shot."

"Yes. The Lieutenant and I, along with certain other parties, believe this would be unfortunate."

"I wouldn't like it much myself."

"We have devised a contingency plan …"

"You don't mean depose him? But—" began the Professor.

"Why not?" asked the Lieutenant.

"Apart from Melior and Plumby, most of us are agreed that this organisation might benefit from a fresh objective," said Colonel Ischzue.

"Now we really are talking treason."

"No, the situation we are discussing is entirely hypothetical. It may never take place."

Yes, of course it wouldn't.

"Who would replace Denarghi? Who could? It would have to be someone who knows everyone, civilian, military and espionage."

"I can think of someone who might fit that description," said the Colonel meaningfully. Did he mean what the Professor thought he meant? Yes, it looked very much as if he did.

"But we'd have a vote, the usual way," said Lieutenant Wright.

Were they suggesting …?

"You can't rig the ballot, you do understand that, don't you? It's really not ethical."

"I doubt we'd have to. There's only one department head who liaises with all the others."

Phew! For a horrible moment, the Professor had thought they were talking about him.

"You mean Mrs Burgess and her ladies and gentlemen in catering," he said.

"No, Professor, we don't," said Colonel Ischzue smoothly.

Oh dear.

"I see," said the Professor non-committally.

"I believe you know the exact being to whom we refer."

Arnold's pants, that was a blow.

"The word is that Denarghi has an informant. Somebody who is privy to the type of technology we can only dream about. There is further word that this entire episode with the portals is a ruse to get rid of you so Denarghi may supplant you with him."

The Professor hadn't thought of that.

"All he has to do is ask me to stand down," he said.

"Come on Prof. He's too much of a daggers-in-the-night kind of bloke. Anyway, you'd be hanging round, getting on the new guy's wick."

Professor N'Aversion heaved a sigh.

"Oh deary me," he said.

"I merely warn you because, how can I put this? Things may be about to change," said Ischzue.

"You're not suggesting a coup are you?"

"Not yet Prof," said Lieutenant Wright, "but if Denarghi throws the book at you then, for all our sakes, something's got to give."

"And come that point, it will be him," said Colonel Ischzue.

"That's rather bad news, but thank you for the warning," said the Professor. "I wish we had longer to discuss this but I must get back to the lab. Be careful, both of you. Denarghi may behave like a fool but don't be deceived; he is wily. If he has caught one whiff of this, we will all be in dire trouble."

"If he does catch a whiff of this it will only be from one of us three," said Lieutenant Wright.

"That is so," said Colonel Ischzue.

"I'm very glad to hear that."

"Good luck, Prof. Let's hope this pans out."
"Yes, here's to the little scrote listening to reason," said the Professor.
"Here's to ..." said Colonel Ischzue.

****

Far away, in another part of K'Barth, Lord Vernon lowered the thimble from his eye and sat back, smiling.
"And now I have you," he said.

Chapter 6

For once, fate seemed to be smiling on The Pan. When he and Doctor Dot reached his snurd, the one in front of it had gone, allowing for a hassle – and embarrassment – free departure. He gave the matter of Doctor Dot's height and the SE2's size some thought and put the top down.

"Thank you," she said as she got in, but it was a very professional clipped 'thank you'.

"A pleasure. I'm afraid I'll have to put it back up. It's better you're not seen."

"Amen to that." She scanned the buttons. "Aviator. Good. We need to move fast."

"We may draw some unwelcome attention—"

"Then we'll say I've commandeered this vehicle. The sooner I can get to your friend, the better the chance that I can save his leg."

The Pan swallowed.

"It may not be as bad as I've made it sound," he said.

"If my past experience is to be relied upon it will be worse."

"You've done this before?"

"OK, let's go," she said.

The Pan shrugged, pressed the aviator button and took off.

As they flew, she questioned him further about Trev's condition and on a couple of occasions, told him to hurry. Her tone was short, businesslike, concentrating on the job in hand. None of the cheerful easy-going chattiness of the time she'd treated him. He flicked the landing lights on and hovered a few feet above the traffic on Turnadot Street.

"Does your friend have a name?" she asked as The Pan noticed a suitable space in the traffic and dropped the SE2 deftly into it.

"Trev," he said. Should he? Oh why not, she'd work it out anyway. "Trev Parker."

"Is that the recently vaporised Trev Parker? The one you bravely helped Lord Vernon to capture?" The Pan reflected that she was rather more up on her current affairs than was convenient, and a great deal more sarcastic than was called for.

"I didn't help."

"I realise that. I'm very clever."

"You're a doctor. It goes without saying."

"Not necessarily – you should meet my army counterpart. Well?"

He shrugged as he switched the indicator on.

"Yeh," he said. "Look, it's not too late to change your mind about this. I can take you back."

"I'm not going to change my mind," she said. Her voice was taut.

"Then … thank you."

He pulled into the blind alley beside the Parrot. A Grongle would stand out in this neighbourhood so it seemed sensible to use the back door.

"Is this it?" she asked. The Pan nodded and with surprising speed and agility, she had grabbed her rucksack from the space behind the seats and was out of the snurd almost before it had stopped.

****

There was no-one about when The Pan let Doctor Dot into the Parrot, including, to his relief, Humbert. However, the sound of his locking the door behind them brought Big Merv downstairs.

"Alright mate?" he asked.

"Yeh. This is—"

"Where's the patient?" asked Doctor Dot.

"Upstairs," said The Pan.

"Good." She strode across the room, "Through here?" she asked as she reached the doorway into the hall.

"Er … yes," said The Pan.

She noticed Big Merv, seemingly for the first time. "Are you my assistant?"

"Eh?"

"It's up to you," The Pan cut in. "Lucy is the one with the first-aid experience. This is—"

"I know who Big Merv is."

"Right."

Big Merv's antennae knotted and unknotted themselves.

"'Lucy' is Lucy Hargraves, I presume," said Doctor Dot.

The Pan gave her the most apologetic you've-got-me-bang-to-rights shrug in his repertoire.

"I'll leave you with Merv. I need to get ready for opening."

"You're going to open the pub?" asked Doctor Dot. "Don't."

"I have to or your friends in the army might wonder if I'm alright. Do you want them dropping in to check? There are Things here they shouldn't see."

She glanced at Big Merv.

"Good point," she said. "Quickly then, where's the patient?"

Chapter 7

Simon arrived at the Parrot and Screwdriver to find that it had changed very little. It was still pristine, the paintwork bright and fresh – if a different colour. It still, quite clearly, served the dregs of society as it always had. He remembered how the old ladies who ran it – Gladys and Ada – had explained it.

"The dregs of society is a great deal more genteel than people thinks," Gladys, the senior of the two had said.

As he drew nearer he realised there was a knot of people outside the pub. At the front was a man holding an umbrella in the air.

A tour? Surely not here?

Simon approached cautiously. The umbrella-holding man didn't look like a tour guide. He was an odd type with straggly hair, crooked teeth and a strange smell about him that Simon couldn't place.

"This pub is run by a man who has survived longer on the government blacklist than any other. Some say he has eyes in the back of his head, some say he is possessed with second sight. All we know is that he was one of this country's finest getaway men before he retired. You are about to be served a pint by the only living being who has outrun the Interceptor, not once, not twice but seven times, seven times, my friends!" The small crowd broke into spontaneous applause. "I thank you. We will now go into the pub and meet The Pan of Hamgee, the one surviving member of the Mervinettes."

Well, one of the last three. Simon recalled Frank and Harry's presence back at Resistance HQ, he supposed he could hardly expect it to be common knowledge.

"I thought he got shot down," said a Galorsh at the back. He was wearing a T-shirt advertising a band that marked him out as an engineer even more significantly than the belt he wore, which was similar to Simon's, laden with technological equipment.

The tour guide didn't miss a beat.

"Yeeees, he was shot down on the seventh attempt but he escaped six other times and on foot after the seventh. No-one else has even survived facing the Interceptor, which makes his feat all the more miraculous."

How long since the Hamgeean lad had been given this pub? Simon thought to work it out … a couple of days, no more than that. The good burghers of Ning Dang Po certainly worked fast. The 'guide', if that's what he was, was still speaking.

"When we step inside, please don't crowd the bar, take a seat at the table by the door – your drinks are included in the price of the tour." The strange fellow's eyes locked onto Simon. "You haven't paid."

"I'm not part of the tour, I'm just waiting for you to finish so I can go into the pub."

The tour guide glared at him.

"Who are you?" he demanded.

"Simon," said Simon, taking his hat off and making a low bow.

"Well, Simon; you listened, you pay."

"If you make me pay, I'll tell The Pan of Hamgee about your tour," said Simon evenly.

"He knows already," the man retorted but Simon doubted it. There was a pause and the 'guide' shifted uncomfortably, "I suppose you only heard the last few minutes, I'll let you off this time."

"I appreciate your generosity."

"If I catch you earwigging again, though, then you'll have to pay double," retorted the man and then, with a snort, he turned his back and went inside.

Simon smiled to himself and followed.

****

If little had changed outside the Parrot and Screwdriver, Simon discovered that even less had altered in the bar since he had last been there, except for the staff. There were two staff, one was an average-looking guy with blond curly hair who was wearing jeans and a shiny leather bomber jacket. He walked out from behind the bar as Simon arrived and went to collect some glasses, chatting to the various punters he encountered as he went.

The other barman was The Pan of Hamgee. Simon watched him as he served pints to the tour group. He had clearly been beaten up, there was bruising on his face, although it was the lurid colour of a retreating injury rather than one that was freshly applied. He wore a sling and there was evidence of a shoulder brace underneath it; perhaps he'd broken his collarbone, or someone had done it for him. But the thing that Simon couldn't take his eyes off was the ring he was wearing. It was a signet ring set with a ruby that flashed a deep red as he gripped the beer pump and pulled. There was something weighty about that ring, as if it carried more than just a stone. Maybe it was its great age, for it was certainly ancient, but no, it was more than that.

Where would a humble publican get a ring like that? Immediately, Simon recalled the rings Lord Vernon wore. Perhaps he'd generously bestowed one of them on The Pan of Hamgee, along with the pub. No. If he had – Simon remembered the video – it was doubtful he'd have been wearing it. Surreptitiously, subtly, Simon angled his phone, zoomed the camera and took a picture.

He wasn't sure what he had expected The Pan of Hamgee to be like, but different from this. He'd done a little digging, accessing the online files from HQ. He had to do something by the proper channels or it would make IR suspicious. However, what he'd found there differed to what he now saw.

By all accounts The Pan was a total yellow-belly. According to the records, Lieutenant Arbuthnot had been her usual incisive self in picking him out from the others as the weak impressionable link. All who had seen him agreed with her: that he was the dishonourable nothing who would do anything and betray anyone to save his own skin. Or to put it another way; the one who was most likely to crack. The young man serving drinks at the bar projected an air of quiet self-possession, possibly even wisdom, which seemed at odds with that description. Then there was the ring. He wore it with the understated authority of a man inured to its effects, as if he'd owned it since birth. Perhaps this was a different person? Maybe The Pan of Hamgee had a brother. No. This was the same fellow, the face recognition software confirmed it, but clearly he had changed – or those at HQ who had met him misread him.

He was about five feet nine and had dark spiky hair. As well as a sling, he was wearing a virulent paisley shirt and a ready smile. His eyes were dark blue and had something of the thousand-yard stare about them, as if he were watching things happen in another plane of existence, far away. At that moment he turned and looked straight at Simon, with an expression of polite enquiry. Simon saw a wariness in him, a resignation, possibly even some bitterness, but if he was nervous he hid it well. The Spiffle hurriedly stuffed his phone into one of the pouches on his belt and ambled over to the bar.

Chapter 8

The hours from midday until three were not hurrying and The Pan felt slightly panicky as he stood behind the bar serving beers, peanuts, cheese sandwiches and trying to chat casually to customers who had no clue of the highly illegal activities going on in the flat above. In a bizarre irony, there seemed to be more customers today. Luckily Pub Quiz Alan was in and for a few K'Barthan Zloty, cash in hand from the till, he'd agreed to help.

There was a loud thud, from overhead, which coincided with a lull in the conversation.

Betsy Coed – or Betsy the Bordello, as she was called, even if she was technically Betsy the Madam – looked up sharply.

"What was that?" she asked.

"Nothing," said The Pan breezily.

Betsy giggled and addressed the wider bar.

"I reckon he has a bit of crumpet up there to keep his bed warm."

"Nothing is further from the truth."

"Well Nareen, one of my girls, says she saw a very dishy blonde drawing the curtains in Trev's room this morning. She still up there?"

"Nobody is up there." There was another loud bang. What in the name of The Prophet was Doctor Dot doing? Please, oh Arnold please, let there not be sawing noises.

Betsy and Janice, one of her 'girls', adopted questioning expressions.

"Is it haunted then?" asked Janice.

"No … I've … I'm having the drains done," said The Pan just as he caught the eye of Stan the Plumber (specialist in drains: big jobs or small jobs). Pants! "I mean not the drain plumbers Stan the er … the other kind of plumbers … the ones that work with … um … not drains."

"Trev and I done the pipework up there," said Stan. He sounded crestfallen.

"If you was having the drains done, wouldn't that be downstairs?" asked another punter. They were all listening. Every conversation, except this one, seemed to have died, much to The Pan's dismay.

"Yes … no … these are special drains … in fact they're not drains at all they're …" The Pan tailed off and looked around the sea of faces, all turned towards him expectantly, "Drinks anyone?"

With a lot of, "Don't mind if I do's" several punters came forward to the bar, while the rest of them started talking among themselves again.

Across the room, The Pan noticed Pub Quiz Alan staring at him, a brace of empty glasses in one hand.

Another one of the regulars, Norris, arrived.

A man of few friends, Norris seemed to be buying an unusual number of rounds for a different group of people every opening time. He was up to something.

"I see you have another gang of mates in, Norris," said The Pan.

"Yes. They're on an exchange programme through work. We're entertaining groups from other companies."

Quick thinking Norris, except for one small technicality.

"I didn't think you had a job, Norris."

"I didn't but they're short-handed at the recycling depot." The recycling depot? That might explain Norris' unusual smell, although The Pan was pretty sure it still didn't explain his uncharacteristic generosity in buying rounds for his sudden number of new 'friends'.

"Are they really?"

"Yes, that's why they took me on, to entertain the exchange groups while the employees are busy working: casual labour."

"Ah." The Pan eyed Norris, very casual by the looks of it. He made a note that he must talk to Alan, who was becoming a stalwart ally, and find out what Norris was really up to.

Someone by the door caught The Pan's attention. He shifted his position so he could use the eyes in the back of his head to check out their reflection in the mirror behind the bar. A new customer had followed Norris in, a Spiffle. Customers didn't often come into the area on their own, let alone the Parrot. New arrivals entering the Parrot were usually subjected to a certain amount of scrutiny from the established punters. The Spiffle leaning casually against the wall beside the door had managed to arrive without anyone noticing. That was a rare skill. Especially in a hat like that. It had so many feathers The Pan wouldn't have been surprised if there'd been an actual bird attached to them somewhere. The Spiffle was taking in his surroundings but mostly watching The Pan. Did that mean he was Resistance?

Cluck?

"Yeh, I know I'm paranoid," muttered The Pan, but as a member of one of the smaller furry genera, the Spiffle would normally look enough like a Blurpon to make the punters wary. However, they seemed blissfully unaware of his presence. That was notable, in itself. "Is he Resistance d'you think?" The Pan asked the chicken.

Cluck, replied the chicken. Immediately, two images flashed past his mind's eye in rapid succession; the Revenue Acquisition Blurpons who'd tried to steal the ring, followed by a pair of large gentlemen – Frank and Harry style – with sawn-off shotguns. He suspected the chicken had put them there.

"Fair point, hen. The Resistance move in gangs or with henchmen and he has neither ... unless they're outside."

Cluck, said the chicken. It sounded doubtful but clearly wasn't discounting the possibility. The Spiffle was fiddling with a mobile phone; another factor that rang The Pan's warning bells. Sure, he could be very rich. As a K'Barthan, he'd have to be, in order to get hold of a mobile phone. After all, possessing one was illegal for most non-Grongles. If he was that well off, what was he doing in a place like the Parrot, though? Anyway, he was using it without fear which suggested a certain confidence in his untouchability. But no-one was above the law, or at least, no-one K'Barthan, and the rich were as easily killed as the poor when you got up close. The model of phone was a recent one as well, pointing to the little guy being, if not Resistance, then a Grongle spy – no, The Pan was certain not – although, he might be part of a cartel. If he was, Big Merv would recognise him. The Pan thought of his friend, upstairs, and wondered if he should run up and ask.

Making sure he was looking away from the Spiffle, The Pan used his extra eyes and the mirror to continue watching him. If The Pan was going to survive the week, he should find a way to make his peace with the Resistance. If his visitor was one of theirs, then now seemed as good a time as any to make contact. The Pan caught his eye.

The Spiffle fumbled his phone back into a pouch on his belt, made his way over to the bar, took a short run up and hopped onto a bar stool. Embarrassingly, it was a wobbly one. The Spiffle stood on the red velvet plush, arms out to balance himself.

"Hello there," The Pan said.

"Good afternoon." The Spiffle whipped off his hat and executed a theatrical bow, which was no mean feat on a stool as rickety as the one upon which he stood. "Simon, at your service."

The Pan couldn't help but smile.

"Wotcher Simon. Nice hat."

"Thank you, and back at you sir, although yours is not quite ornate enough for my taste."

The Pan was surprised. He knew he didn't have his hat on but, instinctively, he put his hand up and ran it through his hair to check. Nope. No hat. Simon had seen him before. Or had he been checking The Pan's ID against a photo on his phone? That was a bit unsubtle. The Pan was intrigued. Whoever Simon was, it looked as if his thirst for information would outweigh his thirst for … well … beer.

"Yes, I can see you're big on ornamentation," The Pan glanced at the Spiffle's hat for a moment. It was difficult not to. There really were a lot of feathers.

The Pan struck his proprietary landlord pose, his hand loosely on the nearest beer pull and watched, with resignation, as Simon's eyes goggled at the ring. He would have to swap it, and soon, but he was making such a monumental hash of being the Candidate and he couldn't face the censure of his predecessors. Soon, but not yet, then.

Seeing Simon's reaction to the ring, The Pan briefly wondered if he was a scout for the Resistance acquisition team who'd accosted him up on the roof. Possibly but unlikely, judging by the belts he was wearing. Like most Spiffles – and their Blurpon cousins – Simon wore two belts, bandolier style. His were heaving with gizmos though, in a way that The Pan had only ever seen on some of the employees he'd dealt with at Snurd. They were the sort of gizmos that said only one word: engineer. The Pan looked at a laser tape measure, a small thing which The Pan thought he had seen being used to test electrical circuits on Big Merv's MK II, a torch, a set of screwdrivers, a monumentally large bunch of jangly keys, a satellite navigation device, a pager and a paper pad – oooh, the little guy must be old school – a sleeve containing a tablet PC? Possibly, it was difficult to tell when it was in its case, then there was the mobile phone. The crowning glory, or at least the piece that Simon clearly regarded as the crowning glory, was an ammunition clip converted to carry clear plastic Biros in assorted colours. Mmm … definitely an engineer, then.

"What can I do for you?"

"I …" Simon started but tailed off, continuing to stare at the ring. It was not unusual but still irritating.

"Up here ..." The Pan moved his hand up to his face, pointing two fingers at his eyes. The Spiffle's gaze followed his hand, although probably because of the ring, until he realised, with obvious embarrassment, what he had been doing.

"Please accept my apologies," he said briskly, "I'd like a pint." The Pan felt a pang of guilt. He could give the little fellow some slack. He was the one poncing about wearing the wretched thing, after all. He reached for the designated non-regulars' pump. "No, this one please," Simon pointed to a different one. The Pan raised an eyebrow.

"You've been here before, have you?"

"A long time ago. I did my MSc at Ning Dang Po University."

"Ah, so you *are* an engineer."

"Yes," he seemed nonplussed, "how did you know?"

"Just a lucky guess."

"The strange smelly chap over there, with the teeth—"

"Norris," said The Pan as he bent down and took a clean glass from the tray under the bar.

"He said you drove for the Mervinettes."

The Pan supposed pretty much everything about him was in the public domain, now that he was reassimilated, but even so he realised he was going to have to have a word with Norris.

"Did he?" he said.

"Yes." He could feel Simon watching him as he placed the beer glass on the drip stand.

"Is it true?"

"It depends who's asking," said The Pan as he took hold of the lever and pulled.

"Me."

The beer gurgled out of the pump with a satisfying squelch.

"Yeh, nice try, on whose behalf?"

The Spiffle hesitated and shifted uncomfortably on the stool, causing it to wobble so much that he nearly fell off. The Pan pointed to the one next to it.

"You might want to try that one ... especially if you're intending to drink any of your beer. Right now you've picked the shuggliest stool and the strongest beer in the house."

"Thank you." Simon hopped over to the next stool.

"That'll be four K'Barthan Zloty," said The Pan.

"It's gone up a bit since I was last here," said Simon, handing over a note.

"Maybe, but it's what the owners charge." The Pan put the note in the till and counted out the change.

"I thought you were the owner," said Simon as The Pan put the change into his hand.

"No. Caretaker manager perhaps, owner, definitely not."

"They said you were the owner on the news."

"You saw that did you?" he asked and heard the nerves in his voice. Bum.

"On GNN Local."

Phew, nobody ever watched that.

"Well, the Grongles had no right to take this place, and since they're the ones who gave it to me, that means I've no right to own it."

The Pan slipped a beer mat onto the bar in front of Simon, checked that the beer he was about to serve had settled, topped up the glass and put it on the mat. Simon took a sip and closed his eyes in something approaching ecstasy.

"Ooo, that's every bit as good as I remember it. Brewed to the original recipe, I assume?"

"Brewed by the original brewer, and I'm going to have to learn how she did it, very fast, before this lot drink me dry."

"So I see, it has a perfect head on it, you are looking after it well; a fine start to your career as a publican."

"Thank you." The two of them fell into an awkward silence. "I'm assuming you're not just here for a drink."

The little Spiffle had the good grace to be bashful.

"No."

"Then, what are you here for?"

"I want to talk to you."

"I might not want to talk to you."

"You are though." Simon took another sip of his drink.

"Fair point. What d'you want to ask?"

Simon cast another sideways glance at the ring and patently chickened out of asking his first question.

"I'd like a round of cheese sandwiches, please."

"Uh-ha." The Pan laughed and the little Spiffle didn't seem to know what to do, which made him feel guilty. "Sorry, I thought you were going to ask about this." He held up his hand and let it drop. Simon seemed even more nervous and took a big pull at his pint. "Would you like pickle with those?"

"Yes please."

The Pan raised his eyebrows.

"Are you sure about that? It has quite a kick."

"I know. I told you, I've been here before, remember? Two rounds, please."

"Coming up."

The Pan went into the Holy of Holies and sawed four slices off a newly defrosted loaf of Gladys' home-baked bread. He was working on a surface close to the door and, as he buttered the bread, Simon continued the conversation through the open doorway.

"You outran the Interceptor," he said.

"Once or twice." The Pan buttered the bread and laid some thick slabs of cheese on top.

"You're the only man who can."

"So it would seem. How much pickle?"

"Oh, I'll help myself, just bring the jar and a spoon."

"Arnold," muttered The Pan. The little guy must have a bombproof digestive tract – or a death wish.

"Believe me, I can eat more of this stuff than anybody," Simon added. "When this was my local I could beat all comers."

"That sounds like a challenge," said The Pan.

"It would be, if anyone dared," said Simon.

The Pan laughed.

"That's what everyone says. Then they actually eat some and change their view."

He finished making the two rounds of cheese sandwiches, without pickle, and put them at two ends of an oval plate. Then he put the jar of pickle in the middle, not forgetting to use a doily as Gladys and Ada would have wanted, and laid a spoon beside it.

"Here you are," he said as he brought the plate through and placed it on the bar.

Simon opened a couple of his sandwiches and ladled the pickle over the cheese with abandon.

"Watch and learn," he said and he picked one up, took a large bite, chewed and swallowed with no discernible effects. He flipped the plate round so the chutney-laden sandwiches were facing The Pan.

"I'm not hungry."

"Can't take the heat?"

"Oh, I know I can take the heat."

"It doesn't look like it. You run the pub, you should be able to handle the fare."

This was definitely a challenge. The kind of macho challenge The Pan normally made a point of ignoring. Unfortunately, his love of cheese sandwiches, Gladys and Ada style, outweighed his sense of caution.

"You want a demonstration?"

"If you're hard enough."

The Pan laughed.

"I'm not hard at all but I'm Hamgeean, which makes me a dab hand at hot food." Simon eyed him with haughty defiance. "Alright," said The Pan. He picked up the fullest sandwich and ate a large mouthful. It tasted fantastic, if blindingly hot, even for Gladys' pickle. He swallowed it. Yep. Hot, but it was simple enough to keep a straight face and not cry. Simon was clearly impressed. The Pan was merely thankful to have pulled it off. He didn't doubt his ability to eat vast quantities of Gladys' pickle, but he usually paced himself, and he wasn't one for machismo consumption.

"May I propose a wager?" said Simon.

Such confidence. Scary.

"Only if you want to redistribute some of your wealth. Trust me on this, I can – and do – eat pretty much anything."

"Then the bet is on."

Arse.

"How much?" The Pan was painfully aware that the cash in the till was Gladys and Ada's – and in their absence, Trev's – rather than his. And he didn't want to put too much of it on a bet because of Simon's worrying confidence. What if the little Spiffle was about to eat him under the table?

"Let's play for something more interesting."

Phew.

"I seek information. I work for some people who spend a lot of money. When they require funds then, like many of us, they visit a bank.

However, there is something standing in their way."

Arnold's toe jam.

"Really?" asked The Pan as innocently as he could.

"Yes and I think you know what I'm talking about."

The Interceptor.

"I might, and if I do, that's a bet I'm not taking." He picked up a cloth and started to polish the bar. "I'm retired."

"Lost your nerve?"

"I never had any. I think you're confusing cowardice with talent."

"Perhaps you're confusing talent with cowardice. There is a saying, never pass up an opportunity to learn."

"Unless I'm your teacher. Seriously, if you're asking what I think you're asking, I doubt I could help." Not unless the Resistance's drivers had eyes in the backs of their heads, too. "Anyway, I'm only going to be here until Saturday." Deliberately, without breaking eye contact, The Pan took another, enormous bite from his chutney-laden sandwich. That flavour! Like angels tiptoeing over his tongue, angels with lava-hot feet. Despite the tears pricking the corners of his eyes, he managed to chew and swallow without altering his expression. This was definitely an extra-hot batch. Half of him was confident, enjoying himself, but that was probably because of the stimulants in the chillies. The wiser part of him wished he'd selected a different jar. He felt a certain dampness beginning around his temples and the back of his neck.

Simon seemed to be a little exasperated.

"We are both aware that no amount of teaching will give my colleagues something they don't have." That was one hell of an admission. "I'm not asking you to teach," he told The Pan, as he snatched up his own sandwich, stuffed all of it into his mouth and washed it down with a swig of beer. He showed no obvious reaction but The Pan thought he detected a slight bulging of the little creature's eyes.

"What do you want then?" asked The Pan as he ate the last remnant of his sandwich. Mmm, three to go. Could he eat three more? Yes, absolutely but he would have to up the pace or slow it right down. The trick in a duel like this was to eat fast and finish before the true force of the heat kicked in or take it slowly and savour it; there was no middle path to victory.

Simon picked up his second sandwich, took a bite and washed it down with some more beer. Schoolboy error. If he wanted to put out the flames he should smother them with bread, adding liquid would only stoke them higher. The Pan saw, with relief, that he would win this contest.

"I need information," Simon continued with his second sandwich, swallowing quickly, presumably in the hope that not much of its burning contents would touch the sides. Even so his voice sounded slightly higher when he said, "I have to find a weakness."

The Pan tore the second sandwich in half, put the two halves on top of one another and took a gargantuan mouthful. He managed to keep his reaction to a minimum but couldn't help raising his eyebrows as he chewed and swallowed.

"There is no weakness. This is Lord Vernon you're dealing with. It's hardly more than a joke for him, picking off your boys for fun." The Pan was pleased that he'd kept the heat of the chutney absent from his voice but he'd failed to hide his emotion.

"I can see that angers you," said Simon and he took a final bite out of his second sandwich and swallowed. His eyes shone with capsicum-induced tears but, power to him, none fell.

The Pan finished his second sandwich too.

"Yeh. It makes me angry. All of this does," he said, keeping his voice calm and level once again, despite the burning in his throat.

"Would you like a second round?" wheezed Simon.

The Pan shrugged.

"I don't think you would."

"We have a wager."

"No we don't."

The Pan picked up the jar and the spoon and as Simon watched him incredulously, he ate the rest of the chutney. Then he put the jar down and ate the rest of the sandwiches, the ones Simon had not put pickle in. The soft bread neutralised the capsicum oils, subduing the heat to a pleasantly warm buzz accompanied by very clear sinuses.

"Arnold," whispered the Spiffle.

"I did warn you," said The Pan. He looked straight into Simon's eyes, which seemed to give the little Spiffle a shock, so he tried to pretend he'd seen the depths of Simon's soul, when what he'd actually seen was a pair of beady black eyes, giving away nothing. "Alright, you weren't to know how much chutney I can put away and you've eaten more than anyone else I've seen. Perhaps you've earned a proper talk, but I love and trust my customers too much to endanger their lives by having it here." There was a sense of deflation from around the room. It told The Pan that despite the low rumble of background conversation going on, the punters had been listening, avidly, to him and Simon. He waved Pub Quiz Alan over from the other side of the room. In the background he could hear the soft rustling and chinking of coins changing hands.

"Norris, if you've been running a book, remember Ada's rule: there's a ten per cent owner's premium on all winnings."

Norris looked both guilty and surprised. Grumbling and muttering he got up and put a banknote in the charity tin.

The Pan turned his attention back to Alan, waiting patiently by his side. "Can you look after the bar for a minute or two? Simon and I need to have a chat."

"Yeh, sure." Alan cast a brief glance at Simon and fixed The Pan with a knowing look. "You OK with that?" he asked.

"Yeh. We're good Alan."

"The snug's free."

"Thanks."

"I'll keep it that way shall I?"

"Please." The Pan strolled round the bar, trying to pretend he was in control and at ease. Alan seemed to be buying it but he wasn't sure about Simon. "OK, Simon, we have ..." he glanced at his watch, "about twenty minutes. Follow me," he said and headed to the snug.

Chapter 9

Lord Vernon returned to his rooms in a black mood. He had just visited the Chosen One. She was shocked and vulnerable at the death of her friends, which should have been the perfect time to press home his advantage.

So why hadn't it worked? He unbuckled his Sam Browne belt and threw it savagely onto the desk chair. If anything she was even more bullish than before.

He strode across the room, wrenching off his jacket and ripping the diamond-encrusted star from the fabric. How dare she think that worthless Hamgeean was a better driver than him?

"I don't think so," he snarled, balling up the jacket and hurling it angrily into the laundry bin by the door. "I brought him down."

He stalked through to his bedroom, tossing the jewelled star onto the bedside table as he passed. Ruth's continued intransigence irritated him and worse, it was distracting. She knew she was his prisoner, little more than his slave so why could she not accept defeat? He wrenched open the wardrobe door. She also must realise that the more obstinate she was now, the more he would make her suffer later on. What could she hope to gain by fighting? He regarded the ranks of freshly laundered jackets in front of him and their ordered perfection. He closed his eyes for a moment and breathed slowly, deeply, trying to relax. Ruth was no different from the rest of them, he reflected, as he selected one of the jackets and put it on. She would give up in the end. They always did; it was just a matter of finding the right application of pressure, he thought, making a pincer movement with his finger and thumb. He stood in front of the mirror, adjusting his cravat and repositioning the jewel-encrusted star just so. When he was done, he looked at the being reflected in the glass, an indomitable being of charisma and power; a being who owned half the world and would have the rest of it by next week.

Lord Vernon exhaled with satisfaction. He would crush the Chosen One's spirit, and the longer it took him, the more intense the pleasure would be when he succeeded.

He went back into his reception rooms, retrieved his belt and buckled it on again, placing it with expert precision. Then he put on his sunglasses. He looked magnificent. He *was* magnificent and no human was going to stand in his way, no matter how strong-willed she was. He strode back into his drawing room and yanked open the door, only to find General Moteurs approaching down the hall.

"What do you want General?" he barked.

"Sir. The High Leader has arrived and awaits your pleasure."

Though the General had predicted it, the news that the High Leader had arrived a day early put a dampener on what had been Lord Vernon's rising spirits.

"You have shown him to his rooms?"

"Not yet."

"Then you will do so, and you will give him my humblest apologies and explain that I am detained. Other more important items of state business await my pleasure."

"Sir." Lord Vernon sensed Moteurs' doubts, but his trusted deputy was wise enough not to voice them. He knew his master's moods.

"And General, I have a particular task for you."

"Sir."

"The Chosen One."

"Sir." General Moteurs' expression did not change but as usual Lord Vernon detected his tension. No surprise, given the strength of his master's annoyance.

"Make her understand her position, General."

Moteurs' features altered a minuscule fraction into a look of resolve as he spoke up.

"She will not be so obdurate, sir, if you change her gaoler."

"Her intransigence is Captain Snow's work?"

"No sir, the Captain's behaviour is exemplary but he lacks tact, and she requires it."

"Then you will deal with her, General."

"You are relieving Captain Snow?"

"No, you have enough to attend to. She will remain under his protection but you will speak to her and make her see reason."

"She is stubborn, sir—"

"And you will win her round, or it will be the worse for you. You have your orders. I will join you with the High Leader when I am done."

Chapter 10

The Pan sat on one of the comfy chairs in the snug and put his feet on the table in front of it. Gladys would have had a word or two to say about that, he thought guiltily, but it didn't stop him. He waited while his visitor jumped into the comfy chair opposite.

"Right then, Simon, ask away."

"I must be honest, this isn't about driving, it's about disappearing into thin air."

Ah.

"That's a difficult secret to share."

"A lot of lives depend on your answer."

"A lot of lives depend on my surviving until Saturday. If I give you your answer, can you guarantee my survival that long?"

Simon swallowed.

"I thought not."

"It may be possible. It depends on my colleagues."

"You are Resistance aren't you?"

"Yes, I'm Chief Engineer of Tech Ops and you're lucky I got to you first. If the other departments find you, they may not be so civil."

"Yeh, I'm aware of that and thank you for the warning." The Pan heaved a sigh. "How did you know about this place?"

"I used to live round here when I was at university."

"That wasn't quite what I meant. Alright, look, I have portals and you can have some but first you need to persuade your other departments to give me amnesty. D'you think you can do that?"

"I can try."

So that was a 'no'.

"You don't sound very sure," said The Pan.

"I'm not."

"Mmm." The Pan narrowed his eyes. "It's like this, Simon. I really want to help you because once I'm gone there'll be no-one else who can get you portals, or at least, not for a long time. But the difficulty is, your organisation and I have a bit of a history."

"Denarghi wants you dead."

Oooh, hardball.

"Yeh. I figured. That's why I'm asking for your help to stay alive."

"I can try, but as I told you, you're all over GNN Local. Everyone's going to know where you are in a few hours." This, delivered with a get-out-of-that verbal flourish.

"Then they'll get me and you'll be back to square one. I'm thinking you may not want that."

"You're in no position to negotiate."

"If that's the case, why are you here?"

"You're a lot smarter than you look aren't you?" said the Spiffle.

"You're very kind – a little flattery goes a long way – but it's not the answer I'm looking for. Look, I can see you're different. If you were like the others, you wouldn't be bothering to speak to me. You'd have cut my throat and ransacked the place. Well no, you'd have tried and I suspect my faithful punters would have ransacked you. The thing is, Lord Vernon is not the Candidate, and I can prove it. But I need an audience, so I have to wait until Saturday, and I'm also central to the demonstration, which means it's pretty vital that I'm alive to do my thing."

Simon cocked his head on one side and gave The Pan a searching look. "Do your thing?" he said.

"Yes," said The Pan, wishing he'd put it some other way. "So, how do we get from here to the bit where we clap each other on the back and shake hands? Have a think and let me know."

Simon was clearly surprised and a little wrong-footed by The Pan's stance.

"This is not how I usually negotiate," he said.

"Indulge me, I'm a maverick. Perhaps if I show you the goods, you'll try harder."

"Maybe," said Simon with a non-committal shrug, but he was almost vibrating with anticipation.

"Alright." The Pan rummaged around in his pocket and took out the tiny jar. "This is a portal." He put it down on the table with a flourish and as he did so the K'Barthan Ring of State reflected little red speckles of light across Simon's face. There was a moment of silence and The Pan congratulated himself on making an impact and then realised it was the ring, rather than the portal, that held Simon's attention.

"Are you a member of the Underground?" the little Spiffle asked him.

"That's a bit of a tangent, Simon."

"I need to know."

"No you don't, not yet."

"You are then."

"I never said—"

"You implied it well enough." Simon grinned delightedly, he seemed excited, "Is it true that Sir Robin Get is still alive?"

"He might be," said The Pan. "It's hard to say because he's in the old Palace. I suppose they might keep him alive until the installation on Saturday. I'd say he's doomed after that; then again, I'd say everyone is." He stopped. "Sorry. Tangent from me there. D'you want to have a look at this or what?" He held up the portal and, once again, he noticed that Simon's eyes were drawn to the ring.

"Yes, please."

The Pan put the jar on the polished wooden surface and slid it along the table. He shoved it far too hard and it hit the end at speed, glancing off Simon's beer glass. With impressive reflexes, the little Spiffle reached out and caught it before it disappeared under the chair.

"Nice one," said The Pan.

Simon turned the pirate portal round and looked into the bottom, then he closed his eyes for a moment and opened them before looking into it again.

"This is incredible," he said. He put the jar down and took another sip of his beer, the glass shaking as hc put it to his lips.

"You haven't come here to ask me how it works then," said The Pan, pointing at the portal.

"No," said Simon distractedly. He was gawking at the ring again. "I mean yes. I know the theory but not how to put it into practice."

"I see. Well, if you use it, smash it afterwards, or the Grongles can track you, unless you're going to use it to jump around, in which case, I suppose you use the same one until you have to stop somewhere for more than a few seconds."

"Thank you, I'll pass that on to my colleagues."

"D'you want to take that one, to show your boss?" The Pan waved his hand at the jar, and after watching Simon for a moment, made a mental note that if he was going to achieve a meaningful conversation with his visitor he must put his hand behind his back, or in his pocket, to hide the ring.

"Yes. Thank you." Silence. "Should you be wearing that thing?"

"What thing?"

"That ring."

"Yes," said The Pan, "it's mine."

"It looks like the K'Barthan Ring of State."

"Doesn't it just. So?"

The Spiffle's black beady eyes looked straight into The Pan's dark blue ones.

"I thought Lord Vernon was wearing the K'Barthan Ring of State."

"So does he, and he should know." Yes! Excellent non-committal answer there. "Shall we get back to the matter in hand, as opposed to on it?"

The Spiffle looked up at him with an expression of … what was that? The Pan wished he was better at reading other beings, but something about the ring had shaken the little chap up. It was clearly worrying him far more than the portals he had come to discuss. Had he recognised The Pan, for who he really was? Surely not. He was in the Resistance. They were all supposed to think Deirdre Arbuthnot was the Candidate.

"I believe—I think—I need to speak to the Professor." Well, that sounded like progress. If Simon's boss was Head of Tech Ops, maybe he could rein in his colleagues. "Will you be here tonight?"

"I'm the publican, I tend to be behind the bar, during opening times, anyway."

"Good, don't go away, I'll be back." Simon downed the remains of his pint. "Oh, one last thing, can I take a photo of that ring?"

"You already have," said The Pan.

"How did you know that?"

"I'm smarter than I look, remember?"

Simon laughed but with pronounced levels of nervous tension.

"I need a close-up."

"Then come back with your boss."

"It's for him."

"All the more reason to make him curious then, so he'll come and look."

"Can you meet us this evening?"

The Pan thought for a moment.

"It'd have to be after closing but you can stay over. I mean, if you're worried about being caught and searched after dark."

"Thank you, yes, then I will return this evening."
"Good, I'll look forward to it."

Chapter 11

Alan rang the bell for last orders and, after escorting Simon from the Resistance out through the side door, The Pan returned to the bar to help politely kick the lunchtime stragglers into the street. He hurriedly stuffed some notes from the till into Alan's hand and dismissed his offers to help cash up. Once he had gone, The Pan barred the door and bounded up the stairs three at a time.

Trev was in his room, peacefully sedated, his leg in a complicated framework of metal hoops with spurs sticking out at intervals. There were several dressings and, in places, the living stitched flesh extended beyond them. The whole thing looked more like an engineering project than a cast. Judging by the holes and screws it was adjustable. Well, yes, he supposed it would be, so it could be changed to fit as the swelling reduced. The Pan could hear low voices in the kitchen. Doctor Dot was sitting at the table with Lucy and Big Merv.

"Everything alright?" asked The Pan.

"Yeh, good," said Lucy. She looked tired but elated.

"You did a pretty cool thing there."

What was he saying? She'd just helped someone operate on a broken leg, in a pub bedroom. It was more than cool, it was smecking brilliant. He said as much.

"Thank you. Doctor Dot has the patience of a saint."

"You're very kind," said Doctor Dot. She smiled but her heart wasn't in it.

"You OK Merv?" The world's only orange Swamp Thing was looking closer to beige.

"Doctor Dot needed both of us in the end, she and I weren't strong enough to get the bone into position on our own."

"Yer." Big Merv took a long pull at his tea. His antennae drooped a little and stood up again. "I done a lot of iffy stuff in my time but that's gotta be top of the pile." He shook his head and his antennae waved backwards and forwards.

"I can imagine," said The Pan. He was guiltily relieved he hadn't had to help.

Doctor Dot pushed her cup of tea away from her, untouched, and stood up. "I have to get back."

"I can give you a lift if you like," said The Pan. "I mean so long as it won't look bad, you being chauffeured about the place by a native."

"Please don't use that word," she snapped. "Who do you think I am?"

"Sorry."

She put her hand up.

"It's fine, I—" she heaved a sigh. "Yes, please. I would appreciate a lift."

"And … it won't get you into trouble with your less laid-back brethren?"

"No." She picked up her rucksack and slung it over her shoulder. "You understand what you have to do?" she asked Big Merv and Lucy.

"Yes," they said – or at least, Lucy did. Big Merv said, "Yer."

"Good. I'll be back tomorrow. If his condition worsens send Defreville to fetch me."

Arnold's bogies. They'd told her his name: his real name. Did the entire world have to know? Then again, Doctor Dot had read his file and he supposed it was in there. He looked over at her but she couldn't meet his eyes. Uh-oh. He glanced at the other two and raised his eyebrows.

"I'll be back for evening opening. Anything you need me to get while I'm out?"

"Food," said Doctor Dot.

"The doc's right. There ain't much in the pantry 'cept cheese an' pickle mate and Trev wants nourishing stuff."

"Cheese is … Alright, you have a point. Have a look in the freezer – Gladys made some frozen meals – and I'll raid the till and see what I can get. Now, if I'm going to get the doctor back and be here for opening time, we have to go."

Chapter 12

Professor N'Aversion's phone rang.

"Simon! Any news?"

"I've found the extra parts you wanted, Professor."

The Professor's stealth tablet, as he and Nar had taken to calling it, beeped. Sure enough the beep was to notify him of a new private message from Simon on the forum.

'Found Pan of Hamgee.'

'Well done! Has he a portal?' typed the Professor, remembering to copy Nar in too, so she had a record on her own account.

'Yes.'

"How absolutely marvellous! Simon, you should have my job," said the Professor as he went to the door, opened it and beckoned Nar into the room.

"No thank you. Not enough time for science."

Professor N'Aversion laughed.

"Too right."

"Tell me, do you have any more information?" asked the Professor down the phone as Nar went to the desk and caught up with their typed correspondence on the tablet.

"That's the thing Professor. I do and I don't. I have one of the items on your list, and my contact says he can't identify what we've requested without meeting you personally."

"Does he have to?"

"He's a useful fellow. I think it's worth you coming up here."

'He wants amnesty.' Simon's message flashed up on the screen of the tablet.

Nar and the Professor exchanged wide-eyed, shocked expressions.

'What? From Denarghi?' the Professor typed.

'Yes.'

The Professor sucked the air through his teeth to give himself time to formulate a reply.

'Didn't you tell him that we're acting on our own?' he typed to Simon.

'No: he might get amnesty 4 himself by telling Denarghi.'

Fair point.

"What do you think, Nar?"

"You have to go there."

He nodded.

"Alright, when does this fellow want to see me?"

"Tonight."

"Then I had better be there."

'What about amnesty?'

The Professor heaved a sigh. His antennae had tied themselves into a knot and, to compound his discomfort, his big toe had worked its way through a fresh hole in his recently darned sock.

'We haven't a chance' Nar wrote on the blotter.

"I know, Nar," said the Professor.

"What?"

"Sorry, just talking to Nar. Where and when?" said the Professor, aloud, down the handset.

'No can do; Melior, Plumby and Denarghi will not agree' he typed on his tablet.

"Ning Dang Po Botanical Gardens, south entrance, gate three at five o'clock," said Simon.

Professor N'Aversion glanced at his watch and read Simon's latest post.

'As a Nimmist u have 2.'

Uh?

"Yes, of course. Nar, I'll leave you in charge," he said out loud.

'What do you mean?' he typed back to Simon.

'He's wearing the K'Barthan Ring of State. QV pic, uploaded from my phone.'

"Arnold's nasal hair!" The Professor spoke before he could stop himself. Smeck. "Sorry Simon, my antennae have knotted themselves again," he said for the benefit of anyone monitoring them, and congratulated himself on it only being a half-lie. "I'll have to go and sort them out."

'Sorry forgot the link.'

'Have link. No more phone pics, just in case they are picked up.'

"OK, Professor, see you at five?"

"Yes, I'll look forward to it."

"Thanks. Goodbye, Professor," said Simon.

"Goodbye, Simon."

Once the two of them had hung up, the conversation on the forum started in earnest.

Professor N'Aversion typed, *'The ring is fake. Lord Vernon's wearing the real one. We all know that, he swiped it from under our noses just over a year ago.'*

'He should be, yes but I don't think so. Seriously, the picture doesn't do it justice.'

"Have a read of this, Nar," said the Professor, gesturing to the picture. Their eyes met and she shook her head.

'We think it's v. good but it must be a copy. Impossible to tell either way unless it's examined by experts.'

'Why wear a copy? It's dangerous. Plus where does GBI get cash for fake that good?'

'Where did he get any of these things?'

'Dunno but think wearing the ring because has to. Is as if he has no choice.'

The Professor realised where the conversation was going.

'No more. Not even here,' he typed. *'Talk at 5.00.'* He signed out.

He glanced up at Nar and put one finger on the side of his nose. She nodded. He knew she was as worried as he was. She was stroking the end of her furry tail, something she only ever did to calm her nerves.

"Bloody suppliers," he said. "I'd better go. You're in charge."

He took a bit of acrylic from the pocket of his lab coat which he kept specifically for the purpose of charging his phone and tablet – more effective than any fur – and rubbed both of them vigorously. He didn't know whether to laugh with delight or tremble in fear, but if this Pan of Hamgee was the person he thought, it changed everything.

Chapter 13

In a different part of the Resistance HQ, there was a dimly lit room containing several banks of computers, staffed by operatives wearing headphones. Each workstation was walled off from the next by screens, with a half screen coming across behind the operator for privacy. There was a low hum of electronics and the occasional whispered conversation but otherwise all was silent. This office sat in the twilight zone between Espionage and Information Retrieval; an espionage agent had planted the bug in Simon's phone, it being considered an 'in the field' operation. However, it was agents from IR who listened to and collated the results from behind the lines, here at HQ. The two departments worked hand in glove and Denarghi congratulated himself on appointing respective senior officers who got on as well as Colonels Melior and Plumby. He finished listening to the recording of Professor N'Aversion and Simon's call and took off the set of headphones he had been wearing. He thrust them at Colonel Melior and moved away, out of earshot of the agents at the terminals, to a bank of empty cubicles nearby.

"This proves it. That smecker N'Aversion is keeping information from me," he said.

"Sir," said Colonel Melior.

"They're up to something. The question is what. If I discover he is building that Grongolian instrument of death, he will pay."

"Sir," said Colonel Melior again.

"Your orders, Your Majesty?" said Colonel Plumby. Denarghi liked the way Plumby always used his full title, rather than calling him 'sir'.

"You will discover what Professor N'Aversion is scheming and you will pass that information to me and no-one else. We will let him go and your agents, Colonel Plumby, will follow him and see what he does. If there is anything untoward then we will let him return here, with that traitorous little pipsqueak Simon, and when he does, I will call them both to account."

"And if they cannot explain themselves?"

"I will make an example of them."

Denarghi noted that he must talk to Colonel Smeen about organising a firing squad since he doubted that the Professor and Simon would account for themselves to his satisfaction.

****

At one of the nearby terminals, a Galorsh called Forrest glanced up for a moment. What had that been about? He wished he'd heard more of it but they were speaking in such low voices he couldn't catch it all. He paused the surveillance recording he was monitoring and concentrated. He replayed the whispered sounds of Denarghi, Melior and Plumby's conversation in his memory. It had definitely contained the name of 'Professor N'Aversion' as well as some trigger phrases that worried him.

Perhaps there were advantages to being stuck on the spare terminals, away from his colleagues, after all. That had been interesting – unlike the two idiots he was monitoring. He sighed and took a swig of water from the bottle by his side. Even so, he hoped he could get back to his usual space for his next shift. This office chair had even less of the stuffing left in it than his usual one. He adjusted his headphones and continued with his duties. Today, he was sifting through the recorded transmissions from a bug in one of the rooms rented for RA agents in Ning Dang Po. How he longed to monitor one conversation important enough to put in the big red 'urgent' file for immediate distribution. No chance of that. This assignment was lengthy, turgid and one of the biggest wastes of resources he'd encountered.

The RA gang staying in the room this week had been denounced for suspicious behaviour. Putting aside that they were thieves and behaving suspiciously was their job, it turned out there was nothing more going on than an affair between two of them. It didn't surprise Forrest, because it must be very boring waiting around for it to get dark enough to go and mug people. What did surprise him was that they thought anyone would mind. The officer in command of their section of RA, Lieutenant Wright, was pretty tolerant of what her operatives did in their spare time, so long as it didn't affect their duties.

Forrest flopped back in his chair and looked up at a black damp stain on the ceiling. It was always the same: they'd be arguing, or they'd be telling each other how wonderful they were and then one thing would lead to another and then he'd have to listen to it, for ages. Today one thing had led to another rather more quickly. As always, he was tempted to fast forward through the squelchy bits but that was forbidden, in case any information was missed. He rolled his eyes. The couple had far more stamina than was natural or tasteful.

At the end of his shift, when it was time to mark up his findings, Forrest would recommend, as he always did, that the surveillance be concluded. His supervisors always overruled his recommendation, or perhaps they were showing it to Melior to overrule, it wasn't as if anyone got to use their initiative round here anymore. Melior micromanaged everything, even the highest ranked officers were little more than their commander's gofers, and Melior, himself, was little more than Denarghi's.

He doubted Lieutenant Wright knew about the surveillance. If she did, he was sure she would disapprove and have it stopped. Although, he could imagine she may well know about the affair. A voice barked through his headphones, "You! Forrest, no slacking."

"Sorry, sir."

"You'd better be. I've got my eye on you."

"Sir," said Forrest.

Great. Now he'd annoyed his supervisor. He fully expected to be lumbered with the same turgid nonsense to monitor tomorrow. He stretched and yawned. Almost his whole shift lay ahead. But at least he had a date tonight with a female of his own species, which is fairly essential for a Galorsh, someone he really liked. The hours couldn't go quickly enough.

Chapter 14

The Pan grabbed a handful of notes from the till and stuffed them into his pocket. Then he escorted Doctor Dot out of the back door and into the SE2. She was very quiet, keeping her face turned away from him, looking out of the window. Well … she'd spent her afternoon breaking just about every law on the statute books against aiding and abetting fugitives. It was probably making her think. He pulled out into the traffic on Turnadot Street and risked a glance at her again. Yes. It was probably making her think a bit too much. He would take her mind off it with conversation.

"Thank you for helping Trev."

"You've said that once, you don't need to say it again."

"So … What kind of foods should I get him? Anything you'd recommend?"

"I'd avoid hot pickle. He needs balance, protein: eggs, meat, fish—"

"He's from Ning Dang Po so I know to avoid the pickle. If he was Hamgeean, I'd cook him seafood broth but I'm not even sure he eats fish, I'm guessing he's more of a chicken soup man."

Cluck?

The Pan managed to think 'sorry' to the eighth Architrave rather than say it out loud.

Doctor Dot heaved a sigh.

"Chicken soup is fine. Use the freshest ingredients you can. They'll contain more vitamins. He may not feel like eating tonight, we knocked him out with a field anaesthetic, so when he comes round he's likely to feel nauseous."

"Right. Thanks. Is there anything else I should know that might help? I need to give him the best start I can and … Alright, look, I'm sorry but you know how it is. I'm an idiot. I'm just worried that I'll think of Arnold knows how many questions the moment I've dropped you back and I won't be able to ask them."

"You can ask me when you pick me up tomorrow."

"Are you—"

"I said I'll be visiting the patient again. I wasn't wagging my tongue around for the sheer joy of it."

"No of course but ... Look, seriously Doctor, are you sure? It's risky."

"Of course I'm sure, it's my ruddy job. And I'm simply doing it the way I'm supposed to. And if someone, anyone, in this rat's arse of a country, had a backbone there wouldn't be any danger in it."

"If you hate it here so much then why don't you just go home? And while you're at it, do us a favour and take the rest of your countrymen with you."

"Oh shut up."

They drove on, in fraught silence. Doctor Dot probably needed some time to calm down. The Pan knew she was smart enough to keep her mouth shut but at the same time, she was definitely speaking before thinking right now. If a couple of well-aimed taunts from one of her army colleagues got under her skin she would be undone, and so would Trev. He took a sneaky look at her. She was sitting straight and tense, clutching the rucksack on her lap. And then there was the way she was biting her lip. She needed to simmer down a bit and after her comments about his home nation, so did he. He took a detour of a couple of blocks.

"Where are you going?"

"We're taking the scenic route."

"I'm a doctor, I don't have time for scenic."

"Today, you do."

He reached a square of town houses round a small green park. The outside was lined with trees – and railings, as the park was reserved for the use of the residents of the houses. It was a place that projected an air of faded splendour. He pulled into a spot next to the park and switched off the engine. She sat rigid, staring ahead. He turned in his seat to face her.

"Alright Doctor Dot—"

"What are you doing?"

"Stopping for a moment."

"Why?"

"Because I can't do this. You're not happy and neither am I. We're both far too angry to risk getting needled by the wrong people. What's more, we have some serious trust issues and I'm not dropping you back until we've cleared the air."

She sighed but it sounded sort of wobbly, and she didn't speak.

"And also, you look as if you need to have a good cry—"

She waved an exasperated hand at him. A 'yes', he reckoned. With difficulty he extracted a clean tissue from among the bank notes in his pocket.

"Here. I should imagine you Grongles aren't supposed to get weepy, but it's only me, so I expect you can get away with it."

She made a game attempt at a smile.

"I'm not going to tell anyone," he added.

"I know and I'm sorry for what I said."

"It was the truth."

"Maybe."

"Definitely." The Pan put one hand on the bottom of the steering wheel, "I'm sorry I reacted the way I did."

"I'm sorry I compared your country to a rat's arse."

He raised one eyebrow at her.

"Well, we're sorry about a lot of things aren't we? But I'm very glad you're sorry about that, otherwise, as a patriot, I'd have to challenge you to a fight, which you'd only go and win, because I'd run away."

She half laughed, half sobbed.

"Friends?" he asked.

"Friends."

"Good. I don't think there's room for a hug in here but we could shake hands if you like."

"OK, Defreville." She held out her hand and they proceeded, with mock solemnity, to do as he'd suggested.

"So come on then. Tell me what's eating you. You did a wonderful thing today and you should be very chipper."

She looked down and tore a small corner off the paper hanky he'd given her.

"I'm so ashamed."

"What? Why?" In so far as he could, in the confined space of the snurd, The Pan held his hands out, sideways for a second, in the standard style that is read to mean, 'uh?' the world over. It hurt his shoulder.

"After our previous conversation I'm surprised you need to ask."

"Look, you didn't have to help Trev. You didn't have to help me, but you risked your life to do what you believe is right. I see no shame in that."

"Then you didn't see your friends' faces when I arrived. They were frightened of me and they hated me. Oh they're civilised and they put it aside but that was their first reaction: fear and loathing."

Although they were parked in the shade it was still bright and her pupils had contracted to two vertical black stripes. If Big Merv and Lucy had reacted the way she said, The Pan could understand it. He wondered if he would ever be able to look into the catlike eyes of a Grongle without apprehension himself. Arnold! Grow some depth. Of course he would, and so would his friends, when they'd met enough decent ones.

"Big Merv and Lucy: they might find the package unnerving – to be honest, I do, too – but we're all sensible enough to know that the important bit is what's inside. If I had half your principles or your courage, or, more to the point, your intelligence, K'Barth wouldn't be in this mess. I just wish I'd realised who I was before—"

There was a deafening flurry of flustered clucking. The chicken, or at least the eighth Architrave, was unhappy. Hardly surprising. The Pan had spoken without thinking and if Doctor Dot was listening in the right manner, he'd given too much away. He trusted her in so far as he didn't believe she'd betray him. However, treating the blacklisted was one thing, helping conceal the most wanted fugitive on the planet was a big ask, even from her.

"I'm ashamed that when K'Barthans look at me they see a Grongle, like Captain Snow. He is not us."

"I believe you." The Pan pinged the end of the indicator stalk idly with his finger.

"It's good of you to try and reassure me. You're a sweet boy, Defreville."

"Thank you. I'm heartened you can say that after seeing my file."

She laughed.

"It certainly makes interesting reading."

"Yeh, well, at least you know who you're dealing with."

She made eye contact.

"Yes, I do."

She was talking about something else. Arnold's bogies! Had she realised who he was – who he really was?

"Meaning?"

"The Mervinettes had a driver who is pardoned. Then Big Merv, among others, is rescued from execution by an anonymous individual in a rogue commercial snurd from your pub—"

He put his hand up, one finger extended in a no-no-don't-go-any-further gesture.

"Stolen from my pub."

"It still has to be you."

"Not necessarily. I'd hardly have used my own snurd and if I did, I'd have used this one." He patted the dash affectionately.

"No. Too obvious. And Captain Snow was flashing one very similar to this around as recently as this morning. More than a coincidence I'd say. I think the lorry was all you had. Even if it wasn't, you'd never have sacrificed this one. I know a man in love with his wheels when I see one."

He laughed.

"Fair enough."

"My opposite number in the army thinks Lord Vernon killed you all. I imagine my commander knows better."

"General Moteurs?" The Pan had suspected she was right but please, Arnold, let the General not tell anyone.

"Yes," she changed tack. "How did you get this one back?"

"Spare keys … and the original thumbprint of course." He held up his hand and wiggled the thumb under discussion.

"Watch out then, Captain Snow will report it stolen."

"Well, it thinks it's mine, so he can do what he likes."

"That's the danger: he will do what he likes and the law is on his side. Be careful."

They sat in amicable silence for a moment.

"Doctor, can I ask you something? You seem to be fighting your own lone battle here. You've spent the last few hours with a bunch your government classes as very naughty people. I'm just wondering why. Is this about more than just medicine?"

"No, medicine is at the heart of it. It's about scientific truth and my integrity. I'm a doctor. It's a position of trust. I swore an oath. My loyalty should be to my patients. Always."

"From where I'm sitting, your loyalty's beyond question."

She looked down.

"It isn't."

The Pan waited a moment, tracing the outline of the snurd logo in the middle of the steering wheel with his index finger.

"Would it help to tell someone?"

She looked down at her hands again and tore another piece off the tissue.

"No."

"Sorry. I didn't mean to pry."

"You aren't. I lost a patient, that's all. It happens to everyone but this was my fault."

"I find it hard to believe."

"Well it was, and now a young woman is dead."

"I think, maybe, you're being too hard on yourself. People die. However much you want them to live and, no matter how hard you try, not everyone you treat will get better."

"This one should have done."

"Even if it feels like that, it may not be the case. It's not necessarily your fault."

"Oh it was." She was animated, "I closed my eyes to the truth. I told myself it would be alright, that it was better if it was I who oversaw her treatment than someone else. It was absolute ethical anathema and I was fully aware of what I was doing. I have to atone."

"So you make a habit of this: treating the blacklisted?"

"I think it's time you drove me back to the Security HQ, don't you?"

"Alright. But before we go, thank you, sincerely, for everything you've done."

"Thank you for listening."

"I owe you more than that and it galls me that I will never be able to pay you back. Please feel free to bend my ear any time … if it helps."

"You are a good soul." She smiled. "Truly, truly good."

"Hardly. I'm an incorrigible rogue. And you, of all people, should know that. After all you've—"

"Read your file," at last she laughed, "yes. General Moteurs trusts you though, and he's a keen judge of character."

"General Moteurs?"

"Yes. He has a very high opinion of you."

"That's … not the impression he gave me."

"He's not one to shell out praise. If you've earned his respect he considers it endorsement enough. Now, young man, if you're going to buy my patient some proper food and still be back to open your pub, we must go. I don't want Captain Snow calling in to check up and undoing all my good work because you've been sitting here with me."

"Can I just ask, how come General Moteurs—"

"Tomorrow, young man. We don't have time to discuss this now."

"But—"

"Drive."

"But—"

"Please."

She laughed and he was glad she was cheerful again.

"Alright, alright." He swiped his thumb over the reader on the dash, pressed the starter, and they set out for the Security HQ.

Chapter 15

Ruth was wondering whether it was safe to work at the trapdoor on the chimney some more with the underwire from one of the bras when she heard a knock on the door. This was a surprise in itself. She waited. Maybe whoever it was would go away. There was another knock. This was extreme politeness from Captain Snow. Normally he would have smashed the door open by now. She moved to the bottom of the stairs.

"Come in," she said tentatively.

The door was unlocked and opened by a Grongle guard. But instead of her usual odious gaoler, it was General Moteurs who stood at the top of the steps. Balanced in one hand he carried a tray with one of those domed silver dishes they keep food warm with in posh hotels. He managed to bow without dropping it which was impressive.

"Good afternoon," he said with precise formality. "My master has sent me to talk some sense into you." He walked down the steps and as the guards closed the door and locked him in, he lowered the tray a little so he could waft it past her nose; it smelled good. "But first, you would have something to eat, I think?" He put the tray down on the table.

"Please," he gestured to the chair. Slowly, hesitantly, she went over and sat down. He pushed it in and placed the napkin on her lap, like a very smartly dressed waiter. He moved round to where she could see him. "This has been prepared by Lord Vernon's own chef," he said, lifting the lid with a flourish. "I give you my personal guarantee that it is unadulterated, by Captain Snow or anyone else."

"Are you my gaoler now?"

"Not yet."

She stared at the meal in front of her.

"You used Lord Vernon's chef and made him prepare shepherd's pie … and peas?"

"It displeases you?"

"No. But I bet it displeased him."

"Lord Vernon?"

"Well, probably, but I meant the chef."

He inclined his head.

"Perhaps, but I do not think so. He likes to cook and he appreciates it when those he cooks for enjoy his food."

"It's very kind of you, and I'm grateful – it's one of my favourite things – but I'm not hungry."

He put the metal lid down on the tray and put his hands on his hips, like some exasperated parent.

"Ruth, starving yourself will only sap your strength and provoke my master to even greater depths of cruelty. It will achieve nothing else."

"I don't feel like eating."

He took a platinum thimble from a pouch at his belt and put it on the table between them. Briefly, she wondered why and then she remembered The Pan explaining that it would make it difficult for anyone using another portal to listen to their conversation.

"I believe I can change your mind."

In a way, that sounded sinister, especially with his habitual deadpan delivery. She looked at the thimble and up at him.

"Once I've made a decision, I don't change my mind that easily," she warned him.

"So Lord Vernon tells me. You are driving him almost to distraction."

"Good. Angry people make mistakes."

The corners of his eyes softened slightly.

"That is your strategy."

"Yes. If I can make him insane with rage—"

"He will do something foolish?"

"I hope."

"Perhaps, but that anger makes him volatile and unpredictable, not to mention obdurate. He will be harder to manipulate while enraged."

"Maybe, but if he's thinking clearly he will be invincible, so it's the only way I can help."

"Then you have a stouter heart than I," he said, continuing smoothly, before she could protest. "Now, to my true purpose in coming here. I have news, and I believe you may be more inclined to eat when you have heard it. Your friends are alive. The Pan of Hamgee rescued them."

"What!" She stood up and he glanced down at the plate of food with a slightly pained expression. "Are you sure?"

"I have an eyewitness account, from a reliable being."

Dare she believe this?

"Someone I would trust with my life," he added. "My medical officer. Your Hamgeean sustained an injury while in custody."

"Yes, Lord Vernon shot him."

He inclined his head.

"Some medical treatment was required so I arranged that he should have it from my MO rather than the army's. Your friend, Trev Parker, was also injured while in custody. He has a broken leg which was infected. He is also, officially dead – a condition which presents some problems when attempting to obtain treatment from the K'Barthan health service. She tells me both are recovering well."

"Is this true?"

"Obviously, or we would be having a different conversation."

"Then, that's amazing … thank you," said Ruth. It wasn't quite sinking in.

"My pleasure."

"And Trev? Will he be OK?"

"Yes, he has Big Merv and your friend Lucy to look after him, as well as The Pan of Hamgee and he is receiving daily visits from my MO."

"Is she a member of the Underground?"

"Naturally."

"And all four of them are alive?"

"Yes."

"Really?"

"Yes."

"Then … that's wonderful! I knew he was driving! I can't believe it!" Ruth ran to General Moteurs and threw her arms round him, hugging him tight. It clearly surprised him but not so much that he couldn't give her an awkward hug in return. "Thank you, oh thank you. You have no idea what it means to me … not just what you have told me but what you have done."

"Perhaps I do now." He stood back and held her by the shoulders, smiling. "I cannot pretend The Pan of Hamgee impressed me initially, but I am beginning to understand why Sir Robin sees him as he does; why you do. He has something. He will make an excellent Architrave."

"If he gets the chance."

"We must ensure he does."

"We?"

"We. You must play your part in this but first, I beg of you, eat something."

"You sound like my father."

"And you are very like my daughter – other than that I might have talked some sense into her by now."

It dawned on Ruth that this was the first time she'd had anything approaching a normal conversation since she'd been taken prisoner. She was grateful to the General for bringing her this small slice of the everyday, as well as such wonderful news, when the rest of her existence was a bad dream.

"Alright then, Dad, just for you," she said.

He dropped the formality enough to chuckle at that and she went back to her place at the table. The shepherd's pie smelled fantastic, up there with her mother's she reckoned. He watched her for a minute or two while she ate. He seemed preoccupied and she guessed he had more to say. He turned and walked out onto the balcony where he picked up one of the chairs. He brought it inside, put it at the table, opposite her, and sat down.

"Thank you for the world-class pie," she said. She still wasn't hugely hungry but she did see his point about not eating and it was good, which made it a lot easier to force down than it might have been.

"A pleasure."

They lapsed into silence.

"How's your day been?" Her attempt at small talk seemed to surprise him even more than the hug.

"The High Leader has arrived for Lord Vernon's installation."

"The High Leader?"

"The Lord of All Grongolia."

"Ah, the most important man on the planet."

"The most important—" he began patiently.

"Grongle, right," she corrected herself. "Sorry."

"Yes. I have been trying to persuade him to choose a set of rooms."

"That was difficult?"

"He is exacting at the best of times but he is here to establish his superiority."

"Which makes this not a very good time and him even more exacting?"

"Yes."

"How come you escaped?"

"I have left him settling in while I attend to an important matter of state: you," a beat, "you are Lord Vernon's betrothed."

"Don't remind me," Ruth put down her knife and fork. "I was almost hungry until you said that."

"Please accept my apologies. Ruth, my master is the other matter we must discuss."

"Yeh well, he has sent you to talk to me."

"Yes. He asked me to persuade you to cooperate."

"Persuade."

"That is the word he used. I understand that you must face him in whatever manner ensures your sanity but ..." he tailed off.

"But?"

"You are not the only person affected by your actions."

"Lord Vernon giving you a hard time is he?" she said and regretted it at once.

"What he does to me is of no consequence. I was thinking of the others. You must find a way to walk the line."

"I cannot give him what he wants. Soon, I'll have to but now ..."

"Understood. But you cannot be at loggerheads with him, or I assure you, he will destroy you. You must make your peace. There is an old Grongolian proverb, 'Iron is harder than water, but iron can be held when water cannot'."

"Which means somebody didn't have a bucket, I presume."

"No," he said patiently. "It means that to be truly strong you must be flexible or even pretend to be weak. Identify those things my master wants which you can give, and offer them to him. Start by eating."

"How can I when Captain Snow—"

"I have already given you my guarantee in that respect."

"What about supper?"

"I hope to persuade my master to assign your care to me, in which case, it will not be an issue. However, I will need your cooperation on this point. Please, I will explain while you eat."

She picked up the knife and fork again.

"It's hard to drum up an appetite when I'm miserable. But I'll try. What do you suggest?"

"That you offer a TV appearance. If you give a good account of yourself you may even persuade him that you are finally coming to heel. He believes you will. His confidence in his power is absolute but if he believes the process has started he will treat you better."

Ruth thought about this. She didn't want to endorse Lord Vernon on TV, she didn't want to make her support of him that public – even though it was the point of the deal she'd made – and she didn't want to because it would hurt The Pan. General Moteurs guessed at what she might be thinking.

"The Hamgeean still loves you and yes it will cut him to see you with my master. But he is intelligent. By the installation on Saturday he will know the truth, I swear it."

Did General Moteurs mean that he was going to tell him? It almost sounded like it. She gave the matter a few more moments' consideration. Appearing on TV, and in the press generally, was what she had expected when she struck her deal with Lord Vernon. Perhaps it was what he expected too, until she'd passed out at GNN. Afterwards she had assumed they would make her try again. She had not offered. It hadn't occurred to her that she should.

"OK. Tell Lord Vernon I will do it."

"You will not regret it. You will have to be taken to the K'Barthan GNN building under armed guard but they will be my troops, and except for the interview, I will not leave your side."

"You blanked me last time."

"Yes. You were not my responsibility and it was expedient that I showed no concern. If I looked at you—"

There was a strange buzzing sound from somewhere and General Moteurs put his finger to his lips, unhooked his mobile from his belt and answered it.

"Moteurs …" there was a pause while someone spoke to him at the other end, "sir …" if Ruth hadn't guessed who it was from his use of the word 'sir' the way he seemed to sit straighter, taller, as if standing to attention showed her, "yes, sir, I will be there directly" he was saying, he glanced at his wristwatch, "certainly, sir, I will return it to you on my way ... three minutes, sir. Thank you, sir."

He gave the phone a quick rub in his hair and hooked it back on his belt. Then he took the platinum thimble from the table and slipped it into his pocket.

"I regret that I must leave you, but take heart Ruth, and please," he gave her another of his almost-smiles, "do not be afraid. I will see you again tomorrow, for even if I fail to persuade Lord Vernon to relieve Captain Snow, I will bring you one meal a day. Now, I regret I must leave you. My master awaits and he is not known for his patience."

Ruth stood up and walked with him to the door.

"Thank you," she said.

"My pleasure. Now," he gestured to the table, "eat the rest of it, if you please."

When he had gone, she was drawn back to her plate by the smell of Michelin-star-quality shepherd's pie. What was left was still warm and the mashed potato top still crunchy. The peas were bright green and enticing. Her mouth watered. General Moteurs was right, she thought, she needed strength, and while she was in reasonable spirits and felt able to, she probably ought to finish it.

Chapter 16

The Pan's chat with Doctor Dot, followed by a trip to the market, had made him later back to the Parrot than he expected. He parked the SE2, bipped the keys and watched as it drove away. Balancing the grocery box on his knee and steadying it with his good arm, he was just struggling to put the keys in the lock with his other hand and cursing the pain in his shoulder when he noticed somebody walking up behind him. Luckily it was only Pub Quiz Alan.

"Hello Alan," he said. There was too much on his mind and he wasn't really concentrating, which was why he mistimed it, speaking just before Alan tapped him on the back. He made to turn round but nearly dropped the box of groceries, managing not to let go of it but only in favour of dropping the keys instead.

"Sorry mate." Pub Quiz Alan bent down to pick the keys up and handed them back to The Pan.

"Not a problem."

"Listen … you and me we've got to have a word."

"Is it about the bar work? I could do with a hand this evening if you're up for it." Please let it be about the bar work or something else simple.

"No."

The Pan put the box down on the ground beside him.

"OK, Alan. What's up?"

"It's about all the extra punters …"

"Right."

"I know where they're coming from."

"You do?"

"Yeh. Let me take that," Alan bent down and picked up the groceries as The Pan unlocked the door. "Upstairs or down?"

"Downstairs," said The Pan quickly. "Come on in Alan, I'll show you where to put those," he added unnecessarily loudly, hoping that if Lucy or Big Merv were on their way down to greet him they'd realise he had company and stay hidden.

Alan reverted to his original topic.

"I reckon they're coming to get a look at you," he said as he followed

The Pan inside and closed the door behind him.

"What because of Lord Vernon's little handover ceremony?"

"Don't be daft—"

"Is this to do with Norris?" asked The Pan over his shoulder as he hung up the keys.

"Now you're cooking. Partly Norris ... and the rumour, of course."

The Pan stopped.

"What rumour?"

"Thinking about it, I s'pose it's Norris's rumour—"

"Out with it." The Pan started walking again and led Alan into the Holy of Holies behind the bar.

"Stick the box on there for now," he said and Alan placed it on one of the work surfaces.

"Norris reckons you got the Architraves' ring."

The Pan followed Alan's gaze to the ring on his finger.

Blimey. Another person who knew the significance of the ring. The first time it had come into The Pan's possession he'd appreciated that it was old, but all he'd really seen was a nice shiny piece of loot he could sell. He had always understood that he was not as clever as he wanted to be, but he hadn't bargained on everyone else being so much smarter: schoolboy error.

"It might be a replica."

"That doesn't matter to Norris—here, d'you want me to unpack this?"

"No, leave it. Some of it's for upstairs."

"Why don't I take it up there then? It won't take me a sec, stop it cluttering up the place down here."

"No," said The Pan firmly. Alan's eyes narrowed a fraction but he said nothing. The Pan changed the subject. "You were saying about Norris?"

"Yeh," a loaded 'yeh', "he says that the ring looks the deal and that's all it needs to give you some kind of authority."

"And he's been spreading that has he? Alan, I'm trying to keep my head down and be a good boy. This kind of cobblers is not going to help."

"You want me to have a word with him?"

"Is it going to do any good?"

"Ner. He's Norris and he's given to over-exaggerating."

"Let's hope everyone else knows that."

"It ain't just Norris. It's other stuff: the delivery snurd turning up at the execution yesterday, out of the blue."

"Yeh? Well I can explain that. Some smecker nicked it last night. I reported it but the police didn't care. They told me to look for it myself. Then he gets it blown up for me. I'll never afford a new one."

"I thought you were going away at the end of the week."

The Pan felt sick at the prospect of what lay ahead.

"I am," he opened one of the drawers and took out the bread knife, "but whoever gets this place after me will need a delivery snurd and now I don't have one."

"Right … yeh." Alan took the breadboard from under the counter top and passed it over.

"Thanks." The two of them prepared the kitchen for 'service', such as it was, in silence for a minute or two.

"Norris and the others," said Alan, "they saw what happened to your delivery snurd, and all."

"Did they?"

"Yeh, and then they seen you here. An' they've looked at that ring on your hand an' they've looked at the comings and goings round 'ere and they reckon SOMETHING is going on."

"Something? Sorry SOMETHING?"

"Yeh."

"What kind of THING?"

"Well, Norris reckons that ring gives you magic powers and that you've magicked them all back here."

"Who?"

"Trev, Big Merv and that foreign bird."

"Lucy?"

"Yeh, 'Lucy'. You know her then?"

Arse.

"No."

"Yeh, right. Course you don't. That's why you're on first-name terms."

"No, I called her Lucy because I don't know her second name."

"Yeh, course."

"Yes, actually. I suppose Norris thinks I grew long blonde hair like the git who nicked my delivery snurd and came back from the dead as well?"

"Well here's the thing. Norris ain't sure how to explain that one. But me … I reckon I can …" Like the detective at the end of a crime novel revealing the identity of the murderer, Alan unzipped his leather jacket and with a flourish pulled the wig out of his inside pocket.

"Smeck," said The Pan before he could stop himself. What with the state of Trev, after they'd arrived he had completely forgotten about the wig.

"That's right, 'smeck'," said Alan. "You want to take a bit more notice of where you leave stuff, my lad. And current affairs … you want to take a bit more notice of them and all."

The Pan tried to keep his expression blank but he suspected he was succeeding about as well as usual, because Alan was giving off a distinct aura of I've-got-you-bang-to-rights-ness.

"You left it on the table. You're lucky I was first in. I can't believe we came this close," he held up his hand, first finger and thumb together, with a tiny space between, to emphasise the extreme closeness in question, "to doing you in."

"Then thank you for demurring."

"Yeh, I bet your mates are glad about that and all."

"I bet they are." The Pan wondered where the conversation was going; the wrong way, by the looks of things unless he could grab hold of the wheel and steer it back in the right direction.

"Yeh, see, Norris reckons you only get to wear that ring because it's yours."

The Pan's throat had gone dry. He swallowed.

"I found it at work, so I suppose it is," he croaked.

"If that's the way you want to play it, we'll say you did but it's not what I think."

"What do you think then?"

"I'm the Reigning Upper Left Central Ning Dang Po Trivia Champion. I know that's the K'Barthan Ring of State. So I reckon the reason there's a lot of people in that bar," Alan turned and pointed to the empty room, beyond the doorway, for theatrical effect, "and the reason Norris is doing tours, is sort of because they believe Lord Vernon."

"Eh?"

"They think there is a Candidate but they know our Lord Protector isn't it. BUT see, they've heard this other rumour, that the real deal is here, in the city, right under his nose, and they say …" Alan paused for even more theatrical effect, "that he's running a pub."

Bum. Why did this have to happen? Mentally, The Pan didn't so much kick himself as beat himself senseless. Not that he could get much less sensible than he already was.

"Norris is telling people that?"

Alan nodded.

"And is he saying it's this pub?"

"Not in so many words."

"Then he'd better stop, I mean it, NOW. And you have to tell him Alan."

"It's not just 'im. They don't need telling; they're seeing you and believing it. That ring's got power and so have you."

"What's that supposed to mean?"

"That me and Norris and all the others, we know who you are."

"I think this—and Norris—might be getting a bit out of control."

"He's only trying to help. There's no time and if you want K'Barth behind you on Saturday, it's got to be more than us. Everyone has to know who the good guy is."

"Listen, Alan. I'm not the 'good guy' and if you or anyone else stands behind me on Saturday, you're going to get slaughtered."

"No. That's not going to happen. Can't."

"That's right, it can't, because you all have to lie low, get organised and wait for the next one."

"The next one? So you *are* the Candidate."

Smecking Arnold.

"I didn't say that."

"Yes you did, by mistake – which makes me, for one, believe it."

"Alright, look, Alan, it's lovely of you, and Norris, to want to help but spreading rumours won't. What I'm trying to say is this: there is going to be a Candidate, a real one who's worth something, soon. And when he – or she – turns up there has to be someone left alive to stand behind them. Who I am is irrelevant, it's what I'm here for that matters and my purpose is to stop Lord Vernon from becoming Architrave. And yes, it's partly about this ring." He held his hand up and let it drop. "But if I'm going to do that, I have to stay alive until Saturday. Believe me, the chances of that are slim enough; the entire world, including Lord Vernon, wants me dead, and having the equivalent, in gossip form, of a big neon sign over this pub going, 'Yoo-hoo! Over here!' is not going to improve my chances."

"How's Lord Vernon going to hear about it? The Grongles aren't going to listen to gossip."

"No but he has spies, and even if he doesn't listen to gossip, the Resistance will. Their Tech Ops already know where I am—"

"That Spiffle who was here?"

"Yes, him. He's bringing his boss to see me tonight about some … other stuff and there's a Revenue Acquisition gang based here or hereabouts who tried to take the ring off me a couple of nights ago. I had to escape from them in a way that …" How to put this? No don't even try, "Well, I expect I've drawn a fair bit of attention to myself. I'm easy enough for them to find, even if these Tech Ops people don't say anything, and even without Norris telling tall stories about me, a bunch of short furry psychopaths with long knives are going to come and ask me for this ring, soon."

"They ain't gonna get it."

"They are if they find me Alan, and unless I'm extremely careful, they're going to be prising it off my cold dead hand because they could take on the lot of you, no problem."

Alan laughed.

"You're a drama queen and no mistake."

"You have me there but, in this case, I'm afraid this is less about drama than realism." He ran his hand through his hair.

"So how did you rescue your mates?"

"I never said I rescued them, Alan."

"Maybe. But I've been thinking about what Betsy said, you know, about you having a bit of skirt—"

"Perhaps I have."

"Nah. I checked with one of her other girls who lives the other side of the alley," Alan waved a hand in the general direction of the Parrot and Screwdriver's back door, "and she also swears blind she saw a blonde bird, the spit of that Lucy Hargraves, closing the curtains in Trev's bedroom. So it ain't just Nareen, that's two independent witnesses telling the same story."

Arnold.

"Alan, I don't know what you're talking about."

"Sure you don't. Let's go over the facts. Your delivery vehicle has been used in a crime, you've been wearing a blonde wig, just like the driver, you got people upstairs what are making a noise—"

"I told you the reason for that."

"No you didn't. If you needed a plumber you'd use Stan. You're harbouring them fugitives upstairs: Big Merv, Lucy Hargraves, and Gladys and Ada's Trev. What's more, you got the K'Barthan Ring of State; I'll bet my arse that's real, and you're wearing it like you own it."

The Pan realised he was staring at Pub Quiz Alan with an expression of something approaching horror.

"An' that look tells me I'm right," finished Alan.

"I—" The Pan cleared his throat. He knew Pub Quiz Alan was reigning trivia champion but Arnold's socks, did he have to be so smecking clever? "I'm only wearing the ring because I can't take it off."

"Why?"

"It's … complicated."

"Yeh. Now that I can believe. I know who you are: who you really are. We all do."

Smeck.

"No you don't."

"Yes, we do. You're the Candidate."

"Smecking Arnold! Don't say it."

"Why not? It's true."

The Pan's eyes went to his hand, currently clutching the bread knife as if his life depended on it, the ruby glowed deep red and the gold shone. His shoulders drooped.

"OK, Alan, you win. Does anyone else know about the wig?"

"Nah."

"Good, because you can't tell a living soul about this; not a living soul, d'you understand?"

"Can I tell them you got Big Merv upstairs?"

"NO!"

"What about if I say the Candidate saved Big Merv but don't mention that it's you and he's up there?"

"NO! I meant what I said. You mustn't say a thing to anyone. Otherwise I'll have to—"

"Have to what? Get him down here to do me over?"

The Pan sighed.

"No."

"I won't tell no-one. You know I won't. Coz if I was going to, I'd have got the wig out when the punters was in."

"I realise that and thanks." The Pan ran his good hand wearily through his hair. "Even so," he looked Pub Quiz Alan in the eye, desperately hoping to communicate the gravity of the situation, “there’s a lot riding on this. After Saturday, you can tell who you like but until then—”

“I’ll keep quiet about it.”

“Yeh, please …” he checked his watch, “and now it’s time to open up.”

“OK. Can I tell them the Candidate—”

“That’s the end of the conversation, Alan.” The Pan went out into the main bar and unlocked the door.

Chapter 17

Lord Vernon sat at the usual table on his balcony awaiting the arrival of General Moteurs. The two of them were to join the High Leader for dinner. Placing the platinum portal on the table in front of him, just so, he sipped his smoothie and enjoyed the view. Having lent the portal to the General, he had demanded it back shortly after the arrival of his Grongolian superior so he could use it to watch his faithful deputy enduring the High Leader's insufferable company. The highlight, so far, had been the moment when his trusted number two turned down a job offer.

After three hours, even Lord Vernon took pity on General Moteurs and went to relieve him, partly as a reward for refusing the job but also to distract his own thoughts from his frustration with the Chosen One: a frustration which several hours spent in the cells, enthusiastically handling state business, had done surprisingly little to appease. Lord Vernon gave the High Leader a tour of the Palace during which his honoured guest found astonishingly little to like. As the tour progressed, the High Leader's taxing presence proved far more effective than Lord Vernon's most extreme indulgences in the cells. To his relief, his private fantasies featured the Chosen One less and less and the act of murdering his opposite number from Grongolia more and more.

A partial success, then. He smiled as the peaceful environment of his balcony worked its magic and he began to relax. The glass doors slid open and a flunky showed General Moteurs into his presence. He seemed weary.

Doubtless his duties accommodating the requirements of the High Leader were a factor.

"Our guest is satisfied with his rooms, General?"

"Yes, sir."

Lord Vernon doubted it.

"He has not complained?"

"Not significantly, sir."

"Almost miraculous. How did you achieve this?"

"I crave your pardon, sir, but I told him they were your rooms."

"Excellent, General. I see you have read him well."

"Sir."

"He is exacting to a tiresome degree."

"Sir."

Lord Vernon stood up.

"And now, I must entertain him at dinner. I fear I will lose control and slit his throat before the week is out. I require more time to compose myself before this evening. You will inform them I shall be late. There is a small matter I must attend to first."

"Sir," General Moteurs hesitated, "he may be insulted."

"Doubtless. Nonetheless, you will do as you are ordered."

"Sir."

Lord Vernon pushed the platinum portal across the table.

"You may keep this, General, as a reward for your patience. I may require you to return it at any time but otherwise, consider it your own."

"Thank you, sir." General Moteurs put the thimble into one of the pouches on his belt.

"You have your orders. Go."

"Sir," said General Moteurs and he did as he was told.

Chapter 18

Deep in the basement of the Resistance's woodland HQ, Forrest, the Galorsh, handed control of his listening terminal to the being on the next shift, a human, at least roughly human – he was Hamgeean – called Bob. Forrest closed the door on Surveillance Room B and headed away, helium-spirited, to prepare for his evening. Tonight he had a date with the loveliest female he'd ever met. He thought for a moment of Nar. Quiet, sensitive and superintelligent. Oh yes, and having dinner with him. Booyacka! He skipped a few paces and flicked the end of his long tail in delight.

"Hey! You got your hot date tonight?" It was one of his colleagues, a Swamp Thing called Maurice, who was heading towards him. Forrest skipped a couple more paces, executed a spin on one foot and landed in a half crouch with one finger pointing at his friend, just as the two of them drew level.

"Yo, Mo!" he said gleefully and the two of them did a high five as his friend walked past.

"Yo, but not in that daggy outfit, right?" said Mo turning and walking backwards so they could carry on talking.

"Nah, I've got me some smooth threads," said Forrest.

"You'd better," said Mo and the two of them laughed. "Gotta split or I'll be late!"

"Wooooah. The supervisor will have your nuts on a spike!"

"Ooo! I'm running! Catch you later."

"Cheers mate!"

Supper at the canteen was less than ritzy but it was all HQ offered, and as he was not authorised to leave, all there was. Not that it would have made any difference, out in the woods there was nowhere to go. His date had been left in sole command of her department so she was trapped there too. He'd managed to 'rent' a candelabra. Forrest could offer little else. Calling it 'dinner' seemed to elevate it to something more shiny. He was hoping they would just chat, like last time, or at least, he would ask her lots of questions so she would chat and he could just sit there watching her, floating on air. He checked his watch.

He doubted Nar would want him to visit her at work and he didn't want her to see him in the outfit he wore for listening. His comfortable tracksuit bottoms, manky T-shirt and sweatshirt would probably come as an unwelcome surprise. But she was loyal to her boss and he knew she would prefer it if Forrest told her what he had overheard sooner rather than later. He picked her out at once, the moment he walked into Tech Ops. She glanced up at him, and then up at the clock on the wall, and seemed surprised.

"Hi, you're early," she said. He couldn't read her expression but he could almost hear what she was thinking: *Did you actually dress yourself this morning?* Yeh, she was definitely thinking something like that because she looked down to hide it.

"Sorry, these shocking duds are for work only. I was on my way back to change into something smoother."

She smiled. There was a vulnerability, a shyness to Nar that turned Forrest's heart inside out. He wanted to put his arm round her and hold her close. But that would not be cool.

"How did the inspection from our Leader go?" she asked. Hey, she'd remembered.

"Well, listen up, that's what I came to see you about."

"Really?" She sounded half pleased and half disappointed.

"Yeh, we need to talk, man, somewhere quiet if you get me."

"Sure."

"It's got to be somewhere real quiet."

She flushed, was she getting the wrong idea? He hoped not. He leaned forward and whispered in her ear.

"They're listening."

"I know. OK, when?"

"Now, sweet sis."

"Excuse me everyone," she clapped her hands a couple of times, "I must talk to Forrest." Somebody wolf-whistled. "Not funny. I'll come back in five minutes. Blimpet, will you take over please?"

"Yes ma'am."

"Please come with me," she said to Forrest and walked past him, out into the corridor.

"Laters guys," said Forrest and ran after her.

She slowed her pace and waited. He could see the bulky outline of the jumper she was wearing under her lab coat. She was cold. She'd got her growback wrong. That was cute: geeky cute. He felt protective again.

"OK, what's wrong?" she asked.

"Where's the Prof?"

"You know I can't tell you that, Forrcst."

"Yeh, OK, sorry. But, I think there's some proper-bad, brown-stinky coming his way. Denarghi brought Colonel Plumby with him today and them and Melior was talking. My terminal malfunctioned so I was moved to one of the spare ones, in an empty bunch of cubes at the back, away from everyone else ... except one other guy, Vogle. He was sitting across from me, but he was listening to something sensitive so he was like, 'stop talking man' the whole time. So I had to sit getting bored out of my skull listening to a couple of RA agents getting it on."

"How come you never get to monitor any enemy activity?"

Forrest shrugged.

"You got me there. It's all our own agents, the recordings I'm given." Her brow furrowed. "Yeh," he continued, "Denarghi's one crazy dude and Colonel Melior? He's even crazier. So, I reckon Vogle pushed the panic button because the next second, right, Colonel Melior's on his back and King Denarghi and Colonel Plumby as well and they're giving Vogle some special attention. Denarghi listened on the guy's earphones, and, sure as I am standing here, I'll swear he was listening to the Professor."

"How do you know?" asked Nar. She was holding her long tail in one hand, smoothing the fur with the other.

"Because after they'd finished with Vogle, right, they all went into a huddle, in the corner away from everyone; everyone except me that is, because I shouldn't have been there so they weren't looking and they didn't see me. I only got bits, but I heard him say 'that smecker Professor N'Aversion' and then he said 'call them both to account' and something about 'making an example'. There was garbled stuff. I didn't get much but, wherever the Professor's going it sounds like he's got company."

"You mean they're following him?"

"Yeh. Word up."

Nar was quiet for a moment. "Forrest?"

"Yeh?"

"Thanks. I really appreciate you coming here and telling me this. I need to get word to the Professor. If you go and get ready ... can we meet half an hour later?"

"Yeh, I can do that."

"Don't tell anyone else what you heard will you?"

“Are you crazy? They’ll shoot me if they find out about this.”

Her brown eyes met his.

“That’s what I’m worried about. Be careful, Forrest, I don’t want anything to happen to you.”

Arnold’s eyeballs. She cared. Cool.

He leaned down and touched her cheek with his: the Galorsh equivalent of a platonic kiss, except it was oh so much more than that.

“Catch you later, babe,” he said and headed for the dorm.

Chapter 19

Deirdre and Snoofle passed an enjoyable day in the drying room with Mrs Pargeter and her 'girls'. Nobody took much notice of them, so before long they took some wooden knives and a cork board and demonstrated their knife-throwing skills. Every now and again, for appearances' sake, somebody hung something up to dry. Deirdre had forgotten how much she hated the cumbersome uniform, long skirt, white frilly shirt – plunge neck obligatory – laced-up bodice.

Their day over, Snoofle and Deirdre left the laundry and made their way to the staff dining hall for supper. It was full and as they cast around, trays in hand, for a space where they could sit together, there was what Mrs Pargeter would call 'a kerfuffle' at the door and five Grongles marched in. They wore the black and red uniform of the army. Two of them waited, barring the door, the other three, a Major and two regular troops, marched into the middle of the room and stopped.

All conversation died as, with a mass scraping of chairs, the staff stopped eating and stood up, as protocol dictated.

"You may sit," said the Major. He spoke with the clipped, upper class tones of an officer and there was another bout of scraping and clattering as everyone in the room sat down again.

"Arbuthnot and Snoofle. Make yourselves known."

Deirdre and her friend stood up.

"Come with me."

Snoofle and Deirdre exchanged glances. She put her hand on her thigh, where, under her laundress's uniform, she wore her knife belt. Snoofle shook his head. The two guards either side of the Major drew their laser pistols and levelled them.

"No sudden moves," said their leader. "I know you are armed."

Deirdre and Snoofle left their trays and walked slowly out into the centre of the room. The two guards lined up behind them and Major Pylup put them in handcuffs.

"Walk," said the Major.

The two guards, still with their pistols drawn, formed up behind them. Mutely, the two friends did as they were told. They were escorted out into the corridor, past the dinner queue and ushered into a lift.

"Doors closing," said the tinny female voice.

Deirdre tried to catch Snoofle's eye. Now was the time to thump them and escape but before she could alert her friend, the Major spoke.

"Please accept my apologies. General Moteurs was most adamant that your colleagues saw you arrested."

"What?"

"You are in great danger." The lift stopped. "Denarghi has declared you compromised."

"Doors opening."

The seven of them stood in silence.

"Doors closing."

"Strike Ops have been ordered to liquidate you. General Moteurs has therefore ordered that you are returned to his custody for your own safety."

"Then why have we been arrested by the army?"

"The General considered it more convincing."

"Doors opening."

"This way please."

Trying to process her shock at the information she'd been given, Deirdre followed the Major as he escorted her and Snoofle along a corridor. She recognised it at once as the one outside their original prison. Sure enough, at the door waiting for them, with their things reclaimed from their dormitories, was a deputation of four Imperial Guards and Corporal Jones. She saluted the Major and her four subordinates snapped to attention.

"Sir."

"At ease, Corporal. Here are the prisoners your commander requires."

"Thank you sir."

He turned to Deirdre, "Excuse me Lieutenant, but your handcuffs are property of the army. I shall not hear the end of it if I leave them with you. If you please?"

"Of course." She held out her arms and he removed them.

"You too, Group Leader."

Snoofle held his arms up and the Major stooped and removed his cuffs, too.

"I thank you. Until we meet again," he said and marched off down the corridor with his troops.

"That was weird," said Snoofle.

"Agreed."

"This way, sir, ma'am," said Corporal Jones holding the door open. "I am informed you had not eaten. I will have your supper brought to you in twenty minutes."

"Good," said Snoofle, "I was cut up about leaving those sausages."

"My commander would speak with you first," Corporal Jones told them.

At the table, waiting for them, sat General Moteurs. Deirdre was glad to see him. He stood up, at once.

"Your prisoners, sir," said Corporal Jones.

"Thank you, Jones."

"Sir." The Corporal saluted, left the room and locked them all in.

Snoofle spoke first.

"What's going on?" he asked.

"Please be patient, I cannot answer questions as I do not have much time. I will speak with you in detail tomorrow. Major Pylup has informed you of the situation, I think."

"He told us Denarghi has ordered our liquidation," said Deirdre.

"That is true. Your superiors here are delaying but they cannot stall for long."

"What happened?" asked Deirdre.

"You were correct in your supposition about Denarghi. He did not trust me. He believes I have turned you and has forbidden Professor N'Aversion to build the portal. You must leave the Palace at the first opportunity."

"How?"

There was more than a hint of steel in General Moteurs' voice when he said, "I will find a way."

"When?"

"Tomorrow," he glanced at his watch, "and now I must leave. I will return when I have more information."

"Tonight?" asked Deirdre.

He couldn't meet her eyes.

"I regret not," he said.

She could feel Snoofle watching but did not turn her gaze from General Moteurs. "Trust me, Lieutenant," he said and to Snoofle, "you too, Group Leader. You are under my protection," he added and for the first time, on hearing him say this, Deirdre felt glad.

With that, he was gone. For a moment there was silence.

"Here we are then, room-mates again." Snoofle hopped across to his bed and lobbed his bag onto it. "Ooo clean sheets."

Deirdre smiled weakly.

"Come on, soldier. It's not so bad, in fact, between you and me I'm pleased; you should hear some of the lads in the dorm snore."

"Ha! The females are no better."

"I'll bet my dorm-mates outsnore yours."

"Frankly, I do not believe that possible."

They sat quietly for a moment, wrapped in their own thoughts.

"What is Denarghi thinking?" asked Deirdre bitterly. "Why? And what can I do about it? I'm a senior officer in the Resistance, I should not just … run away. I should not allow this."

"You aren't running away, Deirdre," said Snoofle, "and you can't do much about it, not from here or the laundry. I tell you what, why don't we have our supper, take another look at those plans and try to forget about Denarghi? There's nothing we can do until General Moteurs finds out more and we're safer here than anywhere else."

"Maybe," said Deirdre, "but if any one of my people comes looking for us they will rue the day. I'd like to make him pay for what he's done."

"Fighting words," he smiled. "And I'm with you all the way, trooper; I'd happily kill him myself."

"Spoken like a true Blurpon."

They stopped as two of Corporal Jones' staff arrived with supper. As soon as they put it on the table, Snoofle hopped swiftly onto his seat and began to eat.

"How can you be hungry now?" Deirdre asked him.

"I'm not, but I'll bet Denarghi will send a seven-agent team for you, and if we're going to take them down, we'll need all the energy we can get."

Chapter 20

When Professor N'Aversion and Simon arrived at the Parrot and Screwdriver, The Pan of Hamgee was nowhere to be seen. Instead they were served by a blond, curly-haired man with a black leather jacket and stonewashed jeans, who introduced himself as Pub Quiz Alan. He wore penny loafers and under his leather bomber jacket, which was hanging open, he wore a red, white, and black striped polo shirt. Though friendly, he was clearly wary of them. They ordered a couple of rounds of sandwiches, without pickle, sat at a table in the corner, out of the way, and waited. The odd glance, thrown in the Professor and Simon's direction, showed them that Alan and a couple of the other drinkers, were keeping a beady eye on them. The owner of the establishment arrived, only a few minutes late, but the pub was already getting busy.

The Professor wasn't sure what he'd expected from The Pan of Hamgee but the young man who joined Alan behind the bar wasn't it. After a brief chat the two of them looked over at the table where he and Simon were sitting. The lad was wearing a sling but he gave Simon a casual wave with his other hand and came over.

"Hi, sorry to keep you waiting," he gestured to their drinks and the sandwiches, "glad to see Alan's taking care of you."

"Yes he certainly is, thank you," the Professor looked up at The Pan. His dark blue eyes, a ready smile and a casual, easy air gave The Pan a relaxed appearance, but he seemed distracted.

"Are you alright waiting until after closing time? Only it's a bit busy tonight. If it's going to put you out, I can see you tomorrow instead."

"No, no. We're fine. We'll wait until you're ready," said the Professor.

"Right, OK, see you later then," said The Pan and he went back to serving.

The Professor watched him. The lad seemed to be very alert, nervous even – but not in the way he had been described by those who'd met him at the Resistance HQ. There was a self-possession about the boy which no-one back there – or at least, no-one the Professor dared ask – had mentioned. Perhaps he was just better at hiding his cowardice on home ground.

However, it was the reactions of those round The Pan that interested the Professor most. The way the Parrot and Screwdriver's other patrons were keeping a protective eye on him. That was respect.

"The only man alive who can outrun the Interceptor," said Simon, as if answering his thoughts.

"Yes ..." said the Professor slowly, "they certainly hold him in high regard. But I'm not sure that's the reason."

"No, me neither."

Chapter 21

Nar knew she had to go about her business as if nothing was amiss, so she sent the Professor a message and did just that. That was the hardest part. He and Simon might check the forum before they retired for the night. They might, but in reality she knew she was unlikely to hear from them until the following day.

She was grateful to Forrest for the information and even more glad of their date. He had understood her predicament instinctively and as she fretted, waiting for a reply to her message from the Professor, he told her gossip about his department, cracked jokes and made her laugh. The time passed surprisingly quickly as they ploughed their way through Mrs Burgess' latest gastronomic offering, cabbage à la crème.

Throughout the evening Nar checked the forum for any sign of activity.

Why hadn't the Professor replied to her message?

She and Forrest had reached pudding now. She broke off from her conversation to glance at the Professor's stealth tablet sitting on the bench beside her. Still nothing.

"Hey, listen, babe," said Forrest gently, "I—"

Someone put their hand heavily on her shoulder.

"Hello Deputy Chief Engineer Nar," said a voice. She slipped the tablet onto her lap, out of sight, and tried to assume an air of innocence as she looked up and met the eyes of a Group Leader from Henching – she didn't know his name. He was flanked by six armed guards. Her mouth dropped open. She closed it. This looked like an arrest. Except it couldn't possibly be an arrest, could it? She glanced across at Forrest and then back up at the giant behind her.

"Can I help you?" she asked, trying to sound calm, and unafraid, and failing. "Group Leader?" She tacked the 'Group Leader' on as an afterthought, almost forgetting it in her nervousness.

"Yeh, you can stand up, slowly, without giving me and the boys here any trouble, and come with me."

"Where?"

"Denarghi wants to see you."

Her heart sank. Something had gone wrong. Under the table, she pressed her leg against Forrest's and slid the stealth tablet towards him.

The Group Leader grabbed her arm.

"I don't think so," he said. "Now you can come quietly or I can cuff you. Put your hands and the computer on the table where I can see them."

She put the tablet on the table and stood up. The case was identical to the ones issued to Resistance staff, only the software was different; there was a chance they wouldn't realise what it was, if they didn't examine it too closely. Arnold's eyebrows, she shouldn't have tried to pass it to Forrest.

"Very nice," the Group Leader picked it up.

"It's standard issue," said Nar.

"Is it yours?"

"Yes."

He nodded.

"I see. OK, little lady, let's go."

"But, sir, proper straight, man, I think there's been a—"

"You too lad."

"No," cried Nar.

"I'm afraid so. This way."

Two of the guards were already at Forrest's side, he looked from one to the other and over at Nar.

"I'm sorry," she said.

"It's OK, we're cool," he said gently as he stood up.

"As you were, nothing to see here," bellowed the Group Leader, and anyone who hadn't noticed craned their necks to see what was going on. Nar and Forrest were made to stand in single file and the troops formed up either side of them. Then, with the Group Leader at their head, they were marched out into the corridor.

Chapter 22

It was closing time at the Parrot and Screwdriver. Most of the punters had gone and the last few dribs and drabs were leaving. The Pan escorted Professor N'Aversion and Simon to the snug and left them there with a bowl of nuts. He tried to ignore the knot of nerves in his stomach as he and Alan tidied up the bar. They washed up, cashed up and put the glasses away. The Pan hadn't actually opened a bank account, there was hardly any point. His assets would be frozen on Saturday morning so it seemed logical to keep them as liquid as possible. In this case, he was putting the money in a box under his bed for Big Merv to find. Even so, for the sake of keeping up appearances, he and Alan counted it all into little bags and kept a tally of the earnings. The pub was doing well enough.

Which reminded him, he needed to write an inventory for Big Merv, soon, so he could find everything.

"You sure you're going to be alright with those Resistance geezers?" asked Alan, as The Pan unlocked the door and let him out into the street.

"Yeh, if things get a bit hot I'll scream like a girl. I'm sure someone'll come to my aid."

"You really are a spanner. You Know Who still up there then?"

"Nobody is up there."

"Course not, that's why the self-styled yellowest bloke in K'Barth is happy to meet two dodgy characters, one of which is a Swamp Thing, on his own. I've got some business to fix up with Psycho Dave. We'll look in later, make sure you're OK."

"Is that wise? You know how suspicious the Grongles get when they see K'Barthans out after dark."

"I've never paid it any mind before."

"There's no need, Alan. In fact, please don't."

"What if they kill you?"

"If they wanted to kill me, they'd have done it this afternoon."

"You think we'd have let them do that?"

"No. But they'd have had a go anyway. And, as Gladys and Ada would say: 'Go on! Git!'"

Chapter 23

Once The Pan of Hamgee had led the Professor and Simon to the snug he disappeared for rather a long time. The Professor and Simon sipped their beers, nibbled at the nuts.

"Sorry I took such ages," he said when at last he rejoined them. "My help behind the bar thinks you're here to kill me." He mentioned it casually, but there was a tension in his voice that betrayed his nerves. "It took me a minute or two to talk him round."

Professor N'Aversion rose to his feet politely, and Simon followed suit.

"Thank you for taking the time to see us," he said.

"It's a pleasure," The Pan said, adding a belated, "don't get up."

They all sat down again, The Pan, awkwardly as if he wasn't sure what to do next.

"Would you like another drink?" he asked them.

"I think that would be illegal, wouldn't it?" said Simon.

"Very probably, I'm rather sketchy on legal. It's not an issue I'm used to."

"Quite so," said the Professor, trying to put him at his ease.

"I'm guessing you'll want to see the goods?"

The Professor's eyes were drawn momentarily to the ring and then up to The Pan's face. Before he could stop himself, he voiced his thoughts, which had nothing to do with portals.

"I think I already have," he said.

"I'm sorry?" The dark blue eyes met his and suddenly there was a shrewdness about the lad that the Professor had neither noticed nor expected.

"Oh dear, forgive me, I was miles away, yes, please … by all means," said Professor N'Aversion quickly and he watched with breathless excitement as The Pan put a tiny individual-portion-sized jam jar on the table and sat back.

"Simon knows how it works, so I assume you do."

A grainy video image of General Moteurs jumped into the Professor's head. He cleared his throat.

The Pan waved his hand towards the jar.

"Help yourself then but don't put your finger in, please."

The Professor put the portal to his eye. Everything he imagined, he saw.

"Remarkable, truly remarkable." This certainly trumped the Grongles' box!

"Not bad is it? I have about one hundred and fifty of these. You're welcome to them. I think you're going to need them, but in return, I want …" He heaved a sigh, "I want quite a few things, actually but the deal-breaker is amnesty."

Simon cast an apologetic glance at the Professor.

"Ah … yes … I was going to talk to you about that."

"It's non-negotiable, so I don't think there's anything you need to say other than yes."

The Professor squirmed.

"It's rather difficult you see …"

The young man raised an ironic eyebrow. "Yes?" he said. Professor N'Aversion wondered why it was that young people always had to be so sarcastic. He looked helplessly at Simon, who shrugged.

"I'm beginning to think you're not strictly here about portals are you?"

"No," said The Professor, "I'm afraid to say, you're correct."

"And I'm guessing the problem with amnesty is that Denarghi doesn't know you're here."

He was remarkably quick, this lad.

"That is also correct."

The Pan heaved a sigh.

"Right. Anything else you want to tell me?"

"There are many, many questions I would like to ask."

"Yeh. I'll bet." The lad gave him another measuring look. "Alright then, on you go."

Chapter 24

Upstairs in the kitchen, Big Merv watched Lucy as she finished making some biscuits. For someone who didn't bill herself as being domesticated she was doing a pukka job. Then again, she was quality and that meant she was the kind of girl who liked to make a proper job of anything she did. Or maybe those ten minutes spent setting Trev's bone … Yer, maybe she was keeping her mind occupied so she didn't have to think about that. Big Merv had seen the aftermath of enough gangland fights to have a strong stomach, but even he'd found that hard, and in the middle of it all, there was Doctor Dot, calmly sorting it out. She was something else that doctor. Merv was an uncomplicated creature, he was used to judging beings by their actions; even so, it was the first time he'd been impressed by a Grongle.

He listened to the sounds drifting up from the bar below, it was quieter now. The Parrot was closing and he could hear the bang of the doors as the punters left and the cheery, beery goodbyes they bade one another in the street.

"You're keeping yerself busy."

"Yes."

"Blimey, girl, what you eating?"

"Another of Mrs Poldark's gnissoids, I found a packet in the bathroom cabinet. I was beginning to feel a bit rough. I didn't want the flu coming back."

He gave her a hug.

"Yer, I get that. Might come back whatever."

"I hope not, on the packet it says I can miss up to four days' worth. I might have just squeaked in. I feel better, anyway."

"Maybe it weren't the flu. What you done today, 's enough to make any rookie feel ill. Smecking Arnold, I ain't so proud I'm gonna lie to you girl. I felt pretty rough an' all."

She smiled.

"Maybe."

He took a glass from the cupboard, went and got a bottle of milk out of the fridge, poured some and downed it in one.

"I think Doctor Dot did most of it … and Defreville … and you," she told him.

"Don't do yerself down sweets, you played a blinder." He rinsed out the glass and put it on the draining board. "'S good to be here." He watched her putting the last of the biscuits on the cooling rack "With you. You wanna hand with those?" He reached out for one and she slapped his hand playfully.

"Not now, in a few minutes, when they're cool."

He laughed. On one level, it would be smart to keep the noise down, on another, now that the punters were gone, it wouldn't do any harm if those Resistance geezers The Pan was meeting downstairs knew he wasn't alone. Which reminded him.

"OK, sweets, if you're good here, I'm gonna have a quick dekko. I don't trust them Resistance blokes."

"D'you need any help?"

"Nah, stay here and keep an eye on Trev. If anything goes down, keep quiet and lie low till I've got rid of 'em."

Trev and The Pan were sleeping in their own rooms while Big Merv and Lucy were sleeping in Gladys' room. Ada, being Ada, had a bedroom that was more of a boudoir; everything in it was pink. Even Lucy agreed it was a selection of hues that would constitute a heavy visual assault first thing. Big Merv knew the old birds had kept a shotgun somewhere because Ada had nearly shot him with it by mistake. From the conversation at the time, he'd had the impression it belonged to Gladys but he checked Ada's room first, just in case. Big Merv's experience of old ladies was restricted to gangland mums. They tended to be a breed apart: doughty matriarchs, armed to the teeth. They kept the guns required to exert their authority over the wayward friends of their husbands – and/or offspring, not to mention said husbands and/or offspring themselves – in the wardrobe, on the wardrobe or, if the weapon was a revolver, under the pillow.

Ada did, indeed, keep a revolver under her pillow. He made a note of it but left it. The shotgun was what he was after. This, he finally located on top of the wardrobe in Gladys' room. It was a pine cupboard, with coving round the top of it that stood a couple of inches higher, making it easy to secrete a gun there. Big Merv's searching fingers soon felt the reassuring shape of the stock and he lifted it off, but this was not the gun he had seen. It was a ten shot pump-action sawn-off. His own personal weapon of choice – when it came to that sort of thing.

He whistled, quietly.

If he hadn't known it was impossible, Big Merv would have thought it was left there for him. All he needed was the ammo. He pulled up the bedroom chair and stood on it. Sure enough there it was. He took it down, loaded the gun and put the safety catch on. He put a few spare slugs in his pocket and then put the box, and the chair, back where he'd found them. He crept to the top of the stairs and, putting his feet at the sides of the steps, closest to the wall, to minimise the chances of them creaking, he moved stealthily down a little way. He listened. They were talking in low voices, mostly seriously, except for a moment when one of them laughed. It sounded as if things were going OK. He crept back up the stairs and peeped into Trev's room. His friend was still asleep. It looked as if Lucy had been in to check on him too; the sheets had been smoothed down and tucked in again and an extra blanket put over him.

Satisfied that his friends were alright for the moment, Big Merv went back to the kitchen to see his girl. There'd been a lot of women in Big Merv's life. It was all part of being the boss. Some were attracted to the power, some just liked a bad boy, but none of them had ever been like Lucy. Big Merv had fifteen years on her but she genuinely didn't seem to care. From almost their first meeting, it was as if they'd always been together. She'd stood up to him, been honest with him and she hadn't been afraid. Not even in awe, just relaxed. He smiled to himself and headed for the kitchen but as he neared the door he was immediately on his guard. She'd turned the light off. When he opened the kitchen door, he didn't want to present a nice easy target silhouetted against the brightness behind him so he flicked off the switch in the hall. The only illumination was from the light in the hall downstairs. He thought about going back and turning that off, too. No. It would take too long. It was dark enough.

He readied the gun, put his ear to the wood and listened.

Nothing.

Slowly, he reached out for the handle and it opened a crack. With lightning speed he stepped silently to the side and flipped the gun up, ready to fire.

"Merv?" he heard Lucy whisper.

"Yer, 's me."

He took her hand and slipped swiftly into the room, closing the door quietly behind him. He waited for his eyes to acclimatise to the dark. Turnadot Street was not well lit, and there were no street lights in the alley to the side of the pub. However, the moon was bright and he could see well enough as his eyes had begun to adjust.

"Wossup girl?" he whispered.

"There's someone out there."

He listened. Sure enough he heard the sound of a person who was not very good at being quiet trying not to make a noise. She clutched his arm.

"They're coming up the fire escape."

"Yer. 'S alright. I got this," he whispered. He led Lucy to the gap between the fridge and the draining board and indicated she should hide there. Luckily she didn't argue. There wasn't room for both of them where she was hiding, there wasn't room for him on his own. But then, he wasn't going to hide.

"Stay 'ere and when I tell you, open the fridge door," he whispered.

"What?"

"It'll turn the lights on wonnit? But if they've gotta gun, see? An' they're thinking of having a pop, you gotta nice chunk of metal between you an' them."

He patted her hand to reassure her and moved on, soundlessly, to the open sash window. He stood against the wall beside it, sawn-off at the ready in his right hand. The footsteps approached slowly and as they climbed the fire escape towards the kitchen he realised there were two sets; the noisy novice and another one who knew what he was doing.

The first one into the room was the noisy one. He had no more idea about fighting than he did about keeping quiet. When Big Merv flung one arm round his neck, pulling him backwards against him, the little nerk hardly struggled and when Big Merv hefted the shotgun so the muzzle was against his temple, the guy did little more than squeak. Then the second one jumped into the room.

"Alright Luce."

The fridge door opened, throwing out a pool of light.

"Grk …" said Big Merv's victim.

"Shut it," growled Big Merv, "you an' all," he added, as the second one drew a breath to speak.

Standing in the light spilling from the fridge, the professional one turned and faced Big Merv, putting his hands out, palms forward. Big Merv recognised him at once. He'd worked on the door at one of the night clubs Big Merv had frequented.

The first one was not a professional, or at least, not at this. He was scared, really scared.

"Alright sunshine," Merv jerked the gun but only a little bit, just so it would move against the non-professional's temple. "Do you know what this is?"

"Grk," the bloke said nodding frantically.

"You wot?"

"A ...sawn ... off?" The snotty little bleeder seemed to be having trouble breathing. Big Merv supposed he was squeezing his neck a bit tight, but you couldn't be too careful in a situation like this.

"Good. Then here's how this is gonna go down. Very slowly, without any sudden moves, specially not from you Psycho Dave. Yer – 's right Dave, I know who you are an' I know you can't do me no damage from way over there but I ain't taking no chances – you're gonna put your hands up. An' then you here who I don't know," he elicited another 'grk' of acknowledgement when he squeezed his arm even tighter round the other one's neck, "you're gonna put your hands up an' all, and then you're gonna go and stand over there next to Dave. Any questions?"

"Grk."

"No," said Psycho Dave.

"Good. Let's go."

Big Merv released his victim, pushed him away, he staggered over to Psycho Dave, turned and put up his hands.

"Alright Tiny. Let's start with you. What's goin' on?"

"Please, Mister Merv—"

"What makes you think you know my name?" Big Merv interrupted. He slipped off the safety catch with a click.

"I'm sorry. Please don't kill me. I don't—I'm j-just—I'm a friend of The Pan's and I know he rescued you. I've been working in the bar and he's got these blokes round and I wanted to—I said I'd look in."

"Yer, I bet you did. That's why you come sneaking up the fire escape innit?"

"We came in this way coz I thought that if there was any trouble we might need to get the jump on them."

"This true Psycho?"

"Yer boss."

Big Merv primed the sawn-off.

"You sure about that Psycho?"

"Yer." Psycho Dave's voice was a little higher when he answered.

The other one looked like the brains of the outfit and in the half-light spilling out of the fridge Big Merv moved forward out of the shadows, not too far, not so he came into close range but close enough for them to see his face. He eyed the small one with a gimlet felt-tip green glare. The little scrote was petrified: close to kneeling and begging for his life, but fair play to him, he didn't.

"What about you, Tiny?" he asked. "You sure you don't mean my friend no harm?"

"Arnold no!" he said. His voice was trembling.

"Sweet. Luce, turn the lights on. Let's see what we got." The room was filled with glare as Lucy did as he'd asked and closed the fridge. "Thanks babe." In full light, he confirmed the identity of Psycho Dave. There was also something familiar about the small intruder but he couldn't place it. He nodded. "Alright Dave."

"Wotcher boss," said Psycho Dave.

"Who are you?" Big Merv asked the other one.

"I'm Alan—" he began, and Big Merv remembered.

"Pub Quiz Alan?"

"Yes."

Big Merv relaxed a little. Everyone knew Alan and everyone knew he was harmless. He lowered the gun slightly.

"I admire your work. You got some smooth answers."

"Thank you."

"Yer, I won some good money on you a few years back. And you, Dave, how's yer old mum?"

"Not so bad, boss."

"She still running that fiddle down the bingo halls?"

"Not yours, boss."

Big Merv glanced over at Lucy who smirked at him.

"Them bingo halls ain't mine no more, the Grongles have fixed that. The way I see it she can scam who she likes. Alright, let's get this little chat we're havin' back on track. You boys reckon my mate, The Pan of Hamgee, has got himself into a tight spot."

"Yes."

"More than a tight spot."

Big Merv flicked the safety catch back on and let the muzzle of the gun drop, sensing a wave of intense relief from Alan and Psycho Dave as he did so.

"Then we gotta check it out."

"You could make it look quite normal if you took them tea and biscuits," said Lucy.

"That's a great idea from your friend, Mister Merv, sir," said Alan.

"Just call me Merv, mate. You too Dave – I told you, I ain't the boss no more – an' this is Lucy."

"Yes boss," said Dave but Big Merv let it go. Old habits die hard.

"You reckon that'll work do you Alan?"

"Yep. They've seen me serving behind the bar all night."

"Nice," said Merv. "OK Alan, wot's the signal if you want the cavalry?" he nodded at Psycho Dave to show he meant both of them.

"How about I drop the tray?"

"Whadda you reckon Luce?"

"It's not a bad plan."

There was a brief silence during which Big Merv heard a noise from downstairs, the kind of noise which he recognised, at once, as the wrong kind. Stealthily, almost silently, someone had forced a door. The others had heard it too.

"What was that?" whispered Lucy.

Big Merv put his finger to his lips and listened. There was someone downstairs moving through the main bar. He motioned to Lucy to turn the light out. Very quietly, Big Merv opened the door and crept out onto the landing. Staying well back in the shadows, he inched along the wall until he could see down the stairs. Six Grongles were moving soundlessly towards the snug. He recognised Captain Snow. He crept back to the kitchen.

"Luce, Alan, stay here. If something happens there's gotta be someone to take care of Trev. Psycho?" Psycho Dave made his way silently across the room to Big Merv's side. He remembered The Pan's pirate portals, there were three on the kitchen side unit. He took one. "If we don't come back you know what to do, girl." He handed the other two to Lucy, beckoned to Psycho Dave and the two of them crept into the hall.

Chapter 25

Lord Vernon was grateful that his dinner with the High Leader was nearly over. The High Leader's social standing was such that despite Lord Vernon being the host, his guest chose who to invite. As a result, the gathered company comprised the High Leader, his entourage and Lord Vernon. He had toyed with the idea of bringing an entourage of his own but decided to attend with a deputation of bodyguards – army, from his own regiment, and General Moteurs. He and the General sat at one end of the table, his guard ranged behind them. The High Leader sat facing them at the other end, with his own bodyguard in the grey uniform of the Imperial Guard ranged behind him. His entourage, in descending order of importance, were ranged along the sides. The least important were therefore at Lord Vernon's end. The message was clear enough.

As the being of most importance, the High Leader made the social running. Protocol dictated that none of the entourage, or Lord Vernon, spoke unless spoken to, except that the High Leader had addressed almost the entire conversation, so far, to the Lord Protector. He had thoroughly disrespected the comfort of his rooms, the unfashionableness of his surroundings, Lord Vernon's taste in art works, beverages and anything else he could think of. The conversation lapsed for a moment or two, while the diners attacked their puddings.

"I see my personal chef is still one of the finest," said the High Leader.

Lord Vernon had taken delight in poaching the High Leader's chef some months previously. He knew the food in his kitchens outstripped anything the High Leader's could supply. He smiled graciously, though having been selected for character assassination over the course of the evening, maintaining the thinnest veneer of civility took increasing effort. He removed his sunglasses and locked eyes with his guest. There was an audible intake of breath around the table as his deformity, those slate grey, human eyes, was revealed up close.

"My chef, Your Divine Excellence," he corrected the High Leader. "I thank you. He is surpassing himself, now that he enjoys a position in which he is suitably incentivised."

"I wonder how he stands it here, among these savages," sniffed the

High Leader. "I wonder how you do."

"Every culture has something to teach us, Your Divine Excellence," said Lord Vernon, quoting The Prophet.

The High Leader cast about him with disdain.

"I doubt there is much to learn here. I am almost sympathetic to your plight. Indeed, if I thought I had a suitable opening in government, I would be tempted to summon you home; if only for a chance to improve the output of my kitchen."

"Of course; but it is a somewhat elaborate ruse to retain a chef, Your Divine Excellence." The Grongle etiquette for this situation would be for Lord Vernon to offer to release his chef back to the High Leader's employ. However, after the day of pernicketiness and one-upmanship he had endured he didn't feel inclined to.

"Nobody is worth what you pay him," snapped the High Leader.

Well that was probably true, not that Lord Vernon would ever admit it. His chef earned more than it was tasteful to pay any member of household staff, but that was the joy of running K'Barth. He could do what he liked. He was one of the richest beings on the planet, so the obscene amount he paid his chef was an anomaly worth every penny for the vexation it caused the High Leader.

"Perhaps you appreciate him less than you think, since he is worth that to me," said Lord Vernon smugly.

"And he is happy in his work?"

"He produces food of the highest quality. It seems he wishes for little more than to perform his art for those able to appreciate it."

"But other than yourself and the good General here perhaps, are there many beings in K'Barth with the levels of sophistication required to appreciate his art?"

"Why, there are always my honoured guests." The High Leader's retinue preened and puffed but the High Leader himself made no acknowledgement, merely fixed his eyes upon his host. "This is your first visit to K'Barth, I would not expect you to understand," Lord Vernon continued, "but I assure you it is not so wild. Not anymore. There are opportunities here."

"Maybe, but I should imagine they are unsuitable for the weak of intent. I'll give you that you've tamed these savages well enough but almost every K'Barthan business has failed."

"They have had some assistance from us in that, in order that they may be supplanted by Grongolian interests. We have space and resources to build," Lord Vernon waved one suede-clad hand expansively as he spoke. He noticed the High Leader's eyes following the rings he wore as they flashed in the light. "We have an abundance of slave labour so our health and safety requirements are … a little less stringent here than at home. K'Barthan production is cost effective and efficient. It makes sense and of course, Grongle entrepreneurs residing here in K'Barth pay less tax. The number choosing to base their operations here is increasing."

"I—"

"But what am I saying? I know you will agree with me. You are privy to the stock reports of my government's salt production facilities. I assume that a being of your great foresight will have been one of the first to invest." Lord Vernon gave the High Leader a conspiratorial wink, all the while knowing his opponent, at the other end of the table, had not invested in any K'Barthan stock. He continued, "As our economy grows and your own business interests with it, I should imagine you will come frequently to Ning Dang Po. I am confident we will see a lot more of one another."

The High Leader's eyebrows went up in surprise, "I'm sure that will be a pleasure," he said and his ministers and acolytes murmured in ironic agreement.

Lord Vernon picked up his glass, leaned back in his chair and took a sip of his smoothie. His gaze swept the faces around the table.

"I'm sure it shall. I will look forward to it," he said.

"Yeeees," said the High Leader, slowly. "However, for all the exciting opportunities here, Grongolia's investors are notoriously cautious. K'Barth is less than stable. Slave labour is all well and good but what if it rises up and destroys the factory?"

"As usual, Your Divine Excellence, you make an incisive point. But K'Barth is extremely stable. Ensuring that stability is one of the reasons why I am holding the ceremony you have so graciously condescended to attend: my installation as Architrave of K'Barth."

"Ah yes, I must ask you about this. It seems to me that you have brought these K'Barthan non-species to heel as well as can be expected. Indeed I commend you for doing so but I fail to see how some piece of K'Barthan ju-ju will suddenly make them docile."

"I thank you, but I strive for excellence. Good is not enough when perfection is there for the taking. Their religion leads them to believe that a new ruler will come, some all powerful half-deity who will vanquish me and save them. On Saturday, when I am installed, I will prove decisively that, far from being vanquished, I am he. I will extinguish their hope of freedom, forever, and legitimise my rule."

"It sounds very appealing, if, perhaps, a little simplistic."

"Oh but I assure you, Your Divine Excellence, it is that simple. If they believe I am their true leader then they will be compelled by their tradition to obey me. But even more importantly, I will have access to certain secrets – the science that underpins their tradition – that will make it very difficult for them to resist, even if they want to. They will be crushed, entirely, permanently."

"These powers you speak of. I am having trouble pinning down exactly what they are. Would you care to enlighten me?"

"I would not wish to bore you, or your retinue, suffice it to say that it is a simple application of reality theory. I doubt there is much that I, a humble servant of the Grongle nation, could explain to a being with your wealth of learning. When I demonstrate these powers, in your presence, at the installation, on Saturday, I know you will understand the principles yourself."

"Yeeees. I am certain I will, when your ruse succeeds," said the High Leader, his tone of voice suggesting he believed the reverse.

"Naturally." Lord Vernon examined the ends of his suede gloves and then he let his gaze drift upwards to the High Leader's face again, "And the power I will hold will be at your service of course."

"Of course, Lord Protector, as I would expect from a loyal servant of the Grongolian State," said the High Leader. He rose abruptly to his feet and, as protocol dictated, so did Lord Vernon and everyone else. "It has been a long day, I have matters of state to attend to before I retire. Thank you, Lord Vernon, for a most interesting dinner but now, I regret that my retinue and I must withdraw."

"As you wish. If there is anything you require, General Moteurs here, or my staff, will be happy, no, honoured to oblige." Lord Vernon executed the low bow required by etiquette with an ironic flourish.

****

"I don't think he likes me very much, Moteurs, and after I was so polite to him," said Lord Vernon as he and General Moteurs made their way across the Upper Quadrangle, to the officers' side, where their quarters were situated.

"Sir," General Moteurs seemed thoughtful. Lord Vernon sensed his concern.

"You think he is aware of my plans for him?"

"It is possible. We must be wary, sir. He does employ some of the world's most deadly and efficient contract killers—"

"And they are here?"

"To my certain knowledge, at least three have entered the country and I'll wager two of his bodyguard are not members of the Imperial Guard. He sees you as a threat, sir. I believe there is a danger he will order your assassination."

"You have verified this."

"Sir."

"Your surveillance team?"

"Monitoring, sir."

"Level of risk?"

"Condition amber, sir."

When they reached the other side of the Quad they went their separate ways. Condition amber, Lord Vernon reflected as, in appeasement for the over-rich dinner, he climbed the stairs. The High Leader was famously ruthless in removing any challenges to his power. So, Lord Vernon would simply have to strike first.

Chapter 26

The Pan sat back in his seat and waited for the Professor or Simon to say something. It took longer than he expected for the Professor to speak up.

"I'll be brief. We have been contacted, via our agents in the old Palace, by a high-ranking Grongle. He claims that there were five ancient K'Barthan portals, one of which you used to escape from us, I believe."

"Yes, I did. Your contact is telling you the truth." The Pan had a feeling he knew who the Grongle might be but waited, to see what else the Professor and Simon had to say.

"This is where it gets complicated. This Grongle says he gave one of the K'Barthan portals to a group of Grongolian scientists working for him. He also claims that they reverse engineered it and came up with a Grongolian portal that works on input map coordinates."

That was bad news.

"Unfortunately, that sounds about right. If you need me to, I can probably find out for certain."

"No need to check. Lieutenant Arbuthnot and Snoofle sent us the plans."

"Then build it. Fast," said The Pan.

"We'd like to but we have a problem," said Simon.

"Denarghi has forbidden us to make it," said the Professor.

The Pan tried not to look too incredulous but he suspected the facade he was aiming to project, of intelligent, pointy-brained leader, had probably slipped a bit.

"Why in the name of The Prophet would he do that?" he asked.

"He distrusts the source," said Simon.

"Our agents claim to have turned the Grongle it came from, but in this particular instance, Denarghi does not believe it possible. At worst, he thinks it is our operatives who have been turned and at best, that we are being played."

"Maybe I can help there. This Grongle who sent you the plans. Do you know his name?"

"Some fellow called General Moteurs," said the Professor. "Do you know him?"

"We've met."

"You don't like him."

"I'm not sure. I haven't had a chance to get to know him. I don't have to like him to trust him."

"And you do?"

"Yes. He's given me a lot of help."

"He has?"

"Yes, he's saved my life, at least once. He introduced me to the doctor who saved Trev's—"

"Trev?"

"We'll get round to that. Going back to your story, why is Denarghi so against this?"

"Partly history; we made contact with what we thought was the Grongle Resistance a few years ago, but it was a set-up and the whole organisation was nearly wiped out."

"Ah."

"Yes, and he says he has another contact of his own who has told him that to build the box will be our doom," said Simon.

"Such poppycock! It's quite safe. But he doesn't understand the science of course, so he can't see for himself."

"But doesn't he trust you?"

"Apparently not. To give him his due, I understand why. I had quite a moment, myself, seeing those plans. It's such a simple, elegant premise that I can hardly credit how it stayed secret for so long. But General Moteurs thinks we are about to be attacked. He says he is Underground and under orders to ensure we have it. I will have to flout Denarghi's authority and build the Grongle version for now. However, I believe that if we want to stay ahead of the game, our version has to be the one you have, with an option to use map coordinates, rather than the one the Grongles are developing."

"Right. But you know mine has strings; it will only take you to somewhere you can imagine, and mostly, I think that has to be somewhere you've been. There are also some places where it won't work, the old Palace is portal proof, you can't get into it by portal from outside, not with the K'Barthan version, and also, if you're trying to watch someone who also has a portal, theirs will interfere with yours and neither of you will see anything."

"Ah," said the Professor, "so that's why they're all over the pub."

"Yes."

"I thought you were hiding them in plain view."

"I suppose there's a bit of that too," said The Pan.

"Then it is even more expedient that we learn the science behind yours, so we can put the two together before the Grongles do."

"Yeh, I can imagine," said The Pan.

This complicated things. A lot.

Chapter 27

The clock on Lord Vernon's smartphone read nearly midnight but he was still at his desk, taking care of some outstanding paperwork. He snorted irritably as he read the document in front of him. He wished he could get some minion to do this, but seeing to these things personally, understanding them, was the way Lord Vernon kept such an iron grip on power in K'Barth. Perhaps when he ruled the entire planet, he could let General Moteurs handle some. Possibly. His mind played on his dinner with the High Leader.

He took a sip of water. The rich food the kitchens had prepared to flaunt at his opposite number seemed to be curdling in his stomach. Perhaps it was merely the High Leader's odious company. And the High Leader didn't trust him, that much was clear. General Moteurs was right to doubt.

He shoved the state papers to one side. His trusted deputy had been kind enough to furnish him with the plans of the High Leader's rooms – not that Lord Vernon needed them, having lived in them himself for two years. Even so, he unrolled them and examined the drawings in front of him. His eyes took in the shape of the space and the positions of the furniture. Lord Vernon knew these quarters were totally secure. There were no weak spots, nowhere for an assassin to hide. The General had marked the most likely positions for any guards. It would be impossible to assassinate the High Leader, or them, in a direct attack. Or at least it would if it was a conventional attack, but with a portal … Lord Vernon smiled to himself.

"Child's play," he said.

He sat back for a moment to think. Drawing his knife he twirled it casually from one hand to the other. He would strike first. He wanted the power of the Architraves – he already owned K'Barth – and he had wanted it before he took control of Grongolia. But such a perfect opportunity had arisen now, that he would be a fool to pass it up. Saturday's installation could just as easily seal his bid for world domination as begin it.

He sheathed the knife for a moment, took the gold thimble out of one of the pouches in his belt, imagined the High Leader's rooms and looked into it. The guards were stationed exactly where General Moteurs had said they would be. The High Leader's bed was in the middle of the room and he was still awake, engaged in the same kind of state paperwork as Lord Vernon.

He was wearing light body armour; not that it would protect him from a properly planned assassination. Lord Vernon wondered why he bothered. The benefits of wearing it hardly outweighed the discomfort. He put the portal down and turned his attention back to the plans. General Moteurs was exceptionally thorough when explaining the details of the High Leader's security arrangements to Lord Vernon. The rooms were impregnable. The High Leader's troops would believe they could protect him from any kind of attack. But the lack of hidden recesses, of weaknesses and places to hide would leave them helpless against any assassin with a portal and quick enough reflexes.

General Moteurs had been subdued and thoughtful after dinner when Lord Vernon quizzed him about the High Leader's motives. If the Lord of All Grongolia failed to survive the night, Lord Vernon doubted his deputy would be surprised.

Chapter 28

The Pan sat in the snug with Professor N'Aversion and Simon, trying to process the information they had given him. He'd borne high hopes for the Resistance, despite having met Denarghi, and he wasn't sure how to proceed. He supposed that it was his confusion and the magnitude of the information his visitors had just shared that overrode his escape instincts. Whatever it was, he didn't notice someone in the hall until too late. The door of the snug was flung open and five Grongles in army uniform spilled into the room, laser pistols drawn and ready.

"Freeze, non-beings!"

With an apologetic glance at his guests, The Pan put his hands up, or at least the one he could. The Professor and Simon put their hands up too. The five troops fanned out into a ring, still covering them with their laser pistols, and Captain Snow stepped through their ranks.

"Well isn't this a pretty picture?" he said.

Very slowly, The Pan stood up.

"What do you want, Captain?"

"You've got something of mine, you little piece of crap. Something I want back and now it seems I've got myself a bonus. Who are your mates?"

"Just friends from out of town."

"You reckon do you?"

"Yeh."

Captain Snow walked round the table until he was standing right in front of The Pan.

"Or have you got something to hide?"

"No, everything's pretty much on plain view."

"Yeh, I'd say it is."

The Pan tried to conceal his fear but he was shaking and what felt like a torrent of cold sweat erupted from his pores. It started to drip down his face and he could feel a couple of buckets more running down his back. Great. The calm and collected thing had been going so well and now this.

"It's not against the law to have some friends in for a drink," said The Pan.

"It is on a commercial premises after hours. If you were going to be legal you should have gone upstairs."

"Ah …" said The Pan, then again, considering who was up there, thank The Prophet he hadn't.

"Let's find out who your friends are. Private Land, you know what to do."

One of the guards holstered his gun and took out his standard issue Grongle Army smartphone. He pointed it at the Professor and Simon and then showed the screen to Captain Snow.

"Isn't that a thing? I got me a couple of suspects to play with. Treason, too. I like asking questions."

"Yeh, and one day you might even understand the answers," said The Pan's mouth, running off without him as usual.

"You think you're invincible don't you?" Captain Snow drew his own laser pistol, pushing the muzzle against the Pan's nose and then he put his face very close. The Pan tried not to flinch at the onslaught of what had to be some of the worst breath he'd ever smelled. "You think Lord Vernon'll give you amnesty for consorting with a couple of smeckers like these two?"

"If you'll excuse me, sir—" The Professor began. The Captain's guards raised their laser pistols and there was a single click as they primed them to fire in perfect synchronisation. They took aim and the Professor stopped talking abruptly.

"That's better," Captain Snow sneered. The Pan looked up beyond the barrel of the laser pistol pressed against his nose into the Grongle's bloodshot eyes. Three more days. Arnold's hair, how was he going to swing those now? "I reckon your luck just ran out. Lord Vernon won't forgive you for this."

"He might," said The Pan with a great deal more hope than conviction.

"Sure, dream on. You're finished. Unless …" he pretended to look thoughtful. Was he going to use this to extort something? Could The Pan be that lucky? Arnold! Please yes. He didn't have much but it was enough to string Captain Snow along for three more days. If he'd just get on with it. And move his laser pistol, because he was dumb enough to fire it by mistake.

"Unless?" The Pan asked. He thanked The Prophet that his voice sounded a lot calmer than he actually was.

"Unless you got something that'll help me forget," said Captain Snow. To The Pan's relief, he removed the gun, with a flourish, and walked round the room. "Nice place you got here, perhaps I should help myself to something special."

OK, don't cave in too easily, pretend to play hardball.

"I doubt I have anything that would interest you."

"Oh you do," after a circuit of the room, Captain Snow ended up in front of The Pan again, "apart from your friends here who I'll be taking with me. You see, you gave me something and where I come from, if you give someone a present you don't take it back."

"You mean my snurd?"

"It isn't yours, you little scrote. It's mine. And now it doesn't work. Some smecking security protocol," he swung back to The Pan grabbing him by his shirt and pulling him towards him, "so if you know what's good for you," he jabbed his pistol into The Pan's face again, "you're going to switch whatever that is off. Now."

"It doesn't have a security protocol that I know of, it just thinks it's mine. Or perhaps it knows you took it."

"It's not sentient, you piece of—"

"I'd watch your mouth, if I was you pal," said a voice. The Pan couldn't see much beyond Captain Snow and didn't dare hope. "Put the wimp down, drop your gun and turn around. Slowly."

Three of the guards maintained their positions, guns trained on Professor N'Aversion and Simon; Captain Snow and the other two turned round, lasers at the ready.

"Looks like we have exhausted all diplomatic possibilities," said the Captain.

"Yeh it does don'it?"

"But there's six of us," said Captain Snow.

"Don't make no difference." Big Merv held the gun low because, like many K'Barthan gangsters, he shot from the hip.

"We'll fry you."

"Yeh? I wouldn't try it sonny. See, you got them flash laser pistols but I gotta sawn-off. It's messy, for sure, but it gets the job done, and I got ten shots. That's more 'an enough for you boys."

"There are still six of us."

"'S right, pal, I can count an' all. But I'll tell you something, I'm bleedin' fast."

"You'll have to be supersonic at these odds, freak."

"Maybe I am. Course, it don't matter to you, coz whatever happens, you're gonna be first, snotface."

Captain Snow glowered at Big Merv.

"Don't call me that, douchebag."

"Don't call me douchebag, snotface."

"Why you—"

There was a click as Big Merv's finger tightened on the trigger and it moved a tiny bit.

"I'm the one with the sawn-off, pal, so I reckon I can call you what I like. Now, I've asked you nice, so this time, I'll make it simple; are you gonna do what I say or am I gonna blow your head off?"

Captain Snow dropped his gun.

"That's a smart move, Captain. I'm glad you ain't as stupid as you look. Kick it over here."

Captain Snow did as he was told.

"And yer mates."

The others put their guns on the ground.

"Hands up."

All six Grongles put their hands up.

"Alright, Psycho, take the gun from Captain Nonce 'ere and check 'im for any other weapons." Psycho Dave appeared from behind Big Merv and picked up Captain Snow's laser pistol, "Sweet. Now, cover 'em, Dave." He nodded to the Professor and Simon, "Maybe you other boys'll do me a favour and get the rest."

Simon and the Professor patted down the first of Captain Snow's men, removing a variety of weapons, which they threw onto the floor between Big Merv and The Pan. Then the two of them frisked the other guards, taking a laser pistol each and adding the other weapons to the pile. Psycho Dave picked up a spare laser pistol and offered it to The Pan.

"No thanks."

"You oughta take that, son."

The Pan shook his head.

Big Merv shrugged.

"'S your funeral. You lot," he jerked the sawn-off at the six Grongles, "go stand over there, by the wall. Nice and easy. No sudden moves."

Slowly and carefully, the Grongles made their way over to the wall.

"You got something we can tie these Herberts up with?" Merv asked.

"I have," said Simon before The Pan could reply. He removed a bundle of cable ties from one of the many pouches on his belts and threw it over to Big Merv.

The Pan was shaking with shock and relief, as well as fear. But now what? This wasn't over. He couldn't let Captain Snow and his goons go, knowing that Big Merv was alive and well, and wielding a sawn-off shotgun. Where in Arnold's name had he got that? He watched, pretending he knew what he was doing, as Dave bound the hands and legs of Captain Snow and his guards and made them sit on the floor in a row with their backs to the wall.

"What d'you wanna do with them, lad?" asked Big Merv and after a slight delay, The Pan realised his friend was talking to him.

He took a deep breath. He might be shocked but his mind was surprisingly clear. He knew exactly what he had to do now, but it was going to be difficult, possibly the hardest thing he'd ever done in his life. He held out his hand.

"Dave, I've changed my mind about that laser pistol, pass it over will you?" Psycho Dave picked up one of the two spares and gave it to The Pan. "Thank you."

He held the sleek, metal instrument of death in his hand. It was heavier than he expected, as if it carried the weight of the lives it had ended. He rubbed it in his hair to boost the charge. The Pan had never held a laser pistol before and he hadn't a clue what he was doing. Never mind, as Big Merv had once said, being a hard man was only ten per cent nails; the rest of it, he'd sworn, was bluff.

"I wouldn't do that if I was you, that's a big boy's toy," mocked Captain Snow but The Pan could hear the fear in his voice.

"Yeh, Defreville mate, what you gonna do?" asked Big Merv.

The Pan kept his countenance deliberately grim while he examined the gun. Luckily, it was designed to be used easily, intuitively and without thought by grunts who weren't very bright. Phew. He handed it to Big Merv.

"'S alright. I got this," he gestured with the shotgun.

"Yeh, but you need this one."

"No I don't."

"Yes, you do. Because if you have to use it, this," he waved the laser pistol, "is easier to clear up. Watch them, I'll be back in a minute," he said.

"Where're you going?"

"To the kitchen. Any trouble, use the laser."

The Pan wondered how his jellied legs held him up as he ran through the bar and into the Holy of Holies, where, with shaking hands and cursing their diminutive size, he emptied bottle after bottle of pub-sized orange juice in the vague direction of a jug. Captain Snow and his goons had to be disposed of, or they had to forget. The Pan was no killer so disposal wasn't an option but he was pretty certain he knew how to make them forget. By the time he had finished there was as much orange juice on the worktop as in the jug but it would do, there was enough. Next, he poured out a tiny measure of Gladys' home-made Calvados, once again spilling liberal amounts over the work surface, and let a few drips fall into the jug. He stirred it, grabbed eleven of the plastic glasses which, much to Gladys and Ada's disgust, they were legally compelled to serve drinks in to the customers at the tables outside, and stuffed them into his sling. Then he picked up the jug and carried it all carefully back to the snug.

Everyone was as he had left them but there was an air of silent expectation. The Pan put the jug down on the table, took the glasses out of the sling and put them next to it.

"Alright. What are you doing you twerp?" Big Merv demanded.

"I had to get some orange juice. Can you give me the gun back?"

Big Merv did as he asked and reverted to the sawn-off. The Pan levelled the laser pistol at Captain Snow.

"We're going to have a drink, and calm down, and talk about this," he said.

Big Merv gave him a look.

"Are you mental?"

"No Merv, far from it. Professor, would you pour?"

"You think I'm going to drink that?" said Captain Snow, all cocky arrogance again, or was it bluff? He sounded different. Was he getting scared?

Of course he's scared, he thinks you're behaving like a lunatic! said a voice. Wait a minute. That wasn't supposed to happen. It was one of the Architraves. Arnold's hair! That's all The Pan needed. They'd found a way round the ring. He put his thumb against his finger and felt the red ruby, turned inwards.

"Yes. I think I can persuade you." The world seemed to slow down. The Pan listened for the Architraves. They were silent but he felt their emotions as if they were his own; frustration, exasperation, anger and in one or two cases, hatred.

"We don't sup with vermin," said Captain Snow.

"Tonight you do," said The Pan. When he spoke, the strength of his predecessors' feelings somehow added itself to his own, their voices to his voice. Seventy-six of them. And halfway through the sentence he realised that the way he was speaking wasn't him. It was the sound of granite; of rocks, of stones, of age and time itself. If worlds and planets could talk this would be their voice. Weird. And cool. And a little bit scary. Everyone in the room who could move stepped backwards, away from him, except for Captain Snow and his troops, sitting in a row against the wall, who merely seemed to shrink slightly. And Big Merv, of course, who just looked over at him and grinned.

"Wow," said Simon.

The Pan cleared his throat and raised one eyebrow.

"Mmm," he said cautiously and was glad to discover the effect didn't last.

"He's smecking mental!" said one of the Grongles.

"He's going to poison us," said another.

"If he does he's done for, aren't you, you scab?" snarled Captain Snow but there was an obvious tension in his voice now. Nobody had ever been nervous of The Pan before, least of all a Grongle. It was hard to press home his advantage when it was such new territory.

"Done for? I expect I would be if there was any poison in here," said The Pan lightly, "but there isn't," he picked up the jug with his good arm, poured a drop of juice into the bottom of one of the plastic cups, put the jug down, picked up the cup and drank it, "see?"

"You've had the antidote," said Captain Snow amid general mutterings of agreement from his colleagues.

"How could he? Unless he knew you were coming," said Professor N'Aversion.

"And you know I didn't, Captain," said The Pan.

"You took it when you were getting the juice," said another of the Grongles.

"No, and to prove it, the Professor, Simon, Psycho Dave and Big Merv are going to have some too."

He had to persuade the Grongles to drink the orange juice. It was the only way. Someone would know where Captain Snow was, and there was enough going on at the Parrot already without making it the centre of a manhunt, or, The Prophet forfend, a murder investigation. However, they were clearly going to need some incentivisation.

"Alright folks, what would you do right now?" The Pan asked his colleagues.

Big Merv laughed humourlessly, "You gotta waste 'em son, or they're gonna blab. You know it, and they know it."

"'S right," said Psycho Dave.

"Regretfully, I must agree with your friends," said Professor N'Aversion.

"You sure?" asked The Pan.

The Professor nodded.

"Simon?"

"'Fraid so."

"Oh dear," said The Pan. The Captain glared up at him with his usual expression of sneering hatred but he was paler, the sweat glistening on his brow, and he seemed to be trying that little bit harder at it. The Pan stood watching him, thinking, weighing the options. He was pretty sure what he was going to say, and the likelihood he would succeed came down to his ability to bluff. Touch and go then.

"Alright Captain, here's what I suggest. We're going to make a deal. I believe the way you Grongles seal a deal is with a drink. I have it here. So this is my offer. I'm going to let you go and in return, you're going to give me your word that you're not going to mention this visit."

"What are you—?" began Simon.

"Be quiet ... please," The Pan interrupted him. "Give the Captain here some time to decide whether he's going to accept."

"What if I don't?" said Captain Snow.

"Then I regret that I'll have no option but to let Big Merv here, put a cap in you, although actually, Merv, as we've already discussed, I think it'd be tidier if you used one of these," he gestured to the laser guns, "we can just vacuum them up when you're done."

Big Merv understood what The Pan was doing at once. He sucked the air in through his teeth, like Gerry, The Pan's favoured mechanic, at Snurd, when he was about to quote for a particularly expensive job.

"They're big lads. You'll have to empty the bag a few times."

"Better than all that blood, you said yourself, a sawn-off is messy."

One of the Grongle guards retched.

"Shut up, fool," snapped Captain Snow. He and his bullies were a very much lighter green and The Pan smiled in a way that he hoped would remind them of Lord Vernon.

"You could stun them and throw them in the river, give them a fighting chance," said Simon, entering into the spirit nicely.

"No I can't afford to give them a fighting chance," said The Pan.

"You smecking piece of—"

"I understand it's difficult," The Pan interrupted. "It's hard to trust a Hamgeean like me when he says he's not going to kill you, but I promise you, you can walk away from here unharmed. It's up to you. You give me your word and drink a toast. Or …" he shrugged and waited to see what the Captain would do.

"I'll drink the smecking toast."

"I'm glad you've seen reason. Killing is not my style. Professor?" The Pan turned to the Resistance's Head of Tech Ops, whose antennae were still knotted, he noticed. Simon set the plastic cups out on the table and the Professor filled them while The Pan stood and waited. "You choose, Captain."

The six Grongles stood up and shuffled forward, Psycho Dave moved back so he was too far away for them to jump him and covered their movements with the laser pistol. The Grongles took their plastic glasses and then Big Merv, Professor N'Aversion and Simon helped themselves. The Pan passed the last clean glass to Psycho Dave. That just left his, which the Professor had refilled. He picked it up.

"Do we have a deal, Captain?"

"Yeh, alright you piece of crap, we have a deal."

They chinked glasses with a plasticky crunch and The Pan's friends drank, but he hesitated, knowing that Captain Snow and the Grongles would wait to see if anything happened to them first.

"You know my terms, Captain," said The Pan as Big Merv put his glass down, picked up one of the laser pistols and primed it, ready to fire.

"Yeh, I smecking know," said Captain Snow, downing the contents of his glass. His troops followed suit.

"Cheers," said The Pan, downing his. "Give them their weapons back boys."

"Listen mate—" began Big Merv.

"Trust me," said The Pan, "and trust the good Captain here, he's given us his word and that counts for something. Merv, untie them."

"I think this is rather ill-advised," said Professor N'Aversion.

The Pan picked up the nearest laser pistol and handed it to Captain

Snow who primed it, switched the setting from stun to kill and pointed it, laughing, at The Pan.

"You didn't believe me, did you?"

"Of course. You're a Grongle, your word is your bond."

"Yeh, with another Grongle, but not with you, non-being. That's funny, right boys?"

They all laughed.

"Captain, I'm so disappointed in you." He managed to keep his voice calm but inside he was beginning to panic.

"Bad luck that," more laughter, "and here's some extra. I'm going to kill you now." Still laughing, Captain Snow turned the laser pistol sideways, gangsta style, and took aim.

The Pan could feel the anger and disappointment of his friends and colleagues. Arnold's underpants, he should have put more Calvados in.

Captain Snow's laughter attained a manic edge and that of his fellow Grongles began to, too. Were they …? Yes, it looked as if they couldn't stop. But The Pan reckoned they wanted to. The mania in their mirth increased.

"I'm going to smecking-schmecking-schmeshing-washte—" began Captain Snow. He stopped as if confused. He was breathing hard, swaying to and fro. "You schmecking—" he slurred and then his eyes rolled up into his head and he tumbled face down onto the floor at The Pan's feet. The guards stopped laughing and there was a moment of stunned quiet before, as one, they did the exact same thing. The Pan turned to his astonished colleagues.

"To quote my ex-landladies, 'That's proper resistance. None of your bleeding all over our nice clean floors'."

"What have you done to them?" asked Professor N'Aversion.

"Alcohol. A couple of drops of Gladys' Calvados. They can't hold their liquor. They won't remember a thing when they wake up."

"That's amazing," said Simon.

"Yes. But next time, a few drops more?" suggested Professor N'Aversion.

"Yeh," said The Pan with feeling. "Sorry, I was afraid they'd smell it. It doesn't last long though so just to belt and brace …" He picked up a laser pistol from where it had fallen and changed the setting to stun. He pointed the gun at Captain Snow. Arnold, it was almost physically painful. He turned his head away his hand shaking, took a deep breath and—

"Gimme that you giant girl," said Big Merv taking it out of his hand. He checked the stun setting and shot all six of the Grongles.

"Thanks Merv. It would be a pity if they woke up and we had to do that all over again."

"Yer, I reckon I aged a year or two tonight," said Big Merv.

"Thanks for saving our bacon."

"'S nothing."

"How did you know they were here?"

"We heard 'em," said Big Merv. "Alan and Dave came to check up on them two," he jerked his thumb at Professor N'Aversion and Simon. "Alan's still upstairs. We was in the kitchen, having a chat when Captain Snot and his mates here forced the door. Front."

"Arnold, I'll have to fix it," The Pan was still shaking only it seemed to be even worse now that the danger had passed. "And look, I'm sorry if I worried you all. I didn't mean to take that quite so close to the wire."

"You ain't never done it no other way."

The Pan shrugged.

"I couldn't kill them because it's too dangerous and—"

"Because you ain't never gonna kill no-one, son," said Big Merv gently. "We get that. It ain't who you are."

"What we goin' ter do with them now?" asked Psycho Dave.

Big Merv answered for him.

"Leave 'em somewhere to sleep it off, somewhere they ain't gonna bother us."

The Pan slapped his friend on the back.

"Exactly Merv."

"Sweet. You want me to sort that?"

"Yes please, but I was joking about the river."

"Ain't nothing more 'an they deserve."

"Merv."

"'S OK. I get yer. So you got a preference then? For where I'm gonna dump this bunch of prannies?"

The Pan shrugged.

"There's a clip joint down by the harbour," Simon volunteered. "It's very exclusive, a lot of Grongles go there."

"You talking about Ditzy's?" asked Big Merv.

"Yes."

"Won't there be door staff? How are we going to get them in?" asked

Professor N'Aversion.

"I can take care of that," said Big Merv. He nudged The Pan and opened his pocket subtly; The Pan could see that it contained a pirate portal. "Do these boys know what I'm talking about?" he asked.

"Yeh, they do," The Pan took a second one out of his pocket and handed it to Big Merv. "You'll need this one too if you don't want to have a long walk back in the dark."

"Nah, 's a waste."

"No it's not. Any Grongles you come across are bound to be suspicious. It'd be a bit dim to escape this lot and then get picked up by a routine patrol."

"OK … thanks mate. Ditzy's," he scratched his head and his antennae waved about. "This time last week I effin' owned half of it."

"Oh dear. Won't it be closed as a sign of respect?" asked Professor N'Aversion.

"Yeh, you know, unfortunate death of the owner, live on world telly," said The Pan.

"It don't never close," Big Merv grinned, "but you gotta point. I'll have a dekko."

He put the pirate portal The Pan had given him to his eye and squinted in.

"They ain't got no respect," he laughed. "'S good and busy, not many Grongles in mind."

"Well, that's a good thing isn't it?"

"Yer, s'pose, these boys here can make up the numbers. 'S a corner booth free; plenty of room, nice and dark. 'S why it's always been a good place to do business. No-one can see what's going down."

He straightened his tie and smoothed down the fabric of his suit. The Pan left Simon, Psycho Dave, Big Merv and the Professor putting the Grongles' weapons back about their persons and went to the garage to get a proper rope. When he returned, Big Merv tied Captain Snow and his unconscious guards together, weaving it round them so there was no chance of leaving any of them behind. Then he slipped one arm through the rope, took Psycho Dave by the hand, put his thumb in the portal and disappeared.

The Pan faced Simon and Professor N'Aversion.

"That was a hell of a thing," murmured Simon.

"Yeh, I guess you know everything now," said The Pan.

They stood there, saying nothing for a moment and then, to his complete horror the pair of them prostrated themselves on the floor at his feet.

"Your Gracious Exaltedness," said the voice of the Professor, or was it Simon, it was so muffled it was difficult to tell.

"Th-th-that's … please don't do that," said The Pan, taking a step back, "I'm not gracious or exalted."

"But you are the Candidate," said the muffled voice, yes, it was the Professor.

Now what?

"How do you know?"

No, no, no, he should have said, 'Why do you think that?'

"You can't kill anyone," said the Professor.

"Oh," no point lying. "Alright, then, between you and me, yes, I think I might be but please, I haven't hoovered that floor since Monday and I don't want you to catch anything and I-I'm not that kind of man. Please get up."

Slowly, reluctantly, the two of them rose to one knee – progress, The Pan supposed. The Professor was emotional, so much so that he actually wrung his hands.

"We have been waiting for so long, hoping and praying that you'd come to save us—"

"Yeh, well," The Pan cleared his throat, "the saving thing … there's something you need to know about that—"

"I feared I'd never live to see this day—"

"Then I'm very happy for you; and for what it's worth neither did I, but—"

"My unwavering loyalty is yours," said the Professor.

"Please, get up—"

"Mine too," said Simon.

"I am yours to command," said the Professor.

"Me too," said Simon.

"Alright, then my first command is, 'Get up'. In fact, that's an order." Finally, they did as he asked. "Thanks. It's lovely of you to say these things but before you get too excited and start pledging your loyalty all over the place, you need to know who I am and what you're getting yourselves into. I doubt things are the way you think and I can guarantee they aren't the way you hope. In fact, look, I need—I'm a bit wired and

I suspect I have a front door to fix and I have to go upstairs and find my other colleagues—"

"There are more of you?"

"Yeh, a few but it's not an army, I'm afraid. While we wait for Big Merv and Dave, shall we make some cocoa?"

"Cocoa?"

"Yeh, it's kind of a tradition round here and you're welcome to stay. I'd like you to meet the others. The Resistance and the Underground need to work together."

Professor N'Aversion and Simon exchanged glances.

"The Underground?"

"Yeh."

"How many of you are there?"

The Pan thought. It looked as if Psycho Dave was in and Pub Quiz Alan had pretty much pledged his allegiance earlier on. There was Big Merv, Lucy. And Trev, of course …

"A handful. It's always been small. Listen, we need to sit down and make a plan, all of us. D'you mind saving the questions until then only … it's been a long day and …" he ran his fingers round his collar and watched their eyes follow the process of the ring. He tried to look pointy-brained and intelligent and in command but he was running on nervous energy. It had nearly run out and he was on the brink of collapse. He wished he could hand the thinking over to someone else for a few hours and go to sleep.

"You mentioned a door that needed mending," said The Professor.

"Yes," said Simon, "we must make these premises safe."

"Well said and there's no-one better equipped to fix a door than an engineer, right Simon?"

"Absolutely. We would be honoured to patch it up for you," said the Spiffle, "until you can have it mended by a professional."

Honoured. Blimey. Still at least they weren't lying face down on the floor at his feet now.

"That would be very kind, thanks," said The Pan.

They both bowed.

"Please, don't do that. I'm just a man, nothing more. Imagine I'm one of your colleagues."

"Which one?" asked Simon.

Arnold's trousers.

"One you like and respect but who is on the same level as you," he said. He glanced at his watch, "Right, it's late, let me show you where things are, then I'll go and make some cocoa."

Chapter 29

LordVernon laid out the equipment he would need on his desk and went to change into a night assault suit. It was patterned in mottled shades of dark grey specially designed to camouflage the wearer, not only in darkness, but also against night vision lenses, which the High Leader's bodyguards would be wearing. Once the attack began, they could not fail to see Lord Vernon at such close quarters, but the grey suit would make his movements harder to follow. The material, interwoven with carbon fibre, also gave the same protection as light body armour. He adjusted it; the fibre had to be pulled skintight to work, but when it was it would reduce the power of a punch and protect the wearer from a ricochet of laser fire or a glancing knife blow. Lord Vernon stood in front of his dressing room mirror, admiring himself. The dark material accentuated his physique, he felt as if it had given him a new body; even taller and more powerful than the real one underneath. He felt invincible.

He went back into the main reception room and checked the items on his desk. First the knife: he ensured that the blade was keen and the balance perfect before strapping it to his back. He didn't expect to use it. He would make the killing with two laser pistols but it paid to have something extra. He bent his arm back to his shoulder and adjusted the fastenings. He kept altering them, positioning the knife perfectly. His hand must find the grip automatically, without thought, when he reached for it. Then he strapped the two holsters onto his belt and checked the laser pistols: that they were fully charged, that the action of each was smooth and that the power setting was high enough to vaporise any target. He would take no chances: not at a ratio of seven guards, and the High Leader, to one; not even when the one was himself. Each gun would give him a maximum of nine shots at such high power and he must make them count. The High Leader's guards would not give any quarter. If he hadn't killed everything breathing in that room within seconds, he would be killed, himself. This must be a swift, clinical strike.

No problem. Not for him.

When he had finished with the guns, he put them in their holsters and checked that he could draw them quickly enough. That done, he slipped a balaclava over his head with night vision lenses in its eye sockets. He did not remove his black suede gloves but he did take off all of his rings, except for the K'Barthan Ring of State. He picked up the thimble and checked his watch. Good, there was time for some mental preparation.

He stood in the middle of the room, centring his breathing and executing a series of warm-up stretches. In his head, he envisaged his target, the High Leader, and his guards. He imagined the quarters in which he would find them, going through every detail in his mind's eye. He used the thimble to make a visual check, to ensure he had remembered everything correctly. He went over his plan: rehearsing the most efficient order in which to take them. It was going to be … intense, but he was ready.

He took some more deep breaths, centring his anger, his will, his desire for the High Leader's death into the strength he would need to achieve it. Then he drew one of the pistols, gave the power a final boost on a patch of fur sewn to the side of his suit leg, curled his thumb over the edge of the thimble and disappeared.

****

It is possible that six of the High Leader's bodyguards lived long enough to hear a few nanoseconds of some strange sound. They might even have survived long enough to see the dark shape appearing in the middle of the room, but it's unlikely.

Lord Vernon dropped the portal almost as he was still materialising, and drawing the other pistol, dispatched six of the guards in a volley of laser fire before they had even reached for theirs. The last guard was quick enough to get a shot off from the hip. It missed, the beam reflecting off a wall mirror. Greatly reduced in strength, it hit a standard lamp which fell. Lord Vernon downed the guard but was not quick enough to avoid the falling lamp, which glanced off his left arm, knocking one of the laser pistols from his grasp. He swung round, legs apart, arms extended, aiming the remaining pistol at the High Leader.

It was at moments like this that he felt truly alive; the adrenaline coursed through his body, sharpening his reflexes, focussing his mind, exhilarating him. The air was filled with the smell of burning and in that brief second, Lord Vernon's heightened senses took in the scene; one set of curtains was open, the orange street lights of the city illuminating half the room. The High Leader had scrambled out of bed and stood facing his attacker, the lightweight body armour he wore was clearly visible under his night clothes. He, too, was armed, his laser pistol trained on Lord Vernon. The two of them stood facing one another.

"Very good," said the High Leader. "Whoever you are, you should be working for me. Surrender and I'll spare your life. No, better than that, I'll give you double whatever that upstart Lord Vernon is paying you if you kill him."

Behind the balaclava Lord Vernon's mouth curled into a smile. This was going to be easy, so easy that he was almost disappointed.

"I am not for sale," he said and he fired first.

A feeble bolt sputtered from the barrel of the pistol and dispersed a few feet beyond. It was spent. Lord Vernon instantly threw himself into the shadows behind a chest of drawers, as the bolt from the High Leader's gun exploded against the far wall. From his hiding place, Lord Vernon threw his spent pistol at the High Leader's head, causing him to duck as he fired the second volley. It went wide, and Lord Vernon leapt at him, knocking the gun from his hand. But he felt a blow as the High Leader kicked his feet from under him, bringing him down. Before he could reach for his knife the High Leader was on him, hands locked around his throat. Lord Vernon smashed his palm upwards against the bottom of the High Leader's nose, causing him to jerk his head back and loosen his grip: not much, but enough to throw him off.

The High Leader rolled, stood up, and made for his gun. Lord Vernon lunged after him, drawing his knife. The High Leader dodged and delivered a jabbing punch to Lord Vernon's back, close to his kidneys. The suit took the brunt of the blow but he faltered and dropped his weapon. It fell onto the carpet, skidding out of reach but only just. Lord Vernon charged as the High Leader threw himself after it, catching him off balance and bringing him down. Still, the High Leader struggled forward towards the knife, his outstretched fingers almost touching the hilt. Lord Vernon flung his arm round the High Leader's neck, pulling him backwards. He tried to tighten his grip but he was still weak from the punch to his back. The High Leader tipped him easily over his head. But Lord Vernon got to the knife first.

Aware that his adversary would be making for the gun again, Lord Vernon turned quickly and ran at him. He knew the High Leader would be expecting a blow to the neck or head so as he charged he buried the knife in the top of his leg, just where it met his groin. The force of the impact smashed the two of them against the wall and Lord Vernon used his forward momentum to drive the knife further in.

It was over now, the High Leader's groan of pain confirmed it. He struggled but Lord Vernon forced his forearm against his neck, using his weight to hold his victim still, increasing the pressure, feeling the delicious sensation of his enemy weakening. The High Leader's hands scrabbled ineffectually at his arm and at his hand on the knife. Lord Vernon felt the warm blood pouring out. He smelled the ferrous stench of it, the victory. The blood flowed even faster when he pulled the knife out of the wound. He raised it high, and drove it savagely into his victim's neck.

It was done.

The High Leader sank slowly to the floor. He was failing fast now. His hands, clawing feebly at the fabric of Lord Vernon's assault suit, were stained dark with his own blood. With the last of his strength he looked up, supplicating, but pragmatic enough not to hope.

"Goodbye, High Leader."

Lord Vernon took off the mask and the orange light of the city shining in through the curtains fell across his features. He was gratified to see the look of recognition on the High Leader's face before his strength finally failed him and he fell sideways onto the carpet.

"It's my turn now."

Lord Vernon kicked the lifeless body over onto its back, bent down and, placing one foot against the chest, pulled out the knife. He tucked the mask into his belt and used the sheets on the bed to wipe the blood off the blade, then retrieved his laser pistols.

As he cast a final glance around the room, he heard a small tinny voice.

"Hello? Hello? High Leader?"

Ah yes, something glowing on the floor by the High Leader's bed; his phone. Lord Vernon walked over and picked it up. The screen was active, a number called up, labelled 'guard'. He must have tried to summon help. Lord Vernon put the phone to his ear.

"Good evening," he said.

"Who is this?" asked a voice at the other end.

"That is not your concern."

"Where's the High Leader?"

"He is here, but you may wish to come to his aid. He appears to have fallen on something sharp."

Lord Vernon pressed the red button to end the call and tossed the phone onto the bloodstained carpet near its lifeless owner. He picked up the gold portal from where it had fallen, pictured his rooms in his mind's eye, curled his thumb into it and disappeared.

Chapter 30

The Pan made cocoa in the kitchen as the sound of Simon and Professor N'Aversion trying to hammer quietly came from downstairs. Lucy was with Trev, checking up on him and Alan was supposedly 'helping' the Professor and Simon but The Pan suspected it was more a case of keeping an eye on them. The Pan had no clue how he was going to hide his friends – especially Big Merv – or what to do next, but it was good to have company about the place, even if it was just as good to be alone, right now, with the cocoa …

Cluck?

Oh yes, and the eighth Architrave. The Pan needed to clear his head and think of a plan. Ideally, to do that, he would talk to someone about it, somebody he trusted.

Cluck?

"Yes, I know," said The Pan, "I need to make peace with my predecessors."

Cluck.

Yeh, put that on the to-do list then. He heard a sucking sound and a pop followed by the crunch of a pirate portal being ground to dust under the heel of a Swamp Thing's boot. Then footsteps on the stairs, just one set. He heard Big Merv go into Trev's room for a while and then he appeared in the doorway. The sound rose up from downstairs of someone wielding a broom. Clearly Psycho Dave was sweeping up the glass. Big Merv greeted The Pan with characteristic tact.

"You look like crap, son."

"Yeh, I don't feel great."

"Good, you effin' well deserve it! You scared the smeck outta me."

Despite his flagging spirits, The Pan laughed.

"Yeh, I'll admit that was a close call."

"You ain't joking. So what's up? You ill or scared?" Big Merv asked him.

"Sick: sick of this whole thing, sick of the massive cock-up I'm making. Sick that I can't make it right."

Big Merv gave him a felt-tip green, all-seeing look. His antennae tied themselves into a knot and then unknotted again, slowly.

"Lovesick an' all I reckon."

"Yeh," The Pan's voice was wobbly.

"We'll get her outta there."

"No, we won't," said The Pan bitterly, "she doesn't want that. She dumped me."

Big Merv frowned.

"Have you got that straight son?"

"Yeh."

"But she—"

"That's all you need to know, Merv. It's not open to discussion." He closed his eyes and bit back the tears.

"That bad mate?"

"Worse. That's why the conversation ends here." He took a deep breath to recover himself. "Moving on, we need to discuss what we're going to do, all of us, everyone here. Hence the cocoa."

"OK mate," Big Merv dismissed the topic with a nod and then his face split into a smile. "Trev says the old ladies made cocoa."

The Pan brightened instantly.

"Trev's awake?"

"Yer. An' he wants to say hello. You wanna say hello?"

The Pan beamed.

"Of course!"

"You gotta be quick, he's proper knackered, but he smelt that cocoa and he wants some."

"Great, I'll take it to him. D'you want one? And Lucy, I'm guessing she's with him."

"Ner, save ours, for that talk you're gonna have."

"Alright. Poor Trev, I owe him an apology, I've tanked his pride and joy."

"You what?"

"The delivery snurd."

Big Merv laughed.

"It was the Grongles what tanked it. Anyway, he ain't gonna worry about that." The Pan poured some of the cocoa into a cup and turned

down the heat under the rest. "Not after you found that Grongle bird to fix his leg. Where d'you dig her up from?"

"General Moteurs introduced us. Long story."

"I'm lookin' forward to hearin' it, c'mon son." He picked up the biscuit tin.

"I'm afraid there aren't any biscuits left. I gave the last one to Humbert last night."

"You dippy twonk! 'S a shockin' waste. Lucky Luce found Gladys' recipe file then ain't it? She made this lot while you was working tonight an' I'll tell you what, they ain't half bad."

The Pan laughed.

"I'm beginning to think Lucy can turn her hand to anything."

"You ain't wrong there, son. She's real class." He saw Big Merv's pride as he spoke.

"And ..." he raised one eyebrow, "are you two serious?"

Big Merv laughed.

"An' if we was? I ain't gonna tell you, am I? Cheeky little Herbert." He took one of the mugs and the box of biscuits and went out into the hall.

Chapter 31

In the dim glow of the bedside light, Trev looked drawn but he greeted The Pan with a cheerful smile as he put the cup of cocoa down. For all his wanness, he seemed in high spirits and put his arms up.

"Mate!" he said. The Pan braced himself as his friend enveloped him in a huge bear hug. It didn't hurt as much as he'd expected until Trev started clapping him on the back but even then he was happy to grin and bear it.

"Ouch ...Trev ... need to ... breathe ..." he said.

"Sorry mate, and, Arnold, yer arm, I forgot."

"Don't worry, it's good to see you looking better. How are you feeling?"

"Like dog eggs but I got both legs and I'm alive."

"Yeh, I can see that's quite a bonus," said The Pan. "I think you can thank Lucy for that."

"I wasn't the one who got the doctor," she said.

"Nah but you done the most important job today," said Big Merv.

"Yeh," The Pan added, "you know what Trev? She made the biscuits."

They all laughed and despite his situation, it made The Pan feel good. He could see that Trev was already tiring and Lucy told them it was time he went to sleep. Big Merv and The Pan helped him into the bathroom to wash, and clean his teeth, then, when he was settled, they left Lucy fussing over him with painkillers for the night, and a glass of water.

Big Merv and The Pan returned to the kitchen, where The Pan went back to stirring the cocoa for everyone else, and Big Merv washed up Trev's cup. The hammering noises downstairs had abated. "Sounds like you've had a smeck of a week, son," said Big Merv as he fished out more cups for them.

"Yeh."

"So what's your plan?"

"Why d'you think I have a plan?"

"I know you have, mate."

The Pan closed the cupboard. He'd put plenty of Gladys and Ada's pirate portals around the house to ensure that there was too much interference for anyone, Lord Vernon for example, to watch him through another portal. Even so, he took one of the tiny jars from the small stash he held in the bread bin and put it on the table between them.

"Alright, it's not a plan exactly, more an intent because I'm not sure how I'm going to do it yet but I can prove that Lord Vernon is not the Candidate, so I have to go to the installation."

"Then what?"

"I doubt I'll be around to worry. He's not going to like it."

"You always was a positive thinker."

"A realist."

The Swamp Thing shrugged.

"So what you doing here? How come they ain't killed you?"

"I dunno. It's … a long story."

Big Merv subjected him to a gimlet felt-tip green glare.

"Yer. I reckon it's gotta be. An' these Resistance blokes. You trust 'em? Only, if you wanna get rid of them, Dave and I can sling 'em out."

"No, I trust them, I think. Mainly because Denarghi doesn't know they're here, and we need to get in contact with the Resistance. We have to sort out something for after I'm—something. The main worry is their colleagues, who I don't trust, who are going to find me, soon."

"They can do what they wanna but if they want you they've gotta come through me."

"Merv, you are the best friend a man could have but, there are rather a lot of them and only one of you."

"Nah, I ain't the only bloke what thinks that way. You got friends. Friends what owe you an' all."

The Pan smiled.

"No-one owes me, but it's good to have you all here."

Lucy arrived.

"You OK, babe?" said Big Merv.

She smiled wanly. "Yeh."

Big Merv didn't think so by the look of it. His antennae were moving slowly backwards and forwards the way they did when he was thinking, or worried.

"Trev all set?" asked The Pan as she sat at the kitchen table.

"He seems pretty good … although the thing that scares me is that I'm afraid I wouldn't know what bad looks like. I think I should sit up with him."

"What, all night?" said The Pan.

"Yes."

"Oh no you don't. We'll take it in turns."

"Yer," said Big Merv. "But not you son."

"You two aren't doing it on your own."

"We ain't runnin' a pub."

"Or entertaining two Resistance suspects and hiding three GBIs," said Lucy.

"But he's my friend, too, and we're in this together. We have to look out for each other. Right Merv?"

"Maybe."

"Good, it's settled, I'm in. What do we look for?"

"Increase in temperature, restlessness, breathing fast and a fast heart rate or at least, any increases, in those respects, on the way he is now."

"Alright," said The Pan.

"And he needs to be woken at three in the morning for another set of pills. I've laid them all out—"

"'S OK Luce, I can handle the graveyard shift," said Big Merv

"No," said The Pan. They both looked up at him. "You two need to rest. If I take the middle watch and we do three hours each then both of you will get six hours straight. It doesn't matter to me, I'm not sleeping that well anyway and I'm a doomed man." Just saying it made him sick and fearful. He grinned trying to put a brave face on it.

"You know what mate? I been thinking about that an' I reckon you don't have to be," said Big Merv.

"Unfortunately, I'm pretty sure I do. It's complicated … and I need to explain." The two of them watched him and like everyone else's, their eyes followed the ring as he put his hand up and scratched his nose. "I think that …" he stopped, he could hear footsteps on the stairs. Sure enough, the large bulk of Professor N'Aversion filled the doorway.

"I am proud to announce that we have mended your door, Your Most—"

"Defreville," said The Pan firmly as he stood up to greet the Professor. "That was quick. Come in, take a seat. All of you." The Professor wasn't alone. Simon, Pub Quiz Alan and Psycho Dave were with him. "Cocoa?"

Everyone said yes.

"Thank you for fixing the door," said The Pan.

"It wasn't any bother, the door's perfectly good and the lock was intact. It was only the strike plate that was broken, so the Professor and I – with help from Alan and Dave here, we've moved the lock up a few inches, replaced the damaged strike plate with a piece of steel and fitted some of the best quality Shadwell bolts – the tip-top quality lock and shut ones – which I just happen to keep with me. Whoever built this place knew a good lock when they saw one. It's a beautiful mechanism. Precision milled from shot-link galvanised steel right here in K'Barth, none of this shoddy Grongolian rubbish. It's a three-quarter inch lock, tight throw round, full turn, with a seventeen position half-inch spindle. The action was a little jumpy but I've oiled it of course, and adjusted the spindle down three and a half microns, which is an amazingly tiny requirement for a lock of such age. It's as good as new now; better," said Simon, breathlessly.

"Er, thanks. It sounds as if you've made the place very secure."

"You can't be too careful," said Alan.

"Yer and we has hoovered and swept up and done the clearing up in the snug," added Psycho Dave.

"I hope you will find everything to your satisfaction," said The Professor.

"Yes, that's amazing, thank you," said The Pan. "Where did you get all the stuff to do that?"

"I carry a few spare pieces of this and that about my person. For emergencies," said Simon.

When the drinks were poured and everyone had settled down and been introduced, The Pan spoke.

"OK, I'm not sure where to begin … I think you might …" he laughed nervously, "well, you are sitting down so that's a start but I'm beginning to wonder if the cocoa is enough. I think you may need a stiff drink, would any of you like to try Gladys' Calvados?"

He didn't wait for an answer, there was a bottle in the larder which Gladys used for cooking. He went and got it and poured a generous measure into seven glasses.

Chapter 32

The Pan sat collecting his thoughts, trying to work out where to start. "OK, Defreville, we're listening," said Lucy as she sniffed her portion of Gladys' Calvados with a nervous expression. "What's up?"

"He thinks he's doomed, the doppy twonk," Big Merv explained helpfully.

"Well, this is the thing. I am. Because I have to go to the installation on Saturday and prove that Lord Vernon is a fake. My job, my destiny, is to ensure the succession."

"No it ain't, you nerk."

"Well, yes it is Merv because," The Pan's mouth had gone dry, "actually, I'm the real Candidate." Just saying it … at the very thought, he almost threw up.

"We *had* realised," Lucy said, looking at the ceiling.

What?

"Yer, course," said Big Merv.

"Dave?" The Pan glanced over at Psycho Dave.

"Alan told me," he said, as if that explained everything.

The Pan was slightly disappointed by his friends' lack of surprise, although he supposed, on balance it was preferable to a reaction like the Professor and Simon's.

"How come I'm the only person who didn't expect this?" he said.

"Because you're a nerk," said Big Merv. "So, what are you gonna do ?"

The Pan got up, took a teaspoon from the drawer, trawled it through the sugar jar and removed the confibrulator – the Importance Detector – and its stand from under the glittering granules where he'd hidden them. He blew on the confibrulator, extensively, to remove all traces of sugar and put it, with the stand, on the table. Next, after a rummage in his pockets, he put the box beside it; The Box, which only the Candidates of K'Barth could open. They watched in silence.

"You know what this stuff is, right?"

"Where did you get it?" asked Alan.

"A bank job originally, driver's perks," he grinned at Big Merv. "When the Grongles captured us, Lord Vernon took it away from me. Then he shot me, drugged me and waved my signed death warrant in my face before pardoning me and sending me here. They'd done over the place but nothing seemed to be taken and when I started to put everything back in order, I found that these had been added."

Big Merv looked up sharply.

"Sounds complicated mate. When they took us prisoner, Lord Vernon wanted you dead. It was bleedin' obvious, he all but done it on the spot. Why'd he let you go?"

"Well, I asked him why he didn't just kill me and he said, I quote, 'Where's the fun in that?' I can't say for certain but I'm beginning to think it was probably General Moteurs' idea to get me freed. He knew who I was and at the time, I didn't."

"General Moteurs? Who's 'e?" asked Psycho Dave.

"Sounds like a Grongle," said Alan.

"He is," said Lucy.

"And you trust him?" asked Alan.

"He left me these," he gestured to the stuff on the table, "and he's Underground. So that's a yes, I suppose. Anyway, this," he held up his hand, palm inwards towards his face, and flashed the ring at them, "was in the box."

"Which only you can open," said Lucy.

"Yes."

"Which is your proof, right?"

"I think so."

"And that is the K'Barthan Ring of State yeh?" asked Alan.

"The real one?" asked Simon.

"Mmm. I'd say so." The Pan stopped to look at the ruby for a moment and it reflected the light, a deep, dark red.

"As I understand it from the database that ring has a particular property …" said The Professor.

"Yeh, it's shrink-to-fit but only on me. Ruth," The Pan's voice broke, "Ruth tried it on and it … didn't."

There was a long silence while everyone took that in.

Lucy gave him a sideways look.

"Wouldn't you be more sensible to wear it on your other hand, Defreville?"

"Yes but at the moment I'm afraid there are … logistical reasons why

I can't take it off."

"Don't tell me it's stuck."

The Pan smiled and forced a laugh.

"Not exactly."

"So, you got some pukka stuff," said Big Merv, "but unless someone's already got a gun to Lord Vernon's head, I reckon it's still game over the second you stand up."

"'S right," Psycho Dave agreed.

"Quite so. He'll kill you before you can speak," said the Professor.

"Do you really have to go?" asked Simon.

"Yes. Because, as some of you already know, if I fail to attend the installation on Saturday, if I don't prove that Lord Vernon is a fake, the thread will be broken and I will be the last Candidate."

"Then we gotta find you an army, pronto," said Big Merv.

"We can help there," said the Professor.

"I don't think you can. I don't think anyone can. It's too late. If I wanted an army I should have been mobilising it a couple of years ago, but I didn't know who I was until now. Anyway, can you see me leading an army? I have a will of marshmallow and a heart of custard. I'm a coward, I always have been. That's why I'm a good getaway man."

"Alright. But if that's the way you wanna play it, how're you gonna make him listen?"

"I don't see how you can without forcing him," said Simon.

"I think, if I can manage to survive the first thirty seconds, I can appeal to his baser side."

"Are you sure, mate?" asked Alan.

"Not a hundred per cent, no, but the thing is, Sir Robin told me, that a long time ago—"

"What, the Sir Robin, Sir Robin Get?" asked Alan.

"Yes."

"You met him?" asked Psycho Dave.

"If he did he'd have to be smecking clever. Sir Robin Get's dead," said Alan.

"He wasn't last week," said Professor N'Aversion, "although, I'm afraid he is in custody; one of my deputies kindly hacked into the Palace mainframe and found out."

"Are you kidding?" asked Alan.

"Nope. The Professor's right," said The Pan, "he was taken prisoner with the rest of us."

"He's been alive all this time?"

"Yeh, he faked his own death and went into hiding," The Pan explained.

"After which, well, actually he met me. He told me there was this one time when no Candidate was found. So they got someone else and she managed to pass the criteria—"

"Could she open the box?" asked Lucy.

"Yes, well … not this box but I'm guessing she could open the box Lord Vernon has."

"Very interesting," said Professor N'Aversion, "which Architrave was it?"

Jennifer Fifteen, said a voice. The Pan glanced nervously down at the ring. Arnold, it was wearing off.

Cluck.

By The Prophet's toe jam. Never mind. At least they were being helpful. He thought a deliberate 'thanks' hoping that, if they couldn't hear it, the chicken would pass it on and then he ploughed on.

"Jennifer Fifteen."

"No way," said Psycho Dave.

"Yes, apparently. Lord Vernon knows all about Jennifer and he also knows he is close to achieving the same thing."

"Hang on a mo, you're the Candidate, a real one. Jennifer Fifteen was a pretend Candidate. That's fair enough when there isn't anyone else but how can Lord Vernon get one over on the real deal?" asked Alan.

"I don't know," The Pan thought about the Architraves in his head. He didn't think they'd go and live in Lord Vernon's, and if they did, he could imagine they wouldn't like the decor. They'd move the furniture. Maybe they'd melt his mind. That would save a job. Yes well, that was probably enough of that. The Pan gathered his thoughts and continued. "All I know is I have to try and hope that, on the day, I win out."

"I don't like the sound of that," said Simon.

"I guess it's a bit of a double bluff. If he's going to listen, and damn himself, I have to convince him that he's cracked it, like Jennifer. Then, I offer him the opportunity to prove he's the real McCoy on world telly."

"And the world watches him fail and wakes up to the truth?" said Lucy.

"Yeh. I hope. It's a gamble, because if I get it wrong, I think he'll succeed. But it's all I can do: turn up, offer him cast-iron proof of his credentials, on a plate, and hope it'll be too good for him to pass up."

"What if he's pulled it off already?" said Alan.

"He hasn't yet."

"How do you know?" asked Simon.

"Because ... if he had successfully taken my place, certain things, which are happening to me, would stop."

"What things?"

Cluck.

"I don't think I can say. You're going to have to trust me on this, but I know. He isn't the Candidate, not yet. If I still feel like this on Saturday and he doesn't, his attempt to be Architrave will fail. He might look realistic but he won't be the Architrave. Not truly: I suppose it's academic, really. He'll still be in charge and I'll be dead, but someone else will come in time: my successor, someone smart, and worth following; someone who knows what they're doing. I'll take dying for that."

"So the ring shrinks to fit you, you can open the box and there's the thing you can't explain, which, presumably, you can't explain on telly, either, but how can you get to prove he's a sham or even get him to listen?" asked Lucy.

"I don't know. I'll just have to put my faith in The Prophet and busk it."

"Isn't that a rather louche approach, Defreville?"

He smiled ruefully.

"Probably. There are three strands to it. First: he has to be installed with the right stuff, he doesn't have that and I do. He's thorough. He'll have read up on the ceremony so I think he'll believe me when I tell him. He knows there were two boxes, I just have to convince him he's muddled them up. Second: there's the ring. I'm guessing he needs the real one. I'm going on little more than a hunch here—"

"We will check the database," said Professor N'Aversion.

"That's the second time you've talked about a database."

"Yes, it cross references all mentions of religious artefacts and practices – in most places," Simon explained.

"And our ambition of course is to make that 'most places' into 'anywhere'," the Professor added. "We have always questioned why it was that the Grongles placed a blanket ban on all mentions of religion: rationalist and theist. We were trying to find what it was they didn't want us to know. I think we may have achieved that already," The Pan followed his gaze to the pirate portal on the table, "but ..."

"Whatever the ring does, it must be important. If you can dig anything up it would be a big help."

"Consider it done."

"Thanks."

There was silence for a moment.

"The third thing?" prompted Lucy.

"Right, yes, the third thing. One of us – Lord Vernon, or I – has to convince the people and they have to believe. It's reality theory and I don't pretend to understand it but the idea behind it is, basically, this: no matter what the odds are, and no matter what the obvious outcome should be, we won't know until the moment it actually happens who has succeeded. It's—"

"Schrödinger's cat!" Lucy exclaimed.

"Where?" asked Psycho Dave, turning to look out of the window, onto the fire escape.

"I'm sorry?" said The Pan.

"We have a theoretical experiment, where I'm from, called Schrödinger's cat. The idea is that you put a live cat in a metal box with some things that may kill it, if a certain chain of events take place … I can't remember it in detail but I think one of them is radioactive and if it decays it will trigger a switch to release some poison gas. The point is that because there's no way of knowing what's going on in the box, quantum physics sees the cat as both dead and alive at the same time until the moment someone opens the box and finds out the truth."

"Ah," said Professor N'Aversion, "that sounds very similar to Natterjack's Box of Frogs, in K'Barthan science, which takes it one step further in asserting that, if you believe and expect to find the frogs in the box, or your cat, alive then your thoughts will reprogramme the outcome. The theory is perfectly sound, but not my field, unfortunately."

"But what does it mean for Defreville?" asked Lucy.

"That Lord Vernon can be two things at the same time: Candidate and not, until the point in time when someone looks at the results. So in theory, if enough people believe one or the other of them is the true ruler of K'Barth that individual will become exactly that, whether or not they were in the first place. The odds for or against have no bearing; the belief, if there's enough, will suffice."

"You saying we gotta get Defreville more believers so he wins?" asked Big Merv.

"Sort of. The theory feels right," said The Pan slowly. "That's one of the reasons why I have to wait until Saturday I think; because it'll go out on TV and the whole world will be watching and all I have to do is convince it." Right, easy. "Sir Robin told me that Saturday is the most auspicious day for me to make my move. However, it's also the last point at which I can act and, surprise, surprise, it's the most auspicious day for Lord Vernon, too. That's why I have to go, even though, being somewhat unprepared, it probably will be a one-way trip."

There was another silence, and Lucy picked up the confibrulator and looked at it.

"That is handy for a lot of things, including showing the importance of people," explained The Pan. "Everyone scores something but only a real, true Candidate will score eight or over. I wish I could explain why but I haven't a clue how it works. If you want to know stuff like that you'll have to talk to Sir Robin. He's the organ grinder, I'm just the monkey."

The Pan waited but nobody laughed.

"So what's your score?" asked Lucy.

"I haven't dared try it."

"My good fellow, it sounds as if the person in the most need of convincing is you, yourself," said The Professor.

The Pan smiled sadly. He was so tired now.

"You gonna give it a whirl, son?" asked Big Merv.

"Alright. I'll just let the machine ..."

He wound up the Importance Detector, turned the pointer to face himself, and pulled the lever. The machine started spinning, and despite his earlier efforts to remove the sugar, it gave off a pleasant aroma of caramel as it gained speed. The seven of them watched and waited. The needle slid slowly down to zero and then snapped to the other end of the dial but it didn't fluctuate like it had the times Sir Robin and Lord Vernon had taken his reading before. It stayed there for a moment and then edged downwards to eight, where it stopped.

"And there we are," he said. He realised that despite the evidence pointing to his identity; the ring, the box, the Architraves in his head, he hadn't really believed it was true. His palms prickled with sweat at the thought. K'Barth was really in the soup.

"Wow," said Lucy.

The Pan took a slug of Calvados but, because of his nerves, he inhaled much of it, with predictable results. Big Merv was beside him, at once, with a glass of water.

"Thanks," he gasped. As he took a few breaths to recover, he scrutinised his friends' faces, searching for a reaction but they seemed to be remarkably relaxed and unfazed.

"How come you lot are taking this better than I am?" Well, apart from The Professor and Simon doing full-on obeisance to him – that had totally freaked him out – but even they seemed to be more relaxed than he felt.

"It ain't hard," said Big Merv, his face splitting into a smile.

"It's alright for you, you're not standing between Lord Vernon and world domination."

Big Merv shifted. Suddenly he appeared every bit his full size; big, very big, and intimidating.

"I wouldn't be so sure about that, mate. Yours ain't gonna be the only dead body he has to walk over if he wants to pull this stunt. 'S a lot of K'Barthans who ain't gonna like it. An' I'll tell you something for nothing. They're gonna be standin' right behind you."

"Amen to that," said Professor N'Aversion, quietly.

"I hope they're not, I hope they're going to be staying sensibly at home, waiting until the time is right to stand behind my successor."

"And when will that be?" asked Alan.

"When he turns up."

"What if Lord Vernon gets to him first?" asked Simon.

"'S right," Psycho Dave agreed, "we'd be stiffed."

"Yer. Dave's got a point. I reckon the right time to overthrow Lord Vernon is this Saturday and I reckon I ain't the only bloke what thinks that way. There's gotta be others an' I'm gonna find them," said Merv.

"Not without a disguise."

"Then you'd better find me a disguise, sunshine, pronto."

"That's Candidate Sunshine to you, big man."

"Do you know Lord Vernon's score on the machine?" asked Lucy.

"It was eight, the same as mine, but I guess things may have changed." The Pan stopped the Importance Detector, and took a bank note out of his pocket. He folded it so it would stay upright and placed it near the Importance Detector with the side featuring Lord Vernon facing it. He moved the pointer and pulled the lever to set it spinning; the needle rose slowly to nine and stopped.

"Smeck!"

"Yer. That ain't good."

"Looks like he's won already," said Alan.

"Shut it Alan! Unless you want a smack in the gob," said Big Merv. "He ain't won, Defreville, I know it."

"I do and all," said Alan, "I said 'looks' I didn't say 'I think'."

"Easy lads," said The Pan. "To be honest, that may be the truth. Sir Robin told me you can only fake it up to eight," he ran his hand through his hair "so maybe Lord Vernon is the Candidate and I'm the faker."

"No." It was Professor N'Aversion who spoke. "This is complicated science. Don't believe things are always as you see. They aren't."

"Thanks Professor, but it looks worryingly convincing to me," sighed The Pan.

"No," said Lucy firmly. "I don't believe it either. Ruth could never love Lord Vernon. That must count for something."

And there was the likely explanation. Ruth. Her betrayal. The thought caught The Pan unprepared. He had to close his eyes to stop the tears from welling up.

"Not necessarily," he managed to say.

"But yes. If she's really the Chosen One, she's supposed to love the Candidate, and whether or not it means anything, she's head over heels in love with you Defreville."

"What if I told you she's not?" he said, his voice was strained, croaky and quiet. He wiped his hand across his eyes hurriedly. Hold onto the anger. It's the only way. With an immense effort of willpower, he suppressed a sob, disguising it as a cough.

"I wouldn't believe you. She's my best friend and has been for years. I know her better than I know myself and I'd swear, on my life, that she's crazy about you."

The Pan shook his head.

"Yes, Defreville. She's not the kind of person who can just drop that overnight. There's something else affecting it ..." Lucy stopped. "You don't believe she could love him do you? How can you even think that?"

"Quite easily, since she told me, herself."

"What? No, she didn't. She couldn't have done."

"She did. End of discussion." He couldn't speak any more and the familiar sense of desolation was threatening to overwhelm him. If he didn't leave the room at once he was going to cry in front of them. He took a deep breath and managed to rein in his emotions, "Guys, it's been a long day, tomorrow isn't going to be any easier and it's time we all hit the sack." He picked up the things on the table, "Lucy and Merv, whichever one of you sits up with Trev first, come and wake me at three," which was in … two hours, Arnold's snot. "Professor, Simon – and Alan and Dave if you want to stay – there's only one bedroom left, Ada's, but there are a couple of sofas in the sitting room and lots of cushions, you're welcome to both. I'll leave it to you to work out who goes where. There are blankets and pillows in the airing cupboard if you need them—"

Big Merv stood up.

"I'll show 'em," he said, "you gotta go." He seemed to understand but The Pan hesitated. "Get outta here."

"Thanks," said The Pan. He could feel his emotions slipping away from his control and turned his back to hide his face.

Chapter 33

Lucy watched The Pan go.

"What was that about?" she asked, when he had gone.

"He's hurting, sweets," said Big Merv.

"D'you think we should go after him?" asked Alan.

Big Merv was silent and Lucy realised she was getting used to the way his antennae waved to and fro when he thought.

"Nah," he said eventually, "not yet. He don't wanna talk now and he's gotta sleep. I'll have a word tomorrow; Thing to man."

"It must be tough for him. There he was, searching for the Candidate all this time … Anyone could see how disappointed, how betrayed he felt when nobody turned up, and now it's him and he's sitting there, thinking everyone feels the way he did," said Lucy.

"Yer, 's a lot of pressure."

"That's why I think I should talk to him." Many of the cases Lucy dealt with, meant literally, life and death to her clients. It was a heavy responsibility to carry. "Imagine it. There's the whole nation relying on him, expecting him to come riding in with a great big army and make everything right—"

"And there's 'im with a few days to go an' he hasn't an effin' clue."

"Yeh."

"Still, that's how he works, Luce. I reckon there's more." Big Merv turned to the Professor and Simon. "You blokes have gotta find out all you can and Luce, have a chat if you want, but first up, we gotta find out what's going on and then we gotta get him his army."

"How? Where from?"

"I used to be the boss round these parts. I reckon I can put together a bunch of tasty geezers."

"Merv, a few geezers versus this Lord Vernon horror and his entire army, is not enough."

"As I said before, we may be able to help," said Simon.

"Nobody first-line combat trained," added the Professor, "but I'm pretty sure RA—"

"RA?" asked Lucy.

"Revenue Acquisition," he explained. She was still no clearer.

"Thieving for funds," said Simon. "Every guerrilla organisation organises its funding that way."

"'S right. We'll sort it. Coz if Defreville don't make it past Saturday, the Underground's gotta, right? I reckon I owe him that." He stopped for a moment, "I tell you something, Luce, this ain't your problem. You don't have to stay. We'll understand if you wanna go home."

"And leave Ruth? And Trev? And you? No. Lord Vernon has to be stopped."

"You sure, girl? You sure Ruth ain't OK with being left?"

"Yes."

Big Merv sucked the air in through his teeth.

"Whadda you reckon to that Grongle bird? She'd be good. No-one'd suspect her in a million years."

"A Grongle?" asked Alan.

"Yer, she fixed up Trev."

"It's risky. We might not be able to trust her."

"I reckon we can but it don't matter. We got one on 'er. If she don't help us, we tell her boss she fixed Trev."

"That's immoral."

"That's business. But it ain't gonna take that. I reckon Defreville's right. She's on our side already, that General Moteurs and all."

"Not him," Lucy was concerned, "he was arrogant and rude."

"He's also highly intelligent," said the Professor. Lucy got the impression that Professor N'Aversion was almost as far out of his comfort zone with General Moteurs as she was.

"Yer, he's a double-'ard smecker and no mistake. There ain't much heart there as I can see, but someone put that kit here for Defreville to find and who was it, if it weren't him?" Big Merv stood up. "C'mon, babe. Get that hooch down yer neck. One of us has to go sit with Trev."

Lucy smiled wanly. Big Merv was making a lot of sense but General Moteurs' motives worried her. He was Lord Vernon's second in command, after all. What if this was a very clever double bluff? She shoved her misgivings to the back of her mind. Right now, she had Trev to think about. She finished the Calvados.

"I'll take first watch," she wheezed – it was strong stuff.

"Sound. C'mon then, you blokes follow me an' I'll show you where you're gonna sleep," said Big Merv.

Chapter 34

Lord Vernon arrived back at his rooms, quickly removed his knife holster and belt, and put them on his desk. Then he ripped off the assault suit and took a very fast shower. Fresh and invigorated, he wrapped a towel about his waist, picked up his sword and scabbard, and padded back, barefoot, to where he had left the assault suit. He drew the sword, used it to lift the blood-soaked clothing and with a deft turn of his wrist, flicked it into the open laundry basket by the door.

He still felt alive and energised by his deed, which was good, because he doubted he would have time to sleep tonight. There was much to attend to. He poured himself a fruit smoothie, drained the glass and refilled it. Then he took it with him to his bedroom to drink while he dressed. He reflected, as he flung the towel aside and put on a pair of boxer shorts, that the higher he had climbed in his bid for world domination, the fewer obstructions he was forced to dispose of directly. He had forgotten how energising it was to take care of the opposition personally.

He opened the wardrobe, selected a set of uniform and laid it on the bed.

Putting an end to some struggling piece of vermin in the cells was always a pleasure, but, even when they fought him, it had nothing on the endorphin hit of an act such as this. Tonight was a memory he would treasure. He closed his eyes to replay the experience in his head, in all its dizzying intensity. It would wear off at some point, and he would fall into a sleep so deep, so peaceful, so free of care that nothing would wake him. Tomorrow night, he thought, as he put on his black britches and adjusted them so that the red stripe down each side was just so. Today, he had things to do.

He looked at his reflection in the mirror, admiring his god-like physique. He had just killed the most powerful being in the world and was poised to take his place. He ran his hand over his perfectly honed stomach muscles. He had been careful to ensure that any high living he indulged in did not affect his levels of fitness. He followed a demanding exercise regimen designed to ensure his physical prowess remained at its peak. It had worked. Still no excess fat, anywhere. But he felt a dull tension around his back and ribs as he leaned over to pick up his shirt. The High Leader had known how and where to punch. Added to the bruising Lord Vernon had already suffered, in that exquisite encounter with the Resistance blonde, it had taken its toll. He took a large gulp of smoothie and, with regret, closed his mind to his memories of her. This was no time to lose focus.

However, a little harmless pleasure every now and again honed the intellect and heightened the senses ... at the appropriate juncture, of course. He would have her again. In the meantime, perhaps if he rewarded himself with a massage? Yes. After all, a body like his was a finely tuned machine, it must be looked after. Any damage the High Leader had inflicted must be given every aid to heal. Captain Snow had a pool of excellent female masseuses.

He stretched languidly. He was in half a mind to summon them now but General Moteurs would already be on his way with tragic news of the High Leader's death. There'd be time enough later for treats. When he was supreme ruler of the entire world. He put on his shirt and finished dressing.

After a final check in the mirror to make sure he looked characteristically pristine, he finished the last of the smoothie and strolled back to his office, where he took up his phone, rubbed it in his hair to boost the charge and called Captain Snow. There was no answer. Usually that would have made Lord Vernon angry but for the moment he was still too pumped to care. Instead he left explicit instructions on the Captain's voicemail as to what he wanted.

He took up his belt to reattach the pouches and holsters he had detached before murdering the High Leader and realised it was covered with blood, as was the blotter where he'd left it.

"No time to be careless," he muttered.

He should have noticed that earlier. He threw it into the dirty laundry bin. He had a batman to deal with that, bat people, to be precise. He never let others touch the knife though, he would clean and polish that himself. Now. He put it on the desk and took the polishing things out of the drawer. He dotted them around, to give the impression he had been working on the knife for some time. Despite wiping the blade, there was still enough congealed blood round the hilt to add to the bloodstains on the blotter. No matter. Returning swiftly to the bedroom, he selected a spare belt and hastily attached the pouches and holsters to that one. He buckled it on, rubbed his favourite laser pistol vigorously in his hair until it was fully charged and slipped it into the holster.

He checked his reflection.

Good.

Now he was ready to receive the sad news of the High Leader's death.

There was a knock at the door. Already?

Lord Vernon went back into the other room and opened it, himself.

Bang on cue, there was General Moteurs.

Chapter 35

Despite the late hour, Lord Vernon noticed that General Moteurs was wearing full uniform. He suspected his number two had still been up when called. The General seemed to sleep even less than he did, but for someone who'd been wearing the same uniform all day he was looking impressively well turned out – almost as immaculate as Lord Vernon himself.

"General, please come in." He held the door open.

"Sir, I bring grave news."

Lord Vernon raised his eyebrows.

"Sir, the—"

"Please sit," Lord Vernon cut in.

"Thank you, sir," the General sat hurriedly. "The High Leader has—"

"Would you like a fruit smoothie?" asked Lord Vernon. He was enjoying this.

"No, thank you, sir," said General Moteurs, his collected demeanour still very much in place. Lord Vernon waited but his number two wasn't falling into the same trap three times and said nothing more.

"What do you want?" demanded Lord Vernon.

"The High Leader has been assassinated," said General Moteurs.

"What a shame," said Lord Vernon quietly. He saw the General's eyes flick briefly to the knife on the blotter and the bloodstains beneath it.

"Sir." General Moteurs hid any other reaction. Even so, Lord Vernon could feel his second in command's fear and it pleased him.

"How did this … disaster occur?" A little too much irony? No, one could never have too much. General Moteurs shifted nervously in his seat.

"An assassin vaporised his guards and stabbed him, sir."

"Do you know how that could be possible, General?" He leaned back in his desk chair and blew an imaginary speck of dust from the tips of his suede gloves.

"Yes, sir."

"Yes," he said, hissing the s, "but then, you always knew, or you would have allocated him different rooms."

"He chose his own rooms, sir."

"Naturally, but you guided his hand."

The General sat straight and calm. He clearly wondered whether he was about to be double-crossed but he knew better than to point out the obvious, that in influencing the High Leader's choice he had only been obeying his master's wishes, even if he had been given no explicit orders. Lord Vernon picked up his knife and began to apply a cleaning solvent to the hilt.

"I appreciate your loyalty, General," he said, as he polished it casually. "When I am High Leader, you will not find me ungrateful."

"Thank you, sir," said General Moteurs. The nervousness in his voice was less audible, or perhaps it was just hidden more carefully.

"However." Lord Vernon held the knife up, pointy-end towards his favourite underling and looked along the blade. He watched as the red eyes widened the tiniest fraction, and waited just long enough to sense the General's unease; his fear, at what his master might be about to say, before adding, "Perhaps it will benefit us to keep the existence of portals secret. They are classified science are they not?"

"Yes, sir."

"Keep it that way."

"Sir."

"What time is it in Grongolia?" he asked as he flicked the knife round and began to polish it again.

"Zero four hundred hours, sir."

"The High Leader's retinue have sent word home?"

"No sir."

"But he alerted his security team?" This question was almost an admission of guilt. He suspected General Moteurs would take it as such.

"He did, sir, but I have persuaded them not to inform his retinue."

"How?"

"They are under house arrest in their quarters, sir."

Lord Vernon arched his eyebrows.

"Really? For what reason?"

"As a precaution."

"His retinue?"

"The same."

"Where are you holding them?"

"In their rooms, under guard."

"You will hand them over to my forces for processing, the security guards also."

"Yes, sir."

"I will give them the option to pledge their allegiance to me and if they refuse I will kill them." Lord Vernon twirled the knife casually from one hand to the other. He couldn't help thinking that a refusal, in at least three cases, would bring him immense gratification. However, he would deal with them later, it was only fair to give them a little time to reflect, and perhaps, a little incentivisation to help concentrate their minds. Yes. He must issue appropriate orders to Captain Snow in that respect, and when that time came, the Captain had better have turned his phone back on. Lord Vernon switched his attention back to General Moteurs. "Your contacts in Grongolia, they are ready to act?"

"They are standing by sir."

"So efficient, General. I believe if you were not so loyal, that you would pose a serious threat to me."

The General paled visibly.

"I pray you will never think that, sir."

How precious, 'I pray' said with such feeling. Lord Vernon made sure the smile he pulled was extra ominous as he put the knife back on the blotter.

"Not at the moment. We must act fast, I want full control of Grongolia in time for my installation on Saturday."

The General hesitated. "You wish to proceed with the installation, sir?"

"Naturally. You have seen the power of Nimmism, General. There is more to this than portals. I want it, and I must be installed as Architrave to have it. You have studied history?"

"A little sir."

The standard military history taught to officers in training, no doubt.

"Good. Then you will know that Grongolia once looked to K'Barth."

"Yes, sir but—"

"We had good reason. Oh we are superior to these K'Barthan insects now, but for all their savage ways, they once excelled in science."

"Sir."

"And with their secrets we will be invincible. We have accessed one parallel world; doubtless there are others. We will conquer them all, one by one, I will be Supreme Ruler of a New Moral State, spanning every reality. Everything in existence will pay homage to me."

"Sir."

"But, enough of our glorious future, General, who is my contact in Grongolia?"

"General Ennui, sir."

The General was from the same regiment, originally, as Lord Vernon. General Ennui was army, through and through.

"Once again, I am impressed by your efficiency, Moteurs. How long before General Ennui is in control?"

"No more than an hour, sir, from the moment I relay your order. They are at the ready."

Unbelievable. Lord Vernon bit back the urge to guffaw.

"I will meet him in Grongolia, at the Palace of Leadership, in the High Leader's personal chambers in one hour precisely. You will inform me if there is any delay."

"Sir," General Moteurs hesitated, "if you have not slept there is time to rest, should you require it."

"No. General Ennui will rouse his colleagues and call an emergency session of the Grongolian House of Ministers. They will vote me High Leader this morning by nine o'clock. I will address both nations immediately afterwards and be sworn in this afternoon."

"That is somewhat irregular, sir."

"But it is my will, Moteurs."

The General could not have failed to pick up the warning tone in his master's voice.

"Sir."

"I will require General Ennui's contact details."

"I have already sent them, sir."

Lord Vernon took his phone from his belt and flipped open the case. Sure enough, he had received a new e-business card from General Moteurs. He saved it to his list of contacts.

"Thank you, General. That is all."

"Sir." General Moteurs stood up and bowed.

"Oh and General?"

"Sir?"

"Have one of your people find Captain Snow and tell him I do not appreciate being ignored. I have left him some instructions. He will contact me to finalise the details within the next twenty minutes or he will pay dearly."

Chapter 36

The Pan looked out of his bedroom window at a gloomy miasma of drizzle seeping out of a leaden sky. Thursday didn't seem to want to get out of bed. Much like himself. Except that despite his tiredness, now that he had woken up, he couldn't get back to sleep. His mind raced as he went over the previous night's events. Yeh, things had been fraught, and yet once he'd got to bed, after a brief bout of wimpy sobbing about Ruth, he had slept like the dead: until now.

He wondered how Trev was and felt a momentary pang of guilt, coupled with irritation at Big Merv and Lucy for not waking him up to take watch. Never mind, they'd meant well and he had to admit that he felt a lot fitter after a few hours of quality sleep.

It was criminally early, but now that his racing thoughts had assumed control, he gave up on trying to rest in any meaningful sense – he knew it wouldn't happen. Instead, he decided he would go to get the post from downstairs and then listen to the early morning news bulletin from the Free K'Barthan Broadcasting Corporation – or Free KBC as everyone called it – while he made some breakfast. Unlike the Grongles' state-funded GNN, the Free KBC was properly impartial which meant the Grongles considered it a threat. It was only on air for a number of single one hour news bulletins each day: at six in the morning, twelve noon and seven at night. It made film reports which circulated virally online but the radio reports were the main news source for all K'Barthans, even though they too were circulated on the internet. Working or appearing on Free KBC resulted in instant blacklisting and consequently, it transmitted from a mobile base. The mere act of listening to it carried a prison sentence, so although most K'Barthans tuned into it when it came on air, they tended to listen in secret and use headphones outside the privacy of their own homes. The Pan didn't have any headphones and judged the kitchen as the safest place to listen.

He slid his feet into his slippers and padded down the hall. He made sure the kitchen windows were closed, turned the radio onto the lowest possible volume and put his ear to the speaker.

World affairs seemed to be fairly quiet. There'd been some speculation about events at the previous day's executions which, though wide of the mark, was an impressive guess, considering nobody had a clue what had really happened. There was more speculation as to who might be involved but the Resistance had denied responsibility, which was unusual. Having listened to the headlines, he switched the radio off, put a pot of coffee on to brew and headed into the hall.

He inched open the door of the sitting room and popped his head in. Nobody had braved Ada's boudoir. Not hugely surprising. Instead, Alan, Psycho Dave, Simon and Professor N'Aversion were all asleep, on makeshift beds of piled up sofa cushions, except for Simon who had an airbed. He'd probably brought it with him on his belt. The Pan closed the door quietly and moved along to Trev's room. Big Merv was on watch and The Pan beckoned him over. He wanted a word about not waking him up but Big Merv shook his head, pointed to the sleeping form of Trev and winked.

The Pan dragged himself downstairs. The pirate portals that weren't dotted around the pub were stacked on some shelves in the cellar. He went and got a suitcase from the cupboard under the stairs and put the jars carefully into it, with lots of newspaper and some tea towels to stop them rattling, then he took it through to the hall and put it by the umbrella stand. As he did so, the post arrived on the mat with a plop.

Four circulars, a sheaf of takeaway flyers and a couple of bills. As he bent to pick them up a sharp rap on the freshly mended door startled him. He glanced at his watch; it was still only half past six.

Arnold. Was it the police? Possibly, but the average dawn raid tended to be earlier, well, more like the middle of the night than dawn. And they didn't knock on the door so much as kick it in.

"Hello," said a voice and The Pan breathed a sigh of relief. It was Doctor Dot.

"Give me a moment."

He undid the extra bolts that Simon, Professor N'Aversion and their helpers had fitted, and turned the key in the lock. It stuck but after a few moments' cajoling, he managed to shift it and unlocked the door.

"Morning," said Doctor Dot when he finally opened it. She sounded cheery, albeit a little surprised to see The Pan wearing nothing but his slippers, a pair of blue and white striped pyjama bottoms, and the shoulder brace and sling she had given him. He grinned.

"You're early, you caught me on the hop."

"So I see," she said as she came in.

"I thought I was coming to pick you up at ten," said The Pan. She waited for him while he closed the door and locked it again.

"I've something for one of your guests, and my commander thought he would want it sooner rather than later."

"Your commander? You've told someone about this?"

"General Moteurs came to see me. He appears to know everything. He gave me these." She opened a pouch on her belt and took out a bottle of pills. "He tells me they subdue natural skin pigment. Some of his troops used it to blend in on an exercise. He thought Big Merv might need them."

"Er …" The Pan took the bottle she held out. "Thank you."

"How's Trev?" she asked as she made her way towards the stairs. The Pan, scurrying to keep up, followed her.

"He's still asleep but he came round last night, said he felt rubbish but he was definitely better."

"Good. Then while we're waiting for him to wake up, shall I take a look at that shoulder?"

"Sure."

He led her up to the kitchen and once there, he slipped the sling off and waited while she prodded and poked at his collarbone. Then she gently examined the healing burns under their plastic dressing. It wasn't as painful as he'd expected.

"Good, this is healing well, except …" she tailed off.

"Except?" The Pan prompted.

"I-I'm sorry, I don't want to make you think about something that will cause you distress but I have to ask this, did Lord Vernon give you any drugs while you were in custody?"

"Yes."

"Which one?"

"Well apparently his minions are too thick to understand the proper names so it was colour coded with a dye."

"Oh I see. Right. What colour?"

"It was red."

She frowned.

"Red? Not … another colour?"

"No."

"Hmm."

"Why?"

"OK, everything's healing up nicely – better than I can believe – it's just that it's … blue. I suppose you, or the drugs in your system, might be reacting with the protective film but it seems to be getting worse, not better. To be truthful, it's not a phenomenon I've encountered before."

"Ah, right, yes. It's a Hamgeean thing," lied The Pan. "We all bleed blue."

"Really," she said. She didn't sound remotely convinced.

"By the way, thanks."

"Just doing my job."

"As you are always telling me. So, how did General Moteurs know to send me the pills?" asked The Pan.

"I thought you must have told him."

"No."

She helped him back into the brace.

"I prescribed 'gentle' exercise. Did you misunderstand me?"

"No, I've been very careful."

"I'm sure you have but I'd try not to crash any more commercial snurds for a week or two."

"You know that was an aberration."

She laughed.

"Of course, you did it on purpose."

"You ain't wrong there, lady."

"Merv!"

The Pan of Hamgee and Doctor Dot turned to Big Merv, who was filling the doorway of the kitchen.

"Wotcher," Big Merv nodded at their visitor and strolled into the room. The Pan noticed that Doctor Dot was clearly as surprised as he was by the way a smile transformed Big Merv's expression. "Doctor Dot. You alright, girl?"

"Very well, thank you."

The conversation was interrupted by the expectorating consumptive-style noises from the filter machine that heralded the readiness of coffee.

"Anyone else want a cup?" asked The Pan as he poured himself a large one.

"Ain't gonna say no."

"Doctor Dot …? No, sorry, you being a Grongle, I'm thinking you'll prefer tea?"

"No. I like coffee in the morning … please."

"Ah, I'm glad to see your time in K'Barth is corrupting you. Merv,

Doctor Dot has given me some de-greening pills, she's hoping they'll de-orange you."

"What colour am I gonna be then?"

"Human-coloured," said Doctor Dot. "Anywhere from pink to dark brown, although, going on your natural colour I would guess you'll go pink, or a creamy brown." The Pan put her coffee in front of her, along with milk, sugar and a couple of extra spoons. "Thank you," she took milk but no sugar, he noticed. Hard core. Very un-Grongolian. Then again, drinking coffee was pretty un-Grongolian, full stop. "Take one of these and you should change colour within an hour or so," she told Big Merv. "It will mask your natural pigments."

His antennae wiggled backwards and forwards and he looked doubtful.

"How's it gonna do that?"

"I'm afraid I don't know. General Moteurs is an intelligence officer, he has access to black science—"

"Black science?" asked The Pan.

"If the military thinks it can use a scientific discovery, it keeps it to itself, and the wider population in the dark, hence 'black'. I can't tell you how these work because, as a humble MO I don't have access to the recipe. I expect one of my pharmacists could give me the formula in time. Although, it's probably better that no-one does or General Moteurs would have to kill them, and me."

"Is it safe?" the Pan asked her. "We're talking about a Swamp Thing, not a Grongle."

"Our DNA is very similar. Even as a separate species, Big Merv is more closely matched to me than any of the rest of you. General Moteurs would not have sent these if they were harmful."

"I ain't sure, lady."

"I can understand your caution. If you like, I'll take one," said Doctor Dot.

"You're a Grongle, sweets. It ain't gonna leave me none the wiser." He cast The Pan a questioning glance.

"I trust him and I trust the doctor here. Your call though, Merv."

"OK, I ain't scared." He opened the bottle and took out one of the pills. In an irony that was not lost on The Pan, it was bright green. "I gotta get some stuff today, so I reckon I'll give 'em a try."

"Use them sparingly, I may not be able to get any more."

Big Merv examined the pill for a moment and then, with a shrug, he popped it in his mouth and swallowed it with a slug of coffee. He held his hands out in front of him and regarded them thoughtfully.

"It takes an hour to work but it lasts for twelve," said Doctor Dot.

The Pan took his first sip of coffee. Ah. Nectar. He closed his eyes for a moment to savour the flavour.

"Is Trev awake?" he asked.

"'S why I came in here. I was gonna fix him breakfast."

"I'll do that. What about Lucy?"

"Nah, she's still spark out."

"Good, she needs to rest," said Doctor Dot. "Yesterday must have been exceptionally hard for her. Field surgery is always difficult, especially the first time. As I said then, she may even need counselling." The doctor drained the contents of her cup. "You might," she told Big Merv as she picked up her black rucksack and stood up. "If you do, I'm here to listen."

"'S OK girl, I'm set … thanks," said Big Merv. To The Pan, he sounded a little bashful.

She turned to The Pan, all business. "Shall we visit the patient?" she asked.

"Sounds like a plan." He poured a cup of coffee for Trev, adding milk and sugar, the way his friend liked it. "You'll stay for a bacon butty afterwards?" There was a rustling and the murmur of voices from Gladys and Ada's sitting room which reminded The Pan of the others. "Then again, you might not want to."

Doctor Dot had clearly heard the noises too.

"You have some more visitors?" she asked.

"Yes but I'm not sure you want to see them."

"More GBIs?" Arnold, she really didn't seem to care at all.

"No, two of my bar staff and a couple of guys from out of town."

"Well, I'm not worried if you're not."

"Oh … right."

"I'm a doctor, not a police officer, Defreville, so, thank you. Yes."

"What?"

"The bacon butty. It would be very nice."

"Right. I'll give you a lift home too."

"Not in your pyjamas, I hope."

"No, Doctor. Not in my pyjamas."

She laughed. She seemed far more relaxed, more the way she'd been when he had first met her. Then again, perhaps she'd unburdened herself to General Moteurs: a trouble shared and all that. The Pan hoped that

General Moteurs' involvement was a good thing. He felt the reassuring weight of the ring on his finger, the ring he had hidden in the box which General Moteurs had left for him to find. Yes, of course it was. He wouldn't have realised he was the Candidate without all the clues left for him in the pub and as he understood it, one of the key beings who had left him those clues, along with Gladys, Ada and possibly Their Trev, was General Moteurs.

"You coming Merv?"

"Nah, I'm gonna make them butties you promised."

The Pan picked up Trev's coffee, as well as his own. As he was about to follow the doctor into the hallway Big Merv grabbed him by the arm.

"Careful big man, I don't want to drop these."

"I gotta ask you something."

Doctor Dot took a few paces down the hall and turned back.

"Are you coming with me?" she asked.

"I'll be along in a moment," said The Pan. He turned back to Big Merv, "What's up?"

"Does she know who you are?" whispered Big Merv.

By The Prophet's toe jam, he hadn't thought about that.

"I'm not sure. You'd better warn the others not to mention it, just in case."

"I can. But I reckon she's got you bang to rights without no help from me."

The Pan rolled his eyes.

"You ain't exactly subtle, son."

"Yeh, right. Well, don't tell her."

"Ain't you gonna trust her?"

"Oh I trust her, it's not that. But even if she realises, I don't want her officially knowing any more than she has to. The way I see it, she's either very brave or she has no idea what she's getting herself into. Until I know for sure—"

"'S your party, mate, but I reckon she don't care."

"That's exactly my point. She doesn't. Something's eating her, she's dropped a few hints but nothing more. I'll have to get to the bottom of it."

Chapter 37

Denarghi sat alone, working on a speech to try and boost morale in the face of Lord Vernon's announcement that he was the Candidate. His mobile phone rang, and somehow, he knew before he even looked at the screen, who it would be.

"Good morning, Your Majesty," said the electronically disguised voice.

"What do you want?"

"I hope you found my information useful. I have some more for you, if you would like it."

"It depends what it is and what you want in return."

"I have already explained, my wish is only to serve."

"And as I have already explained, I know the world better than to believe that."

"Your Head of Tech Ops is laying plans to overthrow you, with Colonel Ischzue and Lieutenant Wright."

"Is this true?"

"Yes," said the Voice, except as usual, even with the electronic disguise, it was more of a hiss.

"You have left me another dossier?"

"It is in the usual place."

Denarghi yanked open the desk drawer.

"How do you do this?" he asked as he looked at the white envelope inside it.

"I will call you back in thirteen minutes."

Click. Dialling tone.

Denarghi ripped open the envelope. Like the previous dossier this one contained photos. The first one was Simon, Professor N'Aversion's Chief Engineer, crossing a street in Ning Dang Po. It was recent, possibly less than a few days old. There were also transcripts of recorded conversations. As he spooled through the pages, he read the names. Most were between various members of his Technical Operations team. Was this what he thought it was? Did he finally have the concrete proof to get rid of Professor N'Aversion and all his cronies once and for all? His phone rang.

"Is this Grongolian intelligence?" he demanded.

There was a moment of silence.

"No, it's Mrs Burgess from catering, requesting your choice of dishes for lunch. There's cabbage a la crème, deep fried cabbage or sweet and sour cabbage or pickled cabbage on oat cakes. All of them come served with the fresh vegetable of the day."

"Which is ...?"

"Boiled cabbage."

"Surprise me," snapped Denarghi and rang off.

He paced the room, waiting, and at last his mobile rang again.

"Good morning," said the electronically disguised voice. Involuntarily, Denarghi's hackles rose. The line was poor, it sounded as if 'the Candidate' was phoning from a long way away. But for all the poor line and its electronic disguise the voice made him feel like prey. "You have read the file, Denarghi?"

Not really a question.

"Yes. This intel, is it Grongolian?"

"Perhaps."

"How did you get it?"

"Surveillance is simple enough with suitably sophisticated equipment. Perhaps your Technical Operations team lack the expertise to construct it."

"And you have that expertise?"

"Naturally."

"And you are prepared to share that with us?"

"I could be ... persuaded."

"What is your price?"

"Duty is its own reward."

"So the Grongles tell us, but in my world, somewhere along the line, someone always pays."

There was a long, long pause. So long that Denarghi thought, for a moment that the line had dropped. He took the phone from his ear and checked the screen.

"I am still here," said the Candidate.

"What do you want?"

"There are those who seek to destroy me and—"

Denarghi interrupted the caller.

"You want me to destroy them first."

"I have not finished." Even electronically disguised the snarl in the voice was audible. Despite the warmth of his office, goose pimples rose on Denarghi's skin, making his red fur stand on end. He resolved not to interrupt 'the Candidate' ever again. He waited, just to be sure but his anonymous conversant did not wish to continue. There was silence so, nervously, Denarghi spoke.

"I'm wondering if you would like to disappear for a while."

"Yes."

"Maybe, I can arrange that, as a gesture of goodwill."

"You will require a new Head of Tech Ops."

Smecking, smecking, smeck. So tempting. Somewhere out there, there was some seriously advanced science, and 'the Candidate' clearly had access to it. This was the perfect opportunity. A cast-iron case to get rid of Professor N'Aversion and his oh-too-faithful deputies, and someone better with whom to replace them, all in one hit. Too good to pass up or too good to be true? Something about 'the Candidate' made Denarghi nervous and stopped him from agreeing outright.

"That's a very powerful position, Mr Candidate. I can't dish it out to just anyone," he said, "you'll have to prove yourself worthy."

"How?"

"Well now, I have my office swept for surveillance equipment every morning. I'd like to know how you are watching me, I'd like to know how you access my desk drawer without being seen."

"Naturally."

"Show me that and I'll be listening."

"Then I will arrange a demonstration."

"Now?"

"No, Your Majesty."

"Today?"

"No, Your Majesty, tomorrow. I will advise you of the time when I see fit. Good day to you."

There was a click and this time, when Denarghi checked, the line really had gone dead. Never mind, now to get rid of Professor N'Aversion. He pressed the intercom.

"Is my Head of Tech Ops back yet?"

"No sir, he's still in Ning Dang Po," said the disembodied voice of the senior officer outside.

"Why?" he asked bad temperedly.

"He has a lead about The Pan of Hamgee, Your Majesty."

Denarghi reached the door in a couple of angry hops and flung it open. The guard looked up from the intercom in surprise.

"That's not his smecking job! Why didn't he tell me?" Denarghi demanded. "I'm Head of Strike Ops. Or Plumby."

"Yes, sir, I don't know, sir."

"Where is his Chief Engineer?"

"He's also in Ning Dang Po."

"Is there anybody with any authority at all left in Tech Ops?"

"Engineer Blimpet, sir. Deputy Chief Engineer Nar was in charge, sir, but she's—"

"In custody. I am aware, I ordered her arrest."

"Sir."

"Bring her to me."

"Yes sir, right away, sir."

Denarghi slammed the door but immediately had another thought and opened it again. The officer was just picking up his hat.

"And get Colonel Smeen."

"Yes, sir."

Denarghi was about to close the door a second time and stopped.

"And when you're done arrest Blimpet."

"Sir."

Denarghi flung the door shut and returned to his desk.

Chapter 38

Doctor Dot was pleased with Trev's progress. He was still weak and he still had a fever but he was responding well to the treatment. She gave him some physiotherapy exercises to do and commended The Pan on his resourcefulness with the crutches. She'd clearly anticipated it though, as she had packed a selection of rubber ferrules in her bag which she fitted over the ends for grip. Then it was time for breakfast.

When The Pan showed Doctor Dot into the kitchen, Professor N'Aversion, Pub Quiz Alan and Psycho Dave were sitting round the table, Simon was perched on the windowsill while Big Merv and Lucy were cooking bacon and eggs. He didn't know how they were going to react – apart from Big Merv and Lucy – but he was pretty certain that Doctor Dot's easy, cheerful manner would win them over … so long as they could see past her being a Grongle.

"Hello everyone, not all of you have met Doctor Dot—"

"Hello again, sweets," said Big Merv cheerfully.

"Hi, how're you doing?" asked Lucy.

"Oh not so bad." Doctor Dot smiled. "Are you OK Lucy? You did a very courageous thing yesterday," Big Merv looked up from the eggs he was busy frying with obvious pride, "you too, Mister," she told him. She smiled at the others, who were looking a little slack jawed. "Hello," she said.

"This is the doctor I told you about, who saved Trev's life. She also fixed my shoulder," The Pan explained. "Doctor Dot," he continued swiftly, "this is Psycho Dave, and this is Alan. They're friends of mine. That's Simon, on the windowsill, and Professor N'Aversion – we've just met but I believe they're working with your boss, so I don't think you need to worry."

"Her boss?" asked Simon.

"General Moteurs," The Pan explained.

There was a brief moment of silence. The Professor looked up at her, in something approaching wonder and then at The Pan, as if to check, before his manners clearly got the better of him and he stood up.

"Your friend here is right, I have been in correspondence with your boss, but I haven't met him face to face." Silence again, but shorter, "Professor N'Aversion, charmed I am sure," he said and put out his hand.

"How do you do, Professor?" said Doctor Dot as she shook it.

Chapter 39

After a quick breakfast of bacon and egg butties and more coffee, The Pan left Doctor Dot to the tender mercies of what he supposed was now the Underground while he washed and dressed. Then it was time to drive her back to the Security HQ – the old Palace. Big Merv was still resolutely orange but it hadn't been a full hour. Perhaps he was just a shade lighter than before.

Once in the snurd, Doctor Dot assured The Pan that Big Merv would change colour.

"It might take longer for a Swamp Thing than for a Grongle but it won't be more than two hours."

"Thank you," said The Pan. He realised he was going to have to broach the difficult topic of what would happen to Trev after the installation. The Pan would be dead, so legally the Parrot would revert to the state. Since Trev was dead, too – officially – he'd have to leave.

"When will Trev be able to move about?" asked The Pan as he stopped, a little too suddenly, at a zebra crossing and waved a flustered-looking Galorsh with a pushchair and several little ones in tow across the road. Doctor Dot seemed surprised at his question.

"Oh quite soon. As I said to him, he must start moving now, getting out of bed to sit on the chair, doing his exercises. He should be up and about by Sunday but he'll be in a lot of pain and he'll need to keep resting."

"Sunday is too late. I … I'm going away."

"Cancel it," said Doctor Dot, irritated. "Defreville, your friend is very sick. He will heal but he needs time and support. If you care about him, and you clearly do, nothing is more important than this. Nothing."

As he turned off Turnadot Street and into the square, The Pan rued his decision not to fly. It was crammed. Visitors were coming in from all over K'Barth for the installation. He sighed. The central streets would be gridlocked.

"Usually, I'd agree, but there is something I have to do."

"Yes, you have to take care of your friends." The Pan realised he was in the wrong lane and flicked the indicator on.

"I can't. I'm supposed to be the only one there. If I'm away from the pub and there are people obviously living in it, things may get difficult."

"But not impossible. Get Alan and Dave in."

"I can't." The traffic in the lane next to The Pan started to move, catching the driver of a red snurd two back napping. The Pan manoeuvred the SE2 swiftly into the space, out-accelerating the other driver, who tried to close the gap. Affronted at being cut up, the driver showed his annoyance by putting his hand on the red snurd's hooter and keeping it there for some seconds. The Pan wound down the window and shouted, "Sorry," reinforcing the words with an apologetic wave of his arm.

"Listen to me, Defreville. You can't leave your friend on his own," said Doctor Dot.

"I have to." The driver of the red snurd shouted a string of obscenities and beeped again. The Pan leaned right out of the window, "Temper, temper!" he said and blew the guy a cheery kiss. "Welcome to Ning Dang Po my friend."

"Will you stop that!" said Doctor Dot angrily.

"Sorry." The traffic ahead inched forward a few feet.

"Listen to me—" she began.

The Pan pressed the aviator button. There was a metallic whine as the wings unfolded, as far as the traffic pressed around them would allow, and locked themselves into position with a clunk. It was aviator slim. Not ideal but there were no warning lights so in theory there should be no problem with take-off, other than looking like a boy racer, but since he was about to act like one … Doctor Dot looked out of her window and then at The Pan in disbelief.

"Now what are you doing?"

"I'm sorry, I have to explain this and I can't do it here," said The Pan. He waited until the traffic ahead moved forward again, leaving some more room. Not that much but enough. He floored the accelerator and executed what was little more than a vertical take-off.

"This is not the time to show off. I'm trying to have a serious conversation with you," her voice was brittle and he was afraid he was going to make her cry.

"I know, and I understand but there's too much traffic here; I can't explain properly while I'm concentrating on something else."

"Of course, you're male, I'm surprised you can walk and talk at the same time."

"Exactly. That's why we're leaving."

As the SE2 rapidly gained height it flashed past a side road where The Pan caught sight of a police snurd. To his dismay, it followed them. He wondered if they'd seen his boy racer take-off. Almost certainly. He was careful to obey the rules of the sky but he suspected that it was his flagrant disregard for the rules of the road that had caught the police officers' attention. Sure enough, the blue lights on the police vehicle's roof began to flash. He accelerated and flipped the SE2 over some nearby buildings before he remembered that he was supposed to be a law-abiding citizen these days.

Arnold. He slowed down and executed a textbook landing in a cul-de-sac which qualified, by the rules of the road, as safer-than-safe: quiet and free from traffic. After a few moments the police snurd landed behind them. Two standard-size – that is, huge – Grongles got out. They wore police uniforms, which was marginally better than army but still worried The Pan, and they were armed. He glanced over at Doctor Dot who turned her head pointedly away and sighed irritably. One of the Grongles stood well back, drawing his gun and covering the SE2. The other approached the driver's side and as he raised his finger to tap on the glass, The Pan wound the window down.

"Good morning, sir," said the Grongle. "That was a tad racy. In a hurry are we?"

"A bit," said The Pan.

"But that's still no excuse for dangerous driving."

"I know, I'm an idiot, I'm sorry," said The Pan, who just wanted to get this over with. There was a pause, presumably while the Grongle tried to decide if he was being sarcastic.

"Very big of you to admit that, sir."

"Thank you."

Another pause while the Grongle stood back and glanced left and right, clearly admiring the SE2's curves. He looked over at the other one with the gun, who nodded. Then he leaned down to the window again.

"Nice wheels, very nice."

"Thank you."

"I don't like to do this to someone who has been so cooperative, but the law's the law and I'm going to have to issue you with a ticket. That means a fine and an instant ban."

Arnold's pants!

"If you'd step out of the snurd and surrender your documents to me, I'll sign for them. You can collect them from your nearest police station in four weeks."

"My documents?"

"Yes."

Smeck. Re-assimilated or not, The Pan hadn't got round to procuring any documents – not for himself anyway, he'd always had the registration documents to the snurd. The police Grongle was obviously suspicious. Not surprising. Looking innocent had never been The Pan's strong suit. The Grongle continued.

"Get out of the snurd, please, sir."

The irony with which the Grongle said 'sir' was more pronounced.

"Right. Yes. Sorry," said The Pan and he did as he was told.

"Your vehicle will be towed away from here and impounded for four weeks during which you will be under caution not to drive."

"Oh."

"I am duty bound to warn you that driving while banned carries an even heavier fine than the offence you've just perpetrated. Do you understand what I have told you?"

"Yes sir," said The Pan.

"I will require an on-the-spot fine of sixty thousand K'Barthan Zloty or twenty-five Grongolian dollars to be paid now."

Typical, non-Grongles were not allowed Grongolian currency so though $25 was the equivalent of about fifty K'Barthan Zloty The Pan had no choice but to pay in K'Barthan currency …

"That's a lot of money. If I mortgaged my business I couldn't give you sixty thousand K'Barthan." Not that he would borrow against the Parrot. Whatever the law said, Gladys and Ada's pub didn't belong to him.

"How you procure the money is not my concern, *sir,* my job is to collect it. If you are unable to pay, your snurd will be forfeit, in lieu of the debt."

Which was the whole point, of course. They wanted the SE2.

"Officer, I'll level with you. I've been on the blacklist but I'm newly re-assimilated, I have a year's free pardon while I adjust, but … I'm rather new to being a 'normal' again … please … can't you give me a bit of leeway?" he asked.

"One moment, sir."

While his colleague continued to cover The Pan with the laser pistol, the police Grongle checked his standard police issue mobile phone.

"I see, sir," he said slowly. "Then I have some good news for you. The ban is waived. However you will still have to pay the fine."

No.

"Look, my snurd isn't worth sixty thousand Zloty," argued The Pan, "and I have nothing else to give."

"That's bad luck, sir," replied the police officer, now dropping any pretence of politeness as he sneered the word 'sir'.

"Can't I pay the Grongle dollars fine in K'Barthan Zloty?"

"I'm afraid not, sir."

"What about if I paid you in Grongolian dollars?"

"I'd have to charge you for being in possession of illegal currency, sir. Do you have sixty thousand K'Barthan Zloty?"

"Of course I don't."

"Then, please hand me the keys."

As The Pan leaned in to remove the keys from the ignition, Doctor Dot, in the passenger seat, narrowed her eyes at him. She seemed angry and he could hardly blame her. He'd been such a massive plank it was embarrassing. He straightened up, keys in hand, poised to drop them into the officer's outstretched palm when Doctor Dot got out of the SE2, slamming the passenger door, in disgust by the looks of it.

"What are you doing?" she asked and The Pan almost answered her before he realised she was talking to the officer.

"Exacting a traffic fine, ma'am," he said and saluted smartly.

"That won't be necessary," she said, and to The Pan, "put the keys away."

"Is that—?"

"Do it."

He raised an eyebrow.

"Alright," he said and did as he was told.

She took some bank notes out of a pouch on her belt.

"I will be paying the fine, in Grongolian currency. Twenty-five dollars, I think you said."

"Sorry, ma'am, but you weren't driving."

"Officer," said Doctor Dot, with a tone of steely authority, "this man was acting on my orders."

"Maybe, ma'am, but you weren't driving his snurd at the time of the offence."

"No, I have commandeered this vehicle in my capacity as Chief Medical Officer to the Imperial Guard," she held up an identity card.

"I can't help that."

"Yes you can. He did what he did because I made him. Now, I have an emergency to attend to and this young man has to drive me there. So, I thank you for waiving his ban and suggest you take your twenty-five dollars, with my profuse apologies for bullying him into such reckless driving, and let us go."

"You can't order me around."

"Really," she glanced at the badges of rank on his arm, "Sergeant? I believe you'll find I can. As I told you, I am Chief Medical Officer of the entire Imperial Guard in K'Barth, and as such, I enjoy the honorary rank of Colonel."

The Pan stifled a smile.

"But—" the officer began.

"No buts, Sergeant, and that's an order. I have an emergency to attend to and you are wasting my time. If you have a problem, I suggest you take it up with my commander, General Moteurs." She held the bank notes out to him. There was a long pause and then the officer took them.

"You won't be so lucky next time, K'Barthan scum," he warned The Pan.

"There won't be a next time or I'll have you on report," snapped Doctor Dot as the Grongles returned to their patrol vehicle. "Get in!" she told The Pan. He jumped over the bonnet and opened the passenger door for her.

"You first."

She slid into her seat and slammed the door before he could close it. He vaulted back over the bonnet and got in his side.

"Thank you," he said as he settled into the snurd. The Grongolian police drove past them and turned into the traffic.

"I've just perjured myself in the eyes of the law. For your sake. So the least you can do is pretend we're in a hurry."

"Righto." The Pan shrugged and took off, at a speed which was only just the right side of injudicious.

"Slow down!"

"I thought you said—"

"We're in a normal hurry, Defreville, not an escape-from-a-bank-job hurry."

"Ah yes. I'm sorry," he said as he put the snurd into a gentle climb, "I wouldn't want your act of perjury to look unrealistic."

For a moment she glared at him angrily. Then her sense of humour appeared to get the better of her and she started to laugh.

"Smeck! What am I doing here?" she said as the SE2 climbed above the buildings.

"Having doubts by the looks of it. Alright, you and I need to talk. Give me a minute, I need to land first."

Chapter 40

Once outside the mess hall, Forrest was separated from Nar and taken away by four of the guards. The Group Leader and the other two led Nar straight to the cells.

She was left there overnight. She didn't sleep. The two guards who had arrested her stood watch in silence. Eventually the Group Leader who had led them returned in the early morning, with Denarghi.

"Hello, Nar," said Denarghi as he walked in.

"Your Majesty," she made a low curtsey. "Begging your pardon, but I believe there has been an error."

"There has been no error, Nar. I know what you are about. You are charged with treason. What is your answer?"

"I can answer no charge, for I am innocent."

"Really?"

Denarghi turned to the Group Leader who handed him the stealth tablet.

"What is this?" he held it up.

"Standard issue, sir."

"No, Nar, the software is different. Tech Ops has been under surveillance for some time. We have film of both you and Professor N'Aversion entering the code to unlock this. Which means we know what's on here."

Nar said nothing.

"I gave Professor N'Aversion a command, one he has expressly disobeyed. You have aided and abetted him at every turn."

"Sir, he does not wish to set himself against you. He doesn't mean any harm. We are compromised and The Pan of Hamgee has access to something that could help us."

"The Pan of Hamgee, who was in Grongolian custody. Do you know why he was freed?"

"No, sir."

"He betrayed his colleagues. Three of them have been executed, or at least vaporised as they tried to escape, by Lord Vernon, who gave the Hamgeean a pub for his trouble."

"Sir, I believe— " she began but he spoke over her.

"There is no grey here, it is a very simple matter. It is even on TV."

"The Hamgeean was not willing, sir."

"And you know this because …?"

"The lip-reading software—"

"Which is in beta, and not yet working."

"It's—"

"I issued an order and you, the Professor and Simon have disobeyed it. Now, I like you Nar, I think you have potential but the company you are keeping is making it hard for me. I want to help you, really I do, but I wonder if you have this organisation's best interests at heart."

"Sir, I—"

"You do have the Resistance's best interests at heart don't you, Nar?"

"Yes, sir."

"Then I know you will want to assist me." He held up the stealth tablet. "D'you know, we can find no trace of this on the network."

"That's very strange, sir," said Nar weakly. This was getting worse and worse.

"Isn't it? But we know it's synchronising because every time it updates it beeps, and when it does, even though it's locked, a copy of the message scrolls across the screen. I see you are a member of a forum. It's very busy this morning, you have a lot of messages from someone there …" He swiped the screen and tapped the code number to activate it. "If you are as dedicated to the cause as you say, I am sure you will want to sign into your account and join the discussion."

Nar felt sick.

"I don't have the password for the forum."

"Really? But you have an account."

"No."

"Oh I think you do. You will sign in, NOW."

"I can't, really, I don't know how to."

"Oh Nar, what has happened to your dedication? My contact has witnessed you using the forum."

Nar knew this was not physically possible. Nobody had ever seen her using the forum apart from the Professor and Simon. Nobody knew about it but them … unless … she remembered what the Professor had said about K'Barthan portals, how they could be used for surveillance. Had The Pan of Hamgee betrayed them? She wasn't sure but it didn't sit right and if he had, Denarghi would be in Ning Dang Po, arresting the Professor surely. So who else?

Grongles. Except that Denarghi would never talk to a Grongle would he? Not knowingly, but what didn't he know? Could the Grongles have tricked him?

"I-I don't see how this can be," she said, more to tread water than anything.

"No, Nar. That is why I am in charge of this organisation and you are not. This is unfortunate. It is not just you. Forrest is an impressionable young man and I fear you have corrupted him. My difficulty now is that I can't tell how far that corruption goes. However, if you can prove you are less corrupt than I thought I might be able to risk dropping the charges against him."

"But, Denarghi, sir, there can be no charges. He has done nothing."

"By mere association he is under suspicion, so you can carry on pretending and he will die beside you or," the word hung heavy in the air as he held out the tablet, "talk to the Professor and I will let him go."

Not Forrest. It wasn't fair.

"I'm waiting, Nar. His life hangs in the balance and it would be such a terrible waste. Go onto the forum and tell the Professor that all is well."

"I can't."

"I think you can."

Trembling, she reached out and took the tablet from his hand.

"Oh very good Nar. I knew you would see reason."

Chapter 41

The Pan took Doctor Dot to the square where they'd parked and talked the day before, stopping in a similar spot under the trees. He turned off the engine and checked that the pirate portal he always carried was still in the pocket of his dark blue canvas jeans.

"I'm not sure where to start with this," he said, "or how much to tell."

"Try trusting me."

"I do and amazingly I trust General Moteurs but ..." he flicked the indicator switch up and down idly.

"Come on. Out with it."

"Alright. Trev's mum, Gladys, runs—ran," he corrected himself hurriedly, "the Parrot and Screwdriver, along with her friend Ada. For the whole of last year, I lived there. I rented their guest room. I thought they were a pair of sweet defenceless old dears and Trev a harmless fellow, looking after his old mum. It turns out that Trev was busy escorting groups of GBIs to safety out of the country – long story and I'm going to skip it because it doesn't add to this one. Meanwhile Gladys and Ada ... well, I think they're Nimmist elders of some sort. All of them were members of the Underground, which I assume you've heard of."

"Yes," she said.

"Yeh, of course you have, you're in it, aren't you?"

"Maybe."

"I'll take that as a yes."

She smiled.

"Well, that's why they were all put in prison. The state seized the Parrot and then Lord Vernon gave it to me. I thought it was so the locals would lynch me. I'm sure that was Lord Vernon's intention, but at the same time, someone's left a lot of stuff there, for me to find."

"Who?"

Should he mention General Moteurs? Possibly not.

"Someone in the Underground, I think: one of the few left at large."

"How do you know they left it for you?"

"Because it was in places where only I would find it. They did the place over, but only a bit, and I think it was to get me looking."

"What did you find?"

"Information: some prophecies, a bit of equipment, that kind of thing."

"Why leave it for you?"

"Because they want me to find the Candidate and when I've done that, they want me to prove that Lord Vernon is an imposter."

"But … that's … even a Grongle like me knows that there was never a Candidate in years of searching."

"That's because you lot banned the Looking although actually, finding him wasn't the hard bit."

"What? You mean—"

"Yeh. There's a Candidate. So now, I just have to go to the installation. I don't really know what happens but I think there's a bit where they ask the audience. You know, 'does anyone have reason to oppose the choice of the elders?' kind of thing. That's where I say 'yes', stand up and prove Lord Vernon's a sham on world telly."

"He won't give you the time. He'll kill you."

"He will kill me, you're right about that, but I think, if I put the right spin on it, he, and therefore the world, will hear me out."

"And that's what you meant by 'going away'?"

"Yeh."

"I see."

"The problem is, the pub belongs to me in the eyes of the law, but come Saturday they'll reassign my blacklisted status, posthumously no doubt, and the Parrot will revert to the state. If they do that, Trev has to move. Ideally, I would give it to somebody so I don't own it when the time comes. That way, the state has to butt out – for a while at least – and my friends have a chance. Lucy, Trev and Big Merv are GBIs so, obviously, I can't give it to them. Anyway, officially, they're dead, and it's better it stays that way. But unless I can find somebody I trust to give the pub to, my friends will have to leave."

"What about Alan or Psycho Dave?"

"I trust them but I'm not sure it would be fair."

"They might disagree. They might be perfectly happy to help."

"Yes, they might. But I'm not happy to lumber them with the job. It's a lot to ask, 'here's my pub, oh and it comes with three poorly concealed GBIs and Captain Snow sniffing around' – which he is, and thanks for warning me about that."

"No problem. What about the other two?"

"The Professor and Simon? No, that would be unfair on Trev."

"Why?"

"They're under suspicion so the security forces would seize it and search it at once. They probably will anyway but if it belongs to Simon and Professor N'Aversion it's an open invitation. They're officially wanted for questioning."

"Where did you hear that?"

"From … a very reliable source."

Just thinking about the previous night's adventure with Captain Snow made the sweat prickle at The Pan's temples.

"Who?"

He raked his good hand through his hair.

"I really don't think I should tell you. It's not a trust issue," he said quickly, "it's just that the more you know, the more firmly you're on our side, as opposed to your own."

"I do what I believe is right, by myself and by my nation's true code of ethics – not my government's warped version. If that puts me on your side, I don't mind. Now, there must be someone you can give your pub to?"

"Sadly not."

"Then your plan makes even less sense. Why do you need to attend the installation? You must know there will be reprisals. Don't give him an excuse to start."

"He'll find one, whatever I do."

"Then don't waste your life! Resurrect the Underground."

"It's too late for that."

"No it isn't. Today, at breakfast, they accepted me because you did. They look to you. Big Merv would die for you. I can see it. Lead them. Smeck, I'll join you, lead me."

He stared at her. He didn't know what boggling eyes looked like, but he was pretty sure Doctor Dot would, after observing his reaction.

"Come on … are you serious?"

"Yes. If you disprove Lord Vernon's candidature what will you achieve? Nothing. He will still be in charge."

The Pan leaned back in the seat and gazed out of the windscreen at the drizzly, windswept street. Why did everything have to be so complicated?

"Listen, I'm playing the long game. If there is going to be another Candidate, ever, that's what I have to do. And, if anyone hopes to depose

Lord Vernon, ever, ditto."

"And what will the real Candidate be doing during all of this, the one you've found? If he's not going to the installation, which he jolly well should be, then why can't he have the pub?"

"He is going. Both of us are."

"You can't both go; if one of you has to be a martyr, the other has to stay behind and be the leader."

"Well, it's difficult for us to separate because he … because I'm …" The Pan put his good hand up, wrapping his fingers round the steering wheel, and racked his brains for a way to be oblique about who he was. Even in the greasy rain-sodden gloom the K'Barthan Ring of State peppered the inside of the snurd with deep red reflections of what little light there was. Doctor Dot took a long slow look at it. He watched her; waiting, wondering if she would understand.

"I see," she said.

"You know, you're about the only one who hasn't noticed this," he wiggled the finger with the ring on it, "until now."

"I'm a Grongle, I wouldn't expect a Hamgeean to appreciate it but we have these wonderful things called emotional control and subtlety."

"Ha, so you've been goggling on the sly."

"I have noted that you are wearing a very presentable copy of the K'Barthan Ring of State … which is probably enough to get you straight back on the blacklist."

"Ah, but I'm still adjusting."

"I don't think you are and I don't think you intend to, in fact, I'm wondering if that ring isn't the real thing."

Arnold's hair.

"How much has General Moteurs told you?"

Her eyes met his.

"Quite obviously, not the whole story."

"Mmm …"

"I—" she began. "I understand that I'm a Grongle and you'll want to give your pub to a K'Barthan," she sounded slightly panicky, "but if it will help, I'm happy to hold it in your name. Although I don't drink."

"No good publican should. If I give you my pub, am I going to get you into trouble?"

"I don't think so." She looked away and stared out of the window for a moment. The Pan suspected she was lying.

"You've done enough for me already but actually, you made a good point about reprisals, and your being Grongolian might help."

"Of course it would. They wouldn't dare search it if it was mine. Not straight away."

"True and they'd have trouble confiscating it from you, too. Anyway, considering who's living there right now, I'd rather leave it to someone I trust and apart from them – and perhaps, your boss – you're the only one at large."

"You trust me," she said, half question, half incredulous statement.

"I think you've earned it. Although, right now, I'm not sure you're telling me the truth. If this is going to put you in danger you have to tell me and I'll find another way."

"You may not need to."

"I'm touched by your faith."

"Defreville, we have a saying in Grongolia. It's naff but in your case it's pertinent: 'Those who believe achieve'."

"I think you flatter me."

"No, all it means is that you can do whatever you want, if you put your mind to it. It's just a question of believing that you can. How d'you think I became a doctor?"

"Oh I dunno, but I am assuming it was a combination of top marks, cheerful charm and an attack of acute deafness whenever anyone tried to say 'no' to you."

"That too but I meant the other reason, that I believed I could do it. You have a whole nation behind you …" she looked down at her hands briefly, "those of us who know about you."

'Us' The Pan noted.

"Thank you, that's … an incredibly kind thing to say."

"It's true. If anyone can depose Lord Vernon this Saturday, it's you."

He laughed.

"Have you ever thought of life-coaching? No, on second thoughts, I'm guessing you already have a qualification: part of being a doctor."

"I'm being serious, Defreville, remember what I've said."

The two of them sat quietly for a moment.

"There's something else," said The Pan. "I need to get into the installation, d'you think General Moteurs could arrange that?"

"He's in charge of the security."

"I'd really like to talk to him, then I could ask him myself, but it's difficult for a K'Barthan like me to get close."

"I'll ask. Speaking of my commander, he has a message for you."

"He does?"

"Yes. He told me to tell you to trust him, whatever happens, however things look."

"That's all?"

"Yes."

"That's very enigmatic," said The Pan.

"Not really," she looked at her watch, "have you listened to the news?"

"Yeh."

"On GNN?"

Ah, should he admit he listened to the Free KBC?

"Actually, no."

"Then you'll understand when you get home."

"That's even more enigmatic."

"And for now it's all I've got. If he can't get you a ticket you can have mine," she smiled. "Right young man, if you really want to make your pub over to me, we both have to find ourselves lawyers and I have a surgery to open this morning. Which means, we'd better fly. We don't want to get stuck in traffic."

He raised an eyebrow at her.

"Your wish is my command, milady," he said.

"Don't flirt with me. I'm old enough to be your mother."

Chapter 42

It was nearly ten o'clock when The Pan returned to the Parrot. He met Professor N'Aversion and Simon in the street on their way back from visiting an internet café to contact their HQ.

"But what about your mobile phones?" he asked them as they made their way to the back door.

"Bugged. All of them, my tablet too," said Simon as The Pan unlocked the door and held it open for them.

"That is the sad truth," the Professor confirmed. "We are under surveillance and not supposed to be here."

"Should you go back at all?" asked The Pan as he stepped inside locking the door behind him.

"I'm afraid we have to."

"Everything's fine though, we've checked with Nar," Simon added.

"Yes and once Denarghi sees the K'Barthan portal I am hoping we will be able to change his mind," said the Professor as he hung up his coat.

"Rather you than me," said The Pan.

Alan, Psycho Dave and a human-coloured Big Merv, complete with trilby hat to cover his antennae, appeared on the stairs.

"Hello boys. Merv, I see the pills worked."

"Yer," said Big Merv and at this point, The Pan noticed that there was what Ada would have referred to as 'an atmosphere' about the place.

"We've been waiting for you," said Alan.

"Oh? You're all looking very serious. What's up?"

"You gotta come upstairs and see this," said Big Merv.

"Why?"

"Something's happened, it's been on the news. Haven't you seen?"

"No."

"Not you boys neither?" Big Merv asked Simon and the Professor.

"I thought you were going to check the net," said Alan.

"Only for messages from Nar, we can use our phones for the news. We have to use them for something or HQ will realise we've rumbled them."

"GNN's been running a news flash that there's going to be some news."

"Mmm well, seeing as it's called the Grongolian News Network, I'd have thought the clue, there, is in the name."

"Apparently there's a big announcement scheduled for this morning," said Alan.

"Yer," said Psycho Dave, "so all the news is about what the special announcement's goin' ter be."

"Right," said The Pan slowly. "I didn't notice anything on Free KBC."

"That's because there's a news blackout; they wouldn't know," said Alan.

"Yer an' it's tight. 'S why. They gotta special tape running to say they ain't got no clue what's happening," said Merv. "A couple a minutes on, then it goes off."

"Yeh, but both are saying Lord Vernon's going to appear on TV at ten o'clock and tell us why," Alan finished.

The Pan looked at his watch, it was nearly ten already.

"Didn't they even hint?"

"Nah. 'S why I reckon it's gonna be big," said Merv.

Arnold! The Pan's stomach lurched. What if Lord Vernon had got himself installed as Architrave? Could he have done that on the sly?

Cluck, said a voice. OK, that probably answered that one.

"Alright, I suppose we'd better go and watch." Heaven knew, there was little else he could do. They all trooped upstairs to the sitting room. There, they found Lucy already seated. Even Trev had joined them, lying on the sofa with his leg raised up on cushions. The TV was on.

"Good to see you up," said The Pan.

"Good to be 'ere mate." He looked tired and strained. The Pan was glad to see Lucy sitting close by, keeping an eye on him.

"He shouldn't really be here but you know what he's like," she told The Pan. "Even so, you need to rest when we've watched this," she warned her patient.

"Gor, she's worse than Mum," said Trev with a wink, but he was clearly grateful for the excuse.

"Shh," said Psycho Dave from the other sofa, "it's startin'."

The Grongolian National Anthem played and then the camera panned in on Lord Vernon, standing on a balcony overlooking a city.

"That don't look like Ning Dang Po," said Psycho Dave.

"No. It's Grongolia," said Alan. "Look, see that pointy building in the background, that's the GNN tower. It's a popular general knowledge question that. There's another one up in Northern Grongolia in the city of Vindalunia. It's easy to confuse which is which."

Psycho Dave's brow puckered.

"What's he doin' there?"

"Good morning, my peoples," said Lord Vernon.

Plural, uh-oh.

"It is with the deepest regret that I must inform you of the sad death of the High Leader. A Grongle of greatness and vision and a close personal friend, he died in a tragic accident last night."

"Accident my arse," said Alan.

"I'm inclined to agree," said the Professor. The Pan had a horrible feeling he knew where this was going.

"My condolences go out to his family as well as all of us, his subjects. He was like a father to me: my inspiration, my role model. He will be greatly missed."

Lord Vernon paused, presumably to convey the gravity of his sentiments.

"I'm sure you told him that as you stuck the knife in," said Lucy into the silence.

"Regretfully, the home Parliament was almost paralysed with distress, barring a group of decisive cabinet members and army officers, who took action. They believed that to ensure continued, stable government for our nation, a new High Leader must be elected without delay and, after an emergency meeting with the Cabinet, when not one of my peers was prepared to take the heavy responsibility upon their shoulders, they appealed to me for help. Unwillingly, I agreed to stand. In the absence of anyone wanting to oppose me they, along with the rest of our National Parliament, unanimously voted that I should become High Leader. As of zero nine thirty hours, this morning, that is what I am: High Leader of Grongolia, as well as Lord Protector of K'Barth. I will be officially sworn into office this afternoon at fourteen hundred hours."

"Smeck." The Pan's knees felt a bit wobbly. Where the hell were the Grongolian Underground? Then The Pan remembered the General's message. Trust him, whatever happens? Is this what it meant?

"I'm sorry son," said Big Merv gently.

"I will attend my predecessor's state funeral tomorrow afternoon," Lord Vernon was saying. "Then, I will return to K'Barth, which from this moment will be called, Western Grongolia. There, I will be installed as Architrave on Saturday as planned, and I will take the Chosen One as my wife. For today and tomorrow, we will show our respect for one of the finest leaders our nation and our world have known, and mourn his passing. Come Saturday, we will turn our backs on this sad event and look forward, with happiness and anticipation, to a brave new era. A time of racial purity, of greatness, when the two nations of this world will become one global state of Grongolia—"

"There's me thinking he'd call it K'Barth," said Alan sourly and Professor N'Aversion chuckled.

"—under one charismatic leader. We have a glorious future ahead of us, which I will reveal, when my position as Supreme World Ruler is ratified early next week. I will address you again shortly. Until then I am your faithful servant: High Leader of Eastern Grongolia, Lord Protector of Western Grongolia, Supreme World Ruler, elect." Lord Vernon made a low, graceful bow. "Good day to you, my dear children." The lights dimmed and he stood tall and statesman-like, silhouetted against the city behind him, as the Grongolian National Anthem played and the credits rolled.

Chapter 43

Lord Vernon's broadcast finished, the TV screen faded to black and the voice of the continuity announcer came on.

"A very moving speech there by His Divine Excellence, High Leader, Lord Vernon. Coming up next, his special message to Western Grongolia, formally known as K'Barth, in which we will meet his fiancée, the Chosen One, for the first time—" The Pan felt the muscles in his jaw clench and concentrated on the sentiment that was rapidly becoming his mantra, 'hold onto the anger'. The rest of the continuity announcer's words seemed distant and unreal. "We will be right back, with the broadcast from our new Supreme Father after these important messages."

Supreme Father? Supreme git of gits, more like. Trev had the remote. He muted the volume as the GNN news station went to adverts and then he and everyone else in the room seemed to be looking to The Pan for a reaction. Arnold, did they really think he was their leader?

"That's a bit of a bombshell," he said. "I don't know why, because I expected it soon but just … Why now?"

"Because he could?" suggested Lucy. "You know, carpe diem."

This was no time to talk about fish.

"Sorry," Lucy added, clearly noticing his nonplussed expression, "it's from a language you probably don't have in this version of reality; means 'seize the day'."

"I wonder what sort of 'accident' the High Leader had," mused the Professor.

"Perhaps he walked into the path of a firing laser pistol," said Simon.

"Ner, there's a body."

"Good point Trev," said The Pan. "Anyway, it sounds more as if he was pushed off a building if they're calling it an 'accident'."

"That's messy for Lord Vernon," said Trev.

"A bit too messy," said Simon.

"Could be anythin', havin' an accident covers a lotta options," said Psycho. He looked over at Big Merv, "Right boss?"

"'S right," said Big Merv, adding quietly, "don't call me boss, son." His antennae wiggled backwards and forward. "I reckon the High Leader mighta bumped into a knife: nice and quiet behind closed doors. Whatever Lord Vernon done, he done it bleedin' quick. Got his feet under the desk before the last bloke's even cold."

"But why's he going to bother getting installed Architrave? He's already Lord Protector, what's the difference? If the coup sticks, he'll own the world already," asked Alan.

"I think he believes being Architrave is going to give him super powers, you know, make him into some uber-Grongle with the strength of ten of his species and—"

"He already is uber-Grongle, he don't need super powers," said Alan.

"Yeh, well … Try telling him that."

"What d'you wanna do?" asked Big Merv.

"The honest answer is run away." The Pan managed a glassy smile. "But I can't. So I'll have to think of a plan."

"OK, Defreville, how can we help you?" asked Lucy.

"I'm not sure yet. We need to move quickly but it's worth taking a bit of time to think before we start. One thing I do know: Professor, Simon, you and I are going to have to find a way to come clean to Denarghi. He has to talk to me because we have to work together and set up something for after I've gone."

"I fear he may not want to cooperate," said the Professor.

"I'm sure he won't but I have to try and persuade him. I'll have to try and do this, with or without him, but if it's with him, it could make all the difference."

"Then we must handle it very carefully; he has a price on your head. I strongly advise you not to tell him who you are," The Professor's glance lit briefly on The Pan's hand, and the ring. "He's not a traditional Nimmist. Indeed, I believe one of the greatest issues he has with me is that I am."

"Neither of us is his favourite being," added Simon, "and if he knows you're the Candidate then unless he thinks you will bow out and let him run K'Barth, he'll see you as a threat—"

"Which means he'll be even more keen to do away with you," said The Professor.

"You're saying he wants to kill me anyway?"

"I'm afraid so."

"Yeh, I believe that. But we had better think about a way we can get him on board, Professor, especially in light of what General Moteurs told you about the Resistance being compromised. And the trouble is, Denarghi's K'Barthan, and as the Candidate, I have to warn him. I can't stand back and let them destroy him."

"I know it's not a very nice thing to say but in all honesty, it would be convenient," said Lucy.

"Maybe, but it's not the K'Barthan way."

The Professor ran a finger round his collar and reached up to unknot his antennae.

"Perhaps some of my colleagues could help," he said, wincing as he finally straightened them. "If I may, I would like to return with them; Colonel Ischzue and Lieutenant Wright from our Revenue Acquisition department."

The Pan remembered his encounter on the roof: the breeze and the sting as the Blurpon's knife had whizzed past his face. He put his hand to his cheek.

"I've met some of their boys," he said.

"We are aware," Simon told him.

"It didn't go well."

The Professor smiled.

"No, so I heard."

"Mmm. Does it have to be them?"

"They are good folk, you will see that, when you become better acquainted and I think ... you see, the Underground has been little more than a rumour for all these years, and for those of us who seek to do something meaningful and organised against the state, the Resistance is the only way to achieve our aim. However, there are many who would prefer a more moderate approach. I think RA and my own department are the highest concentration of these types. But there may be some in other departments, Espionage for one. My friend Snoofle is not alone and possibly Strike Ops ... Lieutenant Arbuthnot's troops, those loyal to her, will be disgruntled with her treatment at the hands of Denarghi."

"Don't they think I brought about her downfall? Why would they team up with me? Then there's the fact there are Grongles in this organisation. And I trust them. And they're staying. Can your people adjust to that?"

He could hear a certain resolve in his voice as he spoke of his Grongle allies, an authority, which he would normally have considered beyond him.

"We can," said Simon.

"Yeh but will the others? Because they're going to have to. This afternoon, I am formally signing over the deeds of this pub to Doctor Dot."

"What?" said Alan. "Why?"

"Because, when I turn up at the installation and Lord Vernon finds out who I am I'll be blacklisted again, dead or not. Unless it belongs to someone else, this pub will revert to the state. There's a strong chance Captain Snow and his mates'll turn up here to search, but you lot have slightly more chance of being left alone if it belongs to a Grongle. She's a good soul, too," he recalled how she'd bailed him out with the traffic cops who had tried to take the SE2, "and she's on our side."

"Straight up?" asked Alan.

"I think so."

"Then that's OK by me," he said.

Wow.

"What about you Professor? Can your people hack that?"

"I couldn't begin to guess, but I believe I must give them the chance." The Pan looked him in the eye, which seemed to catch him off guard, and saw, at once, that he meant it.

"Alright. What do you need to do?"

"Simon and I will have to return to our HQ and speak to Lieutenant Wright and Colonel Ischzue. They are … putting out feelers, as is my Deputy Chief Engineer, Nar. We will also try to get a message to Lieutenant Arbuthnot and Snoofle too, and then, if I may, we will return here with the Colonel and Lieutenant Wright to introduce you to each other."

"Sounds like a plan. In the meantime, I have one hundred and fifty portals. You can have a hundred of them. At the least it'll make it harder for the Grongles to watch you if you put them round your HQ. I'll need a couple of the other fifty myself, and Merv, the rest are for you. Use them wisely, because they're all I have, for now, and probably forever."

"What you giving 'em to me for?" asked Big Merv.

"Because you're the leader of the Underground," said The Pan.

"No I ain't. You are."

"Not after Lord Vernon's installation; I'll have this small problem called 'being dead' to contend with."

"Will you shut it, you girl?"

"Listen, all of you. I'm going to die on Saturday. I know the score and so do you. It's the only way to ensure the succession, and when I'm gone, you lot and the next Candidate are going to need everything I can lay my hands on to help you."

"I've been thinking about that," said Lucy.

"And …?"

"I have an idea, but let me think about it a bit more first."

He caught the tail end of a signed exchange between Alan, Big Merv and Trev.

"'S time for the special broadcast," said Big Merv pointing at the screen.

"Mmm. And before we make any firm plans, we should probably see what else Lord Vernon has to say."

Chapter 44

The waiting was the worst part, not that any other part would be pleasant. Ruth stood quietly next to General Moteurs, shaking so much that, when she looked down, she could see the hem of her skirt moving. Lord Vernon arrived mercifully quickly, or perhaps it was unmercifully quickly, because while waiting for him was bad, actually seeing him again was almost worse. Ruth wished she could fast forward through this bit of her life, to a few hours' time, when it was done.

He knew how to make an entrance, she had to give him that, and he had presence. The moment he stepped through the doorway, the atmosphere in the room electrified as if he'd put several thousand volts through it. All eyes were drawn to him. He waited a moment to allow his arrival to sink in and then moved further into the room. Now that he was High Leader, it seemed Lord Vernon came with a posse; Ruth counted eight Grongles with him, all in the black and red military uniform of the army.

"Your betrothed has arrived," said General Moteurs, somewhat unnecessarily.

Like the previous time, the assembled GNN personnel and general hangers-on bowed low and, having been versed on the correct protocol by General Moteurs, Ruth followed suit. It was difficult to make an ironic curtsey but she had a good try anyway.

"All rise," said a voice. A catchy military march played – the Grongolian National Anthem – and everyone stood to attention, even General Moteurs: straight and tall, one arm held across the chest, fist clenched. If she hadn't been so scared, Ruth might almost have laughed. It was what the baddies did on every single vintage TV show Ruth had seen; except this was real and that wasn't funny.

Despite the over-the-top, gold-braided bling of the entourage around him, Lord Vernon's uniform was understated: a discreet bit of gold braid round the collar, cuffs and epaulettes of his black and red jacket. He wore no medals, unlike General Moteurs, she noticed. Instead, in the empty expanse of black material on his chest, he wore a large diamond-encrusted star.

Such an understated appearance marked him out from the others. A collective sigh rose from all the females in the room as he entered. Perhaps they mistook the dangerous panther-like demeanour for bad boy glamour. It still kept everyone a few feet away from him. He was immaculately turned out. From the velvety darkness of his black suede gloves and boots to the gleaming buttons and belt there was nothing out of place. As usual he was armed to the teeth, wearing a sword, laser pistol and far more. He stood there, tall and brooding, with the power of a god and, vile though his personality might be, Ruth conceded he looked like one. He took a moment or two to search her out and when he saw her, his expression was steely and full of warning. Even behind the blank lenses of his sunglasses she could feel those slate-coloured eyes searing into her soul.

He leaned over, muttered something to one of his accompanying glitterati and started making his way towards her. The crowd parted in front of him, each one bowing out of his way as he approached. Oh yes, she remembered, she was supposed to be pleased to see him. She stepped from the protective shadow of General Moteurs, to greet her future husband and he took her hands in his.

"Darling." He pulled her against him and kissed her, then he stood back, still holding her hands, to admire her – or at least, pretend to. "Ravishing, as always." He was wearing cologne, a nice one and it was strangely out of place on such a monster. Close to, the aura of barely contained violence emanating from him was stronger: so strong she could almost smell it, under that cologne, and feel it, coiling her into its cold embrace, living and thriving on her fear and growing in strength. Did he do this to everyone or was it just her? Maybe it was his way of warning her that she should toe the line. Did the rest of them even notice? No-one had stopped what they were doing but she was aware of a reduction of noise level in the room as everyone listened to her and Lord Vernon's conversation.

"Thank you," she said as the world's ears wagged. Was that normal enough? No. She should say more, a compliment. "You are looking pretty deadly yourself."

"Deadly," he said flatly. Yes, well, it wasn't the smartest word she could have used. His sunglasses hid the expression in his eyes but the corners of his mouth turned upwards in a smile. "Naturally." He slid his arm around her waist and tightened it around her, pulling her closer against him. She shuddered, closing her eyes to hide the fear in them as he put one hand to her face, caressing it. He leaned down and planted a long, lingering kiss on her lips.

"Are you ready?" He held her even tighter. Perhaps he thought she would try and run. No, not this time. She looked up at him, at the shiny nothingness of his sunglasses. She could see herself reflected in them; squished, distorted but – result – wearing an expression of calm disdain.

"Of course."

"Excellent." He moved round, loosening his hold but keeping his arm round her waist and fixed his gaze on Carlton Scrope, "Shall we begin?"

"At once, Your Divine Excellence." Scrope clicked his fingers, "Make-up!" Two Grongles, one female, one male, came running over from behind the cameras and arc lights. Each one had a vanity case. "Please take a seat," Carlton gestured to a pair of director's chairs, side by side, and she and Lord Vernon sat. Lord Vernon took off his sunglasses and looked the female up and down, she was slim and pretty. She stepped forward and put a plastic bib around his neck to protect his uniform from any stray spots of powder. She seemed overawed and nervous and the way Lord Vernon was looking at her clearly wasn't helping.

"What a lovely bone structure," said a voice and Ruth realised that her make-up artist was talking to her.

"Oh, um, thank you," she said. Her voice sounded strained and she was still shaking.

"You're looking a bit peaky though. I should ask him to take you out a bit more, chin up."

She looked up and he folded the bib around her shoulders.

"Or is it nerves?"

"Nerves, I've never been on TV before. I tried a couple of days ago and it went badly."

"You'll be fine sweetie. Head up again. That's the way. Oh! I'll just take these …" he took her spectacles off and handed them to her. "There. Now, a little foundation …" She felt him applying dots of something cold and sweet-smelling to her face. "This is gorgeous stuff. You K'Barthans really know a thing or two about skin care." Ruth hadn't the energy to explain that she wasn't K'Barthan. "I love this product. When are they going to make it in green?" He smoothed it onto her skin and stood back to evaluate the results. "Hmm, let's do a bit of a blend here," he rubbed her cheeks with his finger, "a little highlight there …" He took a thing that looked like a lipstick, only it was white and ran it down the centre of her nose. "Lovely, and blend …" He rubbed it in and stood back. "Pretty as a picture! Let's add a little bit of powder," he said as he applied it vigorously with a brush. "A touch of blusher," ditto, "and a touch of mascara, look up and hold still, aaaaand blink." She did as she was told. "There we are." He whipped out a mirror and held it up. "Lovely, yes?"

"Yes. That's … very nice." It was a lurid colour, getting towards Big Merv's, but she looked pretty, she had to give him that. Her doubts must have shown more than she realised.

"I've had to bring your colour up a bit because otherwise, with the lights and everything, you'll look very washed out. They're designed for green skin."

"Oh," she smiled up at him, "thank you."

Lord Vernon's female artist had finished in what Ruth suspected might have been record time. Judging by the way she was hugging the vanity case to her chest, she hadn't enjoyed being in close proximity to the new High Leader any more than Ruth did.

Carlton Scrope oiled his way up to them again.

"If you would step onto the set," he oozed.

Ruth's nerves were becoming increasingly pronounced and she tripped on the step, but Lord Vernon caught her. He was still wary, she could tell.

"I'm alright," she said, trying to keep the nervousness out of her voice.

Lord Vernon took off his sunglasses and flipped them closed with one hand.

"Of course you are," he said. His tone was light but this was an order, rather than reassurance; the flash of warning in his eyes confirmed it.

"It is natural to be a little anxious." Ruth realised she wasn't the only one who was nervous. Carlton Scrope sounded as scared as she was. "I assure you, once the interview starts, your fear will leave you. Just concentrate on answering the questions and you'll be fine."

"Thank you," she said. He turned to Lord Vernon.

"Your Divine Excellence … about the viewer's question."

"The competition winner?"

This was news to Ruth.

"Yes. It is over and above the acceptable content we discussed."

"Show me."

With shaking hand, Carlton Scrope held out a piece of paper.

"Mr Scrope, if the people ask I must answer."

"Thank you, Your Divine Excellence."

The two of them, Ruth and Lord Vernon, sat on a leather sofa.

"Closer please," said a voice.

"That's the producer," said Carlton Scrope.

Ruth looked over at Lord Vernon, the opposite end of the couch and inched a tiny bit nearer.

"Closer, please," said the producer.

With a vexed sigh, Lord Vernon leaned over and grabbed her. He hauled her along the couch and put his arm round her again, clamping her next to him.

"Thank you, Your Divine Excellence. As per the running order, Carlton will start us off with a piece to camera and then he will begin the interview with the competition winner's question. That is acceptable to you?"

"Yes," said Lord Vernon, "begin."

"Thank you. Silence please everyone. Places. On your mark Carlton, on air in five, four, three …" said the producer, counting the two, one silently on his fingers.

"Welcome back to this extra edition of Begin the Day. Today we have a very special programme lined up for you; an interview with Lord Vernon, our High Leader of Grongolia and Candidate of K'Barth, or Western Grongolia as it is now called, and the Chosen One, his betrothed. Your Divine Excellence, Lord Vernon and Ruth Cochrane, good day to you."

"Good day, Mr Scrope," said Lord Vernon.

"Hello there," said Ruth.

"Your Divine Excellence, we are privileged to have you here."

"Yes you are."

"As agreed I will start with our competition winner's question. Congratulations to Mr Evan Sake, from Glord in Grongolia, who was picked at random in our draw."

"Ask the question, Mr Scrope." The panther-like menace was there again and despite the fact it was all pointing at Carlton Scrope, Ruth felt like Lord Vernon's prey, trapped by his side.

"Mr Sake says, 'The Candidate is a pure-blood Grongle. Why has he chosen a human?' It is a surprising choice is it not?"

Lord Vernon's non-Grongle grey eyes narrowed and Ruth wondered if Mr Evan Sake had just won himself a midnight visit from the security forces.

"No."

"Er, would you care to expand on that?" asked Carlton Scrope, nervously. He was clearly having as much trouble meeting those eyes as Ruth did.

"If he is a loyal subject, Mr Sake will not require elucidation. He will trust my judgement."

"Of course."

"However, on this occasion, I will indulge him since his lack of insight is understandable. This is about science, Mr Scrope. I would not expect you or your viewers to understand the intricacies of reality theory and quantum physics, but science is no respecter of species. Put simply, Ruth comes from elsewhere, a version of reality where there are no Grongles and no sentient beings, other than humans."

"How very strange."

"Not to her. Her native language is Grongolian and many of her nation's ways are as ours, in short, she belongs to a race that is her reality's version of ours. If she were from our world, I do not doubt that she would be Grongolian and since she is clearly one of our counterparts in a place where, for now, we do not exist, her exact species bears no relevance."

Carlton Scrope was looking a bit sweaty.

"Thank you, please forgive me for asking."

"I understand that it was necessary."

"Since she comes from another version of reality, how did you find her?" asked Scrope. Ruth could see from his expression of shock that he had blurted out his thoughts before he could shut himself up.

"Fate has ensured that we connect. In the world of quantum probability, we, Ruth and I, were always destined to be …" he waved a languid suede-clad hand, "lovers."

Ruth choked but managed to disguise the noise as a sneeze. Lovers? No thank you. Perish the thought. Putting aside their wedding night she intended to have a permanent headache for the rest of her married life. Lord Vernon glowered at her. He clearly hadn't appreciated her reaction. She bit her lip and looked down.

"You certainly seem very happy together," said Carlton Scrope.

"Oh yes we are, deliriously happy," said Ruth, seizing the chance to make up for the choke/sneeze gaffe. The life of the man she truly loved was at stake here, after all. Had she sounded too ironic? Probably. Lord Vernon gave her a guarded look as if he didn't believe what he was hearing.

"Ruth, if I may call you that," Carlton Scrope continued.

"Yes, 'Ruth' is fine."

He didn't like her, that much was clear, but it was probably about her failure to be a Grongle rather than anything she'd said or done. She briefly wondered if Mr Evan Sake actually existed or whether the 'competition' was merely a ruse Scrope had thought up to allow him to ask his own question without reprisals.

"How do you know you are the Chosen One?"

"I'm in love with the Candidate," she replied, and he was *so* not Lord Vernon. She sought out the camera with the red light on, the one that was filming, and looked into it. "I love the Candidate with all my heart, with all my soul and I always will," she said. If The Pan of Hamgee was watching, please let him understand that she was talking to him, please, please. Beside her, Lord Vernon tensed, "I can love no other," she said. Was that laying it on a bit thick? Probably. Lord Vernon leaned down and kissed her cheek.

"Very touching, darling," he murmured. Clearly not. The grey eyes were smug, confident of victory. He turned his attention back to their interviewer.

"If I may explain, Mr Scrope," he said, as if anyone would challenge him. "This is about the concept of belief. There is an experiment in science, Natterjack's box of frogs, have you heard of it?"

"No."

"Then you should have researched your subject more thoroughly." Lord Vernon's tone was mainly sneering condescension but now Ruth detected an undercurrent of I'd-like-to-rip-your-head-off. Her betrothed clearly disliked Carlton Scrope as much as she did. Well, she supposed, no two individuals can disagree on everything. Lord Vernon continued. "The essence, in a nutshell, is 'I believe, therefore I am'. And I believe, Mr Scrope. And so does Ruth."

"How did you find out that you were the Candidate?" he asked Lord Vernon.

"That is the same question, rephrased." Lord Vernon fixed his interviewer with one of his multi-megawatt glares and Carlton Scrope paused for a moment, clearly racking his brains to think of a way to steer the conversation onto safer ground.

"I fear I have not put this question with my customary eloquence, I am a little overawed by your presence."

Scared witless by it more like.

"You want proof."

Carlton Scrope's face was rigid, expressionless.

"Yes, I see you do."

The I'd-like-to-rip-your-head-off aspect of Lord Vernon's tone was more than an undercurrent now. Carlton Scrope began to look even more sweaty.

"I wonder why you did not say?" Lord Vernon's voice was soft, hypnotic. Scrope looked about ready to wet himself. "Perhaps you fear me too much to ask."

Carlton Scrope's Adam's apple bobbed up and down as he swallowed.

"I am overawed," he croaked.

"The question is easy enough to answer," Lord Vernon continued smoothly, dropping most, but not all, of the menace from his tone. It didn't seem to relax his victim. He clicked his fingers and held out his hand. A member of his bling-laden retinue rushed in proffering a box, from the side Ruth noticed. It wouldn't do to have the puppets obscuring their master from shot.

Lord Vernon disentangled his arm from her to take the box and leaned forward to put on the table. She had to move away from him to give him room. Thank you, Carlton Scrope for asking that difficult question. Lord Vernon opened the box and removed the machine inside. He wound it up and set it, on its stand, on the coffee table in front of them.

"This is a confibrulator. It determines the importance of all things. You, Mr Scrope ..." their interviewer almost physically squirmed when Lord Vernon moved the pointer towards him ... "are ..." he pulled the lever, the confibrulator started spinning and the needle crept round the dial to four, "more significant than I would have anticipated. But, of course, you are interviewing the Candidate."

"I—" Carlton Scrope's voice came out rather high and he started again, "I—"

"Listen, Mr Scrope and I will explain – for the benefit of your viewers – you, will no doubt have understood this for yourself," the implication, obviously, being the opposite.

"Thank you," croaked Carlton Scrope. "Can we get a close up of this?" he asked and one of the crew, with a handheld camera, came and filmed the Importance Detector on the table. While the confibrulator was being transmitted in close-up, Ruth watched Scrope as he took advantage of a few moments off camera to mop the rivers of sweat off his face with a handkerchief.

"The Candidate will score eight or above," Lord Vernon glanced up, "are you listening, Mr Scrope?"

"Yes," squeaked the beleaguered interviewer.

"Good."

Ruth hugged her arms around her. Among the half-hidden faces behind the cameras she sought out General Moteurs. He was not looking at her but she was more sure of him now and it was a comfort to know she wasn't entirely alone, at least he was a fellow member of the Underground. She looked at the sea of heads in front of her wondering if there were more. The make-up artist, perhaps, he'd seemed nice, and his own man, or at least, his own Grongle.

"Ruth." She dragged herself back to the matter in hand, and turned her attention back to Lord Vernon. She composed her features into a mask of pretend admiration and it felt as if something was dying inside her. "Let us start with you, as the Chosen One your score will be seven. If you affect me particularly you may score more," he gave the machine a booster wind, set it back on the stand, pointing at her and pulled the lever. The needle swung sharply up to just above seven point five and stayed there. He looked up at her. "Very good," he said softly before returning his focus to the hapless Carlton Scrope. "As you can see, Ruth is Chosen. And finally, myself."

He moved the pointer round so it was directed at him and set the machine spinning again. The needle snapped to the top of the dial and stayed at ten.

No. It couldn't be.

"Oh," she gasped. "It's gone up."

"Ooo," said everyone else in the room, as if a particularly spectacular firework had gone off.

She felt the tears coming and closed her eyes. For heaven's sake! Why did she even believe this ju-ju? She didn't love Lord Vernon and she never would. And he'd probably rigged it anyway. And she was NOT going to cry on world telly. Except she was because nothing would hold back the tears. Because somewhere the man she really loved would be watching and she was deliberately hurting him, and yes, it was to save his life, but he wouldn't know.

"I'm so sorry to cry," she hiccupped, "I'm overcome with emotion." Well yes, that was true. "That is such wonderful news."

"Yes it is." Lord Vernon put his hand to her face and wiped away her tears with his thumb, just as if he was a genuine, concerned lover.

GNN filmed everything.

"You have had an emotional time, my darling," he said, his voice was almost gentle but his eyes showed nothing but cruel exultance. "Do not worry," he whispered, but it was not so much of a whisper that the TV microphones couldn't pick it up. He kissed her mouth, a long slow lingering kiss. He was a consummate actor, everything about his body language, his demeanour, showed tenderness and love, except for his eyes which told her differently. "We belong together." He pulled her to him, kissing her cheek. He held her close, burying his face in her hair so he could whisper in her ear, "You are mine now."

The voice of Carlton Scrope cut through her misery.

"Wow what an amazing piece of television. Viewers, don't go away! We will be right back with our new High Leader and Candidate of Western Grongolia and his fiancée Ruth Cochrane after these important messages."

****

In the glass control booth at the back of the studio the technician reached out to cut the transmission. The producer leaned forward and stopped her. Then he spoke into the microphone that fed into the earpieces of the camera crew.

"Keep rolling," he said, before switching to the tannoy.

****

"That's TV gold right there," Ruth heard a voice say over the loudspeaker. "Good work Carlton and a great performance from our revered guests."

"Thank you," said Lord Vernon. He took the confibrulator off the table and then, all business, he stood up and moved to the edge of the set, "General Moteurs."

The General, conspicuous in his grey Imperial Guard uniform among the black and red army Grongles around him, stepped up into the light.

"Sir."

"I fear the Chosen One is overly stressed, take her back to the Palace." To the crew and audience Lord Vernon added, "She has not been well."

"Yes, sir," said the General.

Ruth could not let this happen. Lord Vernon would surely consider it another failure on her part. If she displeased him he would kill The Pan. She wiped her eyes on her sleeve, blew her nose and stood up.

"No, I won't go back."

Lord Vernon did something close to a double take.

"I want to finish the interview. Please."

"No. You are still frail, I cannot allow you to jeopardise your health so soon before our wedding."

"I made you a promise," she said, "and if I make a promise, I keep it."

"Are you certain of that?"

"Yes," she said firmly. "I know how to behave."

He tapped the confibrulator against his hand, thinking.

"Perhaps …" His eyes burned into hers. As usual it filled her with dread and she told herself, as she had many times before, that it was just a trick, and that if he could do it, she could, too. So she returned his laser glare with one of her own – or at least, an approximation; it was difficult to tell, not having practised it in a mirror. She tried to imbue her look with the same arrogant confidence as his, as if the tables were turned and she was seeing into his soul. For a moment they played stare down and then he took a deep breath in through his nose. As he breathed out, almost inaudibly, he growled. "I sometimes wonder if you are unbreakable," he said.

"No. I'm just in love."

Lord Vernon's eyes clouded with anger.

"Ahhhhh," said everyone, completely misinterpreting the conversation.

"And you know who with," she said sweetly. Yeh, and he did too, and it wasn't him. He did not hide his rage. She could feel it, boiling round the two of them like a cloud of white hot acid. The grey eyes met hers as he held her against him: dark, malignant, evil. But he could do nothing here. She smiled up at him, goading him, daring him, and to her surprise the Grongles around them broke into spontaneous applause. Lord Vernon's expression altered, the rage in his eyes was mixed with something else now, not exactly respect but a wariness, or something close.

"It seems I cannot refuse you," he said. Yeh, she'd won this round. She smiled some more. "You!" he pointed at a Grongle in jeans, trainers and a checked shirt. "Fetch a glass of water."

"Right away, Your Divine Excellence," he said and ran off.

****

"Did we get that?" asked the producer, back in the control box.

"Yes," said the technician.

"Excellent. We'll drop the lifestyle section and use it in the third segment," he pressed a button that would deliver his words directly to the interviewer's earpiece and spoke into the microphone again. "Carlton, we have that last exchange on film. We'll need you to do a commentary, be thinking about that in the next commercial break."

"I will," said the nervous voice of Carlton Scrope.

The producer switched back to the studio-wide tannoy system.

"Places please," he said.

****

Ruth and Lord Vernon returned to their seats along with their wary interviewer. "Thirty seconds …" The runner came back and put a glass of water on the table.

"Thank you," she said and took a sip.

"On air in five, four, three …"

Ruth took a deep breath and steeled herself. She would not let Lord Vernon win. She felt defiled by his touch but when he slid one arm around her again she hid her revulsion and pretended to relax. He started playing with her hair and she leaned against him, as if she liked it. She would pretend to be broken now, if that's what it took to destroy him later, because she had made up her mind, he would not be Architrave. She knew that Saturday was the day that mattered. The day upon which all was won or lost and she made her decision. Even if The Pan of Hamgee didn't show, if the installation went ahead, the wedding would not. She would denounce him, herself, at the altar.

Chapter 45

The broadcast finished with the National Anthem of Grongolia, of course. Trev blipped the remote and switched off the telly. The room was silent.

The Pan sat, tight-lipped, unmoving. He must start getting ready for opening soon. Except, what was the point?

Lord Vernon scored ten. And he, the real Candidate, scored eight.

His friends watched him silently, their faces a mixture of sympathy and nervousness.

"I don't know how he did that. He's not the Candidate. I know he's not," said The Pan.

"How?" asked Simon.

"Because he ain't effin' pukka, that's how," said Big Merv.

"No, I meant, how did he do that?" said Simon. "After yesterday, with those Grongles, I'm pretty sure I know who the Candidate is. So how did he rig it?"

"He didn't," said Lucy. "Sir Robin warned us about this."

"Eh? When?" asked Big Merv.

"When he was showing us the box," said Trev, "only the real Candidate is able to open the box, it's how they tells who is what when the scores is level."

"But these aren't level, he scores ten and I score eight," said The Pan.

"Yes," said Lucy. "But only you can open the box. You can still open it, can't you, Defreville?"

The Pan put his hand in his pocket, pulled out the snuff box and flipped it open with his thumb.

"Looks like it," he said.

"There you are," said Lucy.

"Yer, so, it ain't Lord effin' Snotface up there on the telly," said Big Merv bullishly.

"So how come he's got that score?" said Alan.

"I dunno," said Trev, "I wish Mum an' Ada was here, they'd tell us."

"I'll look at the database," said Simon.

"If this is about belief, though, how can I compete with that?" said

The Pan.

Cluck? said the chicken which only he heard. He smiled ruefully.

"No-one what sees you is goin' ter believe it's 'im," said Psycho Dave.

"I dunno, I'd say he looks the part far more than I do."

"No, he doesn't, he looks like a despot," said Lucy. "And you … you look like something else. Anyway, if the ring fits …" she added with a grin.

"The lady has a point. I believe the ring has a peculiar propensity not to fit the wrong hand," said Professor N'Aversion.

"If you all believe me, why doesn't Ruth?"

"Defreville, it's not the way it seems, I'm sure," said Lucy. "It's TV. They're experts, they've edited it and it's choreographed – even the 'spontaneous' bits – and she's scared of him."

"Everyone's scared of him. But you saw her face, she's desperate to please him. She's in love, Lucy, and not with me." Smecking Arnold, just saying that felt like a knife in the guts.

"No she's not—"

"Then what is she? You tell me Lucy. If she's not in love with him, why is she with him, why is she wholeheartedly endorsing Lord Vernon if he hasn't got to her somehow?"

"He has got to her, I'm sure, but not the way you—"

"Enough," he said shortly. He stood up and made for the door but as he got to where Big Merv, Psycho Dave and Alan were standing he stopped. "Guys, d'you mind opening up for me? I'll join you but I-I need to be on my own, I have to think and then we need to sit down again, all of us, and plan something."

"'S OK mate, take as long as you wanna." The Pan put his hand on Big Merv's shoulder and leant on it for a moment.

"Thanks," he said, "it won't take long. I'll see you in a minute." He walked past them and into the hall but almost immediately, he put his head back inside the door. "Prof, Simon, d'you want to stay?"

"I regret that we must return to our HQ post-haste," said the Professor, standing up.

"Come on then, the portals are down in the hall."

****

Lucy watched The Pan of Hamgee leave.

"Do any of you believe that?" she asked the others, after he had gone.

"What?" asked Alan.

"That Ruth loves Lord Vernon."

"Beats me how anyone could love Lord Vernon, but I don't know her."

"Me neither," Psycho Dave chipped in.

There was a short silence. Alan and Psycho Dave nodded at one another, as if reaching agreement.

"We'll leave you guys to sort it out," said Alan.

"Yer, me an' Alan, we're goin' ter go and start opening up."

"I'll be with you boys in a mo'," said Big Merv as the two of them went out.

"As and when mate," said Alan and the two of them left.

"Trev? Merv? What d'you think?" asked Lucy.

Big Merv shrugged.

"I'll give you, girl, it ain't like what I saw of 'er."

"Yer, I is with Big Merv, on this one," Trev agreed. "She's a good girl I reckons, Mum an' Ada liked 'er an' all. If she was dodgy, they'd 'ave see'd it. It don't sit right."

"She could never love Lord Vernon, I know it. Look, I'm going to go and talk to him."

"'S not a good time, girl," Big Merv warned her.

"There'll never be a good time."

"Yer, you gotta point."

"But first, Trev, you need to rest."

"I got that," said Big Merv. "Do what you gotta, girl. C'mon Trev, I reckon Nurse Hargraves there's prescribing a kip. So while she's bending our lad's ear, I'll give you a hand back to bed."

Chapter 46

Lucy ran out into the hall to find The Pan and almost collided with him as he came out of the bathroom. He look strained and tired.

"Defreville? You OK?"

"I have to be."

"That's a worrying response. Have Simon and the Professor gone?"

"Yeh."

"Right. If you have a few minutes, can I talk to you?"

He glanced at his watch.

"We might need to be quick."

Big Merv was right. It probably wasn't a good time, but for the life of her, Lucy couldn't think of a moment that would be.

"Can you come into the kitchen a minute?"

"Alright."

They turned and walked down the hall. From downstairs she heard the voices of Alan and Psycho Dave drifting up from the bar and the sounds of chinking glasses, opening and closing drawers and chairs and tables scraping as they prepared for opening. The Pan sat down at the kitchen table and Lucy took a seat opposite him. Damn, she hadn't meant to do that, it looked like an interview, she moved round so she was sitting at right angles from him. He watched her, clearly appreciating exactly what she was doing.

"First, I want to thank you for saving my life."

"It was a pleasure." He flashed her a smile and seemed a little less on his guard. "Thank you for saving Trev's."

"I didn't, I just followed Doctor Dot's instructions."

"No, the things you told me, I think they made it easier for Doctor Dot to bring the right stuff and I know your being here, and Big Merv, made it easier for Trev to wait for her."

"You're very kind."

"It's the truth. Is there something else? Do you want to talk about the field surgery?"

"No. Thank you. Actually. I want to talk about you."

"Me," he said flatly.

"Yes."

His eyes narrowed a fraction.

"About the pressure you're under."

"You think I need counselling?"

"No but you need to … talk."

"Really. Go on."

She wondered whether she should bail out and try again later. No, Ruth didn't have time for her to do that. Lucy understood that she might not convince The Pan but if she could just get him thinking … She blundered on.

"OK, the people I work for, usually, they run the risk of being tortured and killed if they go back to where they came from. Every time I take a case on I know that, if I can't persuade my government to let my client stay, they may go home to certain death. It isn't the same level but I wanted to tell you that I understand how it feels to be under pressure, I appreciate how hard it must be for you."

"Thank you. That's not all of it, though, is it?" his voice sounded harder, warier. He was far ahead of her.

"No. In my job, I have to gather evidence to make my argument and I have to know the law. However, the most important thing is to get the people I'm dealing with to put aside their own perspective and see the situation from other angles."

"So?" she could almost see his defences going up. Damn.

"So, I think you are putting yourself through a lot of unnecessary pain because you're seeing things one way, when if you saw them another—"

"Lucy, you're being pretty abstruse, although thinking about it, as a lawyer, I suppose that's your job. Is this about Ruth?"

"Yes."

"Then there's nothing to say." Very firm and she could hardly miss the warning in his tone. Even so, she went on.

"I think there is. I think you're reading her actions the way Lord Vernon wants you to instead of looking at the facts and applying logic."

"Logic was never my strong point but I think I have the facts right. I was there, after all."

"The facts maybe. The interpretation? No. You're thinking with your broken heart."

"That doesn't change the identity of the person who broke it, or alter what she did."

"No but it might alter the reason why."

"You think that makes a difference? She said she loved me; she lied."

"No. I don't think she did. Listen Defreville, I know Ruth, she's my friend; she'd eat a bucket full of slugs before she could ever knowingly hurt you. Three days ago she was besotted with you, so besotted she was ready to do the whole white dress thing—"

"What white dress thing?"

"Marriage."

"In this reality, we get married in red."

"Alright, red. Stop changing the subject."

"Then drop it."

"No. This is Ruth we're talking about. She can't switch something like that off."

"Then why do you suggest she accepted Lord Vernon's proposal of marriage, in front of me?"

"What? Was she in the room with you?"

"Through some one-way glass."

"One-way glass? Where on earth were you?"

"In the cells."

"OK, Defreville, are you telling me Lord Vernon proposed to Ruth in the cell next to yours, in prison?"

"Yes."

Before she could stop herself, Lucy burst out laughing with relief.

"Thank heavens! That's alright then. It can't possibly be genuine."

"It looked pretty genuine to me especially when she kissed him. Arnold, she practically ate his face off. Thank The Prophet the lights went out before I had to watch them actually screw each other."

"In gaol?" Lucy said. "You must be joking."

"No," she saw a flash of anger in his eyes but his voice was steady, "believe me, I find nothing of this remotely funny."

Lucy composed herself.

"I'm sorry, I don't mean to laugh but that is *so* not Ruth."

"On the contrary, it was. Maybe they couldn't wait."

"Don't be facetious, Defreville."

"Don't confuse facetious with bitter. After all she came into my cell and dumped me, remember? She was pretty clear about that; by the way, she told me she didn't love me anymore."

"No, she didn't tell you that. That's what you heard. What did she actually say?"

"What does it matter? I got the message."

"No Defreville, that's my point. I don't think you did."

"Who was there, you or me?"

"Who is calm and rational? She's my friend, I know her. You love her but you're hurting and you're not looking at this with detachment."

"I'd say I'm pretty calm and detached right now, Lucy," he said.

"Cold rage is not calm."

He glared at her.

"Rage is all I can give you. Smecking Arnold! Do you know what she told me? That she had no choice – no choice my arse – then she went skipping happily off into the sunset with hubby-to-be."

"Maybe she was telling the truth."

"You think, do you?"

"I don't know but I'm sure it wasn't like that."

"Well I am. Let's beg to differ."

She tried a different tack.

"OK I'm sorry I don't want to hurt you more than I have to or make you angry, but she's my best friend and I need to know. I'm having a hard time believing this."

He sighed.

"It's alright. I can understand that. If it helps you get your head straight, ask."

"When Ruth left, what happened?"

"I don't even want to think about what they did next."

"Not them, you."

"I was freed."

"And were you expecting that?"

"No."

"Oh yes, of course Lord Vernon had signed your death warrant hadn't he? You told us just after you rescued us."

"Yeh. That's what he said. Captain Snow, too."

"Try this then. You're in gaol, about to be put to death. Your girlfriend agrees to marry Lord Vernon and suddenly, you're set free. What's wrong with that?"

"A lot."

"Yes. Because if a man is going to propose to a woman, he doesn't do it in gaol."

He leaned back in his chair and eyed her like a sullen teenager.

"He's not a man."

For heaven's sake!

"OK fine, he's a Grongle. Whatever he is, he's still male and he's not going to ask the woman of his dreams to marry him in some scabby prison. Why would he ruin the moment of a lifetime – even if it does mean his mortal enemy can see it happen? Sure he tells his enemy afterwards, but the proposal? He's the most powerful being in K'Barth, you'd have thought he could have got a table in a decent restaurant somewhere, wouldn't you? She's the Chosen One. He's going to flaunt her in front of the world right?"

"Not necessarily. He's Lord Vernon—"

"Yes. He's Lord Vernon and even if he wants a private tête-à-tête he can take her anywhere. He can put her on top of a mountain with an orchestra to serenade them but he doesn't; he does it in a grotty cell block so you can see. What does that tell you?"

"That the two of them wanted to make me suffer."

God he was irritating.

"NO, you stupid man! Lord Vernon wanted to make you suffer."

"Which is different because ...?"

"Ruth didn't!"

"On the contrary, she clearly did—"

"Don't project your cynicism about women onto my best friend. This is Ruth Cochrane you're talking about. Think about her, think about who she is. Not your jaded conception of how women seem to be. If it really happened the way you say, Lord Vernon must have been completely desperate. You won that round, Defreville, or Ruth did."

"It doesn't feel like it."

"Of course it bloody doesn't! Because it didn't happen the way you think."

He turned his head away from her, blinking and took a deep breath. She waited.

"Lucy," he said quietly, "I know you're trying to help but I can't—I can't deal with this head on right now. My nation needs me and I—"

"You have to. My friend is about to condemn herself to a life of total misery and you're the only person who can save her. Don't tell me you're too busy feeling sorry for yourself to do anything. God, Defreville, can't you see?" her voice broke, "she loves you. No-one else. You. Don't you understand? She—"

"Lucy, stop."

"Defreville, listen –"

"No. You listen," he stood up angrily. "I can't do this, I've told you. I have a few hours to work out a way to save my nation and if I think about her, I am undone. I can't be undone Lucy. For the sake of millions of K'Barthans I have to hold it together. Believe me, it doesn't make me happy but it's the way it has to be. She made her decision and I've made mine. We'll have to live with it."

"Do you have any idea how much of a bastard you sound? And don't you dare malign my best friend!"

"Malign?" he flung up his arm. "She dumped me for Lord Vernon! That's the truth. Tell me, am I a fool or are you in denial?"

"Oh belt up Defreville! Switch your heart off, for one minute, engage your brain and stop being so angry—"

"I'm not angry, I'm smecking incandescent!" He shouted, then stopped. He ran his hand through his hair, "I'm sorry. It's not your fault. It's her I'm angry with. She doesn't deserve a friend like you." He went out into the hall.

"Wait!" Lucy leapt up and rushed after him.

"I can't wait, it's opening time and I have stuff to do." He stalked angrily towards the stairs and she followed.

"Then while you're doing it think about this. Lord Vernon wanted Ruth and he wanted you dead."

He paused for a moment, was he going to listen?

"Yeh. So what?"

"He's got Ruth, but he let you go. It's a straight—"

"We've finished this, Lucy. No more."

He ran down the stairs, three at a time.

"You may be in love with her but I'm the one who knows her best," she told the empty hallway.

My, that had gone well … She heaved a sigh. What could she do now? Someone put a hand on her shoulder, suddenly, and she almost screamed.

"Merv! Don't creep up on people like that." He didn't reply but wrapped his arms round her and pulled her against him in a hug. She hugged him back, clinging on tight.

"'S OK sweets. You ain't gonna get no sense out of him. He's hurting an' he's hurting bad."

“Yes, he is, and I screwed up,” she mumbled into his jacket, “he’ll never see reason now.”

“C’mon,” Big Merv let go of her but kept one arm draped around her shoulders as he guided her gently back along the hall. “He’s pukka brainy. He’s gonna get to the truth.”

“But it may be too late. He’s emotional too and he only has a couple of days.”

“Yer. I gotta ask, Luce. You sure about this? Pressure alters people, makes ’em act like you don’t expect. An’ there’s the prophecies, if Lord Vernon scores more than Defreville, maybe she—”

“No. She’s Ruth, she’s my best friend and I know she’s in love with The Pan. You saw them together, they were besotted. No-one and nothing can switch that off in a few hours.”

“Yer. I saw, an’ I get what you’re saying. I only gotta look at ’im.”

“She loves him as much as he loves her and she’s marrying Lord Vernon to save him. I’m sure of it. Why else would they have let him go?”

Chapter 47

Professor N'Aversion and Simon made good time back to the Resistance HQ. As they reached the last of the hidden checkpoints in the woods the Professor was still undecided as to what he would say to Denarghi. He and Simon had talked about little else on the journey back. He was surprised from his thoughts when, as the sentry was about to wave them through, a party of armed guards arrived.

"We'll take it from here," said their leader.

"Certainly sir."

"What's this about?" muttered Simon.

"A pertinent question," the Professor muttered back. "Are they from Henching?"

Simon shrugged.

A deputation of four humans – two large gentlemen, two human females – and a couple of Blurpons awaited them. The Professor cast a glance at Simon and gripped the suitcase full of portals he was carrying a little more tightly.

"This is a very singular honour," he said. "To what do we owe the pleasure of an armed escort from Henching?"

"We're a little more dangerous than Henching, Professor," said one of the women. "We're Strike Ops, so I'd show some respect if I were you."

"My profuse apologies, no disrespect intended."

The other one stepped forward. "I'm Group Leader Frosby and from now on you're going to call me ma'am. Denarghi wants to see you directly."

"How very fortuitous, I need to see him."

"I'm terribly sorry but is there any chance I could just nip behind a tree and have a wee first?" asked Simon.

"You don't get that sort of luxury. Denarghi's orders are very explicit. Meet you, bring you in. Don't let you talk to anyone."

Simon adjusted his hat. "Bring us in?"

The two males drew shotguns from the long pockets in their coats.

"Surrender your weapons."

"I'm terribly sorry, we don't have any," said the Professor.

"I bet Chief Engineer Simon has. Hand over the belts."

"But they're—"

"Do it."

"Are we under arrest then?"

"You could say that, but we're here for your own safety. You'd be lucky to get to the throne room without being murdered. Everyone knows what you've done."

"I see. Do you know?" asked the Professor.

"Yeh."

"Well, if you are arresting us, Group Leader Frosby, I wonder if you could let us in on it," said the Professor.

"Yes, because we have no idea what you're arresting us for," Simon explained.

"You'll find out. Now move. Oh and Professor, leave the suitcase here."

"I really can't. It's most important that I—"

"I said, leave the suitcase here. It's going into quarantine."

"What? Where?"

"Here."

"I most strongly advise you—"

"Shut up, Professor. Word is you've come home with some Grongle WMD."

"Double u em what?"

"Weapon of Mass Destruction."

"I've never heard such nonsense—"

"I said shut up. We know you're smart and we know your game. We're not listening."

"But you have to. The Grongles are about to attack."

Group Leader Frosby rounded on him.

"Spare it for Denarghi, traitor. I was ordered to bring you in but they didn't specify whether you needed to be conscious. So shut up or I swear by The Prophet, I'll knock you out."

Simon raised a polite paw, "But—"

"Both of you." She snatched the suitcase from Professor N'Aversion and beckoned the guards who were loitering around the entrance to their concealed underground bunker. "Take this."

Gingerly, they came over and took the suitcase she held out.

"Guard it with your lives. A couple of boys from Henching are coming to defuse it."

"It's not a bomb," snapped the Professor, irritably.

Frosby whirled round, drawing her knife as she did so and held it up, ready to strike.

"I said, save it."

The Professor and Simon put their hands out in front of them, fingers up, palms outwards.

"Alright."

"Good, we're going to see Denarghi and I warn you, don't try anything or I'll be forced to hurt you. Clear?"

"Yes."

"OK, troops, let's go. Move out."

She passed her prisoners and headed towards a nearby clearing that contained one of the many entrances to the Resistance HQ. One of the others jabbed the Professor with the muzzle of his gun.

"Move," he said.

Chapter 48

The Pan stormed down to the bar.

"Don't speak to me," he spat, as Alan and Psycho Dave approached, putting his hand up as if to push them away. He was angry because it was the only way he could be. He went out of the back door, slamming it behind him and stomped across the alley to the garage. It had originally been stables, from days when travellers from out of town had arrived in horse-drawn carriages. He stepped through the broken remains of the door, climbed the ladder into the hayloft and closed the trapdoor behind him with a bang.

Right. Time for a word with himself.

He held his breath and slid the ring slowly off his finger.

Silence.

"Alright, I'm warning you, don't shout at me. I'm not in the mood. I know I've been a total arse. I'll eat any amount of humble pie you wish to throw at me but later because I don't have much time, and I really need to talk to someone." In the silence his voice sounded brittle.

How do? said a voice.

Was that hello? Possibly.

"Hi," said The Pan nervously, "who are you?"

Five.

"Mmm, early."

Aye.

The Pan remembered, possibly at the subliminal prompting of his other colleagues, that the Fifth Architrave had come from Ploff, in Eastern K'Barth, where they all talked funny.

"Right, hello Five, first, I want to thank you and the others for helping me last night."

Nice of thee to say so but 't were nowt.

"Well, it was to me, so thank you anyway. I'm wondering, can I ask your advice on something else?"

Eee, I'll try. Though I doubt it'll get us owt.

Five sounded defensive, but not unfriendly. It could have been worse. It could have been that smecker Forty-three.

"Alright, look, I'll be honest with you. I've been an idiot at every turn and no matter what I do it makes this worse and worse." When Five said nothing, The Pan blundered on. "I don't blame you and the others for thinking I'm stupid and hopeless but Arnold's pants—"

I'll thank thee not to blaspheme, lad.

"Sorry, what I mean is, I'm all you have and I really need your help. The Importance—the confibrulator gives Lord Vernon a score of ten and me eight. How does that happen? He isn't the Candidate, I'm sure of it … unless … Arnold's snot – sorry," he put his head in his hands, or at least, his hand because it still hurt his shoulder too much to raise the other arm. "I'd just begun to believe it all, that I am and that you lot are real."

Tha knows we are. We showed it.

The Pan thought about it.

"I guess so. But why can't I do this? What's wrong? It's not that smecking red stuff is it? Am I still asleep?"

No.

"Are you sure?"

Aye. It sounded as if Five was smiling.

Well that was a relief, sort of. The Pan began to pace to and fro.

"Smecking Arnold, Five—"

I've told thee once … Don't blaspheme.

"You'd blaspheme if you were as completely and utterly hacked off as I am." Five kept an eloquent silence. "Sorry. I need you to help me but I don't even know what to ask for. How am I supposed to make anything of this mess?"

Tha can only decide that for thissen. Tha's not a puppet. Tha's a will of thine own. We're 'ere for ter give thee a bit o' help, not ter stick us hands up thine arse and work thy gob for thee.

"Lord Vernon is High Leader already. He owns the entire world. Is that why he scores ten?"

Don't be soft.

The Pan stopped pacing and flung his good arm out sideways.

"Then why? He doesn't even need to be installed Architrave, although he's going to be because he thinks you lot are a superpower."

If 'e gets 'is mucky paws on us we'll learn 'im what we be and we'll learn 'im good.

The Pan cocked his head on one side.

"You made that sound slightly sinister. What do you mean?"

What I said.

Five wasn't going to be drawn.

"Mmm." The Pan put the statement aside for examination later. There was no time for riddles now, not if he wanted to have a proper chat with his predecessors so he could get back and deliver some sort of plan of action to the Underground before opening.

Don't get mardy it won't get thee owt. Life's a gift. Reach out and tek it wi' both hands.

"Nice but you know what, Five? From where I'm standing it looks suspiciously like a dog turd in a paper bag."

There was a pause. Five was clearly counting to ten.

"Sorry," said The Pan. "I talk rubbish when I'm nervous."

Tek t' dog turd lad, Five said the phrase 'dog turd' with some disdain, but he was clearly making an effort and The Pan didn't really blame him if he was feeling a bit put upon. *Accept it wi' good grace so none other has to. And think on how's it'll be when thine hands are clean after.*

The Pan smiled.

"You're beginning to sound desperate there, Five, but, nice answer."

Cheers. Five sounded surprised to be thanked.

"So, what am I going to do?"

I telled thee, there's nowt but thissen knows that.

"Yeh … well … I have an idea but I'm not sure it's a very good one. Sir Robin's plan is that I step up on Saturday and prove Lord Vernon is not the Candidate. It seems to me that's all I can do. You know what, I even have a vague theory as to how I can get him, and the world, to listen. The trouble is, if he gets a straight ten, and I get eight, I can't can I?"

Tha's t' Candidate, son, and no mistake. Tek it from one as knows. Gizza sec, said Five.

That would be, 'hang on a moment' The Pan thought. He waited while, as if a long way away, he could hear whispering. After a few moments, Five returned.

Aye we reckon summat like it happened to Twenty-three. Her kid brother scored ten right up to t' ceremony.

"What did they do?"

Why, they installed her o' course, she were the one with us in her bonce, she were the one who could open t' box but her kid brother talked her into it. She weren't goin' ter tek up her calling—

"You mean there's an option to say 'no'?"

Aye, 'appen. Fer some.

Great. The Pan wondered about asking Five to qualify 'some'. Then again, what was the point in torturing himself by doing that? They'd probably all had the option to say 'no' except him.

"So, it's Lord Vernon's effect on me that's doing it."

Aye, summat like that.

"Whatever I do, he'll kill me. Is that the reason why he gets a ten?"

No. It's coz it's down ter 'im that tha's faced thy calling.

"Hardly. I've spent my life running away from it, and him."

Aye and it's made thee who tha be.

"Perhaps," he shrugged. "But it doesn't help K'Barth. Look. When the time comes, if you guys can help me, you've all done it before—"

Dying's easy, lad, tha just stops breathing.

"Thank you, I meant more about the installation."

There's nowt this side o' tha head's interrupted an installation.

"No, but you've all been to one, which puts you ahead of me. Don't they ask at some point, you know, does anyone contest the choice of the elders?"

Aye, now tha says it …

"Alright, then, if you lot can just keep your eyes and ears open and if you see or hear anything I can use or think of anything that will help me, let me know … quietly."

The time ter speak up's at t' wedding.

"What?"

'E gets 'isself installed – wi' t' wrong kit it's nowt but a fancy dressing-up game – so if tha keeps mum until t' wedding 'e'll think 'e's cracked it like enough. Then when they ask about just cause or impediment—

"I step up when he's least expecting it."

Tha catches on quick lad.

The Pan smiled.

"Thank you."

Trust us, lad, said Five.

"Funny, people keep telling me that."

Then, cop a listen to 'em.

Chapter 49

In his luxury rooms at the top of the Security HQ – the old Palace – in Ning Dang Po, Lord Vernon put the thimble on the table and sat back. He linked his arms behind his head and stretched. The whole nest of vermin in one place. Tomorrow. It would be a bloodbath. Well, he was master of the world in all but name; he deserved a treat.

"And so to business," he said.

He rang General Moteurs and ordered him to assign an officer to monitor Denarghi as he finalised the arrangements.

It was a shame that the General lacked the stomach for a demonstration of power such as Lord Vernon intended but it could not be helped. Captain Snow would deal with it well enough. He glanced at his watch. If the wretch ever turned up. He was thirty seconds late. No matter, after the successes and excesses of his day he was in a very much lighter frame of mind.

One of the guards outside knocked and entered the room.

"Sir, Captain Snow sends his regrets but is running a little late."

Unlike General Moteurs, Captain Snow was always a few minutes late. Normally this irritated Lord Vernon but not today; nothing could ruin his mood.

"Excellent. You will send him in when he arrives."

"Sir."

The door closed.

Lord Vernon had not been so relaxed for some years, perhaps not since the very outset of his quest for power. He stretched and leaned back in his chair. He had slept and enjoyed the attentions of not two but three of Captain Snow's masseuses. Now he felt fresh, exhilarated and invincible.

There was a knock on the door.

He stood up and adjusted his clothes.

"Yes."

Captain Snow walked into the room, sweaty and nervous. True he was insolent enough to be late, but it must have been by accident rather than design because he had clearly been running.

"You summoned me, sir."

"Yes Captain. First I must thank you for this afternoon's … treat."

"Sir, they pleased you?"

"If this is how you redeem yourself, I will upbraid you more often."

This was clearly not a prospect the Captain relished. Lord Vernon flashed him a nasty smile.

"Sir," he said nervously.

"I want them again, tomorrow."

"No sir, they need to rest, sir," blurted the Captain, his mouth clearly going into action before his brain could deliver the tactful version.

"I hardly think I tired them. Tomorrow, Captain," said Lord Vernon.

"Sir." Captain Snow was pale and sweating. Doubtless he spoke the truth and the masseuses did need to rest but when it came to contradicting his master, he lacked General Moteurs' courage. He also lacked the General's scruples, of course, which was why this particular mission was one that only Captain Snow could attend to.

"No matter, they are irrelevant to my purpose in summoning you here. I have some orders for you."

"Sir."

Lord Vernon walked over to his desk and picked up a folder.

"My requirements are itemised here," he said, as he thrust it at the Captain.

"Sir," Captain Snow seemed slightly bewildered.

"Don't look so surprised. General Moteurs can't do everything. When you read them you will understand that this is a matter for the army, not the Imperial Guard. You will be ready, with your troops, for inspection on the parade ground at the time stated."

"Sir."

"And now, I must discuss my installation. Please clean and delouse Sir Robin and bring him to me."

Chapter 50

Headquarters was uncannily deserted but Professor N'Aversion felt the eyes of his fellows on him. Through twitching blinds and doors ajar the members of the Resistance watched as he and Simon were escorted through the passages of their HQ. The party soon reached a junction where a second group of armed guards waited. They took Simon and headed off in the direction of the cells. Meanwhile Frosby took the Professor to the Throne Room.

Denarghi was flanked by two Swamp Things, bigger, faster and fitter than the Professor. They stood tall and square, sawn-off shotguns held across their barrel-like chests, their expressions completely blank and their antennae carefully positioned so as to give nothing away.

There was no sign of anyone else. The Professor was worried.

"Your Majesty, I must ask, what is the meaning of this?"

"You have betrayed me," said Denarghi.

"What?"

"Deny it if you dare."

"I do deny it. Most strongly."

"I'd be careful what you say, Professor. You have been denounced."

"By whom?"

"You don't need to know. All that concerns you is that you are facing three counts of treason. If I decide you are guilty I will have no choice but to order your execution and no amount of talent at science will save you this time."

"Then perhaps you'd be good enough to tell me what I have done that you consider treasonable."

"We will start with item one. Flagrantly disobeying orders. There is no room in this organisation for people who are not dedicated to the cause."

"I am dedicated, Your Majesty."

"Then why have you knowingly and willingly contravened a direct order from me and started to build this portal?"

"I have not."

"No, of course not. You haven't had time."

"In everything I have done, it has been my concern for the cause, which has guided me," said the Professor. He didn't rebut Denarghi's accusation. It was true, after all.

"D'you know what's wrong with you Professor? You underestimate the rest of us. You think we're all stupid because we aren't as clever as you. But you're not this kind of smart. I know I'll find the plans for that device somewhere about your person."

"You won't."

They were on the stealth tablet, which the Professor had left with Nar.

"I think I will; you have even been to Ning Dang Po to buy parts."

"I did not buy parts," said the Professor, because Simon had bought those. "Denarghi, the portal the Grongles have built is based on ancient K'Barthan technology far superior to theirs. I heard word that there might be one last one in the hands of a K'Barthan. So when you forbade me to build the Grongolian version, I went to Ning Dang Po to find it."

"How very tidy that is. Very tidy. Who did you go and see?"

"I promised him anonymity."

"Convenient. Professor, I know what you did. You went to consort with others like yourself, beings with no stomach for a fight and no commitment. You discussed overthrowing me with Lieutenant Wright and Colonel Ischzue before you left. I believe you went to Ning Dang Po to make contact with this Grongle, General Moteurs."

"Poppycock!" the Professor exploded. "Why would I do that?"

"Because you want to overthrow me."

"Denarghi, nobody wants to oust you. Not when we are the only viable opposition against the Grongles. We can't afford to descend into infighting and anarchy. Do you really want to know why I went to Ning Dang Po? I'll tell you why, because I had proof that hundreds of beings, living and working here, were at risk and you, their leader, would not listen to me. So I went to find more proof, hoping against hope that perhaps then, you might."

"And what did you find?"

"What I sought. Proof. Proof that we are being watched, proof that our days here are numbered. Indeed, the only thing that will stop the surveillance is in my suitcase, which Group Leader Frosby forced me to leave with the sentries."

"And what is in the suitcase?"

"It's difficult to say."

"Then I will make you."

"You will be telling the Grongles at the same time."

"I will take my chance with that."

"If you bring me the suitcase, I can show you and we will be able to speak freely."

"Oh Professor, how stupid you must think I am. I will not be fetching your suitcase. Not until its contents have been checked and declared safe. The whole of your story lacks credibility. If the Grongles have the original five portals, then why would they waste time and resources reinventing their own version?"

"Because the K'Barthan version comes with limitations. It's all quantum, and imagination driven. It is very rare for someone using a K'Barthan portal to be able to transport to somewhere they have never been to. They can, but they need a wealth of special equipment which is lost to all of us. I believe the ancients would have circumvented this, in times past, by travelling to new places by portal with someone who had already been to them. It would have been quicker and easier and explains why the technique has passed from memory. The Grongolian version does not afford surveillance, which is good news for us because it limits their listening to five conversations at a time, if they use each of the five original portals. However, it still allows them to go anywhere they like, so long as they have the grid coordinates. They know where we are, they have watched us with the K'Barthan portals, seen us coming and going, and pinpointed our location. Soon they will attack."

"We are well defended, let them come."

The Professor shook his head.

"They will not send the main force against our defences, they may attack them as a diversion but the full force will come from within. They will transport troops, here, into HQ, by portal. We have no defence against that. Denarghi, for the love of The Prophet I can make this place safe. And put us on an equal – better than equal – footing with the enemy. Let me."

"No. You have been to Ning Dang Po consorting with Grongles and very possibly with a mortal enemy of this organisation, The Pan of Hamgee. Then you return here and have the nerve to pretend your treasonable actions are born of concern. You have flagrantly disobeyed me. Where is your dedication, your loyalty, your patriotism? You swore an oath to me."

"No. I swore an oath to defend K'Barth. That was how the original Resistance oath of allegiance went, if you remember, before you changed it."

"Then you have broken your oath."

"No. I am a Thing of honour and I keep my word but the cause I swore to espouse and yours are no longer the same. You seem to have forgotten what we are fighting for. We are not here to put you in power. We are fighting to defend K'Barth; our nation, our ethos, our way of life. I will do whatever I must to achieve that, and willingly lay down my life. But you have warped this organisation and everything it represents: turned it into your own personal army to achieve power for yourself. That is NOT what I signed up for."

The Professor stopped, he was breathless and angry. The heavy silence seemed to last a long time.

"And there we have it," snarled Denarghi. "You have put the noose round your own neck. I could stomach your spineless liberalism while you stood alone, but now that you are infecting others you have become dangerous. It is time to root out the poisonous weeds from the crop. You, Simon, Ischzue and those witches Nar and Wright, will be executed by firing squad tomorrow morning at ten."

"Without a trial?"

"Why would I waste resources trying you in the face of so much evidence?"

"Then spare the others, leave it at just me."

"What, and let your friends spread this contagion further? Oh no. You know how to inspire loyalty, Professor. Too much loyalty for me to allow that. It is bad enough that I must make a martyr of you. You will all be executed tomorrow and I have ordered Strike Ops to neutralise this Grongle General. Don't think Lieutenant Arbuthnot and Group Leader Snoofle will escape, either. They will stand trial for their part in this."

"Denarghi, for Arnold's sake! This isn't about me and you. You must listen—"

"Take him away!"

"No! Wait!" The guards grabbed the Professor's arms, "This is of the utmost urgency—"

"Put him in the cells," said Denarghi.

The Professor thought about fighting but he was unfit, and up against two younger, bigger and heftier members of his species from Henching.

"You do not need to do this, I will come quietly," he told them. They let go and he shrugged his dishevelled clothes back into position.

"Denarghi! You are courting disaster." He tried to make eye contact with the guards each side of him. "If he won't listen, then you two, at least think about what you have heard here."

"If he utters another word, gag him," snarled Denarghi. "I will see you tomorrow morning, traitor, to watch you die. And don't think your Hamgeean friend will rescue you. He'll be dead by the end of the day, and the other traitorous scum you met in Ning Dang Po with him."

"But—" began the Professor.

"We will find out where he is."

"But—" the Professor began, again, and then stopped.

"He's been on GNN Local. Lord Vernon's close friend: pardoned and set up in business. Do you know what for?"

Professor N'Aversion shook his head.

"For duping stupid, gullible people – like yourself, Professor – into the hands of the Grongles. You have done your worst but he will not give them me."

"No. You'll do that for yourself."

"SILENCE!"

The Professor made to say more and stopped. Was it wise to say anything about who The Pan of Hamgee actually was, he wondered. Or did Denarghi know? Was that what all this was about? Was the little so-and-so making sure the old order stayed buried? The Professor was under no illusions. Re-establishment of the original, liberal K'Barth had never been Denarghi's aim, whatever he might pretend. If the Candidate died it would lay the path to power open for Denarghi. How the Professor wished he could warn the lad somehow. Then again, he was pretty sure The Pan understood the danger he was in. He was vigilant and well protected. He might, possibly, escape. But if Denarghi found out who he truly was, he would make certain of The Pan's fate. Best not to talk, the Professor decided.

"I'm glad you thought about that, Professor, I wouldn't want to have you gagged," said Denarghi. "Lock him up," he told the guards, "I want him and his friends in the securest possible custody, one to a cell. Shackle them to the wall, and put five guards on each one. Anyone unauthorised tries to get close, kill them, anything untoward happens, kill them." Then to the Professor he added, "That'll stop your snot-coloured allies. If they try anything, you'll die before they get near you. Take him away."

Gathering as much of his dignity as he could Professor N'Aversion calmly allowed himself to be led from the room.

Chapter 51

Having been dragged from his cell, Sir Robin stood before Lord Vernon maintaining a dignified silence. But Lord Vernon noticed, with satisfaction, that his prisoner's time in captivity had taken its toll. Or perhaps it was the execution of his son. Sir Robin was thinner, his eyes were sunken and his expression resigned. Clearly the Captain had been enthusiastic, if unsympathetic, in delousing the prisoner. The old man's hair hung damply about his head and he was shivering.

"You are cold."

"I am indeed. Your Captain was kind enough to hose me down but it seems the Palace is out of hot water."

"You are in prison, not a hotel." Lord Vernon reflected that Nimmists were annoyingly difficult to break. All the same, he suspected that Sir Robin was past caring rather than truly defiant. If he wasn't, he would be in a few minutes when Lord Vernon had demonstrated his victory.

"Very true, and there's nothing wrong with a bit of cold water, Lord Vernon. It's marvellously refreshing. You should try it."

Lord Vernon felt the muscles in his jaw tighten. Two minutes in and already he wanted to beat the irritating old goat to within an inch of his useless life.

"Nonetheless, it would be inconvenient if you caught a chill. Do not think I will let you die before you have served your purpose," said Lord Vernon. He clicked his fingers at the guard by the door. "You. A blanket, if you please."

The guard went out into the corridor and returned hastily with a checked rug which he flung clumsily about the old man's shoulders.

"Excellent, and now, Sir Robin, I will show you the extent of your defeat," said Lord Vernon.

He set the Importance Detector to take his own reading, pulled the lever and stood back gesturing to the spinning machine. Nothing happened at first and the two of them stood watching as it built up speed. Then the pointer climbed slowly up the dial to ten and stayed put. "You know what this means?" he asked.

"Yes," said Sir Robin quietly. Lord Vernon noticed, with exultation, that the energy, the vitality, had gone from his voice. It was as if that simple demonstration had switched off his life force. He hoped the old man wouldn't die on him … No, he was soundly vanquished but he would never give up hope.

"Good. Then you understand that I am the rightful Candidate. I am also the High Leader of Grongolia. The world is already mine, to use as I see fit but I would like to make things … official, here in K'Barth, as a gesture of goodwill."

"You seek only power, but I warn you it is greater than you are and not to be taken lightly."

So, the old fool knew what he wanted from this.

"Oh I will not take it lightly. I have read your holy books."

"Then you know that if you cannot control it, it will destroy you."

"Don't try to frighten me, you worthless old goat. This is about belief."

"Yes, it is."

"It is too late for your Candidate now. Oh I know there is one: some child who knows not who he is or what he is for. Perhaps you think he can stop me. If he tries, I will slay him."

Still Sir Robin kept silent but Lord Vernon could see that he was biting his tongue. He chuckled.

"You would like to say something, perhaps? To tell me I am wrong?"

"No, Lord Vernon, you are not wrong," said Sir Robin sadly.

"Excellent. Tell me, what happens at the installation? I have been … researching the order of service but I would like to hear it from you."

"It's very simple. First, I ask if anyone present knows of any reason why you should not be installed as Architrave."

"And this is the point when I despatch your boy?"

Sir Robin ignored the taunt but his voice was shaky when he continued.

"If no-one steps forward then, I lead you to the altar and your reading is taken with the confibrulator. We take five readings, which is why an anthem is usually sung. If your score is still high enough—"

"It will be."

"Then, the forty most senior Nimmists surround you and sing incantations as you are given the Ring of State." Sir Robin glanced at the ruby ring on Lord Vernon's hand, glittering against the black suede. "Regardless of whether or not you have already taken it, the ring must be removed, handed to me, and placed on your finger at the altar. You will then be handed the box, which only the rightful Candidate can open—"

"A cheap trick, Sir Robin, which poses no problem to me."

"Nonetheless, you must open the box and put on the ring," said Sir Robin calmly. "You must then lie face down in front of the altar while the forty elders surround you. You must lie with your arms out by your sides and I will stand on your back—"

"Why?" demanded Lord Vernon.

"If you are to be Architrave, the secular representative of The Prophet, you must show that you submit to his will. I am The Prophet's spiritual representative and so I'm afraid you must submit to me."

"We can dispense with this. I am to be Architrave and I already rule this nation. I will not submit to you."

"No, you're quite right, you won't. You will only make a token gesture to show that you submit to The Prophet."

"Which I do not, so I will make some other gesture."

"There is no other gesture. This is not about the personal enmity between me and you, it is about the offices we hold."

"There is no mention of this in the order of service or the eyewitness accounts."

"Of course not! The Candidate is surrounded by the forty most senior Nimmists at this point. No-one has ever seen enough to realise what happens. You will not be humiliating yourself and, providing you can find enough Nimmist elders to surround you, no-one will see."

Lord Vernon laughed. He knew what Sir Robin was trying to do. Doubtless, under K'Barthan law, this gesture would be legally binding. Except that Lord Vernon could rewrite any law in the world, any time he liked. Maybe Sir Robin hadn't thought of that.

"Perhaps you take me for a fool?"

"On the contrary, Lord Vernon. I do not. There is no trickery in this gesture but it lies at the heart of the installation ceremony and you omit it at your peril."

"I think you are trying to frighten me. You forget, I know the so-called secrets of Nimmism. I know that they are nothing more than science."

"That is true and if you know the science, you will know that it is powerful, and if you wish to control it fully you will understand the wisdom of taking the correct steps required to do so, as your predecessors have done."

'Your predecessors'; so Sir Robin knew he was beaten. Beaten or not, though, Lord Vernon did not relish the idea of grovelling to him, not even with irony. He decided he would have to look that up.

"We will leave this ... gesture for now. Once my obeisance, however it is done, has been made, what happens next?"

"Then I take your hand and raise you to your feet – this gesture is also symbolic and shows that The Prophet, or at least His representative on earth, is handing all power to you because he has found you worthy."

"That is all?"

"That is all."

"How quaint."

"I would warn you, Lord Vernon, this is not ordinary science. The ceremony is as it is for your safety and well-being."

"I appreciate your concern," said Lord Vernon sarcastically, "and now, until Saturday, I am done with you." He waited while the guard opened the door and called Captain Snow back in from the hall. "Captain, take him somewhere clean and make sure he comes to no harm. I want him healthy and alive for my installation on Saturday."

"Always assuming it is *your* installation, Lord Vernon," said Sir Robin.

"You really should learn when to give up. It will be my installation, Sir Robin. I am the High Leader of Grongolia and I already control the world in all but name. Once you have installed me as Architrave on Saturday a new order will begin. I will be Supreme Ruler of this entire planet."

"I wonder if you will. Pride comes before a fall, Lord Vernon."

Deluded crackpot.

"This is not pride, Sir Robin. It is the culmination of a meticulously conceived plan. Let your boy do his worst. When the time comes, I will look forward to despatching him once and for all. And you know that I will."

"I wouldn't be so confident if I were you."

Lord Vernon looked into Sir Robin's eyes and saw his fear.

"You say that, yet I see that you appreciate what will happen. You cannot hide your heart from me."

"I wouldn't try, Lord Vernon, and you are quite correct, I do have grave doubts – but then, I am a man of faith, so I am used to that; one simply cannot have a faith without doubt, whereas you are tending towards blind belief. I wonder which of us is the real fool."

"Is it faith or delusion, Sir Robin?"

"Only time will tell," said the old man calmly.

"Yes, and I assure you, it will. Until Saturday, Sir Robin."

After they had gone, Lord Vernon turned his attention back to the state papers on his desk. They didn't take him long to finish and when he was done, he boxed the pile and put it into his out tray. He was expecting General Moteurs in a little over an hour. There was just time to visit his bride-to-be.

Chapter 52

After General Moteurs had come to see her, Ruth had hoped he might find some way of protecting her from any further visits from her fiancé. However, as she sat at the table on the balcony and looked miserably out over the city, she heard the rattling of keys in the door. No polite knock, so she knew it wasn't the General.

She could not be on the balcony with Lord Vernon. Not after the panic-stricken moment back in London, a few nights previously, when she'd watched him throw The Pan off Nigel's. She went back inside, pulling the glass doors closed behind her. Lord Vernon strolled casually down the stairs into her room, putting his sunglasses into the pouch on his belt as he went. She stayed where she was, waiting.

"Good evening, my darling."

Yeh, until he turned up, it almost was, she thought.

"I have come to ..." he waved one hand while he tried to locate the right phrase, "spend a little time with my betrothed."

"Well that's very nice," she said, and yes, it seemed he was still completely impervious to irony. She turned away from him, thinking to head for the table and chairs, but he slid one arm around her waist and pulled her round to face him. She glared contemptuously up at him. "Let go of me."

He ignored her, pushing her backwards against the wall by the window and holding her there.

"Today you were magnificent," he said. He seemed to actually mean it.

"I did what I had to do. I gave you my word, so I kept it."

"Very honourable." He took her hand and looked down at the ring she wore, his ring, and kissed it. "For a human, and, I will concede, brave – especially after the way my demonstration reduced you to tears."

She tensed, holding her breath. Knowing she could not move backwards, she tried to inch sideways out of his grasp but he held her fast.

"I think not, my own one. After today, I believe you finally understand how completely and utterly helpless you are."

She was aware of the uneven surface of the plaster behind her, of Lord

Vernon's arm around her waist and of his presence: close, way too close, and blocking her escape.

"I'm not helpless. I score seven and a half; I have power, too."

"Against ten? Believe me, it won't help you. Your destiny, Ruth – the immutable 'will be' of your future – lies with me."

"How does that work? I'm still in love with The Pan of Hamgee."

"Oh. You can give your heart to whomever you like. I really don't care, because it will make no difference. You will still spend the rest of your life with me."

"Neither my destiny, nor I, will ever lie with you, Lord Vernon."

"Really …?"

He growled; the same deep bass rumble she'd heard before and she wondered, in her terror, if Grongles killed and ate other creatures or even people. No, stop. Those thoughts were not conducive to courageous behaviour and heaven knew she wanted to put on a brave face, even if the rest of her body, shaking like a jelly, was sorely letting her down.

"Don't try to frighten me."

"I don't have to try."

True. His mere presence was like a physical assault, wrapping cold tendrils around her body, sapping her strength. No, no, no. Don't think that. He was just a big, green bully and she wasn't going to buckle. She concentrated on telling herself that he needed her too much to full-on torture her, for a couple of days anyway.

He drew his knife and ran the tip of the blade gently down the side of her face, along her jaw, down her neck … she felt a slight tug at her shirt as he sliced off the first button …

"Soon we will be married; I own you, Ruth, and I will do as I please …" He leaned forward to kiss her on the mouth.

"Not yet, you don't and until you do, no you will not." She glared into his eyes, daring him to continue. "I am not your plaything, Lord Vernon."

"Oh but you are as I am about to show you … or are you going to use all that power you were boasting about to stop me?"

Slowly, without breaking eye contact, he put his nose close to her neck and inhaled deeply. He growled again and she could not suppress a shudder. His skin was warm against hers. She had almost expected it to be cold; like his heart. He forced her head back and she felt his mouth against her throat. His teeth closed over her skin, pinching slightly and letting go: a gentle bite, so full of sinister promise, it turned her blood to ice.

"Oh Ruth. So much spirit," he said softly. "Such a pity I must break it." He spun her round and threw her onto the table. As she scrabbled to stand up, he flung himself over her, pinning her arms above her head, knife still in hand. She kicked out with all the force she could muster but he was too close for her to do any meaningful damage. He forced her wrists together holding them easily with one hand despite her best efforts to free them. It was useless. He was twice her size and far stronger.

"I will not do this," she spat.

"Oh but you will. You have made your bed with me Ruth! And you will lie in it."

"No!"

"Yes," he snarled. With his free hand, he put the knife across her throat once more and increased the pressure. Ruth knew how sharp the blade was. She stopped struggling and lay very still, looking into his eyes with what she hoped was an expression of calm defiance.

"If you rape me, I will not endorse your candidature."

"If I wanted to rape you, *darling,* nothing – especially not you – would stand in my way."

"That's right. You can't risk it. That's my power. My words carry weight. If I speak, they'll believe me."

The rage in his eyes intensified and his nostrils flared as he breathed in. She felt the iron grip on her wrists tighten for a moment, then it loosened and his weight across her lessened. Slowly, without breaking eye contact, he took the blade away from her neck. He straightened up, half turned and then rounded on her, raising the knife high and stabbing it venomously into the tabletop next to her. His grey eyes locked with hers as he leant on it.

"You think you won't break. But trust me," their faces were almost touching, "I'm going to hurt you so very much."

"Not if you want me 'pristine'."

With an animal cry, he yanked the knife from the wood and toppled the table over, sending her backwards with it.

"You infernal witch!" he shouted as she sprawled on the floor. He turned and took a couple of paces away from her before wheeling round and throwing the knife at the wall, where it buried itself in the wooden panelling.

"I've had my fill of you," he snarled.

The grey eyes burned into hers, glowing with rage as she scrabbled backwards and got to her feet. He stepped over the broken table and slowly, giving her fear time to build, he bore down on her. She moved sideways, as well as backwards, towards the open floor – she would not get trapped against the wall a second time. He followed, breathing deeply, obviously struggling to rein in his emotions.

"I know how much you fear me," he hissed, "I can sense it and yet you resist me in everything." He stopped to control himself, "Ruth, Ruth," his voice was soft, almost gentle, underlining the pent-up violence in him. "Why? You are utterly defeated – I have total power over you. Why do you continue to fight?"

"Because I'm not defeated. Not until I give up. While I fight, I am merely losing."

She stood in the middle of the room with her arms hugged round her, waiting for him to go, but he started to move towards her again. She wanted to take an instinctive step back. No, no, no, she stopped herself. Her fear could not be hidden but fear wasn't the issue, it was how she coped with it that counted. She stood her ground and drew strength from this small act of courage. He stopped very close to her and she looked up into his face. She saw a flicker of something in the slate-coloured eyes. Was it compassion, she wondered. No. Not from him.

"You will not break me," she said.

He was very close now, towering over her, the venomous anger radiating from him like hot poison. He was trying to scare her, and succeeding, but still she stood her ground.

He held her gaze. The grey eyes burned into hers for a few moments longer and then, something else had his attention. He cocked his head, listening.

As if from far away she heard the sound of … what was that? Bells? No surely not. Ruth wondered if she were going mad. Not this early on, she hoped. But yes, it was bells; tinkly electronic ones. Lord Vernon turned and moved away from her, taking something from his belt as he went. His mobile phone. Oh it would be. He flipped open the case and frowned as he read the screen.

"Well, well, well … doesn't time fly when you are having fun?" He walked casually over to the wall and removed the knife, one-handed, with an effortless flick of the wrist. "It pains me to disappoint you, my darling, but according to my diary, my presence is now required elsewhere. We will have to continue this … lively debate later."

A few hours' grace. That was a relief, and at the end of them, if her luck was in, he might not be in the mood. Hmm, she could hope. He was holding his phone in one hand, typing with his thumb.

"I have scheduled us a little longer to enjoy ourselves next time." He snapped the case closed with a flourish and put it in his pocket. "I am sure you can't wait."

Once again she saw that flash of something in his eyes and this time she recognised it for what it was: a grudging respect.

"Plucky little Ruth. Always fighting. But you cannot control your fear forever. Soon it will overcome you and then, I assure you, you will do anything to please me."

"You really don't get this do you?" she said quietly. "The more I suffer at your hands without giving in, the stronger I become. After all the thousands of people you must have beaten and tortured, I'm amazed you could be so obtuse."

He turned abruptly away and strode to the door, which was opened as he reached it.

It closed with a slam. The keys and bolts jangled as it was locked behind him and Ruth was alone.

Chapter 53

By the time Lord Vernon had left the Chosen One and returned to his rooms, the General had been and gone. Having discovered his master absent, he'd left a message with the guards that he had some urgent business to attend to regarding security arrangements for the installation and that he would await Lord Vernon's summons. That was sensible and practical but annoying because Lord Vernon had wanted to find the General waiting for him. He did not issue a summons. He was too riled up to sit still and wait. Instead he descended the stairs to the floor below, strode to the door of General Moteurs' rooms and flung it open without knocking. A brace of flustered Imperial Guards who had tried to stop him staggered in his wake. General Moteurs was sitting at his desk, poring over the plans of the High Temple, by the looks of it. He stood and moved swiftly to meet Lord Vernon.

"Sir," said the General. It was plain that, not only had Lord Vernon taken him by surprise, but he could see the mood his master was in.

"Moteurs," Lord Vernon snarled as he squared up to him and jabbed a suede-clad finger at the General's chest. "Bring the Chosen One to heel."

"Sir."

Lord Vernon turned away from him and began to pace to and fro across the hearth rug.

"She tries me beyond endurance. Any more of her antics and I swear I will lose control. And I cannot be wed to a corpse." He stopped and faced the General. "Captain Snow has had his chance. I am placing her under your protection, and you," he extended his arm and pointed, "will make her cooperate. Fully. And I warn you, if I see no change in her attitude you will pay."

"Understood, sir." General Moteurs adjusted his collar. "If I am to carry out your orders, there is something I must know. This morning, at GNN, did she displease you?"

"No, Moteurs, she was exquisite," Lord Vernon grudgingly conceded. "She does my bidding well enough and I will credit you for that. But she needles me and fights me at every turn. I would reckon to break the strongest opponent in three days; I'd wager even you, General, were circumstances unfortunate enough to compel me, would be grovelling at my feet in five. But Ruth ... She fears me so. Her whole being is alive with it every time I draw near, but she refuses to cooperate. Why?"

"She is the Chosen One, perhaps—"

"She is no different from any other female," said Lord Vernon, "and females are straightforward enough; they give me what I want or I take it."

Again the pause while General Moteurs carefully selected his words.

"This situation is unusually complex, sir."

"Perhaps," said Lord Vernon. Maybe that was the problem. In many respects he had passed the point where he would take what he wanted from Ruth and the delay was certainly getting to him. But the moment was worth holding out for when, with all hope lost, she gave herself.

General Moteurs said nothing.

"She is in mortal dread of me. Yet still she stands her ground. I have never encountered such strength. It's as if she is unbreakable."

"Sir."

"It makes me very, very, angry."

"Sir." General Moteurs' expression remained neutral but Lord Vernon could sense his surprise at such an admission, tinged with fear at what it might lead to.

"Nothing must disrupt my concentration on affairs of state," Lord Vernon continued, "nothing." He paused to reflect. This had never happened before. His emotions were easily channelled into other things; but then he had never felt them with such force. "She affects me, General, more than she should: and that vexes me."

General Moteurs shifted slightly from one foot to the other.

"Sir." His voice cracked. He cleared his throat, "She will affect you. You are the Candidate and she is the Chosen One. From what I understand, it is the nature of it."

"And she resists me."

"As she will, sir. It is regrettable but she was deeply in love with another."

"So it appears. And now if anything happens to him she would rather die than acquiesce."

"Sir."

"He is still alive?"

"Yes, sir."

"Naturally, he clings to existence like excrement to a boot. Even so, perhaps I should take him into protective custody."

"I doubt she would appreciate that, sir."

"No. Nor a squad posted outside his door." Lord Vernon gave the matter some thought. "Yet he must be protected, perhaps a de-coloured bodyguard. Two."

"Sir, if you will permit it, there is something less obtrusive. There are K'Barthans we can use."

"Who?"

Again, General Moteurs swallowed. He was paler now and his impassive expression was acquiring a rigidity that belied the fearfulness beneath.

"I-I believe you know who, sir."

"Not the blonde from the laundry?"

"I'm afraid so, sir, and one of her Blurpon colleagues."

As he contained his anger, Lord Vernon came close to grinding his teeth. He had been thinking that, since the High Leader was no more, the blonde could be returned to him. How delicious that would have been, especially in light of the intense frustration he was enduring now. No. He resisted the considerable temptation to overrule General Moteurs. He had allowed his rage, and his desires, to sway him long enough.

"Do what you consider fit," he said.

"I will assign them at the first opportunity, sir."

"Good. You can guarantee that you have turned them, General?"

"Yes, sir. Completely."

"You'd better have."

"Sir, they are utterly loyal to me and since I am loyal to you ..."

"Then arrange it but when their work is done, my previous order stands. You will return the female to me."

"Yes, sir."

Lord Vernon returned to his rooms. It was a pity but his pleasure must wait.

"You'd better behave on Saturday, Chosen One," he snarled, but he would be Architrave by then, and it would be their wedding night. He would teach her who her master was, and when he was done with her, she would not be so rebellious.

Chapter 54

There seemed to be more and more customers in the Parrot and Screwdriver every night. It was packed and The Pan and Alan had their hands full serving, while Psycho Dave made sandwiches in the Holy of Holies or took it in turns with Lucy to collect the empty glasses and wash them up. Lucy had to keep nipping upstairs to check on Trev. She had spent the afternoon peroxiding his hair white blond and dyeing hers brown, while The Pan had been at a firm of lawyers, signing over the deeds of the pub to Doctor Dot.

Big Merv, having successfully changed colour, disappeared off shortly after Lord Vernon's broadcast to try and procure fake IDs for all of them. He still wasn't back.

There were a lot of new customers: strangers from out of town coming in for the installation. The hotels were doing a brisk trade. Anyone with a spare room was hiring it out, as was anyone with a spare bed, and even some who didn't were renting out floor space.

The crowds of unknowns made The Pan nervous. It's easy to observe someone if you hide in a crowd. He wondered if there were any Resistance agents in the pub; if not tonight then there would be tomorrow. Soon, they would find him. He knew he had protection, both from the Parrot and Screwdriver's regular customers and in the form of his friends but he was still jittery. Never mind, in a few minutes he could ring the bell for time. Then he only had to open the pub twice more before Saturday when—just the thought made him feel sick with nerves. One man and no plan versus Lord Vernon. Yes, well, he was pretty sure how that was going to go. Best not dwell on that.

"Pint please … pint please … hello?" Someone was waving their hands in front of his face. Ah yes, The Pan remembered, he was the barman and the punters would be starting to get their final drinks in soon, there was always a rush before last orders. This particular customer was a regular; Fred 'fingers' Davies, one of the best pickpockets in the city. He winked at The Pan and smiled.

"You alright lad?"

"Yeh, sorry Fred, I was miles away." Instinctively The Pan's good hand checked the pocket his wallet was in. Not that Fred ever brought his work to the Parrot. That was another useful side to Gladys and Ada's customer service policy. On the whole, if you let the dregs of society in, they went about their 'business' elsewhere.

"A pint of bitter please."

"How's tricks?" The Pan asked him as he pulled the handle.

"Booming. It's a shame we can't have an installation every year. A few months like this and I could afford to retire."

"Mmm, I'm not sure whether to be glad for you or sorry for your …" not victim, The Pan knew Fred used another word. Ah yes, that was it, 'pupils'. The Pan pulled the pump again. It made a gargling, farting noise and flatly refused to produce any beer.

Arse.

"The barrel's run out. D'you want something else or are you happy to wait while I get this one on again?"

Fred glanced nervously at his watch, or at least the watch he was wearing, The Pan doubted it was technically his.

"If there's time, I'll wait."

"I got that, son," said Psycho Dave, giving Fred a bit of a look for putting The Pan out.

"Thanks, while you're doing that, I'll just go syphon the python," said Fred.

As The Pan pulled a couple more pints his eyes lit on Norris. He and a large group of 'friends' had pushed two tables together in one corner. It looked like another tour. They'd bought a platter of cheese sandwiches and one round with pickle, which Norris had cut into tiny squares and passed round the assembled party. Never mind, they seemed to be recovering. Norris had left them to their own devices, by this time, except for one of them – some hulking great fellow with a leery expression and arms like girders – who was playing darts with him. The Pan didn't like the look of Norris' new friend and blessed the presence of Psycho Dave, even if he was downstairs. He wondered if he should have been firmer with Fred and told Psycho Dave not to bother. Still it would save a job later. He glanced at his watch, reached up and rang the bell.

"Last orders!" he shouted.

As the sound died away, the door of the pub opened and a new customer walked in. The usual scraping of chairs as the punters got to their feet and made to the bar 'to get the last one in' came to an abrupt halt, and while not physically possible for darts to stop in mid air, the one Norris had thrown made a sterling attempt. All conversation faded out as the new customer walked slowly into the room. Three paces and the lack of noise was so acute it was almost deafening, like anti-sound.

"Arnold's bogies ..." The Pan stared in amazement. Today of all days. In full ceremonial uniform, complete with sword. Did he have a death wish?

Perhaps not, the Resistance had also turned up. Two of them. The first was Lieutenant Arbuthnot, the shouty woman who had met The Pan and his fellow Mervinettes outside the Resistance HQ and escorted them inside, the second was a Blurpon. Except they seemed to be with General Moteurs. The Professor had mentioned Lieutenant Arbuthnot and a Blurpon called Snoofle working together. As The Pan watched them slip quietly into position either side of the door it was easy to see they were a team. Apart from The Pan, no-one else seemed to notice, being distracted by General Moteurs' appearance.

"Good evening," said the General. He turned slowly round in a circle, surveying the faces around him.

"Not for you it ain't. We don't want your kind in 'ere," said somebody. It was the gorilla who'd been playing darts with Norris.

"Oi!" The Pan pointed at him. "That's enough of that."

"What you doing here, snotface?" Gorilla Man stepped away from the dartboard and moved menacingly towards General Moteurs. He had friends: other customers, new ones, whom The Pan didn't recognise, and now they gravitated to his side. This was where Gladys and Ada would have called Their Trev.

"Excuse me, I'm talking to you," said The Pan a little more bullishly, but Gorilla Man's attention was focussed solely on General Moteurs.

"Cat got yer tongue, snotface? I asked you a question," he said.

"One I do not deign to answer," said General Moteurs calmly.

Please Arnold, let Psycho Dave hurry it up, thought The Pan. Things were going to get out of hand unless someone calmed it down and with a sinking heart The Pan realised that in situations such as this, that 'someone' was the publican.

"I said, that's enough," The Pan warned General Moteurs before turning his attention back to Norris' giant friend. "And you. What's your name?" he asked.

Gorilla Man finally acknowledged his presence, turning to glare at him and The Pan met his eyes with what he hoped was a calm, I'm-in-control-round-here expression.

"Nordle."

"Well, Nordle, I'm the publican and I say his money's as good as anyone else's."

"And I disagree. Anything he owns is bought with K'Barthan blood."

"I'm running this pub. Not you. I say who belongs here. If you don't like it, there are plenty of other places you can drink." Arnold's underpants, where was Psycho Dave when he needed him?

"I was here first. You better chuck him out, half pint," growled Nordle, squaring up to the Parrot's newest customer, who was a couple of inches shorter. "Coz if you don't I will," he looked around, "and I'd say I got me some help and all."

General Moteurs gave Nordle a glare of the kind of intensity that would not so much fry an egg as melt the entire cooker.

"Perhaps you'd like to try," he said quietly and he put his hands on his hips in a gesture that just happened to involve putting one of them on the hilt of his sword. Oh well, The Pan thought, at least it wasn't his laser pistol. General Moteurs was tense; lithe, coiled tense in the manner of somebody expecting to fight, but also confident, utterly confident, in the manner of someone who expected to win. There was silence. The air fizzed with tension.

The Pan checked the two Resistance agents by the door. Lieutenant Arbuthnot caught his eye, her hand hovering over a knife holster strapped to her leg. He shook his head. Someone broke the silence, thank The Prophet; it was Giant Hairy Ron.

"'S not good manners to dis the publican," he said and he stood up.

Slowly, chairs and stools were scraped back as, following Ron's lead the pub's regular punters got to their feet. The Pan would have been touched by their endorsement if he wasn't so busy being frightened, but there was an added dimension to his fear. The Architraves were nervous and through the fading blocking properties of the ring, he could feel it.

Giant Hairy Ron walked slowly over to General Moteurs and stood beside him looking threatening. Others joined them, fanning out in a line either side of the General, a couple of paces behind him.

Things were about to get ugly.

"No!" Remembering to use his good arm, The Pan vaulted over the bar and swiftly stood between Nordle and the General.

"If either of you starts anything, you're barred," he said, pointing at them in turn, "I mean that. Both of you." He looked past Nordle at the group of customers behind him, "and you lot as well." He turned to the regulars who'd allied themselves to the General, "Sit down, lads … and … thanks." The ring glittered on his hand and, as The Pan pointed, Nordle's eyes tracked the movements of the stone before flicking back up to his face. "Sit down Nordle … please."

"He's a Grongle."

"Yeh, he's a Grongle and he saved my life," Nordle looked in disbelief from General Moteurs to The Pan and back again, "twice."

"How come?"

"Because he's decent."

"But—"

"'Good' is no respecter of species."

"You reckon," said Nordle.

"I know. He saved my friend's life, too. He lent me a doctor."

Nordle glowered at The Pan.

"Did he give you that ring and all?"

"No. The ring's mine." As The Pan said this, he used his useful extra eyes to look the other way and watch the General's reaction. The inscrutable green face showed little but there was the faintest hint of something; pride was it, or, relief?

"You ought to know that, Nordle. You've been on Norris' tour. It may be ninety-nine per cent cock and bull but as the Prophet said, 'in every legend there is a grain of truth'."

The implication of The Pan's words made his guts contract. That was practically a public admission. With the extra eyes in the back of his head, he watched Deirdre and Snoofle, by the door, as well as the General. None of them reacted. The silence lengthened. Nordle seemed to be thinking. He didn't look as if he did much of that, so, in case he was out of practice, The Pan gave him time.

"Nordle," he said, concentrating on trying to channel his predecessors' authority. He made sure the ring was obvious as he pointed and the Architraves in his head were kind enough to help him out with a dash of The Voice, "Sit down." Nordle took a step backwards, which was clearly involuntary and in his own voice, The Pan added, "Please."

Mmm. That had told him.

Don't get cocky lad, said Five and The Pan smiled.

Nordle turned and went back to his game of darts, glaring at General Moteurs all the while, and his supporters went back to their seats. The Pan imagined himself giving the Architraves a high five.

"Thank you," he said, half to Nordle and his posse, and half to the Architraves. He realised the regulars were still standing.

"I said you too, girls and boys," he warned them, and with a mumbling and scraping of chairs they obeyed his request. "Thank you everyone. Norris," he pointed at him to accentuate the gravity of his words and sparks of reflected red light shot from the ring and flashed across the ceiling, "any more tours and you're banned for life." Norris had the good grace to look embarrassed.

"Sorry."

"Yeh you should be." The Pan took a deep breath. "Right. Nordle." At the oche Nordle turned, darts in hand. "Thank you for not starting a fight. As a sign of my appreciation have a drink on the house – same again or something else?" Nordle seemed to thaw a bit.

"Same again."

"Alright—"

"I got that," said a familiar voice. Big Merv was standing in the hall doorway with his leather outdoor coat on, one hand thrust deep into one pocket and beside him stood Lucy, with a tray of glasses. "You OK son?" The Pan felt his eyes widen; by The Prophet he hoped Big Merv didn't have Gladys' – or was it Ada's? – sawn-off shotgun stuffed down his coat.

"Yeh thanks Mer—Colin, I'm good. You can take your coat off," he said meaningfully and Big Merv winked.

"You sure about that son?"

The Pan turned back to General Moteurs who was standing straight, still and dignified in the middle of the room. It was strange how he seemed to be able to look so much larger and more imposing than his size should have allowed.

"General, it's almost closing time, so if you want a drink, you'd better order it fast."

He looked into the red eyes. They weren't giving much away. With a smile, a glance at the ring and a curt nod he said, "A beer. Three."

The Pan shot a brief glance at the door. Deirdre and Snoofle hadn't moved.

"They're with you?"

"Yes."

"They can have beer then, but I can't serve you. You'll keel over for hours and when you wake up, I'll have to remind you who you are."

"You do not trust me?" said the General.

"You know I do, but I've seen what alcohol does to Grongles. It'll knock you right out and you'll have the mother of all headaches when you—"

"I am a general and I command the Imperial Guard here in K'Barth," General Moteurs interrupted him. "I believe I am big and ugly enough to take responsibility for my own actions."

"Maybe, but you being a Grongle, it doesn't mean you will," said someone.

"Easy lads – and ladies," said The Pan, "this one does."

"I'll let that go for now," the General spoke to the whole room, "but be advised that if I was going to 'keel over for hours' as your renegade publican puts it, I would be wiser than to do so here. I wouldn't trust anyone in this rathole to tell me who I was when I came round," a hint of a smile when he turned to The Pan and added, "especially not you. And I wouldn't trust you, or any of these other reprobates, to leave anything worth stealing in my pockets, either."

The Pan laughed and it felt good.

"On your own head be it then, General. I need a mobile phone. I bet yours is worth having. Which beer?"

General Moteurs smiled, properly, and pointed to the pump for the most potent of Gladys' home-brewed efforts. "That one, if you please," he said. The Pan raised an eyebrow, "And, yes, I am perfectly sure," he added as The Pan took a breath to ask.

"Fair enough. M—Colin, would you like to do the honours?"

Big Merv went to the bar and pulled a pint of beer. Lucy followed him, disappearing into the Holy of Holies with the tray of glasses. She came back out again as if nothing untoward had happened. She was one cool customer, The Pan thought, as he took the General's money and the conventional route back behind the bar. He, and everyone else in the pub watched, with bated breath, as the Parrot and Screwdriver's newest customer took a large swig without any discernible effects.

"Your trick with alcohol only works a few times. After that, we begin to build up an immunity." The red eyes met The Pan's, still guarded but more relaxed now – or perhaps General Moteurs was less immune to the beer than he thought. A bit of both The Pan decided.

"You've obviously been working hard at it."

"Naturally, I am not one for half measures."

A joke? Possibly.

"So I notice," said The Pan. He looked over towards the door. "You two had better come and drink these."

They stayed where they were until General Moteurs turned and nodded.

Psycho Dave climbed out of the cellar and dusted himself down.

"Lorks, it's musty down there," he said and then looking around, "wossup? Has I missed something?"

Chapter 55

General Moteurs and the two Resistance agents sat at the bar sipping their beers.

"Come on everyone. Drink up. You too," he warned the General and the agents, "you might have come to see me but you can't be drinking after hours."

The Parrot and Screwdriver's customers took a long time to leave and The Pan guessed the main reason was because General Moteurs and his agents didn't. Finally, the last of the customers gone, The Pan locked the doors behind them, and his colleagues began to clear up. He didn't feel he could leave them to it again, not unless the General was short of time, which The Pan fully appreciated, he might be.

As he approached the three visitors at the bar to explain, Psycho Dave and Big Merv kept close to him.

"You summoned me," said General Moteurs and in the corner of The Pan's vision Big Merv and Psycho Dave's heads snapped sharply round to look at him.

"It wasn't exactly a summons," he said, "I hoped it was more of a hint." It had felt more like begging.

General Moteurs inclined his head.

"I am here on several counts. I have also brought some of my colleagues in the Underground to meet you. You will be working closely with them."

The Pan glanced from Lieutenant Arbuthnot, to the Blurpon, and back to General Moteurs.

"Will I?"

"Yes. You have already met Lieutenant Arbuthnot," General Moteurs continued smoothly. There was a rustle from beside The Pan as Big Merv folded his arms making his biceps bulge, or at least, bulge more, "and so has Big Merv."

Deirdre Arbuthnot stepped gracefully forward and held out her hand.

"Hi, Lieutenant," said The Pan. Once again the difficult conundrum arose as to which bits of Lieutenant Arbuthnot The Pan felt he could safely look at. Despite feeling heartily off women, Deirdre Arbuthnot was a bit of an exception. Pretty much all of her was guaranteed to turn any red-blooded – or formerly red-but-now-blue-blooded – male's thoughts in the wrong direction. However, The Pan noticed a change. Those ice blue eyes were easier to meet. They held a depth and a hint of softness which hadn't been there before. He felt the keen attention of General Moteurs on him and sensed that his reaction to Deirdre mattered to the General somehow.

"Deirdre, last time we met I was an arse."

"Agreed."

Oh make it easy why don't you? Something unaccountably drew his eye to the Blurpon and The Pan almost fell over when he winked and smiled encouragingly. That was a bit laid-back for a Blurpon.

"Mmm," said The Pan, half to the Blurpon, half to himself before returning his full attention to Deirdre. "The way I see it, if we want to work together, we have to get along. Shall we start again?"

Her perfect eyebrows arched in a look of cool surprise although the ice queen effect was tempered by the way her cheeks coloured slightly.

"I was … Yes … please."

Smecking Arnold, she said 'please'. It was The Pan's turn to be shocked.

"Right, then. Hello," the two of them shook hands, "and hello—"

"Snoofle," said the Blurpon, as he shook The Pan's hand.

"Snoofle, right. Make yourselves at home."

"I thank you for making us welcome," said General Moteurs.

"My pleasure," said The Pan. "So, let me introduce my friends. General, you have already met Lucy but Snoofle and Deirdre haven't."

His friend stepped forward.

"Good evening," said General Moteurs as he took her hand and bowed. Snoofle followed suit and Deirdre, who seemed uncharacteristically unsure of herself, saluted.

"Hi," said Lucy.

"Obviously, you've also met—"

"Big Merv," said Big Merv. "Alright General?"

"Good evening," said General Moteurs.

"Big Merv will be in charge after I'm—after Saturday."

Big Merv stepped forward and The Pan watched as he shook hands with Deirdre and Snoofle. Then, with expressions of carefully maintained neutrality, he and General Moteurs tried to crush the life out of each other's hands. Either it was a draw or each one had come out of it thinking he was the winner but when they were done, Big Merv clapped the General on the back.

"Arnold's trousers, you got a grip like a vice, pal."

General Moteurs winced as he massaged the hand Big Merv had shaken with the other.

"I thank you."

Big Merv shrugged. "Thanks for the pills an' all."

General Moteurs made a half bow.

"My pleasure. I am pleased – and grateful – to see you trust me enough to take them."

Big Merv laughed.

"You can thank the doc for that. She's some bird, your MO."

General Moteurs raised his eyebrows, "That is so," he said.

"Yer, course I was desperate an' all. I ain't gonna blend in au nat-relle am I?"

"This is Psycho Dave who is an excellent barman and a handy fellow to have about in a crisis, right Merv?" said The Pan.

"'S right."

Dave stepped up to shake hands with Snoofle and Deirdre and then he and General Moteurs dutifully repeated the big man hand-crushing ceremony – although it was definitely General Moteurs who won that one. Then Alan came over, and everyone was shaking hands and clapping each other on the back and saying hello.

"General, are you guys able to wait a while or are you in a hurry?" asked The Pan when they had finished.

"We will wait."

"Great, then, if you'd like to come with me …" The Pan started walking towards the snug and they followed him through the hall. "If you don't mind waiting here for a moment," he said as he opened the door. "I feel a bit of a crap boss leaving the lads again."

"And Lucy," said Deirdre. Snoofle laughed outright and even the corners of General Moteurs' eyes softened in a smile.

The Pan grinned, taking his cue from the General.

"Yes Lieutenant, and Lucy. Before I start on the clearing up, can I get you anything?"

"Not legally," said General Moteurs.

"Well, obviously, but would you like something?"

"Better not," said Snoofle wistfully.

"OK," The Pan conceded, "perhaps not alcohol. We tend to have cocoa and biscuits upstairs after we're done, but I could get you some cheese sandwiches."

General Moteurs shook his head.

"I may be able to drink beer but I have yet to master that pickle."

Chapter 56

The Pan was on post-closing washing-up duty so he headed into the Holy of Holies. There were already a few trays of glasses in there and someone, Alan, he presumed, had switched the commercial dishwasher on to heat up. He slipped his arm out of the sling and began to sort the glasses. It hurt more but it was easier. He put the tankards on the tray to go in the dishwasher, while he ran a sink full of soapy water for the others, the ones Ada referred to as 'the twiddly glasses' which never came out clean.

Tankards loaded, he pressed the starter button and the gurgling and rushing of the five-minute wash cycle began. Right, now for the washing up. His shoulder had twinged a little when he put the trays in the dishwasher but he could wash the other glasses, pain free, if he held the brush with his damaged arm. Psycho Dave had washed up after lunchtime opening. Where had he put the Marigolds? Just as The Pan was about to start cursing Psycho Dave for losing them, he remembered he'd used them rescuing Big Merv, Trev and Lucy and he hadn't replaced them. Oh well. He shrugged, rolled up his sleeves and put his hand, still wearing the ring worn by forty generations of Architraves, under the suds.

He was soon happily engaged in his task and didn't look up from the sink when someone came into the room, assuming it was Big Merv or one of the others, with another tray of glasses.

"Thanks. Stick them on the side, on the left by the door, I'll get to them in a minute."

He heard the sound of the tray being placed where he'd asked but when the visitor spoke it made him jump.

"Boy, you and I must talk," said the General, "before we meet the others."

"It's alright, I trust them," he said as he scrubbed vigorously at some smears of bright pink lipstick which stubbornly refused to budge from the lip of a wine glass. "I doubt there's anything I need to hear first."

"On the contrary."

There was something in the General's tone, something The Pan hadn't heard before: a resignation, a sadness. He wondered what could possibly be so bad that they had to speak about it privately first – apart from everything. He turned to face the General, drying his hands on his trousers.

"Help yourself," he said. General Moteurs glanced down at the ring with obvious disapproval. "I've run out of gloves."

"You could remove it."

"No, unfortunately I couldn't."

"You realise who you are?"

"Yeh, I know." The Pan put his hand in his pocket, took out the box and flipped it open with his thumb, "I'm the Candidate, Arnold help K'Barth. And I have seventy-six of my predecessors in my head who are pathologically unable to shut up. And the only way I can cut out their deafening yelling is if I wear this ring."

General Moteurs raised his eyebrows.

"Sir Robin warned me of this."

"It's not so bad."

"You have won them over?"

"Not exactly, they think I'm an idiot. But at least that makes them good judges of character." General Moteurs' poker demeanour cracked a tiny bit. "I am trying to win them round. I had a nice chat to one of them earlier, but for the moment, I use this," The Pan wiggled his finger and the ring flashed in the light.

"If you wish to survive, wear it on your other hand."

The Pan smiled.

"Actually, it seems to help as much as it hinders."

"Even so."

"Is that an order?"

"No," he hesitated, "I am not authorised to give you orders. I am at your command," he forced the statement out as if uttering it was physically painful.

"Well, well, well."

"You are the Candidate, and until you are Architrave, I defer to Sir Robin first and you second, naturally, in his absence."

"Is this the beer talking?"

General Moteurs smiled wryly.

"I sincerely regret it but no." The dishwasher beeped as it finished the first wash. With a glance at The Pan's shoulder he said, "Allow me."

"Did you get my message?" asked The Pan as General Moteurs opened the door of the dishwasher and was obscured, for a moment, by a cloud of steam.

"Clearly, since I am here."

"I meant the one about the contract."

"So did I." He lifted the glasses onto the work surface on the right and loaded the tray of dirty ones from the left-hand work surface that he'd brought with him, into the washer. It made a muted glassy jangle as he pushed the tray in and closed the door. The Pan realised he'd already removed the 'twiddly' ones. Talk about attention to detail.

"Seriously General, you shouldn't underestimate them."

"I do not." General Moteurs didn't sound remotely worried. "Lieutenant Arbuthnot is Strike Ops and I have sparred with her. I know what they are capable of."

"Aren't you even concerned?"

"Naturally," General Moteurs pressed the start button on the dishwasher, "but unless I can do so constructively, there is little to gain from indulging my fear." He was paraphrasing The Prophet. Not just The Prophet.

"My dad used to give me that exact same advice. Unfortunately, I have as much trouble following it now as I did then."

"I have grown accustomed to it. As the officer in charge of the Bank of Grongolia, I was a high-profile target for three years."

"Then you're a braver—well, yeh, that goes without saying."

General Moteurs smiled openly and picked up a clean glass and a tea towel.

"Where do I place these?" he asked.

"Oh just bung them on the side there, I'll put them away."

"Bung?"

"Yes."

General Moteurs tutted quietly but put the glass where The Pan indicated.

Big Merv appeared in the doorway and threw The Pan an 'everything OK?' glance. The Pan nodded.

"You got the clean bar mats, Defreville? There ain't none under the bar."

"Sorry, I forgot to get them out; they're in the drawer there," said The Pan as General Moteurs waited.

"Sweet." Big Merv shot another enquiring look at The Pan.

"You good here, son?"

"Yeh thanks," he said.

"Better than I am. Yer friend Snoofle's mucking in like a natural but I asked Mizz Arbuthnot to give us a hand sweeping up and she practically knocked my block off. She ain't half chippy about being a bird." He eyed General Moteurs. "Still, I s'pose I can give 'er some slack."

"She means well."

"Yer. I get that," said Big Merv and he ducked back into the bar beyond.

"Officially, I am here on my master's business: to check if you are still alive."

"As you can see ..." The Pan did the one-armed man version of holding his hands out sideways here-I-am style. "Sorry to disappoint him."

"Doubtless you realise you are also a target."

"Yeh, but I've a fair number of people looking out for me now."

"Nonetheless, that is why I have brought Lieutenant Arbuthnot and Group Leader Snoofle. They will be your protection."

"I won't need them, but they're welcome to stay."

"Good. Lord Vernon ordered me to assign you bodyguards."

Whoa, whoa, whoa!

"Lord Vernon? Who did *this* to me," The Pan gestured to his shoulder, "and set me up for a lynching?"

"The same."

"Why?"

General Moteurs put the glass he was drying down on the work surface and turned to face The Pan. He seemed to be taller and more forceful as if he was trying to accentuate the gravity of this moment. The Pan met his eyes and was surprised at what he saw: pain, sadness, a little frustration, perhaps, and anger, but none of it aimed at him.

"He has no choice."

"What do you mean?" asked The Pan, maintaining eye contact. It seemed to be making General Moteurs slightly uncomfortable.

"Exactly what I say," said General Moteurs.

The seconds passed. If anything, General Moteurs' emotional discomfort had intensified, but at the same time, he seemed to be waiting. The Pan understood that the General was giving him time to think, in the exact same way he'd given time to Nordle, earlier. Unlike Nordle, however, the penny wasn't dropping.

"Could you … give me a clue?" he asked.

The dishwasher beeped to signal the end of its cycle. They both ignored it. General Moteurs sighed and ran one hand over the top of his short brown hair and down to massage the back of his neck.

"You are so young, and Sir Robin does not understand. You lack the self-confidence to see what is clear to the rest of us."

"Yes, I'm young and I'm also not too bright, so if there's something I need to know you're going to have to tell me."

"Did you wonder how you came to be freed?"

"I thought you arranged that, especially when I got here."

"Even after Lord Vernon signed your death warrant?"

"Yeh. I thought you must have stepped in, like you did when he nearly strangled me, and saved my life."

"It is true that I would have done but, she did not give me the chance."

There was a long, long pause.

"Who?"

"Ruth."

"Wait, I'm not sure. I'm—"

"She bought you." The General spoke with quiet, bitter anger.

The Pan's stomach turned over. 'It's a straight swap.' That's what Lucy had been going to say. He felt sick and it was hard to speak. "She … what?" he croaked.

"You heard me."

"But why? She knows I would never ask nor want this of her."

"Because she loves you."

"But she told me she loved Lord Vernon."

"No. You listened to your fears at the expense of her actual words. As I understand it, she said she loved the Candidate and that would be you, I believe."

"But she—" The Pan's voice broke.

"You thought she did not know?"

Miserably, he nodded.

"Then you underestimated her."

The Pan hung his head.

"She understands the convention of your nation: that the Candidate must realise who he is for himself. Even if she were to flout that convention, as you admit yourself, you would never have agreed to her actions. You would have been executed, and K'Barth would be without hope."

"No," whispered The Pan, "smecking Arnold no." The world seemed to slide away from him, his legs felt wobbly, as if they might give way, but worse, he feared he would cry.

"It was better she made the sacrifice without your knowing, not that she would have had an opportunity to tell you. Lord Vernon was watching her every move from the adjoining interrogation room."

The Pan turned his back on the General, clinging onto the side of the sink for support. "Why am I such a stupid, pathetic, moron-headed fool?"

"You are young. It is hard to place your confidence in others if you have none in yourself."

"Arnold's sweaty smecking ..." A tear ran down The Pan's face and dripped into the lemon-scented suds. He thought about the enormity of what Ruth had done. For him. In his mind's eye he saw her, frightened and unwilling, as Lord Vernon forced himself upon her. It made him feel sick and though he fought back the urge to gag, he couldn't suppress a hiccup.

"If you are going to vomit," said General Moteurs, "may I humbly suggest you take the glasses out of the sink."

Despite the situation, The Pan laughed. Wiping his eyes on his sleeve, he turned round.

"What am I going to do? I can't save her."

"She understands that."

"She must be crazy."

"She is in love with you; naturally she is crazy."

They were silent for a moment.

"I have to see her."

"I cannot allow that."

"No. This is not optional."

"I still cannot allow it."

"For the love of The Prophet, General, you must get me in there."

"No, I will not."

The Pan felt the gravelly weight of his predecessors in his words when he said, "Yes, you will."

There was a flash of anger in the red eyes.

"You would try to intimidate me, boy?"

"I'll give it a go—I'm the Candidate—"

"Maybe, but you cannot see her because I cannot achieve the impossible."

The Pan locked eyes with him.

"You can and you will and that's a smecking order."

General Moteurs merely smiled sadly and shook his head.

"By the Creator, she's lit a fire in you. Alas, I regret, I cannot comply. Sir Robin gave me orders covering this situation and they are very clear. You will not see her."

"Listen General, since I must die on Saturday, let me go to my death in peace. I love her and I can't leave her thinking that I'm angry with her, or that I hate her. She has to understand that I know what she did, that I'm grateful and," his voice caught, "I have to say goodbye."

General Moteurs cast his eyes down. His resolution was wavering, The Pan could see it.

"Arnold, General, I'm begging you. I'm a doomed man, and this is my dying wish."

The General put his hands on his hips. He heaved a heavy sigh and his shoulders sagged, but still he didn't relent.

"I will give it some thought," he said. A 'no' put tactfully.

Big Merv appeared in the doorway with another tray of glasses.

"C'mon Defreville you big girl, we ain't got all night," he said. "Last one 'ere," he put a tray of glasses on the stainless steel worktop, "and the rest of it's done." He stopped as he picked up the atmosphere, "Wossup?" He shot a suspicious glance at General Moteurs.

"Ruth," said The Pan.

"I'm sorry mate, it ain't easy, a broken heart. You alright with the General, here, or d'you wanna talk to Uncle Merv?"

The Pan couldn't help but smile. He glanced at the General and back at his friend.

"Maybe, in a while. First I need to apologise to Lucy."

"Yer?"

"Yeh. She was right."

Big Merv sucked the air in through his teeth. "An' I'm guessing that hurts."

"Yeh. Just a tad," said The Pan, "but moping isn't going to help. Come on, I'll do this tomorrow. Time to make a plan, a real one, for Saturday and for afterwards."

"You want me to round 'em up?"

"Yeh, please."

"Sitting room?"

"Yeh. Thanks."

Big Merv went back out into the bar.

"In any conflict the hardest casualties to bear are those who fall in the last hours," said General Moteurs. Though his expression was rigidly impassive The Pan could almost feel his pain. He didn't like his orders.

"Is that your view or are you quoting The Prophet?"

"Commander Thistwith-Mee."

"He was K'Barthan."

"His nationality is immaterial, he was a fine being and a great commander."

"Yeh. Listen, I know you and Sir Robin don't see eye-to-eye."

"Then you learned something from your eavesdropping."

"Perhaps. If it were up to you?"

"That is not a line of enquiry we will pursue."

Very firm. The Pan remembered the conversation he had overheard; Sir Robin had accused General Moteurs of having a soft heart. Without orders from Sir Robin, The Pan was certain the General would have taken him to Ruth. Perhaps he still might.

"Alright. General ... thank you for telling me. It's killing me, but at least I know and however hard it is to take, I'd rather know the truth every time than live with a comfortable lie. If you see her again, will you tell her I love her and that I am grateful and that—"

General Moteurs put one hand on his good shoulder and squeezed it gently.

"I will make it my business."

"Thanks."

With a final half pat, half squeeze, General Moteurs took his hand away and gestured to the door.

"The others will be waiting."

Chapter 57

The Underground, such as it was, gathered in the sitting room in Gladys and Ada's flat, above the Parrot and Screwdriver. Trev had joined them, lying on the sofa with a blanket over him. The Pan gave the seat of honour to General Moteurs and it was only when they were all comfortable that he realised the General was waiting for him to speak first.

"Right then everyone. We all know Sir Robin's plan."

"Yer, we get it," said Big Merv.

"OK, look, I've been doing a lot of thinking."

"Keep practising," said Trev from the sofa.

"Yeh, yeh, and it might become a habit," The Pan laughed weakly. "What I mean is, I think we should change the plan."

"Go on," said General Moteurs.

"Sir Robin was taking into account what he thought Lord Vernon would do and I'm not sure he's got it right."

"He has not. You are smarter than you look, boy."

"Thanks. Before I guess, has he actually told you what he's going to do?"

"No, but it is plain enough to see. He speaks of a new state, of stripping all K'Barthans of their rights, of making them slaves. He may well do so for a while, but long term, I believe he intends to sanitise K'Barth."

"I'll guess he ain't talkin' about fixing the plumbing," said Big Merv.

"No. He believes he can cleanse K'Barth of its entire non-Grongle population in less than four months, six at the outside. I'll wager he will be surprised at the strength of the resistance he encounters but if he declassifies portals and they are made standard army issue, then even I do not expect it to take more than a year."

"Totally?" asked The Pan.

"Completely," said the General.

"Smeck. It's worse than I thought. He needs us as slaves, though, right? Someone has to do the crappy jobs you lot won't all do?"

"Naturally, but he has access to another reality, where every sentient being is physiologically the same. The equipment required could be standardised, which would make it cheaper to produce and the differences in output between the genera, which currently blights the efficient use of forced labour, would be eradicated. Working and organising the slaves would be effortless, compared to the way it is now." As he spoke, General Moteurs' voice was hard with anger at what he was saying. "Furthermore, these alternative humans are technologically retarded and can be easily crushed. Unlike K'Barthans. You are merely the victims of economics.

"This world will become the Pure World; the apogee of Grongolian excellence and the source of Grongolian dominance from which all other realities will be subjugated."

There was a long appalled silence in the room.

Smeck.

"I guess I did ask," said The Pan.

"Yes," said the General bitterly, "you did."

"Yeh, and that's my point," said The Pan. His plan, so far, had revolved around sacrificing himself and leaving his friends and his successor to finish the job. It was probably a bit cowardly, getting topped and leaving everyone else to do the donkey work, and not the K'Barthan way. Except that The Pan was pretty sure that it had been Sir Robin's plan and – judging by his own skill set – that of fate, or Arnold, or whatever other random factor had picked him as Candidate.

"So this is our last stand. All or nothing," he said quietly.

"Yes," said General Moteurs.

"We're not really playing to my strengths here are we?"

"Or perhaps you are braver than you know."

"No General, trust me, I'm really, really scared."

"It don't ever stop you," said Psycho Dave.

"Yer," Big Merv agreed, "'s pukka balls that is." He glanced round the room for confirmation, "Right?"

Psycho Dave, Alan, Lucy and even Snoofle and Deirdre nodded.

"Well, thank you very much," said The Pan. "Seriously though, none of you have to do this."

"No, we do," said Alan.

"Exactly. Count me in," said Lucy.

"But you don't and Lucy, you're not even K'Barthan."

"No but my world's up next and nobody gets their hands on my easily crushed, technologically retarded brethren without a fight." She shot General Moteurs a defiant look and to The Pan's amazement, he smiled.

"If the others are like you and Ruth, that you will fight is understood," he said.

"Alright," said The Pan. "So I'll be up by the High Altar, telling Lord Vernon he's a sham. After he blows my brains out, what comes next?"

"He ain't gonna get that far you giant puff! We're gonna arrest him."

"*I* arrest him," said General Moteurs firmly.

"You and whose army?" asked Alan.

"Yer, we needs an army," said Psycho Dave.

"You have one," said General Moteurs.

"Sadly we don't, the Resistance aren't on board. Not officially. Professor N'Aversion and Simon are bringing two of their colleagues to see me tomorrow but they're all acting independently of their leader."

"Agreed. Unless Denarghi is deposed in the next twenty-four hours, it will be impossible."

"He might be," said Dave hopefully.

"It's unlikely," said Snoofle, who was leaning against the wall over by the curtains.

"Stranger things have happened," said Alan.

The voice of General Moteurs, sounding pained, cut through them, "I was not asking a question, I was making a statement. You *have* an army. The Imperial Guard. The entire Imperial Guard presence in K'Barth is under me and I am loyal to you," he said.

Whoa.

"The—You're—Run that by me again," said The Pan.

"I am their commander," said the General as if explaining it to an idiot. "Is it such a surprise that they are loyal to me?"

"Thinking about the ones I've met, I suppose not."

"I am in charge of security at the installation. I will ensure that you are heard." He opened the pouch on his belt and took out a folded lump of paper. It was bulky, like a book, a large sheet folded several times. "I have something for you," he held it out, "the plans of the Temple."

"Thanks," said The Pan.

"Not you, you know what you must do. This is for your second in command."

When Big Merv glanced over at him The Pan raised a 'go-on-then' eyebrow. Big Merv got up and took the plans from the General's hand.

"Sweet," he said, his antennae moving slowly backwards and forwards as he unfolded the paper. He put it on the coffee table, his antennae continuing to move around as he concentrated on the schematics before him. Trev sat up a little and the others gathered closer.

"The Imperial Guard can secure the High Temple but it cannot hold it without help. Not if we are to take and hold the Palace and other key areas of the city. We have allies among the Grongles in the army but we will be spread thinly."

"But once everything kicks off, surely K'Barthans will join you."

"Not necessarily. They may assume it is Grongles fighting among themselves."

"Then someone needs to tell them. And what about the temple precinct? Surely there'll be a big crowd outside and I'm guessing there'll come a point when that crowd is going to get restless."

"Restless? There's going to be a smeckin' uprising! I mean … probably," said Alan. He hadn't meant to say that, The Pan suspected.

"If there is, I need people out there to take charge when it starts and make sure it succeeds. If I have to die, I'd like to get a result."

"You would benefit from some self-belief," said the General dourly.

"I'd say I'm being realistic. I'm very unlikely to survive, we all know that, but I'll take dying, if it means the rest of you can get rid of Lord Vernon."

"So you wants to get the word out?" asked Psycho Dave. Something in his voice, the tiniest hint of self-satisfaction suggested, to The Pan, that he and Alan might have already acted on their own initiative and made a start. It looked as if Big Merv had spotted it, too.

"'S no problem. I reckon we got that covered," he said with a meaningful expression. Alan and Psycho nodded. The three of them weren't saying much but a whole world was being said. The Pan brought the discussion back on track.

"General, we know the Imperial Guard are with us but what about the army? If some of them are on our side, how can we tell?"

"All forces loyal to the Candidate will wear an armband."

"What colour?" asked Lucy.

"Light blue," said Alan.

"Yer, yellow isn't so subtle see? And blue is the colour of his cloak, the lining, anyway," said Trev jerking his thumb at The Pan for emphasis. Blimey, it looked as if he was in on it as well. Those four were definitely cooking up something, Lucy as well, no doubt. It made The Pan proud and comforted, that his friends should look out for him.

"Alright, that makes sense," he said. "Can you do light blue?" he asked the General.

"Yes. Inside the High Temple, there is a key objective which has to be neutralised. This is where I will need your assistance. It is essential that K'Barthans, beyond the Candidate himself, are involved in this, working alongside us. Lieutenant, please explain to them."

Deirdre moved forward.

"Lord Vernon has insisted that Captain Snow and a detachment of troops be stationed in the upper galleries, which are here along the north side, marked in red." The paper crackled as she ran her finger along it. "For any plan to succeed, he and they must be overpowered.

"I propose Snoofle and I lead the attack," said Deirdre. "We both have a score to settle with Captain Snow."

"Too right. He used a control stick on me. He has some serious payback owing," said Snoofle, from his station by the window, surveying the street through the gap in the side of the curtains.

"You're gonna have to wait your turn, sweets." Deirdre made as if to protest at being called 'sweets' The Pan noticed, but appeared to think better of it. "You too, shortsock." A hush descended as everyone in the room realised that Big Merv had just called a Blurpon short.

"What?" said Snoofle. Everyone held their breath.

"I said are you in?"

"Yes," said Snoofle, "sorry, I didn't mean to be distracted."

"The temple is portal proof but it is easy enough for me to get you inside," said General Moteurs. "Captain Snow will be here." He pointed to the spot on the plans. "He will have ensured that there is no access from below. I will have guards, standing by, at your command. Your objective will be to get up to the gallery, without being heard or seen and overcome the Captain and his forces."

"How're we gonna get in if it's portal proof?"

General Moteurs turned to The Pan.

"When do you intend to show your hand?"

"In the actual marriage," The Pan's voice wobbled, he found the word 'marriage' hard to say knowing how much Ruth loved him. "When they ask if anyone objects. He'll be more relaxed that way, there's a chance I might catch him on the hop."

The General nodded.

"An intelligent choice. The marriage ceremony is due to start at fourteen hundred hours ..." General Moteurs took his mobile phone from his belt and tapped the screen a few times. "Taking the order of service as it is currently, that would be at fourteen thirteen precisely, therefore, the rest of you must be in position by that time.

"There is an added complication. Lord Vernon may trust me but he will have contingency plans in place. Matters may change at a moment's notice. However, you must make your way round to the north side of the temple, where the priests' and temple officers' quarters were. The High Priest's house is currently being used by one of Grongolia's foremost couturiers. He is one of ours. Go in and tell them I have sent you about the uniform he is designing for Lord Vernon's new World Security Force. He will take you out to the High Priest's garden, where there is a door into what was the High Priest's robing room. There will be a deputation of Imperial Guards there guarding that exit, and there will be more Imperial Guards in the garden of the priests' and temple officers' quarters over the wall. They are all loyal to me, and as such will provide any assistance required."

"They gonna let us in?" asked Big Merv.

"You can't go, Merv," said The Pan and the others turned sharply to look at him. "You neither, Lucy. You're in command after I'm gone and the two of you are officially dead, which is a good place to be if you, and Trev when his leg's better, want to run the Underground unmolested. And if we fail tomorrow, you three, Alan, Dave and Doctor Dot will be the only ones left."

"So who's gonna take down Captain snotface Snow?" growled Big Merv. "Coz I wanna piece of that."

"Deirdre and Snoofle and some of the General's Imperial Guards."

"As you wish," the General said. Big Merv didn't look too happy but said nothing. "However, you may prefer to hear your options before choosing your team. I have identified three weaknesses. The main stairs to the gallery will be heavily guarded and the door locked. You cannot take it without disrupting the ceremony, giving Captain Snow longer to enjoy his advantage.

"Therefore, your first option is to gain access to the gallery through a maintenance duct in the side of the collection of organ pipes at the Great Door end. All the anterooms along the North Side are interlinked. I will ensure the connecting doors are unlocked so you can move through them, from the robing room to the Great Door end, without detection. I have marked this route in green. The hatch you will come out of is at the opposite end of the gallery to where Captain Snow will be waiting, with ten of his troops. If you time your arrival to coincide with The Pan's first move, their attention will be elsewhere."

"That sounds like a plan," said The Pan.

"There is a caveat. It is not spacious. Snoofle will need to convince a group of fellow Blurpons, and/or Spiffles. Any other being would be hard pressed to fit."

"Why can't we use a portal once we're inside?" asked Deirdre, "Snoofle and I have visited the gallery with you."

"It makes too much noise," said The Pan. "They might hear you arriving and they'll know what it is too."

"The area is being used for storage," said Snoofle, who was still at the window, watching the street. "There is cover enough and I will find a team."

"Right," said The Pan, "what's option two?"

"The second option is to climb up the outside of the building to this flying buttress here," he pointed to the map. "This is where the roof is accessed, from the gallery. There is a door in the wall, here," again he pointed, "I have marked this route in red. If he anticipates an attack from this quarter Captain Snow will be able to lay an ambush, for you. However I believe it likely he will concentrate his efforts on the stairs."

"Alright, tricky but promising I'd say. What's the third option?" asked The Pan.

"Before my less enlightened brethren closed the Priests' School, the gallery was used for teaching. It was warmed by open fires, one at each end. You may scale the building, using the same route but when you reach the top, take the stairs to the roof and come down the chimney. I have marked that route in blue."

"I reckon we gotta use the anterooms, and come outta the organ," said Big Merv, "an' I reckon I gotta go. If I ain't too big, with Deirdre and Snoofle 'ere, Dave and Alan."

"We need individuals who are combat trained," said Deirdre.

Big Merv snorted.

"They bleedin' are, sweets. This is about havin' a pagga and comin' up alive. You come up from the streets like we done you're gonna know that better 'an anybody."

"You can't go, Merv, I told you," said The Pan.

"No-one's gonna recognise me. I ain't orange no more an' I'm dead."

"Yeh, officially, but I think that even though you are a lot less orange, your presence will be a fairly convincing argument to the contrary – if you decide to own up to your name I think they'll believe it."

"Then it looks like Alan, Dave and I are gonna be in the precinct."

"And me," said Lucy.

"Things might get hot," Big Merv warned her.

"So?" She shot him a warning glance.

"Alright," said The Pan, "you too, Lucy."

"I reckon you gotta attack from both sides though," said Big Merv, "have Snoofle take the organ ducts an' Deirdre go up the side with the guards," he turned to the General, "if you got any blokes what can climb."

"I have."

"What about the chimney?" asked The Pan.

"Nah, that's your reserve. You gotta have some backup, in case something unexpected goes down."

"He's right," said Alan. "Two of your options are reliant on one place of entry. If that goes wrong, so long as you can climb up the building, you can get to the chimney, right? So that's your reserve, right there."

"Listen to your friend. Even if he suspects nothing, my master will have contingency plans in place."

"He must know about the chimney, though. What if he has plans for that, too?"

"We must hope he does not," said Deirdre.

"Thinking about it, how am I going to get in?" asked The Pan.

"You have a ticket. My master wishes that you see Ruth wed to another." General Moteurs opened the pouch on his belt again and took out an envelope with The Pan's name written on it in squirly calligraphic handwriting. He held it out. It bore Lord Vernon's personal seal, gold embossed.

"Thank you," said The Pan.

"My pleasure. You will wait here on Saturday. I will send a snurd to collect you."

"If you insist."

"I do."

"Right then, I think we have a plan. Does anyone have any questions?"

The Pan ensured he made eye contact with each of his friends in turn. Snoofle still seemed preoccupied with the view outside the window.

"I'm taking that as a no."

"Good," said General Moteurs, "then we will synchronise watches." He glanced at his watch. "It is now zero one zero seven hours and fifteen seconds."

Everyone checked their watches and fiddled with them for a moment or two.

"Alright, a second check," said The Pan, "the time I have now is one ten a.m. and … thirty-two seconds, right?"

"'S right," said Big Merv.

"Me too," said Lucy and General Moteurs nodded.

"I must leave you. I doubt we will meet tomorrow. I will be in Grongolia attending the previous High Leader's funeral followed by a state dinner to celebrate Lord Vernon's inauguration as his replacement."

"Right," said The Pan, thinking for a moment, "is Ruth going to that?"

"No. In Grongolia it is considered unlucky for a bridegroom to see his bride the day before the wedding."

"He doesn't buy that does he?" asked Alan.

"Amazingly, he does and should his belief falter, my colleagues in Grongolia and I have taken steps, for her sake, to ensure that he will stay there until early Saturday morning. Gentlemen, ladies …" General Moteurs clicked his heels and bowed low. The Pan couldn't help noticing the way his eyes turned to Deirdre and hers to him. "Lieutenant, Snoofle, look after them."

"Sir," said Snoofle.

"I'll give you a lift back," said The Pan.

"I think not. K'Barthans out after dark are considered suspect. You will stay here."

"What about you out after dark?"

"I believe I can take care of myself."

"Maybe but—"

"I do not require a lift. Thank you."

"Is that an order?"

The General's stern expression cracked a fraction.

"Yes, you boneheaded boy, it is."

The Pan was disappointed. He'd intended to use the journey time persuading General Moteurs to let him see Ruth. Perhaps the General realised that.

"Alright then," he said, "I'll show you out."

Chapter 58

When The Pan took General Moteurs downstairs, Deirdre felt a pang of loneliness. It reminded her of the day her parents had left her at boarding school for the first time. She was very glad of the presence of Snoofle. It was clear that The Pan of Hamgee bore her no ill will. If anything, he was a bit scared of her, she thought, but she still felt embarrassed, about the way she had treated him, or perhaps, who she had been. She was also wary of Big Merv. There was an uncompromising directness in those green eyes. She would have to earn his respect and was unsure where to begin.

She wished she felt less awkward. A few days with General Moteurs and the world was a different place, more complex, and harder to understand, but also richer and subtler than it had been before. She looked around her. Lucy and Psycho Dave had helped Trev to his feet and together the three of them were heading slowly towards the door. With an injury like that, and the pain he must be in, he would need a lot of sleep. She was impressed he'd managed to attend the meeting. Big Merv and Alan were poring over the drawings of the temple. She needed to break the ice and had sort of expected Snoofle to. But he was still over by the window, looking carefully through the gap between the side of the drawn curtains and the wall. He seemed to be uneasy, his whiskers almost vibrating with the tension.

"Snoofle?"

He was holding his night vision goggles up to his eyes with one hand. He took them off and handed them to her.

"Deirdre, I think we've got company. In fact, I'll eat Simon's hat if that's not Group Leader Frosby over there."

"Where?" asked Deirdre as she moved swiftly over to his side. The other two looked up.

"Behind the chimney stack across the street," said Snoofle. Big Merv and Alan stood up. "Careful lads, stay where you are. I'm not sure how thick these curtains are or how much they can see. We don't want to advertise the fact we're onto them. Lieutenant, I'm sure you know not to move the curtain."

Deirdre looked where Snoofle indicated and waited. She could see movement behind the chimney stack and sure enough after a few minutes she saw a familiar figure slip quietly out of the shadows and move across the gap between two chimneys. What the hell was she doing there?

"Who's Group Leader Frosby?" asked Alan.

"She is a colleague in Strike Ops," said Deirdre.

"An assassin?"

"Yes."

"If she comes near the lad it'll be the worse for 'er," said Big Merv.

"I do not believe she is following The Pan of Hamgee," said Deirdre. "It is Denarghi's wish that The Pan stand trial. And you also."

"Yeh, he wouldn't usually send Strike Ops to take someone alive. That would be Military Ops," explained Snoofle.

"Maybe the little scrote's changed his mind."

"I don't think so," said Snoofle.

"I can go take a look. If I slip out up the fire escape—" began Alan.

"The whole district's gonna hear you," said Big Merv, not unkindly, "AND … yer man there—"

"Snoofle."

"Snoofle, thanks son, asked us to stay put. Still, any chance of a dekko?"

"In a minute."

"She is not alone, there are two more of them," said Deirdre, trying to hide the concern in her voice, "and there will be others. We work in teams."

"This don't sound good. How many?" asked Big Merv.

"However many the target warrants. Three, five; on a difficult mission, seven, but if three of them are so close together there will be more."

"An' you reckon they ain't after me an' Defreville."

"No," said Deirdre, trying to keep the concern from her voice.

"We'll know soon enough," said Snoofle.

Downstairs the door slammed and Deirdre heard the sound of a key turning and bolts being shot home.

Across the street, in the shadows made visible by her own night vision goggles, Deirdre watched as Frosby stood, crouched low enough to be invisible from the ground but not from second floor level. The assassin motioned to unseen others, a signal to move along the street and Deirdre saw them begin to head off. They went along the rooftop, just long enough for her to see which way they were going, before they ducked out of sight. Her heart sank. She knew exactly who they'd come for.

"They're moving away," said Snoofle for the benefit of Alan and Big Merv.

"Good," said Alan.

"I ain't so sure," said Big Merv.

The Pan of Hamgee appeared in the doorway.

"What's up?" he asked.

"Looks like the General's got company," said Big Merv and with a nod to Deirdre added. "Tell 'em, treacle."

Deirdre bit back a request that he not call her 'treacle' and repeated:

"They're my colleagues, from Strike Ops. Assassins."

"Out there?"

"Not anymore," said Snoofle, "they're following him."

"Then he's going to need a hand," said The Pan.

Big Merv stood up.

"I'll get the sawn-off."

"No!" said Deirdre with such force that Alan jumped. "I trained Frosby. Two weeks ago we were sparring, as friends. They are my agents and they are loyal to me. Let me go. I will talk to them. I may be able to persuade them and … I know which way the General will go."

The Pan of Hamgee looked straight into her eyes, which unmanned her totally, because he didn't do it often. She feared he had seen the truth, that Deirdre had grown closer to General Moteurs than she'd realised, closer than she'd wanted to admit until now.

"Alright. But be careful Deirdre," he said. "Snoofle, go with her."

"I can't. We are under orders to protect you, no matter what. In theory, neither of us should go."

"Then let Merv go with you."

"Who will protect you?"

"Dave and Snoofle."

"And me," said Alan.

"No. Snoofle's place in this battle is by your side. I do not require any aid. They will not be expecting me."

"You sure about that?" asked Alan.

"Yeh, these people are seriously dangerous, Deirdre."

"So am I and so is General Moteurs. Together we can take them down."

"Then, c'mon, you gotta have the sawn-off," urged Big Merv.

Deirdre put her hand on the knife belt at her thigh to reassure him and more importantly, herself.

"No. Thank you. If I am following them over the roofs it will only slow me down." She wondered about taking Big Merv's gun and staying at ground level. No. It wasn't worth the risk. Her quarry were on the roofs because they could move faster and conceal themselves better. If she followed them at street level she might wander into their field of vision without even knowing. She ended the conversation by walking out into the hall, although she wasn't quite sure where to go next. The Pan and the rest of them followed her.

"If you want the roofs, you may as well start here. Come with me," said The Pan as he walked past her. She followed him into the kitchen where he opened the sash window. She saw the fire escape outside. He gestured to it with a flourish.

"I will return," she said.

"You'd better. Good luck. And be careful," he said. He seemed to actually mean it.

With a nod of thanks, she slipped out of the window, into the night.

*****

"You ain't gonna just let 'er go are you?" asked Big Merv after Deirdre had gone.

The Pan took one of the tiny jars from his pocket and held it up.

"No," he said. "I'm going to watch what happens and if they get into trouble, we're going to help."

Chapter 59

Deirdre followed the roofs as far as she could. There was no sign of Frosby or the others and for a moment she feared she'd overshot and passed them. General Moteurs turned into the park and headed down to the tunnel entrance by the river. Surely they would strike now. He disappeared under the bridge and she slipped down, over the side of the building, onto the roof of a lower building close by. From there she would be able to shin along a tree branch and climb down into the park. As she scaled the branches she imagined she saw a group of shadowy figures following him into the darkness.

If she'd been leading them she would have been intrigued by the General's actions and followed him to see where he went. She couldn't bank on Frosby's curiosity though. When she was sure the coast was clear she shinned silently down the tree and ran across the open space.

At the bridge all was quiet. She put on her night vision goggles and from within the shadows where she couldn't be seen she checked her surroundings. She was as sure as she could be that no-one had seen her and no-one was following. The others were still ahead of her. Keeping her back to the wall she drew one of her knives and moved stealthily into the darkness. She heard the soft click as the metal door swung to, but ducked into the tunnel and caught it before the latch clicked into place.

She listened.

Silence. She slid inside and moved soundlessly into the far corner of what seemed to be a pump room. Pipes and air conduits ran along the ceiling of the passage and the occasional LED glowed, illuminating small patches of red and green in the blackness. She waited, in case Frosby realised the door hadn't closed properly and returned to shut it.

However nobody returned. That was careless of Frosby, or very confident. Unless … had she noticed Deirdre following? Was this a trap?

Deirdre stood still and listened. She heard the faint echo of the General's footsteps receding inside and felt rather than heard the presence of the others closer to, just round the corner ahead of her. She listened for the soft rustles that heralded their moving on and followed.

She was glad of her night vision lenses. There was no other light.

Lurking in the gloom, she thought she counted seven shadowy figures moving round the corner at the passage end. It dog-legged there and she imagined them moving slowly, scoping the turns. After the dog-leg was a shorter straight stretch, which led into an open space that the Grongles appeared to be using for storage. When the General had led her and Snoofle out of the Palace through the secret exit, she had noticed how it was stacked with stuff: drums of liquid, crates of looted artwork, broken computers. This is where Deirdre believed they would strike. Swiftly, silently, knife at the ready, she covered the length of the passage. She knew she was faster than Frosby, faster than almost anyone in Strike Ops and she was aided by the fact that the team of assassins ahead of her would not expect to be followed.

She made her way down the second passage and into the store room. Slowly, carefully, she inched along the wall past the stacks of boxes. They had to be hiding here. She crept across the cleared pathway and as she reached the boxes she was pulled suddenly backwards, her hand wrenched behind her back. She cursed as the sudden pain forced her to drop the knife. The attacker was clinical and methodical. He, she believed it was a he, put his arm round her, pinning her against him. She struggled and flung her head back. She heard her assailant breathe out as he avoided her attempt to headbutt him. His grip tightened. He put his other arm round sideways, over the top of her head. Smecking Arnold no, he was going to break her neck. She must not die. She had to save the General. She struggled, kicking backwards at his knees but it had no effect. He held her fast and she lacked the strength to stop him. She felt his fingers under her chin, felt them dig in for a split second and waited for the sharp jerk that would end her life. It did not come. He still had her pinned but she heard a whisper right into her ear, so quiet it was almost without sound.

"Deirdre?"

It was him. Thank The Prophet, she'd found him. In her relief, her tension levels reduced a tiny bit and he clearly felt it, taking it as confirmation that he was right. Gently, slowly, he released her and turned her round so they were facing one another. He was wearing night vision goggles too.

He signalled to her that he was being followed and she nodded and ran one hand across her throat. He pointed at her, and she nodded again, assuming he had been asking if they were Strike Ops. Then someone switched the lights on. The sudden glare turned the lenses of her night goggles white, blinding her. During those few vital seconds before she could rip them off, Frosby and the team of assassins attacked.

Deirdre heard shouts, she felt rather than saw the General reach for his laser pistol, there was a ping as it fired once, and she thought she heard a thump as one of their attackers fell, stunned. General Moteurs didn't fire again. They must have knocked the gun out of his hand. She must find it. Someone drove a fist into her stomach. She punched out unseeing, finally managing to wrench off her goggles and fling them away from her.

She hit out again, making contact with a crunch but another punch, from an unseen assailant flew in sideways, bowling her over. She slammed into a pile of boxes, knocking them down, and the metal cans they contained clattered and banged to the floor. Her attacker came after her and instinctively she picked up a can and hit him square in the face with it. He flopped sideways, half on top of her, unconscious. She threw him off and weighed into the group surrounding General Moteurs. There were four of them. She swung the flat lid of a metal box down onto the head of one of the Blurpons and then upwards to bat away a knife, which was heading straight for the General's back. She turned, steadying herself in a second and threw one of her knives. It buried itself in the shoulder of Anna Marie, one of her most promising recruits. As Deirdre returned to the fray, Anna Marie rolled backwards over one of the metal drums and lay still.

Deirdre and General Moteurs were back to back now.

General Moteurs had drawn his sword. Out of the corner of her eye Deirdre saw him flick it round, hitting one of Frosby's throwing knives as it spun through the air and sending it into the wall. She saw him lunge forward and then two of the assassins were bearing down on her, knives drawn. Now that her eyes were accustomed to the light, she recognised them, as she had recognised Anna Marie. They were her people, doing the job for which she had trained them. Arnold, a few days previously she'd have helped them. She knew, even as she attacked that she could not bring herself to kill them outright. She had one knife and they were fully armed with weapons of stealth: knives, throwing stars, garrotting wires, instruments of silent death. She had beaten them all in sparring matches back at the Resistance HQ, but that had been individually. She had not fought for her life against Lord Vernon beforehand, either. Even six days afterwards, that encounter was taking its toll. She could feel her energy waning, the power in her punches weakening, the speed of her reactions slowing. With only one knife left she knew she must keep the fighting close to and hand to hand. But that meant she must make the running, keep attacking, keep her opponents defending. It was taking all her stamina and every bit of determination. They were going to kill her. They knew it, and so did she.

She dodged a knife thrust from one but the other had got behind her and kicked the back of her knees bringing her down. Through the heat of the fight she heard three rapid rounds of laser fire behind her. Smeck no, don't think about that. Even if he didn't get out of this alive, she had to. She tried to get up but they fell on her. One sat astride her grabbing her arms, the other took a fistful of her hair, using it to pull her head up. She saw the knife in his hand as he reached out to cut her throat.

"No."

Another round of laser fire rang out. The one with the knife jolted and fell backwards. General Moteurs wrenched the other off her back and shot him in the chest at point-blank range. He went down like a sack of potatoes.

For a few seconds, the General stood over her, one foot planted either side of her, laser gun primed, ready to fire. She lay on her side, panting, and watched him as he checked their surroundings: intelligent, incisive and in cool command. He calmly shot any of their attackers who were still conscious, then, after rubbing it in his hair briefly to boost the charge he holstered the gun.

"Do not fear. They are stunned, not dead," he said.

"Thank you," she whispered. Her throat was dry, her voice croaky. He took a canteen from his belt.

"Here," he pulled her to her feet and handed it to her. She drank and then held it out to him; he took a small sip and handed it back. "Your need is greater, I think." He gave her arm a gentle pat as he put the canteen into her hand with the other.

As she drank some more he turned away from her, taking out his phone. He made a brief call, his voice quiet and authoritative as he issued orders. She put the canteen on a pile of boxes and bent over, resting her hands on her knees trying to centre herself. She took deep breaths: in, out, in, out. Her endocrine system was in overload now, making her tremble so much that she was almost afraid to move. She felt his hand on her shoulder.

"Deirdre?"

Slowly, carefully she straightened up. Holding her by her arms he looked into her face, his expression full of concern.

"By the Creator, you are hurt. Let me see."

He put his hand under her chin and turned her head slightly. His touch felt almost electric and made her skin tingle. It frightened her. Arnold, where was her self-control? Her emotions were running away with her. Deirdre reminded herself that General Moteurs wasn't the only cool, calm commander round here. She felt shocked and shaky. She put her hands out and held onto the only thing to hand with which she could steady herself: him.

"I am … fine," she said. "Thank you." His uniform was soft and she could feel the warmth of his body beneath it. Suddenly she was filled with an intense yearning to touch him, to feel his skin against hers. She felt her fingers moving, interlocking with his.

"Deirdre?" His eyes met hers. Dilated, the pupils looked rounder. Like all Grongles the red colour came from a pigment rather than any lack of one. There were flecks of different hues in his irises – some lighter, some darker – like a human's. Deirdre realised she had begun to think of him as human. Or perhaps he had changed her view of Grongles. She felt surprisingly wobbly but it was not because of the fight. It was because of her emotional response to the General's touch.

"It's nothing."

She looked up into his face, the strong jaw, the fine eyebrows, his mouth … and suddenly, vividly, in her mind, she was kissing him. Arnold! Where in The Prophet's name had that come from? She started to tremble in earnest.

He misinterpreted the cause and slipped his arms around her, tenderly, pulling her closer and supporting her. She closed her eyes for fear they would somehow show him the images playing in her mind's eye: his fingers caressing her face, that mouth on hers. It made her tremble more.

"You are in shock," he said.

"Yes, I believe so." But Arnold, he wouldn't begin to know why. She put her arms round him, hugging herself against him, trying to assuage her need for contact without revealing her feelings – she wanted to make sense of them and come to terms with them herself before she showed them to him. "Forgive me, I cannot understand why I should react this way … I am an assassin."

His arms were tight around her, holding her close.

"We are sworn enemies, my species and yours. Until recently, these attackers were your own troops. I do not think your reaction is so unusual: not after fighting them alongside me."

"Maybe." She was still shivering. He put his hand up, moving a stray wisp of hair off her face and the force of her emotions made her stomach contract; she felt as if she was being turned inside out. Was it possible that she was in love? With a Grongle? It was difficult to tell. In matters of the heart, Deirdre had always prided herself on being too aloof to have one.

"We make a good team, you and I," he hooked the hair behind her ear. "We are well matched, I think."

As he smiled down at her, as they stood there, together, Deirdre's world went into slow motion, unlike her pulse, which speeded up. Arnold, was he going to …? He wasn't? Was he …? Was this …? She closed her eyes and tilted her head up, her lips parted, she could feel herself softening, relaxing against him and … No! What was she thinking? She wasn't so much as a blip on his radar, he was talking about combat.

"We …" she croaked as she tried to recover herself. What in The Prophet's name was happening to her? She could hardly speak. From the beginning, something about the General had turned her head but now, it was as if fighting beside him had flicked some switch in her mind and she couldn't turn it off. She cleared her throat. "We work well together, but your skill exceeds mine."

"I have a laser pistol. Perhaps without it I could match your skill – but I would not vouch for that – and, had I spent two hours fighting my master for my life, I know I could not fight the way you have just done so soon."

"You are older than me."

He hugged her to him tighter, for a second, and then laughed, throwing her completely.

"That is exactly what my wife would have said." He let go of her, slowly, as if he were unwilling but he kept one arm about her shoulders.

"And now you are trying to flatter me."

He smiled down at her.

"You know I am too honest for that."

"She was younger than you, your wife?"

"Three weeks younger, and she never let me forget it!" Deirdre stepped away from him.

"There are eight years between us."

Her head buzzed. His phone beeped. Again, she leaned down and put her hands on her knees. With a glance at her, he unhooked the mobile from his belt, flipped open the case and consulted a message on the screen.

"You have trained them well," he said as he snapped it closed. She picked up her knives, apart from the one in Anna Marie, which she left. He stepped over to the wall, removed the dagger Frosby had thrown and held it out to her. "A replacement for …?" he nodded at Anna Marie's prone form.

"Thank you." She could not meet his eyes as she took it from him. Smecking Arnold, how old was she? Five? He gestured to the side of her face, which was bruised and bleeding a little.

"That needs attention."

"No."

"You require a medic."

"No."

"Then, a bandage?"

"No, thank you."

"As you wish." He squatted down next to Anna Marie, took a field dressing out of one of the holders on his belt and started to cut away her clothes from around the hilt of knife. "She will live. A medical team is on its way."

"Thank you."

He looked up at her and raised his eyebrows.

"For …?"

"Not killing them."

He grunted non-committally and, dressing applied to Anna Marie, he went over to one of the male prisoners and started to remove his weapons.

"It is you who deserve thanks," he said matter-of-factly. "You saved my life by coming here; I am in your debt." He took a knife belt from the leg of one of them.

Knowing Grongle protocol dictated he should not, she patted down Frosby, the only other female attacker besides Anna Marie, who wasn't going anywhere, searching for concealed weapons.

"You saved mine so the debt is cancelled," she said as she removed several knives and a garrotting wire from about Frosby's person.

"On the contrary, since you saved mine a second time, when I was set to gather a knife from that female—"

"Anna Marie."

"Anna Marie," he corrected himself, "it stands."

"I didn't know we were keeping score ..." she said as she rolled Frosby carefully onto her back and removed another cache of concealed weaponry.

She moved onto the next assassin and he joined her, close again. His presence, so near, affected her far more badly than the shock. Seemingly oblivious of her confusion he took a folded canvas bag from one of the pouches in his belt. Deirdre wondered if she was concussed. She had taken a blow to the head. Perhaps that explained her emotional turmoil. Smecking Arnold, she hoped so. But what if it didn't? What was happening to her? It was that thing, wasn't it, when you grow to love your gaoler. She was going mental. Except she knew she wasn't. The matter was so much simpler than that.

Maybe she should seduce him; get it out of her system. Except that she doubted she could seduce General Moteurs. She helped him put the weapons into the bag. While he was concentrating on this, she tried to steal a glance at him, but he looked up. Their eyes met. She cleared her throat and turned her attention swiftly back to the bag. He put his hand on her arm.

"Deirdre?" he said softly.

"Please, I am fine. It's nothing." He sat back on his haunches and watched her. She could feel his eyes on her as she worked. When she was done, she zipped up the bag. He grabbed the handles and stood up, slinging it over his shoulder. Deirdre paused for a moment, taking a couple of deep breaths to calm herself. He helped her to her feet and one of the supine assassins caused a welcome distraction by stirring slightly.

"They are only stunned, they will wake soon enough." He drew his gun again.

"And when they do they will attack."

"Then perhaps I should stun them a second time."

"If we followed the training I gave them, we would kill them and neutralise the threat ..."

"Anyone I trained would do likewise. I am glad to see you are as unwilling as I."

"They are my own troops and we have been fighting for the same goal," she stopped again. The General waited. His face was expressionless but his eyes had narrowed the smallest fraction. "It would not be the K'Barthan way," she said.

"When the lines of battle are as blurred as this, it would not be the Grongolian way, either," he said. He moved closer.

"Take this." He handed her the gun. One-handed, he opened another of the pouches on his belt and took out an antiseptic wipe in a foil packet. He hefted the bag on his shoulder so it stayed out of the way and left both his hands free. Then he ripped open the packet and cleaned the wound on Deirdre's face. He was careful not to hurt her but it stung and she couldn't help but wince. "I apologise. I do not mean to cause you pain."

"Understood. It's just a scratch."

He folded up the antiseptic wipe, put it back in the packet, folded the open end over and put it in his pocket. He seemed remarkably calm for somebody who'd just survived an assassination attempt. Deirdre, on the other hand, was in turmoil.

A group of Imperial Guards and two medical orderlies arrived, led by a female doppelganger of Corporal Jones, who glanced quickly from General Moteurs to Deirdre. It made Deirdre even more uncomfortable. Did her feelings show? Arnold she hoped not.

The Imperial Guards handcuffed the unconscious assassins and put them onto seven stretchers. One of the medics made to treat Deirdre but she waved him away.

"Please see to the prisoners. I am alright," she said. They might have tried to kill her but these had been her troops and she had trained them. General Moteurs, who was speaking to the Corporal, glanced over at her briefly. Then the guards and the medical team took the assassins away.

"Your friends will be held until the installation, after which, since they will pose no danger to us, I have ordered that they should be freed."

His words starkly reminded Deirdre that neither she nor the General were likely to survive the installation themselves. She felt even shakier now.

"I have also given two of my troops orders to inform your allies that you are safe."

"I-I have to go back. The Candidate is unguarded."

"Tomorrow. Not now. He is safe enough and there is something you and I must attend to first." He strode off along the corridor.

****

Shock or no shock, this was no time for jelly legs. Deirdre ran after General Moteurs' retreating form, finally catching him as he rounded the corner. They walked – or at least he walked, Deirdre had to jog to keep up with him – to his apartments in silence. His mouth was set in a determined line and she could feel his tension as she ran beside him. He strode inside, throwing the bag of weapons on the floor as he went and held the door open for her. As she passed him, he grabbed her arm and in one swift movement pulled her round in a circle. Wrapping his other arm round her waist he pushed her against the back of the door as it slammed, pinning her against the wood. He held her there, his breathing fast and ragged, his red eyes burning with emotion.

"Deirdre …" he said huskily.

She looked up at him, daring but at the same time, also begging him to kiss her. And without breaking eye contact, General Moteurs, the antithesis and yet the embodiment of everything she desired in a male, leaned slowly forward. She felt his breath against her face, smelled his cologne and that softer, muskier scent of him, and she wanted him. Arnold she wanted him. The intensity of it almost killed her. He brushed his lips against her cheek, and she tried to speak, but all that came out was a wordless, animal sound. Smeck. He pulled back a fraction, looking down at her. Then his mouth was on hers, and she lost herself, crooking one long leg round his waist. The heat in his kisses increased as she pulled him closer. She arched herself against him as he moved one hand slowly down, under her thigh. She ran her fingers over his arms, feeling the muscles flex as he lifted her and took her weight, and when she wrapped her other leg about his waist he pushed her tighter against the door, kissing her harder and with an urgency that approached abandon. There was no going back, now. Nothing else mattered. Nothing but him and her. She could no more refuse him than die. She loved him, and she wanted him and when Deirdre wanted someone … she threw caution aside and surrendered to her instincts.

Chapter 60

It was the small hours and everyone was supposed to be asleep, but in the Parrot and Screwdriver, nobody was, apart from Trev who had been forced to retire earlier by 'Nurse Hargraves'. The Pan sat in an armchair in Gladys and Ada's sitting room. Psycho Dave was watching over Trev. Alan, Snoofle, Lucy and Merv were with The Pan. They sat in silence, each wrapped in their own thoughts. The Pan's eyes felt dry and strained from looking into the jar for so long but he dare not drop his concentration, not for a moment.

It was obvious that the General had a portal with him, The Pan couldn't see his movements at all. However, he'd watched Deirdre until she went under a bridge in one of the city's parks and through a doorway in the wall there, after which she disappeared. Either the room beyond it was portal proof or there was someone with a portal waiting for her inside. He was pretty certain it was not someone with a portal; there had been no interference outside and no hint it was coming until she stepped through the door into an instant grey fog. All the while he told his friends what he was seeing.

"Norris thinks there's a secret passage into the old Palace," Alan told them when he reported Deirdre's disappearance.

"I know there is," said Snoofle. "It's how General Moteurs got us out."

"I did wonder," said The Pan. The old Palace wasn't far away from the place where they'd disappeared, and after Sir Robin was first blacklisted, he had allegedly been cornered in one of the state rooms there before he escaped. The old boy must have got out somehow. "It would fit. The interference I'm getting is different, not like I was getting from the General's portal. If there is a secret passage it could be protected by the Palace's portal proofing system."

Since he didn't know what had become of Deirdre and the General, The Pan had watched the doorway through which they disappeared and waited. The others waited with him in tense silence.

"OK, it's been twenty minutes. Is there still nothing?" Lucy eventually asked.

"Still nothing, although my arm's getting tired."

"I'm not surprised. Is there nobody at all?" she said.

"No-one."

"I would call that a good sign," said Snoofle.

"Yer," agreed Big Merv. "If them assassins had done 'em in you'da seen 'em leave."

"I guess."

They waited some more. The minutes slipped by, thirty, forty, fifty and The Pan kept watching.

Still nothing.

When somebody rapped at the door, downstairs, everyone jumped.

"Smeck," said Alan.

The Pan stood up.

"Merv everyone. There are eight portals in Trev's room. Go in there, all of you and tell Psycho Dave what's going on. If anything happens to me, Lucy, you know what to do. It might be Deirdre. I might have missed her leaving or she may have come out of there a different way so hold off unless I shout."

"OK," said Lucy.

"Come on then, look lively."

They all trooped out into the hall, the others went into Trev's room and The Pan went downstairs to the door. The knock came again. He turned on the outside light and looked through the spy hole. Grongles, a male and a female. Not good. But they wore the grey uniforms of the Imperial Guard and the female bore a striking resemblance to Corporal Jones, the one he'd met in the cells, when the General had introduced him to Doctor Dot. He put the chain on and opened the door.

"Hello?"

"Message from my commander, sir," she said.

"And that would be?" he asked. It seemed smart to check.

"General Moteurs," she said with a puzzled frown and a tone of voice that said, 'who else?'

"Alright, give me a second." He closed the door, slipped the chain off and opened it. "Sorry, but you know how it is, you can't be too careful," he said as she stepped into the hall.

"Yes, sir, understood."

'Sir' The Pan noted. He closed the door behind her and her colleague.

"Is he alright?"

"Yes, sir. That is the message, sir. That he is safe, Lieutenant

Arbuthnot, too. He craves your pardon in detaining her for another night, sir. She will return to you at dawn tomorrow."

Did it have to be dawn? It was such a painfully short time away.

"She can make it later if she needs to sleep it off," he said. The guard appeared nonplussed for a second or two and then explained.

"My commander is on duty at six, she will need to return here before then."

"Of course, I understand. I'm glad she saved his life," he added, trying to steer the conversation onto easier ground.

The Imperial Guard exchanged a look with her colleague. It spoke volumes but in a language The Pan wasn't a hundred per cent confident he could read.

"I'll wager, so is she, sir," she said.

"Agreed," said the male, "and if she is not, he will make her glad before the night is—" The female one shut him up with a contemptuous look.

"You forget yourself soldier," she said with a meaningful glance at The Pan.

"My apologies, sir," he said.

"That's fine," said The Pan. "I'm delighted to hear they are OK." Having received the message, he wasn't sure what to do next. "Do you want a cup of tea or anything?" he asked weakly.

"No, sir. We must return to our duties directly," said the female.

"Righto. Then … thank you."

"A pleasure, sir."

He let them out and listened as the sound of the female giving the male an earful for his impropriety receded into the distance. Chuckling, he turned to discover Snoofle hopping down the stairs.

"Did you hear that?"

"Yes," said Snoofle, adjusting his whiskers. He was positively radiating happiness.

"Good job Deirdre."

"Yes," said Snoofle and The Pan got the impression he wasn't just talking about saving General Moteurs' life.

"Right. I wondered … Deirdre and the General are they …" The Pan felt delicately for the right word, "close?"

Snoofle was not so reticent.

"Besotted. Completely. They're in denial, of course."

The Pan beamed, "I'm wondering if, perhaps, they're a bit less in denial than they were."

"If that is true, it would be wonderful."

"You know," agreed The Pan, "I think it would. I'm glad they've had the chance to spend some time together. Come on then, dawn's not far away. We should try and get some sleep. Ada's bedroom is the only one left but if you'd prefer it, you can always sleep on the sofa."

Snoofle laughed.

"Never fear, sir. I like pink. It reminds me of Itzal Bluff."

"The artist?" asked The Pan.

"Oh, I'm impressed. There's not many folks who know about Itzal Bluff."

"Well, I've heard of him, That's not exactly the same as knowing anything. He was a Blaggysomp wasn't he?"

"Yes, from some one-yak town in Smirn; Smeal it's called. He believed pink was the colour of revelation. He said if you stared at a big enough expanse of pink for long enough you would see visions of the cosmos. He tinkered with different shades to promote different types of vision but if you ask me, with the cocktail of hallucinogenic drugs he took, he could have looked at any colour and seen visions."

"Mmm," said The Pan. "I think the kinds of pinks Ada likes actually *could* induce hallucinations without the drugs, especially first thing in the morning."

"Never fear, you will find me unaffected. I have experimented extensively with Bluff's techniques and I can confirm that they don't work at all. Not without the kinds of industrial quantities of narcotics that only a Blaggysomp's system can stand."

Chapter 61

Deirdre woke slowly, her brain clawing its way muzzily to the realms of consciousness. She lay in bed with her eyes closed, taking a few moments more to luxuriate in the warmth and softness of the cotton sheets. The highest quality. Nothing less for General Moteurs. She gave herself a moment to collect her thoughts. Deirdre, being Deirdre, didn't have too much trouble attracting males. Indeed, back at the Resistance camp, pretty much any of her humanoid male colleagues would oblige with breathless eagerness if she showed the slightest indication of interest. But that was sex. She had never experienced anything like this. With General Moteurs it had been so much more. There had been no confessions of undying love. They were not required. It was tacitly understood.

She opened her eyes. Outside it was still dark. Slowly she sat up, there was an empty space next to her, a reading light on the table beside the bed cast a pool of light on the pillow. She breathed deeply and put her arms up, stretching the muscles in her back. General Moteurs returned, already dressed, with a cup of tea and a plate of toast. He put them on her bedside table.

"Ford," she murmured, and when he leaned down to kiss her she put her arms round his neck. If only every day could start like this.

"Breakfast," he said.

"Thank you."

"What time is it?"

"Zero four hundred hours."

"Ugh," she rubbed her temples, "have we slept at all?"

"Half an hour. Actually, I let you lie in." He smiled down at her. "You've had forty minutes."

"Pure luxury," she said drily. "I have to go now, don't I?"

"For your own safety, and that of the Candidate yes, you do. If you are seen here—" he stopped.

"I know, it will not go well for either of us."

"I regret that is so. Even if they know about the assassination attempt, my master has marked you as his own. It is improper enough for me to have a female here unchaperoned but in your case it is also extremely dangerous."

Yeh. She could imagine.

She washed hurriedly and then drank the tea and ate the toast as she dressed. He watched her. Neither of them spoke.

"You are ready?" he asked quietly when she was done.

"Yes."

He stood up and moved over to her side.

"I will kiss you now, because in public, I cannot," he said. He pulled her into his arms and proceeded to do just that. She closed her eyes and lost herself until slowly, reluctantly, he broke off.

"I would that things were different," he said.

"Me too," she said as they hugged each other close.

He sighed and stepped back, straightening his uniform.

"It is time," he said, with a glance at his watch and taking her by the hand, he led her to the hall.

They kissed again before leaving his rooms and then, side by side, they walked the length of the corridor, to the stairs and upwards, this time, to the roof.

"Welcome to the Officers' Landing Stage," he said as he opened the door onto a flat reinforced platform. A dark green snurd landed as they arrived. It was a model Deirdre was familiar with – her father had owned an earlier version – and although neither she nor General Moteurs knew it, far away, in another version of space and time, it was a Maserati Quattroporte. "My staff snurd."

It pulled up in front of them all sleek, shiny, understated expense. A driver got out, walked round and opened the back door. Again, General Moteurs checked his watch.

"I cannot come with you," he said. "My master is expecting me at zero five hundred hours."

"Then this is goodbye." Her military side reasserted itself as she smiled stoically but her heart wasn't in it.

"Apparently so."

He took her hand, bowed low and kissed it. Her eyes filled with tears. For heaven's sake what was happening to her? She was a soldier, a senior officer and an assassin. She didn't do crying. It was for wimps. She took a breath and tried to think calm thoughts.

"I will see you tomorrow," she said.

"Yes, you will." His eyes met hers. He stood before her and for all his outward calm she could sense the emotional storms raging within. "Deirdre, on my oath, I swear I will die before Lord Vernon touches you again."

"I would hope I can spare you the trouble. If I face him again, I will be better prepared."

"Then good luck." His voice was tight with emotion. He took something from his belt, a smartphone. "This is Grongolian army issue. If you are in danger, if you need me, use this. No matter where I am, or what I am doing I will find a way to reach you. My details are programmed in."

He put the phone into her hand.

"Thank you," she said.

"This is not goodbye. I will not allow it to be that. We have unfinished business, you and I. Believe and the boy will prevail."

"I'll see you on the other side."

They walked to the snurd together, and she felt his hand gently touch the small of her back as she got in. He stepped away and nodded to the driver who closed her door, walked round the back of the snurd and got in his side.

"Where to ma'am?" he asked as Deirdre stared out of the window. General Moteurs saluted.

"Turnadot Street," she said and she saluted back.

The driver pressed the starter and took off smoothly into the darkness. Through the back window Deirdre watched the receding form of the being she loved above all others. He stood unmoving, looking after her, until the snurd left the Palace behind and he was lost from sight.

Chapter 62

The Pan slept fitfully and was awoken by the sound of an engine. He got up, went through to the sitting room where the windows looked out onto the street and peered through the crack in the curtains. A sleek dark green snurd was parked outside. He padded downstairs. The knock on the door came as he was crossing the hall. He opened it to find Deirdre Arbuthnot. She had her arms hugged around herself and she seemed lost, smaller than usual. If he didn't know better he'd have thought she'd been crying. She made a game attempt at a smile.

"Hi." She wiped her nose on her sleeve.

"Hi … and well done." He opened the door wider. "Sorry, that's …" he shrugged. "I seem to be out of good lines right now but what I'm trying to say is, I'm sure future generations will thank you."

"Yeh," her voice was hard.

"Are you alright?"

Of course she wasn't.

"I will be. I need to sleep."

"Yeh, I can imagine," said The Pan and then remembered that all the rooms, even Ada's, were full. "You'd better use my bed, but I'll need to change the sheets. Are you alright waiting a moment?"

"Yes. Thank you, you are very kind."

Blimey. The Pan nearly did a double take but managed to disguise it as scratching his head.

She looked close to collapse. He wondered whether he should put his arm round her, or even carry her but decided against it. Whether or not she needed it, she'd probably hit him. But he offered, anyway. "Do you want any help?"

"No."

"Come on, then, quietly as you can though, we don't want to wake the others."

They crept up the stairs and with a wave at Alan, who was on watch in Trev's room, he showed Deirdre into his bedroom.

"Give me a minute," he whispered, "I'll just get the sheets. The bathroom's down the hall, first door after the stairs."

He made his way to the airing cupboard, grabbed a new set of sheets, an eiderdown and some blankets, thinking to retire to the sofa with the duvet. He popped his head into Trev's room and had a quick chat with Alan. Trev was doing well, sleeping soundly, and Alan seemed as glad as The Pan that Deirdre had successfully saved General Moteurs' life. He declined The Pan's offer to take over, saying that Big Merv was on duty next.

The Pan supposed all this had taken him a few minutes, but not more than five. However, when he returned to his bedroom Deirdre was curled up on top of the duvet, asleep. Gently, trying not to disturb her, he put the sheet over her and laid the blankets and eiderdown carefully on top. She sighed and stirred but she did not wake.

Quietly, he retrieved his things from the chair where he'd left them.

"Sleep tight Deirdre," he whispered, and closed the door.

He went into the sitting room. The sofa looked inviting. He went and found his cloak, wrapped it around himself and lay down.

Chapter 63

Lord Vernon liked to be up early. He enjoyed having time to collect his thoughts and plan before he started his day. That's why he rose at four o'clock. He was not pleased with Captain Snow when he arrived, in some agitation, shortly after that. However, he was even less pleased with General Moteurs, when he discovered the reason for the Captain's agitation.

Now, half an hour later, he sat on the balcony sipping a fruit smoothie, the remains of his breakfast before him – muesli, toast and a boiled egg – and General Moteurs sitting opposite him.

Lord Vernon appreciated that Captain Snow was wont to make sweeping accusations, but if he was right, the General would answer for this and he would pay a high price.

"General, I wonder if you would explain something to me."

"Sir?"

"I have an eyewitness report stating that you were seen entering your apartments with Lieutenant Arbuthnot, last night," Lord Vernon paused for a few seconds to allow General Moteurs to fully appreciate the weight of what he was about to say, "and leaving early this morning."

"Sir?"

"I have given you orders, General, that she be reserved for my pleasure."

"Yes, sir."

"I am sure you know how I feel about insubordination." Lord Vernon's grey eyes burned into the General's red ones. His second in command feared him more and more each time they met. He saw it now in the sweat running down the side of the General's forehead, in the pallor of his skin, in the way his hand went briefly to his face. He saw it and rejoiced in it.

"Sir."

"Perhaps you would like to explain yourself?"

"I—"

"Well, General?"

"She is loyal to me, sir, and nothing more."

"Loyal? I've never heard it called that before."

"Sir. Last night I delivered her and her colleague, Snoofle, to guard the Hamgeean, as you ordered. I thought it prudent to do so subtly, through the secret passage into the park. I believe a group of assassins were watching the pub. She saw them follow me from there and in turn, she pursued them. They attacked me in the tunnel and she set on them and saved my life."

"That sounds a trifle melodramatic, General."

"It is the truth sir. There were seven of them and I was too complacent. They knocked my pistol from my hand and without her they would have killed me."

"I believe she swore an oath to expunge our species from the face of the earth."

"I have heard it said, sir."

"And now she is saving your life."

"Sir."

"I'd like to know how you did that, Moteurs."

"Sir, I—"

"You understand my concern?"

"Sir?"

"So tell me, how did you effect this wondrous …" Lord Vernon waved a hand as he attempted to pin down the right word, "transformation?"

"Trust, sir."

"Trust? And how, exactly did you win her trust, General?"

"A little economy with the truth, sir."

"You lied to her."

"Naturally, sir."

"Of course you did. And that is all, you did nothing … else?" The accusation hung in the air unanswered for a moment. General Moteurs shifted in his seat.

"I did what I had to, sir."

"That is what concerns me." Lord Vernon steepled his hands, leaned back in his chair, and looked into the General's eyes. As usual, Moteurs returned his gaze, as usual his expression was calm but this time it was not so inscrutable. His eyes were guarded. He was hiding something, and Lord Vernon wondered … He'd better not have touched her.

"Are you sure 'doing what you had to' did not include anything … unsavoury."

"Unsavoury?" For a moment the General seemed to be genuinely puzzled, "No, sir."

"Good. In that case, General, I would advise a little less economy with the truth around Captain Snow. He has formally denounced you."

That had hit home, the General's expression remained impassive but he took a sharp breath in.

"It is not only what he saw tonight, Moteurs. But what he has heard from others. He believes you are working against me."

"His concern is understandable, sir. As you know, that is what I have led the Underground to believe."

"I am aware. But their belief may be a little too ... fervent for your safety, General."

"Sir."

"Captain Snow may lack your subtlety and intelligence, but he can be very astute. That is why I value him so highly."

"Sir."

"However, I have formally dismissed his accusations."

"I am in your debt."

"Yes, Moteurs, you are," Lord Vernon paused to give the gravity of the idea time to sink in.

"You understand that your ability to manipulate others makes you unpopular with those who ... covet your gifts as well as those who distrust your motives."

Lord Vernon congratulated himself. General Moteurs could and would take that remark on so many levels.

"Sir," said General Moteurs. This was the first time his fear had been audible in his voice, Lord Vernon noted. Perhaps he wasn't so bulletproof, or perhaps he did have something to hide? Had their positions been reversed, Lord Vernon knew he would have taken the blonde and had his fill. He must speak to Captain Snow, arrange a little surprise at the installation.

"Very well. To business, then," he changed the subject abruptly. "I must congratulate you on an extremely inspired strategy with regards to the Resistance. They are split, exactly as you predicted. Denarghi has vanquished the ... enemy within. Barring a handful to guard the perimeter they will all be gathered in the mess hall at zero eight hundred hours this morning to watch the rebel department heads executed. We have the coordinates, we will transport there by portal and slay them."

"Sir."

"I commend you, General, on a truly excellent piece of work."

"Sir." General Moteurs was very pale. Perhaps the shock of being praised after being accused was too much for his system. "Do you wish my troops to accompany you?" the General asked.

"No General. Exterminating the blacklisted is arduous work, a matter for the army, not the Imperial Guard."

"Sir, I—"

"No buts, General. While I am detained at the Resistance Headquarters," – and oh what a pleasure that would be – "you will travel ahead of me to Grongolia. You will ensure that General Ennui understands my requirements. He is expecting you in," Lord Vernon consulted his watch, "five minutes."

"Sir," General Moteurs was really pale now. "What time are General Ennui and I to expect you in Grongolia?"

"Ten hundred hours at the latest. I will keep you informed."

"Sir." The General shifted, he seemed to be gathering his courage.

"There is a problem?"

"No, sir. I am at General Ennui's service – and yours."

"Excellent. I am glad to hear that, General."

Lord Vernon almost laughed. That had put a bomb under him.

"Sir." Or not. General Moteurs was clearly in dread of contradicting him but, Lord Vernon realised, he was going to, "If I may be permitted?"

"Go on."

"My scientists have improved on the current version of our portal. Tests are scheduled for this morning, in and around Ning Dang Po."

"Your attendance is necessary?"

"Not strictly, sir, but—"

"You think it will motivate them?"

"Sir."

"Yes," said Lord Vernon, only as usual it was more of a hiss, "I notice you lead from the front. We will compromise. You will join General Ennui as you are ordered. However, I will inform him that he is to release you briefly, if required, to liaise with your scientists. If you use the portal I have given you, it will allow ample time to congratulate them."

"Yes, sir, thank you, sir."

"Until ten hundred hours, General."

"Sir," General Moteurs stood up, bowed and was gone.

Chapter 64

As ever, further sleep evaded The Pan. After half an hour lying on the sofa staring at the ceiling he threw in the towel and got up.

Cluck? said the Eighth Architrave.

"You and me both, hen," said The Pan as he dressed and went through to the kitchen.

The first streaks of light were appearing in the night sky.

He wrapped his cloak around him, slipped out onto the fire escape and went up to the roof. There was one particular spot, hidden, secluded, between two chimney stacks. It was there he went now. The fire below had been lit and the bricks were warm against his back as he sat, huddled in his warm cloak, and watched the stars retreat. He let his mind wander and then, absent-mindedly, without really realising what he was doing, he took off the ring.

The Architraves were easier to deal with now, or perhaps The Pan was more used to them. He managed to have a whole conversation with Five and the chicken without actually speaking out loud. Neither of them had any answers but they were understanding and willing to listen as The Pan outlined his various ideas for ensuring the succession. Between them, Five, the chicken and The Pan came up with a plan of action that his predecessors were prepared to, if not endorse, then at least, live with.

Eee up, tha's company, said Five just as The Pan was about to put the ring on.

He glanced up. Sitting on the ground, a few feet away, was Lieutenant Arbuthnot. Her knees were drawn up to her chest and she had her arms round them.

Thanks for the heads up, he thought to Five. He stood up and coughed, to alert her to his presence. She didn't move.

"Hi," he said.

Still no reaction. He could feel the chicken watching as he went and sat beside her. It seemed to be concerned.

"D'you want to talk about it?" he asked her.

"There's nothing to say."

"I can imagine."

They sat there in silence, watching as dawn painted the sky pink.

"Looks like it's going to be a nice day. And now I've said that it'll probably chuck it down relentlessly, the whole time."

Still nothing.

"You know what they say. Red sky at morning, shepherd's warning."

She sighed, kind of in agreement, The Pan thought, rather than to make him go away, so he carried on.

"Listen, if it helps, I do know."

"What?"

"How it feels to search all your life for a soulmate and find them when it's almost too late."

She was quiet for a moment.

"I was not searching."

"You still found him, though, didn't you?"

"Yes."

"I'm sorry …" smecking Arnold, "well, no, that came out wrong, I'm happy for you but I'm sorry it had to be the way it is rather than—"

Quit while tha's ahead.

Yeh, good point Five. He stopped. Why did he have to be so unbelievably crap at this kind of thing? He suspected she might be wondering the same thing, which is why it surprised him when she turned towards him.

"How do you find the courage to face it?" she asked.

He shrugged.

"I try to tell myself that a few snatched hours is more than many lovers get."

"And this has helped you?"

He turned the ring over in his hands and put it on.

"To be honest, no," he smiled ruefully. "Not at all."

As she gazed out over the roofs, she ran her hands through her hair, gathering it up and tying a band around it. Was that a good sign? He couldn't tell but he blundered on.

"I just wanted you to know that if you need to talk to anyone, you can bend my ear whenever you like. While you're guarding me."

"Thank you."

"It's a pleasure."

They sat together for a while and then The Pan stood up.

"I'm going to go and get breakfast on. D'you want some? I'm guessing a fry up's not your thing but I can do porridge."

"I would appreciate that but not yet. I'm not hungry."

"OK, as and when, but," he took off his cloak and handed it to her, "if you're going to be up here long, wrap up. There's a nice spot between the chimneys over there," he pointed to where he'd been sitting, "it's warm and nobody'll see you."

"Thank you."

"Any time," said The Pan as he headed back down to the kitchen.

Chapter 65

Rank on rank of the Grongolian Army's finest stood shoulder to shoulder in the cobbled courtyard at the back of the Palace; just over a hundred of them. In the dim light of the early dawn, Lord Vernon, or to give him his full title, His Divine Excellency, High Leader, Lord Vernon, eyed them critically and moved forward to take the salute. There was a loud crack as just over one hundred pairs of heels snapped together in perfect unison. It was time to inspect them.

"Captain." He strolled over to the end of the first rank of troops. Captain Snow joined him. He walked along the rows, the Captain a respectful pace behind him. To one side waiting, engines running, stood a convoy of armoured personnel carriers. Each had been fitted with a Grongolian portal to transport the troops and Captain Snow, to their destination. Parked at the head of the convoy, dark and menacing, was the Interceptor, in which Lord Vernon would lead them. When he had finished his inspection, the Captain gave the order and the troops started getting into the vehicles.

Lord Vernon watched, appreciatively. He was about to wipe out the only military force K'Barth could throw against him, and with the use of portals, and the element of surprise, it was going to take no more than a handful of troops. If he could do this, with these, what could he achieve with the rest of them? Thousands of them: disciplined, highly trained, a supreme army. So much power at his fingertips, an invincible force, to use as he wished. His forces would sweep through every reality: dominating, cleansing, renewing. Nothing would stand in his path. He maintained his expression of steely authority, but he wanted to laugh. Captain Snow returned to his side.

"We are ready, sir."

"Good. You understand your orders, Captain?"

"Sir. Once we reach the forest we will take a deputation of troops, transport inside and kill anything that breathes. Outside, the rest of my troops will establish a cordon and kill any agents trying to escape."

"Correct. There will be no quarter. I want the Resistance laid waste. I want them annihilated."

"Move out," shouted Captain Snow as Lord Vernon strolled to the Interceptor and got in.

Chapter 66

Once again, Doctor Dot arrived before The Pan could go and collect her, only this time she was not on foot but in the same dark green snurd that Deirdre had returned in.

"Nice wheels," he said as she got out of them, "yours?"

"My commander's. Now we must go inside at once." She walked past him, taking him by his good arm as she did so and shepherding him swiftly into the pub.

"What's going on?" he asked as she shut the door behind them.

"They're attacking the Resistance HQ."

"What?"

"The HQ. Captain Snow and Lord Vernon. General Moteurs has been sent to Grongolia but he managed to get word to me, before he left. Denarghi is going to execute Professor N'Aversion and some others this morning. Everyone in the Resistance will be forced to watch, so Lord Vernon is going to transport into the audience in an armoured personnel carrier. Those who aren't crushed will be gunned down."

"Smeck. When?"

"Zero eight hundred hours."

He glanced at his watch. There was very little time.

"Come on." The two of them ran upstairs, him shouting, "Wake up everyone, we have an emergency."

Big Merv and Psycho Dave were at his side by the time he reached the landing, followed shortly afterwards by Deirdre, and Snoofle, who came out of the kitchen.

"In Trev's room," he said as Alan and Lucy came to the doorway. They went inside. The others sat but The Pan could not. Instead he paced backwards and forward across the patch of floor between the bed and the window.

"What's up?" Trev asked him as he paced to and fro.

"They're going to attack the Resistance and we only have a few minutes to stop them," said The Pan. "Deirdre, Snoofle, if Denarghi wanted the whole organisation to watch where would he do it?"

"The mess hall," said Snoofle.

"Then we have to be there. D'you have your phone?"

"Yes," said the Blurpon.

"Then warn everyone you can."

"Consider it done," said Snoofle. "If I send a secure text I can get it to everyone in my address book."

"Good plan, and if there's anyone you would ring …?"

"Of the three I trust, one is about to be executed, and if he is, I'd bet the other two are going to die with him."

"Fair enough."

Snoofle took out his phone and started tapping away at the screen.

"Defreville you can't go. You're the Candidate," said Doctor Dot.

"Which is exactly why I must. Alan, can you get me some of the portals from the bar downstairs? We need to take a couple each, get to the crowd and start transporting them to safety. And while you're doing that, I have to find Denarghi and explain."

"As your bodyguard, I advise against that," said Deirdre.

"Too right, he'll kill you," said Snoofle.

"I have to try."

"Nah, you don't," said Big Merv. "Denarghi's made his choice and it ain't you."

"He's right," said Lucy.

"Then we have to save the rest of them; every agent we can. Smeck." He kept moving. It was helping him think. "Deirdre, Snoofle, can you take us to the mess hall by portal?"

"Yep," said Snoofle, without looking up from his phone, and Deirdre nodded.

"Good."

"It's dangerous," said Doctor Dot. "What if you're killed?"

"Yeh, and what if Lord Vernon gets to hear there's been portal use?" asked Alan.

"At least that's one problem you won't have to deal with, portal use, I mean. The General's team of scientists is conducting field tests for a new model of our version this morning," said Doctor Dot, "I should imagine he ordered that for a reason."

"D'you know how long for?"

"No, I'm sorry."

"Don't worry. That makes life a lot easier," said The Pan, "but I think we should still operate on the premise that any portal use could be tracked by hostile," he stopped, he didn't want to use the word 'Grongles', "forces."

"Yes, go carefully," said Doctor Dot.

"We may need weapons," said Snoofle.

"We gotta sawn-off, a revolver—" began Big Merv.

"And a laser pistol," said Doctor Dot. "I am the Imperial Guard's MO. I bear arms."

"And I have my knives," said Deirdre.

"That ain't gonna get us far."

"Exactly," said The Pan. "And is it issued to you, specifically, Doctor? If one of us dies using it, will they be able to find it and trace it back to you?"

"Yes but—"

"No buts, Doctor, we're not using the laser pistol. It's too incriminating and it'll make so little difference there's no point."

Alan came back.

"Here," he said and he laid the portals out on Trev's bed.

"Alright," said The Pan after taking a brief moment to count them, "here's what we're going to do. We split into two groups and two of us go with Deirdre and two with Snoofle. You two will take us somewhere near the mess hall, as near as you can get without drawing any unwelcome attention. You'll have three portals each so you can smash the one you use to take us through. We'll have two portals each, one to use and one to give any agents we find who know Ning Dang Po well enough to help. Once we arrive, Deirdre and Snoofle will have to take us to the mess hall itself. Then we dive in, grab anyone who'll come with us and transport them out."

"What if the entrance is guarded?" asked Alan.

"Then we'll have to go in there by portal under cover of Lord Vernon's arrival."

"That is seriously dangerous, son," said Trev.

"Better than doing nothing, which is the only alternative."

"If we are successful getting in, where do we take them?" asked Deirdre.

"Here. No. Wait. If there's any pursuit, we have to spread it as thinly as we can." The Pan thought for a second. "Go to public spaces around the city: parks, precincts, the tow path along the canal, the banks of the river Dang. That way you can keep going without smashing the jar, so long as you make sure you never transport them to the same place twice. Warn them to run like smeck as soon as they land and tell them to come here to regroup."

"There may be several hundred of them," said Snoofle.

"Only if you moves quick," said Trev. "See, you has got ter limit yerselves to five or less each time. An' that is counting the person who is usin' the portal. Any more an' that and you'll get yerselves into the plop."

"How much plop?" demanded The Pan.

"Big time plop son." He looked pleading and glanced over at Lucy.

"No, Trev, you can't help, not in a million years. You have to stay here," she said.

"She's right, I'm sorry," said The Pan. "OK everyone who's coming. You heard him, five and NO more so speed is of the essence. We have to do as many trips as we can." The Pan doubted there'd be more than a handful of agents left after the first trip, not unless he and the others could get a warning to them. "Unless anyone has any better ideas."

Nobody said anything and The Pan read it as a 'yes'.

"Alright, looks like we have a plan. When you transport them out, we don't want any hiccups, so to keep the pursuit on their toes, and avoid mix-ups, we'll do it by district: Alan take Left Central; Dave, Upper Left; Snoofle, Lower Left; Deirdre, Upper Right; Big Merv you take Lower Right and I'll take Right Central. Lucy, you don't know Ning Dang Po, so you're going to have to stay here, Doctor Dot, you're staying too."

"But—"

"Both of you need to take care of Trev till he's better and Doctor, if you're going to own this pub you can't afford to get seen."

"Neither can you, Defreville."

"Fair enough," and he started unbuttoning his shirt.

"What are you doing?" asked Lucy.

"Removing any distinguishing features," he explained as he took it off to reveal the white T-shirt he was wearing as a vest.

"It's not just you though, what about Deirdre and Snoofle?" asked Lucy. "If they're seen by the Grongles, won't Lord Vernon realise who sent them?"

Good point.

"Yeh, he will." The Pan turned to the two agents, "Deirdre, I've a bald cap in my room. Maybe if you wear that, and my shirt?" He threw it to her.

"You're overcomplicating it," said Alan as he and Dave took nylon stockings out of their pockets and slipped them over their heads.

"I got spares," said Dave holding onc out towards Deirdre.

"I will not require it."

"Maybe you should," said The Pan, "Lucy has a point, everything hangs on General Moteurs and if either you or Snoofle are recognised it could compromise him. You shouldn't be coming at all. I'm only letting you because you know where the mess hall is."

"Understood," said Deirdre, taking the stocking from Dave and, with a show of reluctance, putting it over her head.

"They'll cover your features. Make you hard to identify," said Alan.

"Peppermint?" she asked.

"Me Gran's foot lotion," said Dave.

Deirdre turned to him, her expression of horror clearly visible under the nylon as her hands went to the stocking to remove it.

"It's clean I promise," he added hastily. "An' it hasn't got on there from her feet. When she was wearing them like."

"Yeh, it's on there for us. If you wear them a long time they get itchy. A dab of foot lotion stops that."

"I got enough for everyone," added Dave, helpfully.

"Stockings or foot lotion?" asked The Pan dubiously.

"I don't need one," said Snoofle, "Doctor Dot aside, I've never met a Grongle yet who can tell one Blurpon from another."

"OK everyone, put the stockings on," said The Pan. What was he doing? Shaking with fear, he put the one Dave had given him over his own head. Then, he took Deirdre's hand and Big Merv took his. Snoofle, Psycho Dave and Alan held hands, too.

"Ready?" asked The Pan.

Everyone assented.

"Good luck," said Doctor Dot.

"You too. Right, one last thing, remember, if you find anyone who knows Ning Dang Po, give them a portal, show them how to use it and get them rescuing people. The rest of the portals are in the HQ somewhere. I'll try to find them so we have more to hand out. Now, it's time. Deirdre, Snoofle, is the coast clear?"

The two of them looked through their portals.

"Yes."

"Good. Then let's go."

Chapter 67

Professor N'Aversion finished the last of the fried breakfast in front of him. It was like forcing feathers into his mouth but Mrs Burgess and the ladies and gentlemen in catering had made it specially. He couldn't disappoint them. For all Denarghi's efforts to paint him as a Grongle sympathiser, he was clearly going to be missed. It was touching, like attending his own memorial service and discovering hundreds had turned out to say goodbye. However, it made the precarious situation of the Resistance all the more worrying. Denarghi had made attendance at the executions compulsory for all agents other than those on essential duty. The doors and sentry posts were guarded by nothing more than a skeleton staff and everyone would be gathered in one place.

Colonel Smeen arrived with an armed escort.

"Alright scum, time to go."

The Professor stood up.

"Hands behind your back."

"Smeen, this is a terrible thing you are doing. The Grongles are going to attack."

"Save it," said Smeen but he came closer. "I'll check those, lads," he said as one of the guards handcuffed the Professor's wrists. "You know the score. Go into the corridor, I'll bring him out."

They went.

"The handcuffs are closed but not locked," whispered Smeen. "Same for the others, this is a coup. Wait for my mark."

"Thank you. You ought to know, the Grongles are going to attack us, soon, and I am almost certain that my execution will be the moment they choose to strike."

"I'll have to move quick then. You ready? Only I got to black your eye now."

"I'm sorry? D'you mean hit me?"

"Yer. We're not supposed to touch the prisoners, the blokes think I'm sending them outside so I can put the boot in. Sorry. It was the only way I could think of to get each of you alone."

"No, that's quite alright. Go on then."

The punch, when it came, was harder than the Professor expected.

"Arnold's toenails!" he shouted and Smeen winced apologetically.

"Your suitcase, it's in my office, under my desk."

"If this comes off we'll need it," said the Professor.

"Then you'll have it."

When the Colonel pushed him out into the corridor the guards snickered.

****

The Professor was escorted to the mess hall under armed guard and led onto a stage. There, he was positioned next to Lieutenant Wright, Colonel Ischzue, Simon, Nar and—

"What is Blimpet doing here?" asked the Professor. "He has done nothing."

"He is surplus to requirements."

"Then let him go."

"I don't think so. I told you, we can't have your contagion spreading, and he has been peddling black market coffee." Denarghi addressed Smeen, "Position the prisoners for execution."

The guards lined their prisoners against the wall in pairs, The Professor and Lieutenant Wright, Nar and Simon, Colonel Ischzue and Blimpet.

"Blindfold them," Denarghi ordered.

"No. Thank you. I would rather see it coming," said the Professor.

Denarghi glared at him.

"Oh very heroic of you, Professor. Making a martyr of yourself, true to form. As you wish; I will give you a choice, and the others. Who wishes, like the Professor, to eschew the blindfold?"

"Me," said Lieutenant Wright.

"Anyone else?"

Nar, Colonel Ischzue and Simon all made the same request.

"Ready the firing squad, Colonel Smeen," Denarghi ordered.

"The Grongles will attack soon. Indeed, with all of us gathered here I fear they will do so now," said The Professor. "It's not too late. I can save us if you'll let me."

"I am done with your lies, Professor. You will kill him first, Colonel Smeen."

"Yes, sir."

There was no fanfare and no drums.

"Ready," said Denarghi.

"Aim."

"The Prophet bless you, Professor and all," shouted somebody from the audience.

"Who is that?" demanded Denarghi.

More voices joined in, wishing the prisoners luck in the afterlife, invoking the blessing of The Prophet, the Creator, even some of the early architraves.

"Shut them up!"

"They're just praying for us," yelled the Professor over the swell.

"Then they will stop."

Over and above the shouts of farewell the Professor began to hear another noise, it sounded like bathwater disappearing down decrepit pipes.

"Smeen!" called The Professor. "They are coming. Get out everyone!" he shouted at the gathered agents. "Run while you may!"

"Don't think your friends will save you," shouted Denarghi.

"These are not my friends," shouted the Professor. "The Grongles are coming. NOW. Leave!"

Denarghi snatched a rifle from the nearest of Smeen's firing squad and raised it to fire at the Professor, but just then the bathwater noises resolved themselves into a loud pop, and the crowd was screaming as a Grongolian armoured personnel carrier appeared from nowhere, ploughing through the press of beings in front of it. The vehicle drove forward, the wheels squishing and cracking over the living beings in its path, to a crescendo of agonised screams. And before he could pull the trigger and kill the Professor, a laser-gun round turned Denarghi to vapour.

"Smeck!" Professor N'Aversion was crying and his hands shook as he took off the cuffs.

Then the cannon on the personnel carrier spoke. A round hit the stage and the Professor, along with everyone else on it, was thrown upwards. Perhaps he lost consciousness for a few seconds, or maybe his senses were overwhelmed by events, but the next thing he knew he was lying half buried in the splintered wreckage. As he clawed his way forward, he saw Colonel Ischzue and Colonel Smeen vaporised in front of his eyes. The air was thick with dust and smoke and his throat was dry. Someone hauled on his arm.

"Professor. Come on."

It was Lieutenant Wright. Her voice sounded faint behind the ringing in his ears.

"Where are the others?"

"Dead, I reckon." She ducked, pulling him down with her, and a round of laser fire pinged over their heads. "Us too if we stay here. But we can make it. Stick with me."

She led him under cover of the pile of wreckage towards the kitchen area. The mess hall had a row of arches to one side where the size of the trees above had precluded the complete removal of their roots. There was a colonnaded section here, where the ceiling was lower. In the wall of the space, which made up the side of the mess hall, was the serving hatch from the kitchen. The armoured personnel carrier was too big to fit through the arches and the remnants of the gathered crowd who had not fled through the exits on the other side moved there. The Grongles were still strafing them with fire but while many fell, the Professor saw, with relief, that many more were climbing over the serving hatch and escaping through the kitchens.

Meanwhile, Mrs Burgess herself, wearing the metal mixing bowl from an industrial mixer on her head, appeared to have procured a couple of heavy machine guns from somewhere. She stood fast with her team of staff, who were similarly attired, and returned the Grongles' fire with gusto. Her catering assistants, with the other gun, laid down covering fire for the last few agents as they made their escape. The bullets rattled off the personnel carrier's shields but at least it kept the detachment of Grongles, which it undoubtedly contained, inside it.

The Professor's ears rang and his head buzzed as he followed in Lieutenant Wright's wake. But he had recovered enough of his wits to dive through the hatch with her.

"It's getting dark," said Lieutenant Wright.

"They'll be targeting the mirrors," shouted the Professor as Mrs Burgess sent off another volley of fire. "They want us to panic."

There was a tinkling sound as another mirror bit the dust and the light in the mess hall descended to twilight level.

The last handful of agents dived over the serving counter crashing onto the floor. Mrs Burgess sent off another volley of fire and slammed the hatch closed.

"It won't hold 'em long," she said.

"No. We must regroup. How many of us?"

"I'd guess a couple of hundred," said Bob, Mrs Burgess' sous chef, "maybe more. Trick will be to get out. Word is there are more Grongles on the surface."

"We're trapped," said Lieutenant Wright.

"No, not if we can get to Smeen's office," said the Professor. "There are portals there. Two hundred of them."

"Where are the senior officers?"

"Eee, there's only us this side, pet," said Mrs Burgess.

As they picked their way towards the exit they heard a noise from the mess hall. It was the distinctive sound of portal use followed by the squealing of tyres halting abruptly. Another vehicle, smaller by the sound of the engine, drew up in front of the closed hatch. There was a metallic whine.

"That sounds fishy," said the Professor, "time we were gone."

There was a dull thunk, the unmistakable sound of a torpedo-firing mechanism priming.

"Ruuuuun!" shouted Bob. As the four of them dived into the corridor, an all-purpose torpedo detonated against the closed hatch, blowing it inwards. The force of the blast flung the heavy, catering-sized mixer against the back wall of the kitchen. Professor N'Aversion felt the shock wave, like a hand on his back pushing him out into the corridor. The kitchen appliances exploded and the ceiling fell in, metal air-conditioning ducts crashing and banging onto the twisted remnants of the stoves.

"Smeck," said Lieutenant Wright.

"At least it's blocked that exit."

They'd use the one the other side, no doubt.

"Where's the best place to regroup d'you reckon?" ask Lieutenant Wright as they ran down the passage.

"I have an idea or two."

"What d'you think to the cells?"

"At the top of my list. But we need to move fast."

"Too right," said Lieutenant Wright as they swiftly retreated, "they'll be coming."

Together, Professor N'Aversion, Lieutenant Wright, Mrs Burgess and Bob the sous chef ran down the corridor along with any number of agents who had escaped with or ahead of them. The survivors were regrouping into armed units of five, as their training for this situation dictated, and moving forward to cover the retreat of any last stragglers.

"Wait here, I'll go and take a dekko," said Lieutenant Wright. "Come on Bob," and the two of them ran off.

The Professor cast about him.

"What do you want the rest of us to do pet?" asked Mrs Burgess, as they continued to retreat.

"The bulk of you must fall back to the cells. It's the most heavily protected part of the building and it's the most central. I think the Grongles will try to get in through the exits as well as here, and trap us."

"There's an armoury there, too," said Mrs Burgess with a glint in her eye. "We'll take some trapping."

"There is so. Stay in the cell block and hold it for as long as you can. In the meantime, I need more armed units to keep the Grongles busy while we establish ourselves and two more to come with me to Smeen's office. If I can get there, I can get you all out."

Smeen's office was near to the Throne Room, on the other side of the mess hall, behind the line of advancing Grongles.

Everyone carried on moving back except for the volunteers, who began moving forward. A filing cabinet and some other furniture were taken from the rooms close by and piled across the corridor to provide cover and two groups of volunteers waited, guns at the ready.

The Professor could hear the sound of laser fire and running feet. Lieutenant Wright came belting down the passageway towards them with Bob hot on her heels and another large contingent of agents, about fifty, following on behind.

"Quick," she shouted, "they're out of the vehicle and coming this way."

As the last of the agents reached the safety of their armed colleagues, two more figures rounded the corner. Who in The Prophet's name were these? They looked like RA, judging by the nylon stockings they were wearing over their heads. It was only when they got closer that The Professor realised who they really were: Big Merv and Lieutenant Arbuthnot.

"Hold your fire. These are ours," he shouted as the agents ranged across the corridor took aim.

As Big Merv and Deidre reached the line, the first of the Grongles rounded the corner in attack formation.

The Resistance agents opened fire. The Professor knew how this was done; the groups would work in pairs. The one at the front would engage the attacking Grongles and then run for shelter while the second, further back, laid down covering fire and then, in turn, became the front line.

"By The Prophet, what are you two doing here?" The Professor asked as he retreated down the corridor with Big Merv and Lieutenant Arbuthnot.

"Trying to keep up with 'er," said Big Merv, jerking his thumb at Lieutenant Wright, "oh yer, and we're onna rescue mission."

"Where are the portals The Candidate gave you?" yelled Lieutenant Arbuthnot over the gunfire. Straight down to business, thought the Professor, with a smile.

"Smeen said they were under his desk."

"Smeck, that's all we need," said Lieutenant Wright.

"'S alright," said Big Merv, "we gotta couple o' portals here, we're gonna go get 'em but first we gotta get this lot outta here. Where're they gonna regroup?"

"The cells," said the Professor.

They beat a hasty retreat to an open area where Big Merv and Deirdre gathered everyone together for a quick debrief.

"Alright sweets, you know what to do," he told her.

"Affirmative, swampy."

The Professor wasn't sure which surprised him most; that Big Merv had called Deirdre 'sweets' without her slapping him down or that Deirdre had called him 'swampy' without him punching her lights out.

"Listen up soldiers," bellowed the Lieutenant. "Professor N'Aversion is going to get some kit from Smeen's office and then, we are going to get everyone out of here." The bedraggled group of agents cheered. "That's right troopers, this is a rescue. But if we're going to make it, you must be disciplined and obey orders. This is Big Merv and you treat him with the same respect you show me. Understood?"

"Ma'am, yes ma'am!" shouted the agents.

"Nice," said Big Merv to Deirdre as she moved back and stood next to the Professor. "Sweet, thanks babe. OK here's how it's gonna go down. We gotta take the injured first." Deirdre threw him a questioning glance. "It's what the lad would want," he told her in his normal voice before raising it again to address the agents. "The fitter you are, the longer you stay. It ain't good, I get that, but it's the way it's gonna be. You gotta stand by yer mates."

"Sir, yes sir!" shouted the agents.

Big Merv turned to Deirdre and winked.

"Everyone's gonna get outta here by portal. You won't know what that is and there ain't time to explain. You gotta trust me and the Lieutenant here. It ain't gonna take long but if the Grongles attack, some of you gotta buy us time. And that means some of you gotta volunteer to hold the line. You gotta stand by me and kick some royal Grongle butt. If we're lucky we ain't gonna have to for long. The Professor, here," Professor N'Aversion bowed when his name was mentioned, which got another cheer from the gathered agents, "reckons he can lay his hands on some extras. I need twenty volunteers. The rest of you, get yerselves into groups of four. We're gonna hole up in the cells and then Mizz Arbuthnot, here, an' my blokes, are gonna take you to Ning Dang Po, group by group. Mizz Arbuthnot and I ain't the only ones. Snoofle's here and our leader, The Pan of Hamgee and two of my blokes from the Underground, Alan and Psycho Dave.

"When we get there, you gotta run. Get yerselves to the Upper Left Central District and go to the Parrot and Screwdriver pub, on Turnadot Street.

"Any questions?"

The agents clapped and cheered but no one asked anything.

"Sweet. Deirdre, I reckon you got this covered. See you down the cells. As for you, sunshine," Big Merv turned to the Professor and put a tiny jam jar in his hand, "you know whatta do with this?"

"Yes."

"Alright. Go get those portals, Prof, pronto."

Chapter 68

Lord Vernon stalked through the smoking corridors of the Resistance HQ with a laser pistol in each hand. He used the pistols in turn, charging one while he vaporised everything in his path with the other. A tableau of greasy shadows along the walls where he had passed bore testament to the number of his victims. It was all that remained of them, along with the ash that covered the ground round his feet. So much killing, so much power over life and death; he was almost drunk with it.

It was a complete rout, and so easy it was laughable. The mess hall had been full, as he had determined. Every available agent was watching the planned execution under pain of death. Those agents the armoured personnel carrier had not cut down, Lord Vernon and his troops did, laying about them from the bulletproof safety of their vehicles with laser weapons: cannon, rapid-repeat rifles and pistols.

Oh, a few had made it out. Lord Vernon, at the wheel of the Interceptor, had dealt with the group in the kitchens. The handful left alive ran and Lord Vernon and his troops had left the personnel carrier and pursued them – moving outwards, through the corridors, killing everyone they found. Up at ground level, detachments of troops stationed at the entrances attacked and overpowered the agents on guard and took down any others who were foolish enough to try and escape. The Resistance vermin were caught like rats in a trap. Another few minutes and it would be over.

Chapter 69

The Pan closed his eyes, gritted his teeth and waited. There was a loud sucking sound and a pop, and he, Deirdre and Big Merv were rolling across the floor of a corridor. As he got to his feet a door opened and fleeing agents spilled out of it, along with the sounds of screams and acrid smoke.

"Smeck, looks like they've begun already," he shouted.

"Then we gotta get started," said Big Merv and he disappeared into the crowd. The Pan looked around for Deirdre but she, too, had already gone.

He hadn't thought about this. Beings who are running for their lives seldom have time for conversation. The Pan ran alongside a couple trying to explain but they wouldn't stop so he grabbed one, thought about a quiet corner of park in the area of Ning Dang Po he'd allotted himself and transported there.

"What the—" began the agent.

"No time, listen," said The Pan. He clearly communicated some of his urgency to the Architraves because they helped him out with The Voice when he said 'listen'. The agent stopped trying to speak and, instead, simply stared at him, open-mouthed. "Regroup at the Parrot and Screwdriver on Turnadot Street when it opens for lunch. Got that?"

The agent nodded, dumbly.

"Great. Off you go." The agent began to walk away. "A bit faster if I were you. The Grongles may be here any minute." The agent began to run. Good. Time to go. He imagined the corridor he'd just been in and put the thimble to his eye.

"Smeck!"

It was overrun with Grongles.

Cluck?

He was pleased to hear Eight. He was completely out of his depth and somehow he found the presence of his avian predecessor comforting. Especially in the light of what he'd just seen.

"Yeh. Now what?"

Cluck, said the chicken.

Oh yeh, The Pan remembered, he had to run, too. He took off at speed towards the riverfront. Right Central was a swanky area. The Planes was only a few blocks away so there were wooden pavilions dotted along the towpath, facing the river Dang. They had seats in so that the idle rich of Ning Dang Po could come and watch those who were unfortunate enough to have to work going about their daily business: in this case, on the river. He ran into the first one he came to and sat down.

"Alright, calm thoughts, panicking won't help," he whispered to himself.

Cluck, a mental picture of himself with the nylon stocking on his head sprang to mind.

"Yeh right, thanks," he took it off and stuffed it into his pocket. "Think, think, think."

He pictured his friends in turn but when he looked into the portal he saw nothing of them or their surroundings.

"Of course they have portals, too, you idiot. Theirs are jamming yours."

He thought about the other two Resistance agents he'd met, Simon and Professor N'Aversion but the result was the same. They were either dead or the others had found them and given them portals. He imagined the handful of places in the Resistance HQ he'd actually been to. A few lengths of corridor, Denarghi's throne room and the cells. They were deserted. He could transport himself to one of them and wander around until he found someone. But he didn't even know how to get from one to the other, let alone how to track down the last remaining Resistance agents. Presumably they'd all be regrouping somewhere and sure, he might find them. He might. Or he might find the Grongles.

"OK, let's call that Plan B."

Cluck?

The Pan screwed up his eyes and shook his head. But the chicken had a point. He looked down at the ring.

"Alright," he said, and took it off.

Silence.

The Pan's stomach turned over. What if they weren't there? What if they were with Lord Vernon?

"No. That can't be. Eight's here," he told himself.

He remembered how, when he was young, the local priest had visited his class and tried to explain the concept of prayer. He'd described it as something that had to be done by instinct, because, as a way of putting positive energy into the universe at the infinitesimally small level where the blocks that build all life reside, only a person's instinct could ask for the right thing. He'd stressed that it was not about pestering Arnold to present the Creator with a bucket list but about opening the heart and letting it speak. The poor man had done his best but it was only now, years later, that his words made sense. The Pan concentrated, his panicking thoughts, the bitter self-recrimination, the frustration and the anger became no more than noise and as he waited, a single phrase surfaced.

"Help me."

Still silence, but now he knew there were people in it, thinking.

"Please. K'Barthans are dying, I have to get back there, I have to save them. In the name of The Prophet, help me."

Ah'm glad tha's nor afeard ter ask.

"Five?"

Aye. Don't put t' ring on lad but tek a hold on it. And put t' portal in t' pocket.

"I need the portal."

No tha' don't.

"Are you—"

Does tha' doubt me? There's seventy-six of us in 'ere lad. Tha believes enough and we can tek on most things.

The Pan stood up. Worth a go. He closed his eyes and tried to relax. He felt strangely still and yet energetic, or at least, tingly as if he were statically charged. His toes and fingertips, especially, seemed to be almost vibrating. He held his arms as far out in front of him as his injured shoulder would allow and spread his fingers, turned his hands over and then brought his fingertips against his thumbs. It felt as if there was something gritty between them, like grains of sand, except he knew there was nothing there, or at least no sand. This was some form of energy. He concentrated on the sensation of the grit and began to feel lighter. Then he was moving and he wondered, briefly, what anyone watching from the park would see, before he felt the familiar sensation of portal use. Except without one.

"Where will I end up?" he asked somewhat belatedly.

Where tha's needed most, said Five and then The Pan was tumbling across a room and rolling to a stop against a wooden surface. *Very swish,* said Five dourly.

"Yeh, I need to work on my landings."

Cluck, agreed the chicken.

Tha's done alreight, lad. Put on t' ring, said Five.

"But—"

Eight'll tell us when tha' wants us, and before he could thank them, the pair of them were gone.

"Thank you. That was amazing," he said anyway, because it pays to be polite.

Nothing.

"Hello?" whispered The Pan.

Still, nothing. They really had gone, except he believed Eight, the chicken, was listening.

He got himself the right way up and clambered to his feet. The wooden surface he had collided with was the side of a workbench, except the space he was in couldn't really be called a workshop. It was more high tech. A lab? Perhaps. He stood up and put on the ring as Five had instructed.

Chapter 70

The Pan looked around him. It didn't take a genius to guess that this was Tech Ops. If the equipment lying about hadn't told him, the film posters on the walls, the action figures on the desks and the discarded graphic novel left on a bench would. He made his way over to one side where a partition ran across the corner. The top half was glass and he guessed it to be Professor N'Aversion's office. There was a sofa with a small occasional table and a desk. Along one wall was a workbench like the ones in the main workshop. It was very tidy and looking at the chaotic state of the desk, The Pan suspected the Professor's work in progress had been removed, either by Denarghi or the Grongles.

As he stood thinking, he began to become aware of an uncomfortable sensation that he wanted to be elsewhere, fast. Never one to go against his instincts, The Pan moved swiftly out of the office and headed for the door in the opposite corner of the lab. As he did so, he noticed that there was another door behind him. He stopped for a moment, wondering which of the two exits to use. Maybe he should use the portal, which he still had in his pocket, or see if the Architraves would help him again.

Then he heard a sound, footsteps approaching both doors. It was difficult to distinguish the sound of one but the other was a group, marching.

Arnold. Grongles.

He hesitated for a split second as he put his hand in his pocket and his fingers closed around the reassuring shape of the tiny jam jar.

No.

Scratch portal use unless all other options were exhausted. The Grongles might hear it. And then they would know. And at the moment they didn't. So right now he must hide.

He turned and headed for the office. Noooo not the office. He'd be trapped and if they searched it he'd be cornered. He must stay in the lab, that way, he might be able to move round, keeping out of sight.

No time left, no choice. He dived behind one of the heavy wooden workbenches where he waited, crouching, ready to bolt, or creep further out of sight.

The sound of marching grew louder until the door was flung open and a small detachment of Grongles arrived. Another set of footsteps, arrogant, swaggering, approached from the opposite direction. The Pan risked a glance. A tall figure entered the room. Oh it just had to be, didn't it?

"Captain," said a voice, a voice The Pan knew only too well. "Where are the rest of them?"

"We believe they're heading for the cells, sir."

"Naturally; all but two of the exits are taken. They know they are trapped. Have we taken any casualties?"

"Private Partee has cut his finger. He caught it in the door of the personnel carrier. He'll need stitches."

"Get him seen to, and … the females?" something in Lord Vernon's tone of voice, when he mentioned the females, made The Pan's blood run cold.

"We have over a hundred now, sir."

"Really? I was expecting more."

"It's difficult to take them alive, sir."

"I am aware of that, Captain. Try harder or I will have to keep them all for myself."

"They fight like demons, sir."

"Yes, Captain. That is why I want them and that is what the stun setting on your pistol is for. Those you have taken thus far, you will send back to Headquarters. The choicest specimens will be allocated to me, for my own pleasure. Bring me more and I may leave some for you."

The Pan's skin burned and his head thrummed with the righteous indignation of his predecessors. They wanted to act. They wanted him to use their power against Lord Vernon, and Arnold knew, so did he, but something told him that if he tried before he was Architrave it would destroy him. He remembered a conversation he had overheard between General Moteurs and Sir Robin about him suffering horribly now that he had released his predecessors. Soundlessly he gritted his teeth and tried to show them this knowledge. Hiding behind the bench, sweaty and breathless he fought them for control of his body, while trying not to make any noise.

"Sir. What of the lab?" Captain Snow was asking.

"What of it?"

"All this equipment, sir."

"It's safe enough, they can't get to it now."

"Do you want it destroyed, sir?"

"No, fool, I want it preserved, General Moteurs' scientists must see it. Give me the map."

Captain Snow clicked his fingers and there was a papery rustling, as one of his troops handed over the map. Lord Vernon snatched it and unfolded it on the surface of a nearby worktable.

"We are here, sir, and the cells are here."

"How long will it take to drive the rest of the rats to the centre of the nest?"

"Five minutes? Less. The cells are central and secure. That is why they are heading there to regroup."

"Excellent. Then when they are gathered we will place units in the passages, here, here, and here, so there is no escape." He snorted derisively. "Five troops and a cannon on each will be enough."

"They will counter-attack, sir."

"No they won't Captain. They know they are defeated. Their plan, now, is martyrdom. They will wait for us to attack and try to destroy themselves, and us with them. I will not give them the gratification – much as I would like to take care of them personally. We will have to be a little less ..." he paused to pin down the word he wanted, "hands on. I have almost everything I want and I know that I can rely on you to rectify the situation with the females. I am due in Grongolia in one hour and ten minutes, and I must prepare myself. We will gas them, like the pestilential disease they are."

"Sir."

"You will find a team on the surface. They have already positioned the lines. Your troops will drive them into their lair and then withdraw, after which I will start the pump in three minutes."

"Sir."

"We will rendezvous on the surface here," there was another papery rustle as he tapped the position on the map, "and then your troops will return, with breathing apparatus, to collect and identify the bodies."

"Sir."

"I want every last one of them accounted for."

"Sir."

"And call GNN, I want the collection process filmed. K'Barth must be shown that it is crushed."

"Sir."

"You may go."

"Sir."

The footsteps of the Captain and his troops retreated and a door banged. The Pan's anger burned fiercely, eclipsing his fear but he could not take on Lord Vernon now. He must wait. His legs were cramped and sore, his jaw tightly clenched with the effort of containing his predecessors but he stayed where he was, still, silent, waiting. Lord Vernon had not left yet. The Pan was sure of it. After a few seconds, he risked a brief glance. Sure enough Lord Vernon was there, phone in hand, concentrating on the screen. The Pan ducked quickly back as he looked up, suddenly, and put the phone to his ear.

There was a moment of silence and then Lord Vernon spoke.

"Moteurs."

A pause as he listened.

"Your portal tests, they were successful?"

A second pause.

"I am glad to hear that. How soon can the prototype be put into production?"

Another silence.

"What teething problems, General?"

Lord Vernon was quiet again and, from the phone, came the faint sound of a voice uttering indistinguishable words.

"Very well. Continue testing. I am all but finished here, I will join you and General Ennui in fifty minutes for a debrief before the ceremony."

There was a snap as Lord Vernon closed his phone.

The Pan risked the movement of glancing at his watch. Up on the surface, Captain Snow would be relaying his orders to the gas team. Big Merv and the others were running out of time. Why wouldn't Lord Vernon just go away?

He was moving slowly around the room. Arnold's pants. Surely the smecker wasn't going to examine the lab now? Lord Vernon's footsteps grew louder as he approached the bench. His breathing was audible to The Pan, huddled behind it. He moved closer and The Pan crept stealthily backwards. As Lord Vernon emerged round one end, The Pan crawled silently round the other. His heart pounded and his throat was dry. Arnold, he must not cough. And what about his hands? They were wet with perspiration. What if he'd left sweaty prints on the floor? What if

Lord Vernon heard his heightened breathing? But no, it seemed the Lord Protector was too wrapped up in his own thoughts. After standing for a second or two in silence, he turned and strode from the room. The Pan did not move until the footsteps had receded into the distance.

The Pan had been to the cells at the Resistance HQ and he lost no time transporting himself there by portal.

Chapter 71

When The Pan arrived at the cells, the gassing had already started; there was a hissing sound and the air smelled acrid. He took a breath and held it, removed his sling and wrapped it round his face. He ran round the corner and found a sea of prone agents, along with Big Merv who was lying on his side with one hand across his face, still clutching the handkerchief he'd been holding over his mouth.

The Pan put his hand to the Swamp Thing's neck. There was a pulse, he didn't check the others. No time. He just hoped.

Big Merv was holding something in his other hand too: a khaki-coloured box with an on-off switch and a single red button. It had a wire running from the bottom to the wall where there was a hole packed with, yes, that looked like explosives. There was another wire running down the wall to similar holes at regular intervals all the way down the corridor. So the red thing was a detonator. Lord Vernon had been right. They'd been going to blow themselves up. It was a good plan, a bomb would make it hard to look for bodies. Like as not the Grongles would never find out that there weren't enough.

For the sake of those who had already escaped, The Pan had to blow the bomb.

And he had to rescue his friends.

And everyone else.

If he could.

Yeh, and by any time yesterday would be fine.

"Eight!"

He yanked off the ring.

His chest was burning and his lungs felt as if they were about to explode. In a few moments, he knew, he was going to take an involuntary breath and it would probably make him pass out. Except that ... He thought about the park in Ning Dang Po, put the portal briefly to his eye to check and then he held the open end against his mouth and took a breath. Wow. Air. Tank up then. He breathed out, put the portal to his mouth again and took another breath. This time he held it. His thoughts bombarded him at lightning speed, along with those of his predecessors.

They'll die before you can tie them together. One of the voices. Brusque and female.

"No need to link them up. If you help me, I can get them out, I know it," thought The Pan. He remembered what Five said, "If you can give me the power."

It may kill you.

"Then do what you can and let's all try to stop before it does."

Concentrate on what is required and surrender your body to us. The Pan didn't like the sound of that and she clearly realised. *You must trust us. You are the conduit, we are working through you.*

This in a few seconds.

The Pan did as she had asked and concentrated, trying to imagine the HQ as a whole, and with it any Resistance agents inside, no matter where, who were still alive. He felt a dull pressure building in his head.

Concentrate harder, said the voice. He reached out with his mind and his imagination. It made his stomach churn and the pain in his head increased. Or was that the gas? The crushing pressure around his brain intensified. Much more of this and it was going to come squelching out through his ears. Or explode. No, no. But the effort! He sweated and strained like a circus strongman pulling a commercial snurd up a hill by his teeth. Except that it felt as if it was the whole planet he was dragging using his actual brain. He hoped it wasn't really melting the way it seemed to be. But what if it was going to be sucked out of his head? No, no, don't be stupid. It wasn't.

"Help me," he begged them.

No, no more, said the voice.

"Just a tiny bit," begged The Pan. The pressure in his head turned to pain, but he felt the tingling sensation in his fingers. Bright lights exploded against the backs of his eyelids, he felt unconsciousness closing in. Arnold! No, he was so close. It had to work, it had to. He tried harder. The last thing he thought about was the detonator. He hadn't pressed the button. Then it felt as if his whole body was imploding under the weight of the power he was attempting to channel, there was a flash of searing pain and he passed out.

Chapter 72

The Pan rolled over onto the wrong shoulder.

He sat up and immediately started coughing. Around him were fifty or sixty beings of assorted genus and gender who all appeared to be at various stages of regaining consciousness. They were coughing, as well.

"Thanks," he said although he wasn't sure his predecessors heard him.

His clothes felt damp and clammy with sweat, and his hair was wet with it too, hanging lankly over his forehead. He put his hand up and pushed it away.

Someone was standing over him, two people, indistinct black outlines silhouetted against the bright morning sun. He looked up at them. They were big, one had his arms folded and a physique like a comic book superhero, the other was carrying a suitcase. The Pan put his good hand up to shield his eyes.

"Are we dead?" he asked.

"Nah, we ain't," said one of them.

"Merv!"

"Yer," said his friend, starting to chuckle until it turned into a cough. The Pan leapt to his feet. Too fast.

"Here's the Prof an' all. Whoa, easy mate," said Big Merv, catching him by the arm as his legs buckled under him. Merv put The Pan's good arm round his shoulders and gripped his wrist firmly, holding him up. The movement made both of them cough again. "Arnold's socks! You spotty little Herbert. How come you gotta be late for everything?"

The Pan laughed until the coughing took over again.

"It's the way I roll," he wheezed. "Hi Prof," he added pausing for another round of coughing. "Arnold's bogies, what was that stuff?"

"Standard lethal gas," said the Professor. "It shouldn't do any lasting damage." He sounded calm but he was trembling, visibly, and The Pan could hear it, too, in his voice.

"Good to know, that," he felt incredibly weak and even to his own ears, his voice seemed faint.

"You wanna sit down again?" asked Big Merv.

"No, I'm fine, it'll wear off in a minute. You alright Professor?"

"I think I have fared better than you," said the Professor.

"Maybe," The Pan grinned. He nodded at the suitcase in the Professor's hand.

"Is that what I think it is?"

"Yes."

"Nice one."

"Your Most Gracious—"

"Defreville."

"Defreville," the Professor corrected himself. "That really was remarkable."

"Thanks," said The Pan, "I had a lot of help."

The Professor paused for more coughing and Big Merv stepped into the conversational gap.

"You done good, though, mate," he said. "C'mon, we gotta get you back to the Parrot. Doctor Dot's there. I reckon she'd better take a gander at yer."

"Fine by me." The Pan smiled wanly. His chest still burned as if his lungs had been filled with acid.

"I'm wondering, do you know where we are?" asked the Professor.

"He'd better coz I ain't got no effin' clue," said Big Merv, looking at The Pan.

The Pan squinted round him. At first, apart from the recovering Resistance agents, there wasn't much to go on. Then, on the ground, closer to, his eyes lit on a hammer. There was something familiar about that hammer.

"Yeh, I know where we are but I think we should go."

One of the voices spoke.

Wait a while. Give them time to recover. Portal free travel is untraceable.

Aye, tha's safe enough, said Five.

Yes, said the other voice, *but you must put on the ring.*

Aye, said Five again, tha's not t' only one as needs a break.

Cluck, agreed Eight.

"Sorry guys, Five, Eight and … all of you. Thanks."

"Whadda you on about you tart?" asked Big Merv.

"Sorry Merv, forget it, I was talking to myself."

The Pan's fingers felt numb and were possessed with the dexterity of someone else's sausages but he managed to fumble the ring back on.

"You wanna rest up a mo? You ain't lookin' good."

"No, I'm right as rain, having a gas."

"'S not effin' funny."

"I think I know where we are … This is where I left the delivery snurd on the morning I rescued you."

"Is it really?" asked the Professor. The Pan watched as the erstwhile head of Tech Ops looked around him, alert, watching, listening. It was hard to tell what he was thinking. Standing, propped up on his friend, The Pan doubted he was looking much like a leader.

"I'm OK, now," he said, trying, without much headway, to remove his arm from Merv's shoulders, "I can stand up on my own, really."

Big Merv let go of his wrist.

"Thanks."

One of the agents approached. A Galorsh. He was nervous, holding his tail in one hand, stroking it with the other.

"Hello," said The Pan.

"Alright son?" asked Big Merv.

"Yeh man, I'm good." He turned to The Pan, "I-I wanted to say, we're proper grateful, what you just did, I mean whoa it's—"

"It's no big deal," The Pan interrupted him, "although, having said that, please don't ask me to do it again. Or at least, not for a very long time." He was completely drained and he felt as if he'd been awake for a thousand years. He turned to the Professor, "Are your people ready? Only we should probably be going. It's a long walk back." He thought longingly of the SE2. That was a point. It was illegal for K'Barthans to move on the streets in large groups. They'd have to split up but follow each other. It would be mayhem. "On second thoughts," he said taking his snurd keys from the pocket of his trousers and pressing the button, "it'll take a while but I suspect it's better if I give everyone a lift."

"Thanks dude," said the Galorsh.

"You might not be so thankful when you've tried it," said The Pan.

"Yer, the way that little squirt drives, you're gonna need a strong stomach," said Big Merv.

"Are you sure you have the strength?" asked the Professor.

The Pan straightened his back and looked him in the eye.

"Yeh," he said and to the Galorsh. "What's your name?"

"Forrest."

"Nar's Forrest?" exclaimed the Professor.

The Galorsh looked down at his fingers.

"Yeh," he said quietly. "She's not here."

"No," said the Professor sadly.

"Don't lose hope, she might be back at the Parrot," said The Pan.

"Thanks," said Forrest, and over his shoulder, The Pan saw Professor N'Aversion shaking his head. Both he and Forrest seemed about ready to cry, but luckily the SE2 arrived and distracted them, along with everyone else.

The agents were all up on their feet now and they gathered round it making approving comments, stroking the paintwork and generally being excited. The Pan watched, impressed, as Professor N'Aversion anticipated and defused the argument as to who would go first before it broke out. He looked at his watch. They'd been there five minutes. Big Merv shifted, beside him.

"He's solid, the Prof, knows what he's doin'," he said voicing The Pan's thoughts.

He tried to concentrate on how many agents there were and how many trips he would have to do. There were some Blurpons and Spiffles, he could squeeze five of them in at once if he put one in the footwell each time. As for the others, he reckoned on two or three. Not so bad. Quicker than trying to keep groups of them together on foot and it was a short journey time if he flew.

"OK, let's go. Professor, can you stay here and look out for this lot?"

"Of course, as Commander Thistwith-Mee said, 'a good general never leaves his troops'."

"Yeh. Come on then Merv, I'll need you taking care of things the other end, and you Forrest."

The roof of the SE2 began to retract.

"Yo, smooth," said the agent as he squished himself into the space behind the seats.

The Pan pressed the button to put up the roof.

"Put yer seat belt on, son," Big Merv warned Forrest as The Pan selected aviator mode.

The agents in front of them cleared a path as the snurd's shiny silver-grey wings morphed out of its sides. Then without more ado, The Pan gunned the engine, to cheers from the assembled agents, and took off. He was still so tired he could hardly think, but being at the wheel of the SE2 automatically lifted his spirits. He circled, checking for any signs of suspicious locals or approaching Grongles but the surrounding area was deserted from the air. As they flew over the agents on the ground The Pan could see them waving.

Ah what the heck? He did a 360 roll.

When he looked down at them again they were jumping up and down and pumping the air with their fists.

"Have you gotta do that?" asked Big Merv.

"Oh yeh."

Chapter 73

By the time The Pan pulled up outside the Parrot and Screwdriver with Professor N'Aversion and the last of the agents, he could hardly keep his eyes open. Waving away their thanks with a wan smile, he stopped for a moment to steady himself. It was all he could do to put one foot in front of the other. He'd been running on adrenaline and it was spent. He needed to sleep, possibly for the rest of his life. But he couldn't. Not now. He had a pub to open and it wasn't as if he could leave it to the others. They'd been through the same thing as him and they would be just as drained.

Tha 'as ter lead from t' front.

"Yeh, Five," The Pan yawned, "I know."

Hang on. He checked his hand. He was wearing the ring wasn't he, so how come—?

It's wearing off lad. If tha's not installed at t' end of this week tha'll be insane afore t' end o' t' next.

"Great. Marvellous news."

With a sigh The Pan followed the Professor and the agents inside. Through the hall he could see that the main bar was crammed and to his surprise he realised it was open and serving. Snoofle was waiting for them.

"The hero of the hour returns," he said.

Hero? Where?

"Do you guys want to go and rest up a bit?" asked The Pan.

"In time," said the Professor. "I think I'll have a snifter first, and one of those cheese sandwiches."

"Alright. Snoofle, d'you know how many we saved?"

"There are three hundred and thirty two agents making the best of your workshop and hayloft until we find them somewhere to stay."

"Wow, really?" The Pan was delighted and as such, a bit more energised. "That's a fantastic result, amazing." It was a fraction of the personnel at the Resistance HQ but it was still over three hundred beings, alive and well, who wouldn't have been there otherwise. "Thank you, thank you so much for what you did, you and the others." He wondered where Big Merv was and chided himself for not thanking him, or the Professor, before.

"It wasn't just us sir," said Snoofle.

Sir? Arnold, this being in command thing felt weird.

"I think we can call it a group effort," said The Pan. "Is everyone accounted for?" he asked, as Big Merv came out of the bar, partially answering that question, with Alan, who was looking somewhat singed but otherwise none the worse for wear.

"Wotcher," said Big Merv striding over to him and enveloping him in a hug of such ferocity he almost collapsed. "You alright mate?"

"Yeh," said The Pan trying to look lively. "You?"

"I reckon, right lads?" said Big Merv and the Professor, Snoofle and Alan agreed.

"Did you get yourself kippered, Alan?" asked The Pan.

"Yeh. It's not bad. My jacket smells like bacon, have a sniff," he proffered an arm at The Pan who dutifully complied.

"It does too," he said and before anyone else could sidetrack him, asked again, "Are you guys alright, do you need to rest?"

"Nah," said Big Merv, "but you do son. We got this ain't we?"

"Right," said Alan. Snoofle and Professor N'Aversion nodded.

"Sweet. So get upstairs, get showered and get yerself sorted."

"Do I smell?"

"Like a warthog's armpit."

"Thanks Merv, consummate tact there. As ever."

"Yer, I'm surprised them agents survived the journey what with you gassing 'em a second time."

"Smecking cheek! Next time I'll leave you there, you get," said The Pan. "OK, a bit more seriously now on the subject of rest and baths and stuff, what about you lot, and the agents?"

"What about us?" asked the Professor. "We'll wait."

"Yeh," agreed Alan.

"And so will the agents," said Snoofle.

"You bet they will if they reckon it's gonna stop the pong round you," said Big Merv.

It was so good to be back in the pub.

"I can see you're feeling chipper," The Pan told his friend, "but I—aren't you feeling tired, too?"

The Pan desperately wanted to accept their offer and sleep. But he was supposed to be in command and he wasn't sure that was how it was done.

"Not like you son. We done 'em in batches of five, remember? Not fifty, right Prof?"

"There were sixty-one of us," said the Professor quietly.

"Arnold," said Alan.

The Pan didn't say anything.

"The usual practice is to take it in turns," said Snoofle, "and since you did the most work, you go first."

"Yeh, it's quiet enough," said Alan. "Doctor Dot and Lucy are behind the bar."

"Please, rest first," said the Professor. "We'll wake you."

"Yep," said Alan, "it's not like you have to fix much. Some of the punters and their friends … and anyone else they trust enough to drag into this, have volunteered to take the agents into their own homes. Betsy's taking six of them."

"Yer, 's a lotta them," added Big Merv.

"What, agents?"

"Nah, punters."

"Yeh, looks like Norris might have done you a favour with all his clap-trap," said Alan with a chuckle.

"That's-that's great," said The Pan, "but isn't it dangerous? I don't want to put anyone in harm's way."

"Nah, 's no trouble, not with the installation, 's a lotta strangers from outta town."

"And after the installation, they'll be gone," added the Professor.

"That should be their accommodation fixed up if the customers take a couple each," said Snoofle.

"Wow, that's terrific. I can see you have it organised," said The Pan. "How can I ever thank you, and all the others? I could never have pulled off today without you."

The Professor drew himself up to his full height, suddenly serious.

"Defeat him," he said. "Nar and Simon and hundreds like them are dead," his voice broke. "Don't let their deaths be in vain."

The Pan looked him in the eye, trying to appear strong, to hide his doubt and fear.

"I'll give it my best shot."

He looked round at the four of them.

"Right then. I'll just pop in the bar and say hello to the others, then I'll turn in for a bit. Don't let me sleep too long. Come and wake me in an hour or two," he said and headed into the bar to find Lucy, Deirdre and Doctor Dot.

Chapter 74

It was the end of the day. The Pan sat on the sofa in Gladys and Ada's sitting room. Everyone else had gone to bed. There wasn't even anyone sitting up with Trev. Doctor Dot was so pleased with his progress that she'd told Lucy she could stand down the night watch.

Alone, The Pan reflected on his situation. He'd serviced the bar one final time, the washing-up was done, everything put away and the rescued Resistance agents had been patched up by Doctor Dot, where required, and taken home with the punters. He had spent an hour after closing time with his friends, with the schematics of the newly rebuilt temple spread out in front of them, going over the plans they'd made with General Moteurs one last time: who was to do what, where they would be and when The Pan would make his move. Deirdre had chosen some volunteers from among the handful of agents left from Strike Ops for her mission and Snoofle had chosen some Spiffles and fellow Blurpons for his. The only other two senior Resistance agents left, Professor N'Aversion and Mrs Burgess, were working with Big Merv coordinating the efforts of the K'Barthans outside the temple. All the decisions had been made while The Pan was sleeping off the mind-numbing tiredness caused by moving sixty-one half-gassed Resistance agents from their HQ and blowing the bomb they'd set. The entire thing had been presented to him as a finalised plan, and in the absence of any better ideas, he'd given them the green light.

"It might work. I may even survive," he muttered. Except ... Lord Vernon would have thought about every angle of this. Even if General Moteurs had won his trust, he would have contingency plans, and contingency plans for the contingency plans, and so on.

The Pan had spent most of the hours since he woke up wondering what those plans would be. He hoped he and his friends had covered the options but he knew his limitations; he was a pantser, not a planner. And acting on instinct was fine on your own but when other people were involved the thinking had to be done in advance and he wasn't so sure of his ground. His predecessors seemed to approve. There was a continual buzz of conversation going on in his head now. The ring was losing its power to contain them, indeed, he doubted he could restrain them any more, not if they became really angry. If they unleashed all their power before he was installed as Architrave, he knew instinctively it would kill him. But he could also tell that they were holding back, trying to contain themselves, trying to preserve him, and they were starting to suggest things and work with him rather than simply rant and tell him off.

"I just hope I've done enough."

Cluck.

"Thanks."

He got up, went through to the kitchen and looked out of the window. Somewhere, among the roofs of the city, across the sea of twinkling lights, was the Palace, and Ruth. He wanted to see her, wanted to so much that it hurt. He leaned his head against the glass and looked up. The night was clear, with an autumn nip in the air and the stars were bright. K'Barth, the world, was so small and insignificant in the grand scheme of things. A snurd motored slowly down the street. He listened to the engine as it faded into the distance.

General Moteurs would be in Grongolia tonight, at the inauguration dinner for the new High Leader, which, the new High Leader being Lord Vernon, meant he'd be there too. The Chosen One would be on her own, and a visit from Lord Vernon looked unlikely. The fact that Grongles regarded it as unlucky for a bride and bridegroom to see each other the night before their wedding also increased the odds against hubby-to-be paying her a visit. In theory, The Pan might creep into the Palace and see her – if he was feeling like doing something dangerous and reckless. In theory, it shouldn't be a problem. And it would be so easy. He would go to the doorway under the bridge where Deirdre had gone and then he would step inside and use the portal to find Ruth.

"No," he said aloud.

He couldn't. He mustn't. It would jeopardise everything.

"Big picture," he reminded himself. But he didn't believe it.

He turned away from the window, filled himself a glass of water, went out into the hall and stopped.

He wanted to do the right thing for K'Barth, for his friends, for the world. But he was going to die for them in a few hours and if he was going to do that, he wanted to be at peace with himself, too. And if he wanted to be at peace with himself then, reckless or not, he must make his peace with Ruth.

"I have to see her," he whispered. "I have to."

Cluck? said Eight who didn't actually sound all that alarmed by the idea.

"Yeh," said The Pan.

His mind made up, he put on his jacket, cloak and hat, grabbed both sets of keys for his snurd and put a couple of portals into one pocket. He wanted to give her something to remember him by. He looked down at the K'Barthan Ring of State on his finger, well, no, probably not that but it gave him an idea. He went and had a rummage in the kitchen drawer, the one where Gladys and Ada kept the kind of useless items you keep because they might come in handy and then throw away a couple of days before they actually do. There were broken handles from pots, pencils, the knob off a drawer which in no way matched any of the other drawers anywhere on the premises, several buttons, a penknife with half a blade and yes, there it was. Pinker and plastickier than he remembered. Ada had won it in a cracker when they had flouted a Grongle ban to stage a 'secret' celebration of The Prophet's birthday at the Parrot, for the entire neighbourhood.

"Good days," he said quietly as he remembered.

Aye, and beggars can't be choosers, said the voice of Five into his ear, if tha wants a ring that's all tha's got.

"Yeh," said The Pan. He dropped the gaudy piece of plastic into his pocket with a smile. Then quietly, he moved to the window and opened it. He slipped out onto the fire escape and carefully, silently, slid it closed. He made his way up to the roofs. It would be less dangerous than the streets, even at this time of night, and it wasn't as if he had to worry about any Resistance agents any more. The air was chill with the first hints of winter and he took a lungful. He walked the length of the street, along the tops of the moonlit buildings feeling alive and invigorated.

He supposed his imminent death was to blame, but it was as if he could sense the vibrancy, the energy in everything. And it felt good. Being doomed wasn't so bad and if he was going to be murdered on world telly, than at least it would be quick. He pressed the button on his keyring and the SE2 appeared, top down, heater on. There was nowhere for it to land so it made a slow pass and The Pan jumped off the gable and landed, with easy precision, in the driving seat.

"Nice," he said. The pleasure he felt at pulling off such a manoeuvre was only slightly dulled by the absence of anyone else to see it.

Cluck, said Eight.

"Can't win 'em all hen," he said.

*****

Up on the moonlit roofs, a few hundred yards away from The Pan, Lieutenant Arbuthnot watched with grudging approval. She had misjudged The Pan of Hamgee, or he had grown up since they first met. He was definitely a better leader, an all-round better man, than she'd first thought. She slipped quietly back down the fire escape and into the kitchen.

"That him gone?" asked a voice in the darkness.

"Big Merv?"

"'S right treacle."

Arnold, did he have to call her that? She blinked as he turned the light on.

"Ford warned me of this," she said as she shut the window.

"Yer, 'e's smart your General."

"Yes. He is."

"Yer, an' you're pretty tidy yourself."

"Thanks," she said.

"'S the truth. You done alright today girl."

"You too," she said.

He smiled and she was surprised at the way it lit up his face.

"You wanna sit down?" he asked. "I'm guessing you ain't gonna want cocoa but I got some herbal tea," he added as he flicked the switch on the kettle. "Luce drinks it."

"Thank you." She shut the door, in case their conversation woke anyone else, and took a seat at the table.

"We must contact Ford." She removed the phone General Moteurs had given her from her pocket and put it on the table.

He stood there, looking down at her, the piercing green eyes watching, gauging, weighing her up. His antennae were waving backwards in thought. She felt almost as if this were some test and her actions would determine his view of her. The two of them were quiet for a moment.

"In a while," she said, "let's have some tea first."

He laughed. Whatever the test was, it appeared she had passed. She was surprised at how pleased that made her feel.

"You catch on quick, girl," he said.

"I would hope so."

Chapter 75

Lord Vernon watched General Moteurs move among his aides, a single grey-clad figure in a sea of black, red and gold braid. He wore a dress uniform, as custom dictated, but apart from the medals, he had eschewed all but the most subtle indications of rank. The medals said it all, Lord Vernon reflected, as did the bejewelled K'Barthan star of office he, himself, wore. Both of them stood out among the bling-festooned aides around them.

"Two of a kind," said Lord Vernon quietly.

His eye swept the room, searching for the female General Ennui had introduced him to at the champagne reception. She was wearing the tiniest sequined dress on the most deliciously pert and athletic body. She'd been commanding much of his attention since they had met. He soon spotted her and watched as she spoke to a mixed group on the far side of the room. Even at this distance he could see how the males in the company were competing for her attention.

He smiled to himself. Oh they could try but he knew she wanted something a little more … alpha … than them. She'd been giving subtle indications, all evening, that she was his for the asking, if he wanted. She must have felt his eyes on her as she glanced up suddenly, her skin flushed and her pupils dilated under his gaze. He made sure he had her full attention and glanced briefly at the open balcony doors, watching as she excused herself from her conversation and walked seductively over to them. She paused in the doorway to cast a glance back at him, a lingering, smouldering look, before drifting out into the darkness. He smiled to himself. He would not return to K'Barth tonight.

He cast about for General Moteurs and soon spotted him talking to the Minister for the Interior.

As Lord Vernon's second in command in K'Barth, anyone in the room with a government post in Grongolia was senior to the General. Yet he moved with a quiet confidence and authority that was striking. His behaviour, as always, was impeccable but the respect the others showed him went well beyond deference into the realms of fear. It was only natural and Lord Vernon congratulated himself that it was not General

Moteurs they were wary of but his relationship with his master.

As Lord Vernon watched, the General excused himself from the Minister and withdrew to the side of the room. Opening the case at his belt he took out his phone and stood motionless for a few seconds while he read the screen. Lord Vernon moved quietly to his side.

"Bad news, Moteurs?"

General Moteurs snapped the case closed and put his phone hurriedly back in his belt.

"Nothing of import, sir."

"You do not appear relaxed."

"In truth, I am not."

"Why?" Lord Vernon asked, giving him the kind of ominous, searching look that was guaranteed to rack up the General's tension levels.

"Seating the Grongolian Cabinet is somewhat onerous at present. The deputation from the Finance Ministry refuses to be positioned further back than the Minister for the Interior."

"These pompous fools would have the entire congregation placed in a single row."

"It would seem so, sir."

"They will sit where they are told," said Lord Vernon.

General Moteurs looked up at him, his expression determined.

"Indeed they will, sir."

"And your message?"

"It is nothing. My subordinates will take care of it."

"No need, General. I will be staying here tonight. I have ..." Lord Vernon glanced over at the open balcony doors, his mind on the delight awaiting him outside, "business to attend to. I will return tomorrow morning at zero four hundred hours precisely. Until then, I leave K'Barth in your hands."

Chapter 76

The Pan reached out and twisted the brushed aluminium knob to turn the heater down. As usual the rows of shiny buttons on the dash filled him with something approaching awe. Even over the course of the week, running the Parrot and Screwdriver, The Pan hadn't really had time to examine the capabilities of the newly rebuilt SE2 very thoroughly. Now he discovered there was a button he hadn't noticed, just above the heater knob.

"Stealth?" he read.

Cluck.

"Mmm. Only one way to find out." He pressed it and the bonnet in front of him disappeared. He could see the wing mirrors still but not the metal in which they were mounted. "Smecking smeck," he breathed, "are we invisible?"

He took it lower and buzzed along a nearby street for a hundred yards or so, at first floor level. In the shiny mirror reflection of the darkened windows he saw his head and shoulders fly by, but the snurd didn't show up.

"Arnold's sweaty sandals. No way. That is the coolest thing I have ever seen," he took the snurd upwards into the sky again, "pity I won't live to use it. Then again …"

The place he was aiming for was coming into view so he turned the snurd's headlights off; if he was going to do 'stealth' he reckoned he might as well do it properly. He landed the snurd on the grass in a park. In front of him was the bridge under which Deirdre had followed General Moteurs.

"Oops. Sorry." There was a bump as the snurd ploughed through an ornamental flower bed. "Arnold's armpits, I should have been looking where I was going."

Trailing soil and flowers behind him, he drove the snurd along the path and under the bridge.

The Pan got out of the SE2 and stood looking at the door Deirdre had gone through. He hadn't really expected to find it unlocked. However, when he tried it and found that it was indeed, locked, it was still a disappointment. He knew how to pick pockets but locks were beyond him. He stood leaning against it for a moment. Now what? He might be close enough to get to Ruth, he took the portal out of his pocket.

Yes and no. He could see her but the picture was cloudy and indistinct. He didn't fancy trying to transport himself into her presence. He wasn't sure all of him would get there. He wondered if he could transport there without using a portal, the way he had that morning. He put his thumb against the band of gold round his finger. The buzz of his predecessors' background conversation died, completely. Apart from the fact the very idea made him feel queasy, he sensed something akin to a wall of disapproval from them.

"Couldn't I just …?" he left the question hanging.

When tha needs to lad, not whenever tha wants.

Cluck, agreed Eight.

"Yeh, sorry, I didn't mean to take advantage," he whispered.

Nowt ter mither thissen abaht.

Cluck, agreed Eight.

"Now what?"

Tha's got ter ask? Five sounded incredulous.

"Well … yes."

What Five is wondering, I believe, is why you aren't using your Snurd and stealth mode? asked one of the others.

Aye, she's on t' veranda.

The Pan knew exactly whereabouts in the Palace the 'veranda' – as Five called it – was. It ran from the corner of one tower along a sizeable portion of the front of the building: more of a roof terrace in size than a balcony. He thought about Ruth and looked into the portal again, taking more notice of the background this time. Yep. Five was right. He checked her surrounding area for activity. There were guards outside her door but to his relief he realised they were Imperial Guard rather than army. Otherwise, the coast seemed to be clear.

"Good point. Thanks Five and …?"

Forty-three.

Whoa, help from unexpected quarters.

Forty-three clearly sensed The Pan's surprise, *You've been a lot more interesting this week, he explained, more action, less mooning after your girlfriend up there. I'm almost beginning to like you.*

He got the impression his predecessors wanted him to look at the SE2 to the point that, when he did, he had a slight feeling that they were moving his head for him. He walked over to it and got in. He pressed the button to put the roof up, checked that 'stealth mode' was still activated and took off.

Arnold's pants, this might just work. Unless he was wrong. At the very idea he felt the nerves knotting his insides. What if he was wrong? What if Ruth really did love Lord Vernon and General Moteurs had told him otherwise to make him feel better?

"No, stop," he told himself and he headed for the Palace, considering his options as he drove.

He could get to her if he timed it right, but he would have to be careful, because the Palace was heavily guarded by highly vigilant troops. If he flew in at about second floor height …? Yes, that seemed to be the best option.

When he arrived at the square, he approached slowly, hoping to drown any noise from the engine. Even in stealth mode it might make some. He drew up alongside the balcony, below the parapet, out of sight, the SE2's engine idled soundlessly as he drifted it gradually nearer. Staring dreamily out over the balcony, into the distance, was the woman he loved more than life: Ruth. The Pan moved the SE2 even closer, too close; as it rose upwards to Ruth's level, the wing tip brushed the side of the building with a gentle scraping noise. He stopped. He wanted to be absolutely sure there was nobody with her.

Chapter 77

Ruth stood on the balcony of her penthouse prison looking longingly out over the lights of the city. Somewhere out there was The Pan of Hamgee. She would give almost anything to see him, even if he still believed she loved Lord Vernon and showed her nothing but cold disdain.

"I wish …"

She sighed, turned and walked back inside.

Her last night of freedom. Alone. The rest of her life. Alone. Her wedding night—

No, no. Don't think about that! Living through it was going to be bad enough.

Back inside she felt hot and trapped and, almost immediately, decided that she'd rather be outside.

"Blimey, you're not a cat. Make up your mind which side of the door you want to be on," she told herself.

She went back onto the balcony again and walked past the table and chairs to the far end. She looked up at the stars: thousands and thousands of them. Ning Dang Po was lit at night. Strings of twinkling lights showed the position of the streets. There was the odd snurd in the sky still and a few lights in windows. It was mostly just the street lights now though, it being the middle of the night. Even so, less of it seemed to reflect up, or perhaps the stars were just brighter here. Maybe they were closer. Maybe this version of the universe wasn't expanding as fast as hers. Whatever it was, they seemed bigger and shinier and there were more of them.

She listened to the sounds of the city drifting up from below: sporadic traffic, distant shouts, music from somewhere across the square and … hang on, what was that? It sounded like something scraping the wall just below the balustrade. She went gingerly to the edge and peeped over.

No.

Nothing.

She listened.

Nothing but laughter and voices and the soft purring of an engine outside one of the houses opposite. Strange how geography played tricks on the ears. The sounds of the city were two hundred yards away but carried so clearly that they seemed far more immediate. It made her feel like a ghost. There were people there but she couldn't reach out to them even if, in some ways, it felt as if she were standing among them.

Wait a minute. There it was again; a scraping sound just over the balcony.

Someone definitely was climbing up the side of the building.

She froze, her heart in her mouth.

What if it was an assassin? No, she was pretty sure a proper assassin wouldn't make so much noise. She thought through her options with a calm that surprised her. She had to stay alive. If The Pan failed to show at the installation it was going to be down to her to denounce Lord Vernon. Probably a good idea to go inside and bolt the balcony doors.

She turned towards her room, took a couple of brisk steps and stopped in her tracks. Her hand flew to her mouth to stifle a scream as a man stepped casually out of thin air, into her path. He was tall, but not quite tall enough, five nine? And wearing a hat and cloak. He smiled and she felt her breath quicken, her pulse rate pick up and a bubble of insane happiness rising inside her.

"Ohmygod," she whispered. Could anything she wanted this much be happening to her? "Please tell me this isn't a dream."

"I hope not," he stepped forward. "You have no idea how badly I want it to be real."

He was wearing a sling and he slipped his arm out of it.

"Defreville?" she stopped. He moved a little closer.

"Ms Cochrane." He bowed and smiled and her heart skipped.

"What are you doing here?" she asked him.

His dark blue eyes twinkled.

"I could ask you the same question."

She said nothing.

"If you really want to know, I came to see you."

He did that smile again, and she tried to concentrate but an important part of her brain was doing the mental equivalent of skipping through rose petals.

"It's dangerous," she managed to say. "If you're found here you could get yourself killed."

"Ah, no. That's on my busy agenda for tomorrow. This evening, I thought I'd do something different." He took a step closer. "Wouldn't you like to spend your last night of spinsterhood with an old flame?"

As if she needed asking. She looked at him, standing there, smiling and she sighed with more longing than she'd intended.

"I don't want to make him a dead flame," she said.

"Neither do I. You know me. I'm a coward."

"I disagree, but putting that aside, Mister Pan, there is a girl involved and we know how you think with your trousers."

He chuckled.

"Only sometimes, Ms Cochrane," he said and he raised an eyebrow. "Anyway, Lord Vernon will be very busy tonight. He's away in Grongolia at his inaugural dinner as High Leader," he moved a little nearer, "I'm surprised you aren't there with him. If I were him, I'd be flaunting you at every available opportunity."

She still wondered if she was dreaming.

"What if he comes back?" she asked. It was so difficult to concentrate when every sensible molecule of her brain was away with the happy fairies, frolicking.

"I'll hide."

"He may well; I don't think he trusts me," she said.

"I AM surprised," The Pan raised an ironic eyebrow. "Then again," he covered the last of the space between them, "you're in love with the Candidate aren't you?"

"I think so," she said. Yes, just a little.

"You think so? You sound a bit unsure."

"Don't mock. I know exactly who I'm in love with but he may not realise who he is."

"And you can't tell him, can you?" The eyes were twinkling again. "What about Lord Vernon?"

"What about him?"

"He wanted me to think you couldn't get enough of him." He slid his arm round her waist and her breath caught as he pulled her close. "Does he know you're in love with another or is he under the misguided illusion that you've fallen under his spell?"

"Oh he knows." She stopped. He didn't let go of her but she felt him tense a tiny bit. There was no hiding the truth from him.

"Mmm, I did wonder," he said, suddenly serious. "There's Lord Vernon waving my death warrant in my face, and the next thing, they've taken me off the blacklist and given me amnesty for a whole year to adjust."

"Oh?"

"Yeh, 'Oh.' I can't help wondering if someone bought me."

"And what if they did?"

He sighed, as if the weight of the whole world was on his shoulders.

"They paid too high a price. Oh Ruth, I'd rather have died right there than see you marry him."

"You're not the only one," her lip trembled and she looked down. "But as even you must have twigged, by now, there are complications."

"Ah yes. You know me, a bit slow on the uptake but I got there in the end. Life is never simple is it?" he said.

"No. Are you angry with me?"

"No," he said gently, "Arnold no," he hugged her. "I'm in awe of you; I would never have the courage to do what you've done."

She looked up at him.

"Yes you would."

He shook his head.

"I don't think so. I know my limitations."

"Well, Defreville, I think you're a very brave man. Whereas what I did wasn't courage. Not really. I had no choice."

"Trust me, Ruth, you did and it was. Look, there's something else that you have to know and there's no easy way to tell you. I'm coming to the installation tomorrow but—" his voice cracked, "I'm coming to die. I'm hoping I can take Lord Vernon with me but I might not and whatever happens, it means—it means I can't save you. You understand that, don't you? I have to stop Lord Vernon from becoming Architrave and I can't do both. It's that or you and it has to be …" he tailed off.

"That. Yes. I know. I did this with my eyes open, it doesn't matter."

"It does to me. You shouldn't have to do this. In fact, now that I'm here, I'm seriously tempted to whisk you off."

"You know we can't do that."

"Yeh, I do. But this isn't how it should end."

"Maybe, but you're the Candidate, Defreville. It's who you are and what you have to do." Yeh, she thought, and Sir Robin had pretty much told them how that would turn out. "Anyway, if you were the type of person who would run away with me, instead of saving your people, I probably wouldn't love you. As it is, I always will, even when you're long gone."

"Oh Ruth." He ran his hand through his hair. "I've made such a cock-up of this. Tomorrow, I can't make anything right. All I can do is prove who I am and what he is not."

"No, you will make everything right by doing that."

"Not for you. That's why I had to come here, I couldn't die without telling you that I love you and it feels wonderful. That I'm sorry I've got you into this and," he stopped and took a deep breath, "I want to say 'goodbye'."

"Thank you," a tear escaped. No. She mustn't cry. This was their last time alone. He put his hand up and tenderly wiped it away with his thumb.

"It's OK," she said and tried to smile, "I told you. I knew what I was doing."

He gathered up the cloak he was wearing and wrapped it around her, along with his arms, enveloping her in a warm hug.

"So stoic, Ms Cochrane and always doing the Right Thing," he murmured.

"As ever, Mister Pan," she smiled sadly and laid her head on his shoulder.

"I wondered-I-I thought you might like something to remember me by. The trouble is, I didn't really have much warning—"

She raised her head and looked up at him, grinning.

"Not flying by the seat of your pants then, Mister Pan?"

"You know me." He sounded a little hesitant but at the same time, his voice had the smile in it that heralded the approach of a joke. "The thing is, because I didn't know I would be able to see you, I haven't anything very appropriate. All the same, I have brought you a gift."

"I see."

He rummaged in his jacket pocket and pulled out something plastic and shiny. "It's this."

He put it in her hand. It was a pink, spangly ring, the kind of thing that comes in a cracker. She started laughing.

"It's hideous!" she said before she could stop herself.

"It is rather, isn't it? Would you like to put it on?"

Giggling she put it on her finger and held her hand out.

"Look! It's almost as good as yours."

He put his hand up, beside hers, chuckling, as they compared the pink plastic ring on her finger with the K'Barthan Ring of State.

"So. You're giving me a ring, Mister Pan?"

"Yes …"

"Defreville—"

"As a sign of friendship, no strings attached. Although, if things were different, it would come with a freebie."

"A freebie? Don't tell me you have a bile-green one for my other hand."

"No," he started laughing and as always, she got a small buzz from amusing him, "it's actually a man."

"I see. Any particular man?"

"Well I was thinking this one." He looked down at the ring on her finger.

"Defreville, are you proposing to me?"

A beat.

"Yes. I know it's all academic but if I asked you, and we weren't up to our necks in the doo-doo, would you marry me?"

"At the drop of a hat."

"At the drop of a hat? That's not a phrase I've heard," he said and she started to cry. He put his arms round her. "Ruth, I'm sorry, please don't. I shouldn't have. I never meant to upset you."

"You haven't," she pointed to her brimming eyes. "These are happy tears. At the drop of a hat means 'yes', Mister Pan."

"Oh that's wonderful," he hugged her, "and yet it almost makes it worse. Ruth, I'm so sorry I got you into this mess."

"It's OK," she said. "I would rather live like this than never have met you."

He held her tight and she clung to him, shaking, as if she was drowning and he was a life raft. She felt him kiss the top of her head and looked up into his face. His blue eyes held hers: deep, dark, limpid.

"Ruth," he whispered. He put one finger under her chin, and she felt the electricity between them crackle and spark as he tilted her head up and kissed her. Her heart sang, and her spirit soared. She kissed him back with enthusiasm, hardly believing he was real. When they finally stopped, they stood dreamily gazing at each other for a few moments.

"I love you Mister Pan." Her voice sounded husky and speaking felt strange and unfamiliar, as if a few simple kisses had erased her memory of how it was done. "And I always will."

His eyes closed for a moment and he sighed as he held her close.

"And I'll always love you."

They stayed like that for a few wonderful seconds until slowly, unwillingly, he broke the spell.

"Well, Ms Cochrane, this is our last time together, what would you like to do with it?"

"You could always come inside for a while …" Her voice still sounded husky. She felt hot and fizzy and she wasn't a hundred per cent certain she would actually be able to move, if she were required to try.

"Not here. Not with guards outside your door. I want us to be alone, properly alone, just us. Come and watch the sunrise with me. I promise I'll bring you back."

"You're completely barking mad, you know that, don't you? And we'll have to be back way before sunrise. They get up criminally early round here."

He laughed.

"Then we'll look at the stars," he said and he kissed her again, urgently, passionately, making her lips tingle and her knees distinctly wobbly. Then he took her by the hand and led her to the balustrade. As they approached, the inside of the SE2 morphed out of the air, just as if its metal top was liquefying into open top mode, except there was no metal top to be seen, indeed, nothing to be seen but the interior. She watched it, in fascination and then turned back to The Pan.

"Is that, actually, here?"

"Yes."

"It's amazing."

"It's stealth mode. I have no idea how it's done. I only found out about it a few minutes ago. But when I put the roof on, we will be invisible."

"No way. That's totally awesome."

"Isn't it— What was that?"

Ruth was aware of a sound, the metallic noise of bolts being drawn back and a key in the lock of her prison.

"Quick, hide!" She dodged past the table and ran towards the glass doors as The Pan leapt over the balcony and into the snurd.

Chapter 78

With her heart hammering, Ruth ran into the room, fumbling the doors closed behind her. The rattling of bolts and keys finished but whoever was out there didn't come in. Perhaps the door was still stiff. She risked a glance back towards the balcony and saw the last traces of The Pan disappear as the SE2's roof slid into position.

Someone knocked on the door. Well, they had knocked instead of barging in. That was hopeful. She took several deep breaths and smoothed down her clothing.

"Come in," she called. Her voice sounded tight with tension.

"Good evening," said General Moteurs. He must have noticed her wide eyes and flushed cheeks, not to mention her nervousness, even if it was tinged with relief as she realised who it was. "I hope I find you well." He hesitated and his habitual Grongolian officer air of absolute confidence slipped a little. "If it is not an imposition, I would speak with your visitor."

Ruth felt the colour rush to her cheeks and then disappear with equal speed as the implications of discovery, even by General Moteurs, dawned on her.

"I—"

He walked down the steps and stopped at the bottom.

"I know he is here."

"Well, I'm sorry to disappoint you but, honestly, he's not. Take a look around, there's no-one but me."

He raised his eyebrows and breathed out heavily.

"Ruth, had I not a gift at reading others, I would not have been given this mission. The Candidate is in love with you. He would bid you goodbye, I think. If he is not here now, he will be soon." The corners of his eyes crinkled in the ghost of a smile. "Although, I will wager my life he is on your terrace."

"Would you? Well, I don't know what makes you think that."

"You," his eyes travelled down to her fingers and, too late, she hastily covered the pink plastic ring with her other hand. His expression was impassive, a little stern even but at the same time benign.

"Please give him my best," he said. "Now, you have little enough time. I will not waste more than is necessary. General Ennui and his colleagues have kindly ensured that my master remains in Grongolia tonight, but he rises at zero four hundred hours without fail. It is zero two hundred hours now. I will return here at three thirty to ensure the Candidate leaves the building in safety."

"You won't need to do that," said Ruth. "His snurd has stealth mode."

"Nonetheless, it would be safer." He took a phone out of his pocket and handed it to Ruth. "Take this. I will have some warning of my master's arrival should he decide to return prematurely. When it rings three times, you will have fifteen minutes – twenty at the outside – to say your farewells. At the end of that time, you must be in bed feigning sleep and the Candidate must be on his way out of the Palace. Should my master decide to come here, I cannot stall him any longer than that."

"Thank you," she said and took the phone.

"A pleasure. I will be outside, in the hall, with the guards. If the Candidate has brought his snurd then you, I should imagine, will be elsewhere."

"Not necessarily."

"I think so. Please, give him my compliments."

She gave up.

"I will," she said as she turned the phone over in her hand.

"Tell him, not to take you far, in case you need to return." He ran one hand over the top of his short brown hair. "I should not let you go at all but … I find I cannot refuse." He bowed and was gone.

Almost before the door closed Ruth turned and bounded back out onto the balcony where The Pan was already climbing out of the snurd.

She explained what the General had said and showed him the phone.

"Very nice," he said and then he picked up one of the chairs and put it against the balustrade. "Ma'am," he said, bowing.

"Thank you," she climbed onto the chair and stopped. As she looked over the edge, it seemed such a very long way down.

"Are you going to be alright? I know you don't like heights."

"It's OK."

"Here," he jumped onto the balustrade and held out his hand, "hold onto me."

He helped her into the seat, both of them ensuring the process was achieved with the maximum amount of bodily contact. She was pretty sure that, as they stood there on the balustrade, he came close to kissing her again and then thought better of it. Once she was settled in her seat, he vaulted neatly over the top of her into the driver's seat. The roof moved back into position and the inside of the cabin glowed with dim ambient light.

"Pink?" she began to giggle. "If I hadn't strong evidence to the contrary I'd be asking questions about your sexuality at this point."

He laughed.

"It likes pink. I prefer green, myself, but it's clearly having none of it. Is it too cheesy?"

"Yes but that doesn't mean I don't like it."

"I aim to please."

"Is this a good idea?"

"I'm a fully re-assimilated, bona fide, paid-up member of K'Barthan society AND, as I believe I mentioned, I have full amnesty for the next year."

"Only because they don't know who you are."

"Then let's make the most of the short time we have before they find out."

They drove off into the night.

****

Ruth lay in The Pan's arms, with his cloak around them both, looking up at the stars. They were lying on a lounger on the top of the Quaarl Futures building. For the first time in almost a hundred years, the Quaarl market had closed, at midnight, and would not reopen until after the installation. She lay with her head on his chest, and it lifted and fell as he breathed.

"Three fifteen, we have to go," he said.

"I know," she sat up, "thank you for bringing me here."

He stood up and took her hand, helping her to her feet. She smoothed down her shirt and pulled on her jacket as he picked up his cloak and hat and put them on. Hand in hand, in silence, they walked over to the snurd. Its exterior was still invisible but the roof was down so the interior was in plain view.

He made to open the passenger door for her and stopped.

"Hang on, I almost forgot," he said.

"What?"

"There's just one thing I need to do before we go."

He took her hand and pressed it against his so their fingertips were touching, then he took the snurd keys and put the fingerprint reader between her first finger and his. The hazard lights of the snurd flashed on and off.

"Fingerprint ID checked and assimilated," it said.

"You can drive it now, as well as me, and I've told the people at Snurd that, after my death, she's yours."

"You can't—"

"I can. I am sure there will be times when you need to escape. What better way?" He handed her another set of keys, identical to the ones he was holding. "These are the spares," he said as he put them into her hand. "I'm afraid I'll have to keep the others because I may need it tomorrow but when I'm gone, promise me you'll look after each other."

The snurd's hooter peeped and for some reason, even though it was inanimate and a machine, Ruth thought it sounded mournful.

"I don't think it's very happy about this."

"It might be sad that I'm leaving, but if it has to have a new owner, I suspect it would much rather belong to you than anyone else."

She bit her lip; she mustn't cry, not now.

"Thank you. I promise I'll look after it. Her," she rapidly corrected herself.

He kissed her. "Come on, we'd better not be late," he said.

For a moment she thought about running.

"I wish ..." she said as they stood there together, and stopped.

"Yeh," he said sadly, "so do I."

Chapter 79

The Pan drove reluctantly back to the Palace. He began to think he should have stayed in Ruth's prison with her. Having freed her, if only for a short time, it was so hard to take her back. The two of them were silent, as he drove. Where she had asked him, excitedly, about everything she saw on the way out, she now sat still and stoic, absorbed in her own thoughts.

When they arrived, he coasted the snurd into position next to the terrace outside Ruth's prison. The engine hardly made any noise in stealth mode, but it made some, so as he flew in, he was relieved to see that the long terrace near to hers was empty and the windows facing onto it dark.

"Can you see anyone?" he asked her.

"No."

The SE2's wing bumped gently against the stone as he positioned it. "Smeck! Right, let's get you back."

They waited; the few seconds the roof took to retract felt like aeons. He fidgeted. She sat calmly. Slipping off his seatbelt he stood up, walked swiftly along the back of the cockpit and stepped onto the balustrade where he turned and held out his hand.

They stepped onto the terrace away from the quiet hum of the hovering SE2 and he glanced at his watch. Three twenty-five. Not so bad.

"You'd better have this," he handed her the phone.

"Thanks."

It was almost time for The Pan to go. To leave Ruth to her fate and prepare to meet his. He had known it would be hard to walk away from her – he'd expected it to be nigh on impossible but the reality was it was way, way worse than that.

"We have five minutes," he whispered.

"Defreville," she sighed.

"This is more difficult than I thought it would be and I wasn't expecting much, I've never been too hot at goodbye."

"Me neither but you have to go."

As ever she was doing the Right Thing.

"Arnold, but I'm tempted to take you away with me," he breathed.

"You know it wouldn't work. If I go AWOL, Lord Vernon will only come looking for us."

"I know but, by The Prophet, leaving you here ... it's the hardest thing I've ever done. I feel like a special kind of bastard."

"You aren't. You're doing what you should, and it's never easy."

General Moteurs appeared in the doorway.

"Good, you are here." He spoke in a low voice. "Ruth, you must be ready and Defreville, you must leave. Now. Ruth come with me if you please."

The Pan didn't move.

"Defreville, he's right," said Ruth.

"Yes. But do I get to kiss you goodbye?" he said.

"You've already kissed me goodbye Mister Pan. Several times. Stringing it out is only going to make it worse."

"I know," he said but he kissed her anyway and for a moment he closed his eyes and lost himself.

The Pan had never experienced anything like this. He felt as if his heart were physically tearing itself apart. His predecessors, who had given him a blissful evening's space, were awake, agitated and asking questions. Through the muzz of his emotions and their shouting it was difficult to concentrate. He closed his eyes but it only made the noise louder. An insistent beeping from the phone General Moteurs had given Ruth added to the din.

Cluck?

No.

"Tell them to shut up," he thought, "please, hen."

General Moteurs grabbed The Pan's good arm.

"Do not tarry. You must go. Now. I have given you all the time I can." He stopped speaking abruptly, putting his finger to his lips. The Pan and Ruth turned as, over the partition wall, they saw the light go on a few yards away, on Lord Vernon's terrace. The three of them stood, silent, listening to the sound of the Lord Protector, himself, opening his glass balcony doors.

The General beckoned them and quietly they fled into Ruth's room.

Inside four members of the Imperial Guard were removing sheets and towels from a laundry basket and spreading them on the floor.

"What's this?" asked The Pan.

"A cover story to explain my presence here at this hour," said General

Moteurs. "When—"

"But what are they doing?" The Pan interrupted him.

"No time to explain. When I give you the word, run to your snurd and leave."

"But won't Lord Vernon hear it?"

The General's phone beeped and he glanced at the screen.

"Not from the corridor." He held the balcony door open and addressed The Pan. "Go or you are a dead man."

The Pan ran to the balustrade and bundled into the SE2. Quickly he engaged stealth mode. As the roof slid back into place and he flew out across the square he risked a glance back. But the balcony was empty.

****

Back inside Ruth's room, General Moteurs closed the doors and stopped to listen. As he did so, she heard it too, footsteps, outside in the hall. "I believe that is Lord Vernon, now," he said.

The four Imperial Guards closed the laundry basket and stood to attention, one at each corner.

As the door was unlocked General Moteurs looked sharply down at her hand and with wide-eyes he pointed to the plastic ring The Pan had given her. She yanked it from her finger, hiding it hurriedly in the pocket of her canvas jeans just as the door opened and Lord Vernon stood at the top of the steps, surveying the scene. She stood still, hardly daring to breathe.

"I came to wake you, my darling, but I see General Moteurs has preceded me."

He didn't sound altogether pleased about that.

General Moteurs bowed.

"Sir."

"What are you doing here, Moteurs?" he asked as he walked down the steps and into the room.

The General's hand went briefly to the buckle on the Sam Browne belt he was wearing, as if to check it was still there.

"The Chosen One requested I rehearse the marriage ceremony with her."

"Really," said Lord Vernon. "And that?" He waved an imperious suede-clad hand at the laundry basket and the jewelled rings flashed in the light.

"Laundry, we are laying out the floor plan of the altar steps and the positions of those involved."

"Interesting ..." Lord Vernon strolled over to the basket, wedged his boot under the wicker lid and flipped it open. He thrust his arm deep into the laundry inside and lifted a towel from the bottom. It unfolded as he raised it up. He gave Ruth a brief, appraising glance and dropped it back on top of the rest, sucking the air in through his teeth, half a tut, half as if he was thinking. He paced across the room to her side.

"How very lateral. Ruth, this was your idea, I assume."

"Yes."

"Then I will leave you. General," he swung round, the rings on his fingers glinting again as he rubbed his gloved hands together, "it appears you have everything under control." He added, to Ruth, "I will see you at the altar."

"There is little time and I must leave you," said General Moteurs, as soon as Lord Vernon was gone. "But you have my word, I will do everything in my power to protect you. And the lad, if I can," he told her.

"Thank you," she swallowed a sob. "I doubt I will live long as Lady Vernon."

"I am beginning to believe you will live longer than you think and, as long as you continue to do so, I am your servant and he," General Moteurs nodded to the shiny glass doors through which The Pan had just left, "he will be a fine Architrave, if he gets the chance."

She could hear the respect in his voice and it made her proud.

"Believe, Ruth. That is what this is about. Will you be—?"

"I'll be fine. Thank you."

"You require a sedative?"

"No. Save that for tomorrow night."

"As you wish. Ready lads?" The troops formed up. Two carried the laundry basket, one each end. The other two stood behind them.

He knocked on the door, it was opened from outside by two more Imperial Guards who saluted and stood back as the others carried the laundry basket into the hall.

Chapter 80

Saturday. The installation of the new Architrave would be taking place. In the old Palace, now the Security Headquarters, two of the new cleaners were in the Supervisor's office. He was already at the installation, along with practically everyone else of any import in the building, which is how two of what he thought were his new staff had managed to get into his office, unnoticed. It helped that they were good at acting as if they were a tiny bit ditzy and red hot at cleaning things.

"Typical they had ter be late with slop an' porridge today," grumbled Gladys as she spun idly backwards and forwards in the Supervisor's swivel chair.

"I know dear. I suppose they're running a skeleton staff," said Ada from her station on the floor next to Gladys', or at least the Supervisor's, chair. She was kneeling with her ear clamped against the locked door of the safe, listening.

"Yer, still, I is not sorry to have had my last bowl of that porridge. Someone needs to give them cooking lessons."

"I think you might be missing the point dear."

"Humph." Gladys looked around the room. "I has forgotten to water that plant."

"It won't be your job after today."

"Ner. How long does you reckon this is goin' ter take?"

They'd been there an hour already, Gladys was very glad that anyone going to the installation ceremony had to be in their seats by ten thirty. It gave her and Ada more time, but the lateness of the slop and porridge crew had almost negated the benefits. She leafed through a copy of the magazine the Supervisor had left on his desk, Cleaning Products Monthly.

"It says in here that they is releasing a new version of Super Clean Loo Sploo, to squish away scale."

"Hmm," said Ada.

"Huh. Can't say as I rate it more than a bit of vinegar or lemon juice."

"Quite, and a little elbow grease ..." Ada sounded distracted. "Aaaaand ... Ah!" There was a click. "Here we are dear."

Ada put one hand on the desk, the other on the corner of the opened door of the safe and with an 'ooof' heaved herself arthritically to her feet. She handed Gladys a key.

'Master key, Supervisor's office, Domestic Engineering' the label said.

Gladys held it up to the light and Ada beamed before her brows furrowed, just a little.

"Gladys, are you sure about this?"

"Yer, I done my dippy look and he told me everything. I is certain sure this key will unlock the key box in the guardroom what is two floors down. Then as soon as things is kicking off, as Trev would say, we has got ter get them keys an' let them prisoners out of the cells."

"Hmm ..."

"They is youngsters and we is respectable ladies. They is not going ter suspect us of foul play."

Gladys and Ada both knew that there are few things the young consider less dangerous than the elderly ... with the odd very rare exception.

"Best get the pinnies on then," said Ada, knowing, as she did, that the only thing more invisible than two old ladies, was two old ladies with mops, buckets and dusters.

"Yer."

Chapter 81

The Pan paced backwards and forwards across the Parrot and Screwdriver's hall. It was getting late. The others had gone. Only Trev and three of the walking wounded from the Resistance, who were keeping him company, remained. The Pan was the last to leave. He had already said goodbye to Trev and the agents upstairs, also wishing them good luck, after which he'd made his way downstairs, put on his cloak, collected his keys and grabbed his hat. Now all he could do was wait. The congregation had instructions to be seated by half past ten so the Grongles could conduct a security sweep. It was ten minutes past. General Moteurs had promised he would send a snurd but it hadn't arrived and the Pan knew that if he was going to drive himself he must go in the next few minutes. Even now he might be too late.

"Come on General. It's not going to be too clever if I'm too late to get in," he muttered.

The Pan wondered if he should give up on getting in the standard way and join one of the groups going in through the High Priest's garden. It might be sensible now. A rap at the door made him jump.

"Thank The Prophet! Talk about cutting it fine."

However, when The Pan went and looked through the spyhole he was dismayed to see Captain Snow standing outside with four guards. Behind them was the sleek dark green snurd that, he had originally believed, belonged to General Moteurs.

He took the chain off and opened the door.

"Why aren't you in the temple, you moron?" demanded Captain Snow.

"I—"

"Where's your invitation?"

The Pan took it out of his pocket and held it out.

"Can't you smecking read? You're supposed to be in your seat *by* ten thirty so we can do a security sweep," grumbled the Captain. "It says clearly, right here," he read it woodenly, "'Latecomers will not be admitted'."

"It's only ten past," said The Pan.

"Listen to it," Captain Snow sounded disgusted, "you've got to be seated by ten thirty hours, not rolling up at the door. That's why I've had to leave those Nancys from the Imperial Guard doing the sweep, and schlep all the way out here to this slum and collect your sorry scumbag arse. Because when Lord Vernon stoops to waste a seat on a non-being he expects it to smecking turn up, right boys?"

"Right," said the four guards in unison. They moved closer, presumably to maximise any feelings of intimidation The Pan might be experiencing.

He tried to appear breezy and unafraid.

"Well, well, well. I must be popular. I'm sorry to put you out Captain. As you can see, I'm ready." He adjusted his cloak and put on his hat.

"Then get in the snurd." The Captain grabbed The Pan by the bad arm and yanked him out into the street.

"I'd watch it if I were you," said The Pan's predecessors, speaking through him before he could stop them. Even the ring couldn't contain them now, they were too powerful. The Pan hoped the knowledge that any rash actions on their part would fry him would be enough to stop them from doing anything else. As it was they had a marked effect on Captain Snow and the four guards, who took a step back. "That's better. Just remember, if he's sent you to fetch me, he won't want me damaged."

"What have you done to your voice?"

The Pan smiled what he hoped was a sinister smile.

"Nothing," he said. The Architraves wanted to do more, he could feel their rage, feel the power of it building inside him, they wanted to take control of him and smite the guards. His temples burned as he resisted.

"Nobody is smiting anyone," he muttered, "and trust me, it's for the greater good."

"Shut up, you useless K'Barthan dingleberry," sneered one of the Captain's troops.

"Smecking nutter," said another.

The Pan took the opportunity to lock the door of the pub while Captain Snow was telling them to be quiet. Then he went and opened the back door of the snurd and raised an eyebrow at them.

"Are we ready?" he asked.

"You don't get to ride in the back. That's for us real citizens. Get in the front with the staff, where you belong."

"I'm sure he's better company than you." The Pan vaulted over the bonnet and got into the passenger seat while Captain Snow and his heavies piled into the back. The driver was wearing the uniform of the Imperial Guard.

"Hi," said The Pan.

"Good morning, sir," he said.

"Yeh, yeh, cut the crap. Take us to the temple and step on it," said Captain Snow from the back.

"Sir," said the driver.

Captain Snow shut the glass panel between the driver and the seats with a snap. Then he and his goons leaned back in the luxuriously upholstered leather and talked among themselves. The Pan watched as the driver selected aviator mode and accelerated smoothly into the air.

"Nice wheels," he said, more to take his mind off his nerves than anything. "Funny gear stick though, is it a racing box?"

"Yes, sir."

"Ah, fun to drive?"

"A pleasure, sir."

"Mmm, I can imagine. How come you're driving Captain Snow?"

"This is General Moteurs' staff car, sir. On occasion I am required to collect and fetch his colleagues."

"Well, I'm sorry it had to be that lot," said The Pan.

"So am I, sir, heartily."

The Pan smiled.

"Mmm, is this thing a pukka snurd or is it Grongolian?"

"Oh, it's a snurd, sir."

Yeh, that figured. Only the best for General Moteurs.

"What's the time from nought to sixty?"

"Three seconds dead, sir."

The Pan whistled. "Not bad."

To avoid thinking about his impending doom, The Pan continued to quiz the driver about the General's wheels for the rest of the journey and in no time at all they were landing smoothly, in a specially cleared space outside the High Temple.

"Here we are, sir," said the driver.

"Thanks," said The Pan, "nice landing."

"I take that as a great compliment from you, sir," said the driver. Mmm. Perhaps he knew The Pan was the Mervinettes' getaway man. There'd be no escape this time, though. The Pan swallowed and looked out of the snurd's smoke-black windows, trying to think about something else. There was a huge crowd gathered in front of the High Temple, closely watched by the police and army. As the law dictated, they were silent. On the front of the building, held in place by giant ropes and cables like some strange glowing medallion, was an enormous TV screen and speakers. Presumably the Grongles were going to relay the proceedings to the crowd gathered outside. Currently it was showing a split screen with a view of the inside of the temple and a photograph of Lord Vernon and Ruth gazing adoringly at one another.

As the snurd came to a halt, one of Captain Snow's colleagues leapt out and wrenched open the passenger door. Then he stood aside to allow the Captain himself the pleasure of bullying The Pan out of the seat.

"Get out," snarled Captain Snow as he hauled The Pan upright, almost throwing him towards the stairs that led up to the Great Doors.

"I see I get the red carpet treatment as ever," said The Pan.

"Belt up, you tool, or I'll show you red carpet, I'll give you the smecking stick." Captain Snow put his hand on the crowd control stick hanging off his belt and was interrupted, before he could say anything else, by one of his companions.

"Oh what? Look at the queue." The Pan looked where he was pointing, taking in the long line of Grongles waiting to be admitted to the High Temple. Security was tight and everyone entering the temple was being searched. Females were emptying their handbags onto two tables for inspection while both sexes, male and female, were being patted down for concealed explosives and weapons. These were Grongles; they lived in a military society. All weapons were permitted, but only worn openly on the uniformed classes. It seemed completely pointless to The Pan, especially when the uniformed classes were practically everyone, anyway. He saw no evidence of any other K'Barthan guests and wondered if he was the only one. Unlikely. If the Grongles were searching their own kind this thoroughly, the K'Barthan guests were probably all in an ante-room somewhere being strip-searched. No, no, no. Don't think like that.

The Pan had sort of expected this, and had put the confibrulator, the real box and a couple of portals into the poacher pocket of his cloak. But his heart hammered in his side at the thought of taking off the ring and hiding it. Arnold knew his predecessors were becoming harder and harder to control. If he took it off and the guards made them angry who knew what would happen, they might take him over completely. Luckily his cause for panic turned out to be short-lived.

"I'm not smecking waiting for that lot," said Captain Snow. He hauled The Pan up the steps, one of his goons either side of him and took him inside. "This one's clean so you're going to let him in," he told the security teams on the door.

"Sir," said the Grongle in charge, a corporal, and he saluted.

"Come on, you piece of crap." Captain Snow pushed The Pan roughly through the Gathering Area, a small area under the organ loft, where people met and had a chat before they went into the main body of the temple and sat down.

"That's your seat, scum." He pointed as he dragged The Pan into the temple proper, stopping almost at once at the bottom of the aisle, "And it's too good for the likes of you."

"Care to join me?"

"Don't be stupid. I've more important things to do than sit on my lazy arse," said Captain Snow. The temple had raised stalls round the sides and back wall, where dignitaries could sit and watch the proceedings in lofty elevation. The seat the Captain had indicated was in the row of stalls along the back wall: the first one, next to the aisle.

"This one?" asked The Pan, just to check.

"That's what I said. Are you stupid? Now sit. Enjoy watching your girlfriend marry Lord Vernon," he added, snatching a green-bound book and an order of service from an attendant close by. He shoved them into The Pan's hand and went off snickering.

"Go boil your head," muttered The Pan at his departing back before realising a couple of Grongles two rows up had turned to look at him suspiciously. "Hello there," he smiled and they eyed him stonily. "Right … o."

He turned to the seat the Captain had indicated, climbed the two steps up to it and sat down.

The Pan sat fidgeting nervously, waiting for the ceremony to start. He read the order of service, several times, and looked around him. There were GNN film crews everywhere, and one which he suspected was a Free KBC crew pretending to be from GNN.

The Grongles had done a good job of rebuilding the High Temple; then again, The Pan wasn't entirely surprised. As far as he knew, General Moteurs had overseen the project.

As a child, The Pan had been there once a year, like all good Nimmists. One notable occasion was to see his father receiving an award. He realised he didn't know what his dad had done and that neither of his parents had ever said what the award was for. He looked around him, taking it all in. The long, slender sandstone columns along the sides of the building drew his eye upwards to the vaulted ceiling high above. The sunlight shone in through the clear glass windows, brilliant golden autumn light. It reflected off the crystal chandeliers, peppering the columns with diamonds of white and refracted rainbow colours. The bulbs were on too, not that any artificial light was required, but they twinkled prettily among the glittering crystal.

Flowers festooned the aisles and the pew ends. Two huge arrangements on great pedestals stood either side of the High Altar, and behind it in front of the tapestries, was a huge TV screen, which would relay the minutiae of the event to the congregation.

The Pan reread the order of service. The chants were the best traditional, thumping shout-as-loud-as-you-can tunes and the responses were the original language version, written some 600 years before in an older, more stately form of K'Barthan. Lord Vernon, or General Moteurs, perhaps, had gone for heritage, and The Pan had to give it to whoever, it was good. Elegant. A bell rang, the incense burners started to swing to and fro and the congregation stood. The team of six Spiffle organists stepped up to the famous seventeen manual High Temple organ – which had been shipped over from wherever it was in Grongolia that it had been looted to and then reinstalled for the ceremony – and took their positions. There was an electronic whirring as the pump filled the bellows and then it thundered into life.

Lord Vernon entered and walked the length of the aisle in slow state, followed by the officiating clergy and the choir. He looked every inch the Supreme World Leader he claimed to be, but he would not be Architrave. The Pan slipped his hand into the poacher pocket of his cloak, the cloak which had been his father's and was the only thing he had left of his family. He transferred the confibrulator and the box to his pocket and put his thumb against the ring, moving the stone round his finger until it was on the outside. Then he picked up the book he had been given, the K'Barthan Chantinal, which contained the top 600 most famous Nimmist chants. His palms were clammy against the green fabric cover, his fingers white as he clutched it and his stomach churned. Well, these were the last moments of his life.

The Architraves in his head were as nervous as he was. He could feel their fear; his fear, to the power of seventy-six – or at least seventy-five and Eight the chicken.

"Prepare to meet thy maker," he muttered and somebody in the row below turned round and looked up.

Sir Robin was presiding, and as he began the service, the long-forgotten responses came to The Pan, unbidden. He didn't need the service sheet, he and the handful of other K'Barthans sat and stood, knelt and turned in perfect synchronisation as the rites continued. They spoke the words and performed the actions of forty generations of their forbears as if it were hot-wired into their genes. Arnold let this not be the last time. The Pan spoke the ancient mantra while his mind wandered, remembering his childhood, his family, the people he loved, the good days, even the bad days and the many trips to his local temple with his class, not to mention the visits to his school by the priests. It was always the same basic service, with special sections for events, holidays and the like bolted on. The rites were familiar, like coming home, and as he spoke them The Pan began to feel calm.

He watched the sea of Grongles in front of him getting it wrong, sitting when they should be standing, turning left when they should be turning right, bowing in confused silence when they were supposed to be speaking. The Architraves in his head were angry with them.

"Give them a bit of slack. They can't help it, they don't get it. They look at the world a completely different way to us," said The Pan. "They're Grongles. Most of them are completely clueless about K'Barth and they're just … lost, trying to be something that they're not."

As he looked around him he tried to drown out his doubts and the sound of his fear by putting his heart and soul into the responses and chants.

The Architraves in his head waited in increasing agitation. There was no silencing them with the ring, not now. They screamed in anger and frustration as Lord Vernon was installed, their rage filling The Pan's head with pain. White-faced and sweating with the effort, he fought with them, calming them, begging and cajoling them, and he fought with the agony. He continued to sing the chants with gusto because it seemed to reassure them, and battled to hold them in check. He knew he must die but he could deliver K'Barth, if they would trust him and let him. As he held the K'Barthan Chantinal in his trembling hand, and sang the calming words for all he was worth, dots of red light, reflected from the K'Barthan Ring of State, danced on the heads and backs of the beings in front.

When it was done, the entire congregation sank low, making obeisance. In his stall, The Pan did not. He stood and watched as across the rows of bowed heads between them his nemesis lapped it up. If Lord Vernon noticed his show of disrespect he did not act. Perhaps he would save that for later. Lucky there wouldn't be a later, then.

The first part of the service finished, obeisance made, Sir Robin invited the congregation to stand for the wedding. General Moteurs, who had been by Lord Vernon's side throughout the proceedings turned and walked back down the aisle towards the Great Doors. He kept looking forward but his eyes flicked sideways for the briefest second as he passed The Pan.

Chapter 82

Ruth spent the morning with dressers and stylists and make-up people but was pleased to find that they were prepared to do as asked rather than doll her up willy-nilly. So she got them to arrange her hair the way she wanted: up, but with a few strands artfully hanging down at the sides of her face. Female K'Barthans were married in red, so now she knew what the beautiful velvet dress in her wardrobe was for. It was on the shoulder, just, with long sleeves, a split up the side and a low-cut back.

Well, this might be the most miserable day of her life, she thought, when they were done, but as she took in the vision in the mirror, she had to admit, she was certainly going to face it looking her best. She looked far more attractive than she believed she could be – to the point where she felt as if the woman reflected in the glass wasn't really her. The dress had been adjusted to fit and flattered her with a precision that only bespoke tailoring could achieve. She was pleased. The Pan would be impressed. She wasn't dressing like this for Lord Vernon, but for her real – and secret – betrothed. Reluctantly, she took the pink plastic ring off her finger and concealed it in her cleavage.

Finally, when she was ready, a member of the Imperial Guard collected her and escorted her upstairs to the roof. There was a reinforced landing area there and a green snurd was waiting. Ruth noted, numbly, that in her version of the universe, it would have been a Maserati Quattroporte. The guard travelled with her and when they drew up outside the High Temple General Moteurs was waiting on the steps.

"You are looking very beautiful," he said.

"Thank you."

"I think he will like it," he added and she had the distinct impression that, like her, he was not thinking about Lord Vernon. He took her arm. "You are ready?"

She blinked back her tears.

"Yes."

"Good. Take heart Ruth." He leaned over and murmured, "Look to your left as you enter."

An Imperial Guard handed him a hammer. He stepped up to the Great

Doors, raised it, and banged theatrically three times. With a great creaking and groaning, which went beyond theatrical to hamminess in Ruth's opinion, the doors were unlocked and swung slowly open. She and General Moteurs stepped inside. They were in a low-ceilinged area. He led her across it to an archway, which opened into the High Temple proper. Behind her the doors closed and two Grongle guards moved a tree-trunk-sized piece of wood slowly across, through iron guides, barring them shut. She felt hemmed in, trapped, and for a moment, she almost lost control and ran. Then General Moteurs gave her arm a squeeze of reassurance.

"This way, Ruth."

From inside the High Temple Ruth could hear organ music. They moved across the porch area, to an arch at the bottom of the aisle. The High Temple was oval, but otherwise very reminiscent of a gothic cathedral, except the glass in the windows was clear, making it lighter and airier. There were chandeliers hanging from the ceiling and at the far end, hung luxuriant red tapestries with depictions of ... saints? Arnold The Prophet? Something like that. It was difficult to tell because there was a big TV screen over them, showing close-ups of everything that went on at the High Altar. Ruth did as the General had asked and looked left. A row of raised stalls surrounded the vast space and at the back, in the one next to her, sat The Pan. Her heart skipped as it always did. He looked pale and he was sweating but at the same time he seemed calm. He mouthed the word, 'Hi.'

She could not speak to him but she hoped he could read in her eyes that she loved him and always would. Then the organ voluntary began and with a gentle pressure General Moteurs was moving her onwards up the aisle, away from the man she loved, to the High Altar and, could she call it her doom? Yes, she decided, she could. She steeled herself. No tears. She would not give Lord Vernon the satisfaction. Somehow she would get through this. She would stay strong.

Chapter 83

There had been plenty of volunteers to go with Snoofle and Deirdre. In the end, he had chosen two Blurpons and three Spiffles, while Deirdre had chosen the only one left from Strike Ops, Adamine, and Forrest the Galorsh. He was uncannily accurate with a throwing knife and wanted to avenge the death of Nar, or, as he described her: the only female he'd ever loved, who was worth ten of each of them, and whom they'd killed before he had the chance to tell her, the smeckers.

They went to the house General Moteurs had indicated and delivered their message. A servant took them into the High Priest's garden to the door into the temple, which was guarded by four Imperial Guards, one of whom was Corporal Jones.

"Ma'am. Sir," she said as she and her colleagues snapped to attention and saluted them in perfect synchronisation.

"Good to see you, Corporal," said Deirdre, "you know the plan?"

"I let Group Leader Snoofle in and he and his team approach through the maintenance ducts in the section of the organ which lies at the Great Doors end. In the meantime, you and my team will climb up the buttress onto the spur and then attack through the door to the roof."

"Good, we must strike at fourteen thirteen hours, precisely," said Deirdre.

"Synchronise watches?"

"With mine," said Deirdre and the party did so.

She looked down at Snoofle.

"It is time to go."

"Yep," he said.

"Good luck troops," she said.

"You too my friend," said Snoofle and she knelt down and hugged him. "I will see you later," he said.

Corporal Jones swung the door quietly open and the six volunteers disappeared inside.

Two of the Imperial Guards remained by the door, the other one, along with Corporal Jones, Forrest, Deirdre and Adamine made their way round behind the flying buttress. There, the Corporal had already counted out belays and cams and laid out a rope on the ground. Deirdre and Forrest, who were making up the advance party, divided them out and began to climb.

Chapter 84

Big Merv, Lucy, Alan and Psycho Dave had finally convinced Trev that he should stay back at the Parrot and Screwdriver with three Resistance fighters who were also too wounded to get through the crowds. By the time they arrived at the Temple Precinct, they knew Lieutenant Wright and Professor N'Aversion were already there, somewhere, along with the rest of the Resistance agents who had survived Lord Vernon's attack on their HQ.

Lucy and Big Merv moved through the silent throng. Alan had got some body armour from somewhere and had insisted everybody wear it, 'in case things get dicey'. However, it was old, heavy and although Alan said his mum had aired it thoroughly, it still smelled faintly of mothballs and stour. It also appeared to be filled with lead, or possibly something even heavier like, say, uranium. Big Merv assured her it was simply material: a thick overweave of one of the strongest fibres known to K'Barthan science. He seemed to be more at ease in his than she was in hers. Trying to adjust to the cumbersome bulkiness of it, not to mention the way it made her clothes itch and the fact that it seemed to be as heavy as several whole other people, Lucy followed Big Merv through the crowd. Maybe, as a former gang lord, he was used to wearing it. He'd put it on under his shirt while Lucy wore hers like a gilet, over her clothes. Eventually, he slowed up and stopped.

"You alright girl?"

She nodded.

The trilby hat he was wearing shifted slightly as his antennae moved underneath, confirming that he was thinking.

"I ain't forgotten how heavy this stuff feels the first time. Let's rest up a mo."

She looked around her. She knew that K'Barthans were only allowed to gather in groups when the state permitted and that when they did they were banned from speaking. What amazed her was how much a crowd could say without actually talking. The air hummed with an angry tension which their silence seemed to amplify.

"Scuse me," whispered Lucy as Big Merv eased her past a large purple hairy creature with a tail, which, she believed, was called a Galorsh.

"Silence!" shouted a harsh voice and some of the troops came forward, crowd control sticks primed and ready, barging into the crowd which surged backwards as the leading Grongle trooper advanced, swinging his control stick from side to side.

"Anyone want a taste?" the Grongle asked, menacingly. Nobody spoke. "Good, that's better."

Big Merv took Lucy's hand and they moved further back, to a spot where they were about as far away as possible from the Grongles guarding them on any given side. Now there was conversation, whispered through the sides of mouths. Big Merv was wearing his trilby, charcoal grey suit with a light blue pinstripe, zip-up leather boots, blue shirt and a long leather coat. He had his hand in the pocket of the coat at all times. Lucy didn't want to speculate as to why but assumed he had Ada's sawn-off shotgun.

Finally they reached a part of the crowd where, regardless of genus, the beings seemed to be bigger, uglier and generally more menacing than their contemporaries. Here, she could catch more whispered exchanges around her, but once again, they were too far away from the Grongles to be heard.

"Wotcher, Smirk, I been looking for you," whispered Big Merv, without moving his mouth.

The creature in front of them, another Galorsh, Lucy realised, turned and rapidly swallowed the exclamation of surprise he was about to make, although he did whisper, "Shmeckin' Arnold, boss," before he could collect himself. "We thought you wash dead," he added. He had a big scar up one cheek which made him speak differently and gave him a permanent leer; Smirk, of course, Lucy thought.

"Nah, just pretending," whispered Big Merv, "right Luce?"

She nodded and as the Galorsh realised who she was he nudged his neighbour, a Swamp Thing with a little orange furry creature, that Lucy believed was called a Spiffle, sitting on his shoulders. All three of them stared at her for a moment. She watched the looks of realisation dawn as they saw through her disguise. Then she smiled at them and winked, all the while trying not to look too hard at the incredibly ornate hat that the Spiffle was wearing. Slowly, all three of the gangsters she was addressing nodded their 'hellos'.

They adjusted their positions so they were alongside one another. All of them were wearing light blue ribbons like hers and Big Merv's.

"So whatsh going down?" asked Smirk as he stared straight ahead.

"We're gonna rise up," said Big Merv. "Anyone who's got a light blue scarf on's with us."

As Lucy followed Smirk's gaze she realised she could see a reasonable number of light blue scarves and armbands among the crowd. Probably about a third.

"Crusher? Growler? D'you get that?"

"Yer," whispered the Swamp Thing and the Spiffle on his shoulders, in unison. Lucy wondered which one was whom. The Spiffle was probably Growler, she thought.

"I'm serious," said Big Merv, "you an' the others still in?"

"Yer."

"You all kitted up?"

"Yer," said Crusher, Growler and a few other voices beyond them.

Smirk looked left and right, clearly checking his forces, and Big Merv and Lucy waited.

"Schmeck. What about the othersh?" he gestured to a group of rough-looking beings a few feet away.

"Lucky I gotta few spares," said Big Merv putting his hand in his pocket and removing some strips of blue ribbon.

"What if we run out?" asked someone nearby, Lucy couldn't tell who, but she was pretty sure it wasn't any of the beings they'd been talking to.

"Tell em to do what she done," muttered Big Merv, jerking his head sideways in the direction of a woman, a few feet away, who was wearing a white silk head scarf with 'light blue' written across it in wobbly felt tip. There was a pause while everyone looked at her in turn, so as not to arouse suspicion.

One of the guards at the edge of the crowd stood on tiptoe, craning to see, looking in their direction, Big Merv coughed and the guard turned away, seemingly satisfied that what he'd heard was phlegm rather than conversation.

"Looksh like shome operation," whispered Smirk, bending down and pretending to look for something in his pockets, so the army Grongles watching the crowd wouldn't see his mouth move.

"Yer. Couple a hundred, the Resistance, the Candidate ..."

The Spiffle wobbled on the Swamp Thing's shoulders and had to grab his antennae so as not to fall off.

"Gnnnrgh," Crusher hissed as he stifled a cry of pain.

"The Candidate?" whispered Growler.

"'S right Growler, you 'eard me. He's gonna make his move at the wedding," muttered Big Merv, "an' we gotta make sure it sticks. Word's out. Be ready an' pass it along."

The three of them nodded and turned away. Big Merv took Lucy's hand and the two of them moved on.

Chapter 85

Snoofle waited in the darkness. The General was right, the stored items were still in the gallery. A large pile of stacking chairs with some velvet curtains thrown over them was obscuring the exit of the maintenance duct in which he and his colleagues were hiding from Captain Snow's view. There were other items between them, too: boxes of service sheets, piles of dog-eared spare copies of the K'Barthan Chantinal and other liturgical detritus.

Slowly, he opened the door a crack and slipped silently out; nothing. Excellent. Whiskers quivering, he checked and rechecked his surroundings. No. All was safe. He ran to the cover of the first box and beckoned to the others. They followed. In two groups, they moved past some wooden crates and a pile of old wall hangings. They passed the main gallery stairs which would be guarded at the bottom but were not at this level.

He glanced at his watch, waiting. Deirdre would be coming through the door in five, four, three, two—

Something cold was pressed against Snoofle's neck.

"Well, well lookee here. The Captain'll be pleased to see you."

Snoofle spun round, kicking the gun from the hand of his attacker before he could react and delivering a powerful punch to his solar plexus. The Grongle crumpled to the floor, but as Snoofle turned there was a click, the kind of click that stopped him in his tracks.

"Save it, you nothing. Unless you want to die here," Snoofle sighed resignedly and put his hands up. His colleagues did likewise. More Grongles stood around them, laser guns poised and ready. There was nothing to be done now. He would have to wait. As he looked towards the end of the gallery, where Captain Snow was, he saw the point where Deirdre and her forces were about to enter, saw the Grongles waiting for them. He willed her to realise, to go back, to take the stairs to the roof and come down the chimney but she didn't. The Grongles waited one side of the door, concealed behind the curtain which hung across the fireplace in the end wall, while he and his companions were dragged away down the stairs, out of sight and earshot.

*****

When Deirdre and her forces crept into the gallery they could see Captain Snow ahead of them with twenty or so troops. There was no sign of Snoofle but before she could even process this, let alone order a withdrawal, Forrest rushed past her, throwing himself at one of the guards, knife raised, shouting,

"This is for Nar!"

A Grongle guard stepped out from behind the screen and brought the butt of his laser pistol down hard on the back of Forrest's head as he passed, knocking him out cold. More Grongles stepped from behind the screen, laser pistols and laser rifles at the ready.

"Anyone else want to have a go?" asked Captain Snow.

He and his guards kept their distance, making sure none of their captives could get close enough to disarm one of them. Adamine put her hand on her thigh but Deirdre shook her head. If she and her team attacked they would die here and tempted as she was, if it meant she got to take Captain Snow with her, Deirdre would bide her time. Her party might yet overcome their guards and escape.

While Captain Snow and a couple of guards covered them from a distance, two of the Grongles disarmed Deirdre and her colleagues, pushing them forward. For a horrible moment Deirdre thought the Captain was going to make them walk over the gallery edge, instead, he glanced down at the events unfolding at the High Altar and strolled over to her.

"Looks like my master gets to have you back," he leered at her. "He's going to like that."

She didn't dignify his words with a reply.

He spoke to one of his troops.

"Corporal Puneschment, take them downstairs with the others," he said and with studied unconcern he strolled back to his position.

Deirdre, Adamine, Corporal Jones and the others were led roughly down the main staircase, to the temple below.

Chapter 86

The Pan looked towards the High Altar, to where his salvation, Ruth, and his nemesis, Lord Vernon, stood facing one another, holding hands. She was wearing a long, straight wedding dress of scarlet velvet. It had a demure split up one side; neither plunge nor split were so revealing as to be disrespectful in the High Temple but in The Pan's view they were still insanely alluring. He could feel his blood pressure rising and imagined taking Lord Vernon's place, pulling her to him and—

Alreight lad, keep it above t' waist, said a voice.

"Sorry Five."

Concentrate … Wait for it lad, wait … said Five.

Cluck, added Eight, helpfully.

"Does anyone know any just cause or impediment why these two persons may not be wed?" said Sir Robin.

Count wi' me lad, said Five, *one, two, three!*

The Pan jumped from his seat into the middle of the aisle.

"Yes." And his voice came back to him, picked up by the microphones above and relayed through the speakers on the columns: calm and in control, like someone else's.

A murmur of consternation ran through the crowd and as if it was needed, a TV spotlight picked him out.

The Pan did his best to stand tall and proud, to look like a national leader, even if, in his heart of hearts, he knew he was just a frightened young man from Hamgee. Lord Vernon turned and scanned the packed aisle, disappointingly unperturbed. The microphone relayed his words to Ruth.

"A moment, my precious," he said, the smarmy smecker.

Lord Vernon moved away from his bride-to-be and stood at the top of the step. He was studiedly relaxed, his arms hanging loosely by his sides but at the same time he was clearly ready to act, with extreme violence.

"What do you want?" he snarled. He didn't need to raise his voice, even without the microphone, his words cut though the tension like a razor.

How to say that without getting shot? Tricky.

He can't kill you, said one of the Architraves, breaking into The Pan's thoughts.

"You reckon?" muttered The Pan, "I wouldn't bank on it."

I would. He made a deal with the Chosen One.

"He can break it."

No. Not when he's this close.

Precisely, said someone else, *she hasn't said 'yes'.*

Very, very good point. Please Arnold, let it be enough. The Pan took a deep breath.

"That's no way to talk to your honoured guest." He held up his invitation. "Sorry I was late. Never mind, at least I haven't missed anything and I do love a wedding." No, no. Babbling. Stop. "In fact, I've actually come to give you a hand."

Lord Vernon snorted derisively.

"Of course."

"No, seriously. I'd like my ex to be happy."

"She is."

"She won't be, not unless she marries the Architrave—"

"Which she will. I am taking her as my wife."

"Maybe but you're not the Architrave yet."

The silence was heavy.

"You lie," said Lord Vernon. His voice, ice cold.

Smeck.

"I'm afraid not," said The Pan, trying to keep the turmoil inside him out of his voice.

"On the contrary, I have been installed, by the High Priest."

"Then where's your power?"

Lord Vernon laughed without the faintest trace of humour.

"Here. Guards. Take him outside and kill him."

To The Pan's left and right, several army Grongles closed in. Lord Vernon turned and started to walk back to Ruth, at the altar.

Mentally The Pan gathered the Architraves and all of them put their authority into his voice when he said:

"Wait."

The guards stopped and slowly, Lord Vernon turned round.

"Perhaps I should have you killed where you stand."

"I wouldn't."

"What will stop me?"

"Your curiosity."

"Because …?"

"You know I have what you need."

"Where you're concerned, I have everything."

The Pan smiled and shook his head.

"Not this thing. I can give you cast-iron proof that you're the Candidate, oh and did I mention the power?"

Lord Vernon said nothing, so The Pan interpreted his silence as a signal to continue.

"I'm not talking about earthly you-there-do-that power Lord Vernon – you have the lot on that front – I'm talking about something else. You have some of it already, as any one of your retinue who is wondering how you can get from here to Grongolia and back just like that," The Pan clicked his fingers, "will know. But there's more." He gathered the fabric at the bottom corner of his cloak and threw it over his shoulder with what he hoped was a flourish. Having only one fully functioning arm made it tricky, and the fact he was shaking like a leaf didn't help either.

"I know the power you speak of, and it is mine."

The Pan waited a couple of seconds, for dramatic effect and then began to walk.

"Well yes. In theory … but can you access it?"

"Oh yes," said Lord Vernon softly, and again, though he spoke in little more than a menace-laden whisper it was clearly audible, with or without the microphone, anywhere in the temple.

"I don't think so," The Pan told him calmly. "Not the kind of stuff I'm talking about." As he moved forward he kept repeating to himself that Lord Vernon couldn't kill him yet, but he believed it less and less as he walked the length of the aisle. The air fizzed with silent expectation as the rows of guests watched him pass. When he reached the final pew and he and Lord Vernon stood a few feet apart, The Pan stopped. There, behind the Supreme World Leader in all but name, stood Ruth. The Pan dared not look at her, could not, because his expression would show Lord Vernon everything he was trying to hide. Next to her stood General Moteurs, who was giving her away in the absence of her real father.

"And why would you bring me this power?"

"Because K'Barth needs me to. It needs a real Architrave, whoever he is. Even if he's you, he has to be the genuine article and right now, Lord

Vernon, you're not."

"Which part of the last forty minutes did you miss, vermin?"

"None of it actually." From the back of the temple came a nervous bark of a laugh. "I understand your point," said The Pan, trying to conceal the fearful wobble in his voice. "But it doesn't mean a thing because you've got the wrong kit. That's not the real ring you're wearing, and it may be old but that's not the real box."

"You are mistaken," said Lord Vernon in a tone of voice that suggested this was life-saving advice as well as conversation.

"Would you bet on that?"

"I am the Architrave and I have proved it." Lord Vernon drew his laser pistol.

The Pan flinched but he took another step.

Lord Vernon flicked off the safety catch and took aim. The Pan's stomach clenched and his fear gripped him. He knew he couldn't avoid a shot at this range. But surely, surely, until Lord Vernon had married Ruth, until the Chosen One had said 'yes', he would not fire. Not when The Pan's continued existence was the deal-breaker. He took another shaky step forward. He hoped he wouldn't be sick, or worse.

"It certainly looks as if you're the real deal – and with your confibrulator score, you should be," said The Pan. "But are you feeling it? 'The Architrave stands on his predecessors' shoulders,' isn't that what they say? Most commentaries interpret that as power, all their power, channelled into him. Correct me if I'm wrong but I'd say you want a bit of that, and if you really had it, right now, you'd have fried me already."

"And I say you lie," sneered Lord Vernon, "and you know what I do to people who lie to me, don't you?"

"Yeh, well, I realise how this ends but I'm just trying to do you a favour. You know what the eighteenth Architrave said? 'You need eyes in the back of your head to rule this place.' You want the science, Lord Vernon, trust me on this, and it isn't going to work unless you use the right kit. You'll have to get installed again." The Pan stopped at the altar step and looked up at Lord Vernon. With a trembling hand, he held up the box. Then he turned his hand round, palm facing inwards, and wiggled the finger with the ring on it. "With these."

As GNN replayed his actions on the giant screen above the altar the congregation gasped. Oh yeh, thought The Pan.

Lord Vernon turned to Sir Robin.

"If the Hamgeean speaks the truth it will be the worse for you, old man." He fixed his attention back on The Pan. "I thank you for your advice," he said, putting his hand over the microphone he was wearing, to add, "Perhaps I will dispatch you, now, and take heed of it."

"You'd be foolish to do that straight away. Because I'm the only person who can prove that this is the real box." OK that was a slight lie but it was all The Pan could think of. He risked taking his eyes off Lord Vernon for a second to glance at Sir Robin. He was as certain as he could be that the old man understood, "Are you a gambler, Lord Vernon?"

"No."

"Of course not. This is science isn't it? Natterjack's box of frogs."

"I see you have prepared for this."

"Yeh, a bit, and I saw your broadcast. So I know this is about belief. Whether you think you've done enough; if you believe enough, if these good people believe," he swung his arm in the direction of the packed aisle, "if you have, this isn't a gamble is it?"

"Correct."

"So it shouldn't be a problem. The power, the knowledge … Ruth. The reasons why you're here. They'll all be yours if you use the real ring, and the real box."

"They are all mine, without."

"If they were, you wouldn't bother with all of this."

Lord Vernon was silent for a moment. His anger had given way to something else, an incisive calm. The Pan had got him thinking. Please Arnold let this work.

"If what you say is true, I shall be installed again and take my rightful place. Show me your proof."

"Alright," said The Pan, "may I?" He gestured past Lord Vernon and Ruth, to the High Altar where the fake box and the confibrulator still stood.

Lord Vernon stood calmly to one side. As The Pan moved past he could feel the hatred emanating from his nemesis, a negative energy drawing his courage from him. Lord Vernon walked beside him to the High Altar and the rest of the wedding party, as well as Sir Robin, followed. The Pan walked round to the other side of the altar, partly so that the congregation could see him and the GNN camera operators could film more easily, but mostly to put the huge slab of stone between Lord Vernon and himself. All he had to do was believe. All the people had to do was believe the impossible was possible: that someone could defeat Lord Vernon. Arnold let them want this enough.

The GNN camera team positioned themselves beside The Pan and a large furry outdoor microphone was lowered towards him. With the extra eyes in the back of his head, he watched the images on the big screen behind. He moved the fake box to one side and put the real one on the stone surface of the altar, next to the confibrulator. Oh yes, he'd sort of forgotten that he was going to have to explain. He glanced up at Lord Vernon.

"Begin."

"Right." The Pan couldn't quite believe he had managed to get this far but it gave him, if not confidence, then a feeling that he was a little more in control. He cleared his throat nervously. "Hello everyone, I'm going to prove the authenticity of Lord Vernon's claim to the Candidacy. This thing is an Importance Detector: a confibrulator. Some of you might have seen him use it on TV the other day, to take his own reading. As well as showing the importance of people it can demonstrate the importance of things. I'm going to use it to determine whether or not the box is the real article. If it is, when I set up the importance detector the right way and put the box beside it, the box will glow green." He closed his eyes made the hand movements to change the settings and started the importance detector spinning.

Nothing happened. His stomach lurched.

It's too bright lad, said a voice. Ah. Yes. Thank you, Five.

"Could we dim the spotlight please?" asked The Pan. Lord Vernon removed his sunglasses and clicked his fingers. Somebody did as The Pan asked. The picture blurred as the Grongle from the GNN team with the camera refocused and then, there it was, the box glowing green, and vivid green sparks arcing towards it from the Importance Detector.

"'No glow, no show'," said The Pan.

"Indeed," said Sir Robin.

Lord Vernon looked over at him sharply. "Silence. You will pay for your part in this."

"Now, children," said The Pan. "Thank you GNN, if you want to turn the spot back on you can …" Because I want K'Barth to see this. He thought. Their surroundings brightened to TV level.

"So, Lord Vernon, Sir Robin, anyone else who should know, do you accept that's the real box?"

Lord Vernon shot a laser glance at General Moteurs, who returned it with calm equanimity.

"Yes," he said but it was more of a hiss.

"Sir Robin?"

"Yes."

"So, Lord Vernon, we know you score ten."

"Yes."

"But that doesn't make you the true Candidate on its own."

"The Chosen One loves only me."

"Yeh well, there's no accounting for taste," said The Pan, who had no intention of making trouble for her after he'd gone. "But there have been examples of the Candidate scoring lower than the person who affects them the most and this box … this is the decider. If you can open it – you're the real McCoy."

"And your terms?" sneered Lord Vernon.

"What terms? If you're the true Architrave, who am I to argue?"

Lord Vernon laughed, a snarling, hissing sound which wasn't remotely to do with humour.

"I grow tired of this," he drew his laser pistol and without taking his eyes off The Pan he began to rub it casually in his hair. It beeped to indicate a full charge and slowly, deliberately, he aimed it. General Moteurs moved closer to his master.

"I never had you down as a poor loser," said The Pan as once again, Lord Vernon flicked off the safety catch.

"On the contrary, I never lose because I appreciate the value of fully utilising my time. And you are wasting it."

"Really? And here's me thinking you're just too chicken to take me on."

"I. Am. Not. Chicken."

"Then I'm sure you'll be happy to prove your credentials."

"They are already proven."

"Well here's the thing. They're not. This box is linked to the minds of the Architraves, or at least, whatever it is that astrally relates them. There are only two types of people who can open this box, the rightful Candidate and any person they decide to allow. Which one are you?"

"I am the true Candidate. You know that."

"Then you'll be able to open it won't you?" said The Pan.

The burning grey eyes narrowed.

"Natterjack's box of frogs. It's all about belief. Do you have enough? Do you believe? Does everyone else? Do the previous Architraves? Because if you can tick those boxes, it'll be child's play for you to open this one. And if you can do that, you truly will be the Candidate and it's all yours, by right."

Lord Vernon holstered the laser pistol.

"Very well," he held out his hand and the jewelled rings flashed against the darkness of the suede, "I will open your box."

The Pan picked it up, walked back round the altar and held it out.

"I hope you're feeling lucky, Hamgeean."

The Pan swallowed.

"Not really."

Lord Vernon's face twisted with burning hatred. He snatched the box from The Pan's outstretched hand and faced the congregation. Arnold let this work. Lord Vernon held up the box, giving the TV cameras time to zoom in. He didn't have eyes in the back of his head so he glanced over at one of his aides who checked the screen and nodded.

"Give me the signal, General," he ordered.

"Sir," said General Moteurs and he counted down. "Three, two, one, begin."

Lord Vernon flipped the lid with his thumb.

It stayed shut.

A muted 'oooooo' rose from the congregation and was echoed, with a few seconds' delay by the crowd outside.

He wrenched at it and then stopped, realising, perhaps, that he was being manipulated.

The Pan took the box from his hands. Once again, Lord Vernon's eyes met his, merciless, mesmeric, searching the deepest recesses of his soul, and for the first time in his life, The Pan looked right back into them without fear. He could see the concentration in them but knew that Lord Vernon had failed. He would never be Architrave. It wasn't even that he didn't have the power, he just didn't have seventy-six other Architraves in his head, showing him how to use it.

The Pan pushed the lid with his thumb. He felt it move. He waited a moment, to make the point and then flicked open the box.

"Nice try but no cigar," he said, looking straight into Lord Vernon's murderous eyes. "You're not the Architrave and you were never the Candidate." The Pan closed the lid of the box with a snap. "I am."

There was an audible gasp from the congregation, and even some screams from the crowd outside, a fraction of a second later.

Lord Vernon was pale, his snarling mouth framing a silent 'how'. He put one hand on the altar, leaning on it. The Pan could see his jaw clench, his eyes glittered with rage.

"Well done, my boy!" said Sir Robin.

"Shut up, fool," sneered Lord Vernon.

"I believe you are the one who has been foolish, Lord Vernon," said Sir Robin.

"Yeh. All those times you could have killed me," said The Pan, "I bet you're pretty sick about that now."

"Someone gag that old dotard before I vaporise him." He turned his attention back to The Pan. "As for you, it makes no difference who you are. When you are dead I will take your place."

"K'Barth will not allow that," said Sir Robin.

"I said gag him! K'Barth will have no choice."

"The next Candidate will overpower you," said Sir Robin.

"D'you think?" Lord Vernon cast a contemptuous look in The Pan's direction, "This one couldn't. Moteurs, detain them."

"Sir."

Chapter 87

General Moteurs stepped up and with a glance summoned six Imperial Guards. They moved quickly to his side, carrying rapid-repeat laser rifles, but instead of aiming them at The Pan and Sir Robin, they trained them on Lord Vernon.

"So, General, finally you show your true colours," he said. He stood still, tall and confident and The Pan wondered how it was that, cornered as he was, he still looked deadly.

"Regretfully, sir," said the General, "I must ask you to surrender the rest of your weapons. You will be taken to Grongolia to face trial."

"You think I did not foresee this?"

"I would not be so foolish as to underestimate you, sir."

"No, you are very intelligent, Moteurs – it is one of the things I truly admire in you – so you'll understand that I have bought your allies in Grongolia."

"Sir, but you forget that they are honourable officers and they took your attempt to bribe them as an insult."

"Everyone has a price, General, even you."

"Agreed, sir. That is why I was compelled to double your offer."

Lord Vernon laughed nastily.

"You will bankrupt the Treasury."

"I'll wager not, sir. Your assets will be seized for the duration of the trial. The interest alone will pay them."

"So very, very certain General."

"You cannot fight this. You would be wise to come quietly."

"Now, Captain," commanded Lord Vernon.

The world glowed red for a split second as, with an explosion of sound, laser fire flew from the gallery above.

Smeck! The Pan cast about him. Where in The Prophet's name were the others?

The six guards surrounding Lord Vernon were instantly vaporised and one shot hit the polished stone at the General's feet. Someone screamed and a worried susurration rose from the congregation; increasing in volume it filled the temple with an echoing sound like running water.

Ruth whimpered, turning her head away. The Pan longed to comfort her.

Captain Snow strolled to the edge of the gallery above.

"General Moteurs, I always thought you were a stuck-up prig. Not so full of yourself now are you?"

The General didn't dignify his taunt with a reply but turned his head slowly upwards with a look of utter disdain.

Lord Vernon's troops flooded in from the Gathering Area at the far end of the aisle and moved through the congregation, taking key positions along the aisle and around the High Temple. Some surrounded the altar, their laser pistols and rapid-repeat laser rifles trained on The Pan, Sir Robin and the General. And at the centre of it all stood their master, Lord Vernon, calm, all-powerful, all-controlling and insufferably smug. The Pan looked down the barrel of the laser rifle pointing at him and wondered if anyone who'd smelled a being getting vaporised was ever able to eat a roast dinner again

Chapter 88

Outside in the precinct at the front of the temple, Lucy watched with the silent crowd as Captain Snow fired from the gallery and then with a great roar, the K'Barthans set upon the Grongles. The troops kept firing into the mass of K'Barthans pressing down on them and many of the first surge fell. For a moment everything was still.

"C'mon, let's get 'em," shouted Big Merv.

The angry mob surged forward again.

The Grongles loyal to Lord Vernon were armed with superior weaponry but their numbers were inferior. They were overwhelmed by the sheer quantity of K'Barthans coming at them but it was their colleagues, who slipped on blue armbands and turned their laser pistols on their contemporaries, who made the difference. Beings of all different shapes and sizes were pressing in from the nearby streets, and, Lucy noticed, the Imperial Guard had arrived, about a hundred of them, along with another scattering of black and red clad army, all wearing light blue armbands. They, too, attacked the troops loyal to Lord Vernon.

"Take as many of 'em alive as you can!" shouted Big Merv and from a few feet away a Galorsh turned round and she recognised the lopsided face of Smirk. "Saves ammo! Pass it on," shouted Big Merv as the ranks of army split and groups of them were engulfed by the crowd.

The mob was pouring round the High Temple now, and into the streets, engaging the Grongles loyal to Lord Vernon in running battles.

"C'mon sweets, the Prof's got this down, we gotta get in there, we're the cavalry," said Big Merv pointing to the High Temple. "I reckon we start with General Moteurs' bloke round the back."

"What about the main entrance?" said Lucy doubtfully as Big Merv began to move in that direction.

"Nah. They're more than wood, them doors. Nothing's gonna get them opened 'cept us, on the inside."

As the crowd pressed around her, Lucy began to realise that the mob of K'Barthans, though angry, wasn't as random and disorganised as it appeared. Big Merv, Professor N'Aversion and Lieutenant Wright had coordinated their forces with surprising precision. The fighting seemed to have ceased for the moment – or moved elsewhere – with the odd isolated incident breaking out in places, but little else. As she and Big Merv moved through the crowd, it was concentrating on opening the doors and he was right. Even a captured laser cannon was making no inroads.

The next being that approached them was Pub Quiz Alan, with a Grongle army trooper in the black and red uniform of Lord Vernon's troops but he was wearing a blue ribbon round his arm, and Lieutenant Wright.

"The Temple Precinct's ours," said Alan, "and Colonel Saunders from the Imperial Guard is taking care of the city. Professor N'Aversion is with him."

"Good. Listen, we gotta take care of business in there," said Big Merv pointing at the temple, "an' we're gonna want some help."

"Count me in," said the Lieutenant, "how are you going in?"

"The High Priest's garden, I reckon. If we can get in and then we gotta climb up the building."

"Then I'll come with you. I can climb."

"Climbing's OK, sweets, but it ain't so simple; you gotta kill."

"I can do that, too," said the Lieutenant grimly.

"Well, we got another complication. It ain't gonna be Imperial Guard in the garden no more, Lord Vernon's troops are gonna be there."

"I can help with that problem," said the Grongle. "Apologies, I forget myself." He saluted. "Major Pylup, at your service."

"Alright, then let's get moving, pronto," said Big Merv, "coz I gotta be up there, taking out Captain Snow, like, yesterday."

"Two ticks, sir," said the Grongle and he ran off.

"Back in a sec myself," said Lieutenant Wright.

"Merv," said Lucy. "If the Major controls the door we can get reinforcements in. They can use the doors to go into the anterooms and attack from the side. We can get lots of troops in, undetected and I can lead them. If you want me to. There's no point taking me up to the chimney. I've never climbed in my life. I'll only hold you back, but I can take the team below."

Big Merv nodded.

"Smecking Arnold you're smart, babe. Take the Major and his blokes."

Within moments, Major Pylup returned with four black and red clad troops. He and two of his troops removed their blue armbands.

"Wait for my signal," he said and the five of them ran off.

"Smeck, he'd better get a wiggle on. We gotta get in there," said Big Merv, and he grabbed Lucy's hand and started to move towards the High Priest's house.

"Not without us," said a voice as Lieutenant Wright and a small group of assorted beings caught them up, "and Beatrice here." The Lieutenant gestured to the fiercest looking of their number.

Beatrice had short blonde spiky hair and Lucy judged her to be about the same age as her, late twenties, but she was extremely intimidating. There was a glint in her eye that said she was a cold-blooded killer. True, Lucy conceded, Deirdre had that look but it wasn't the full picture. You could see in her eyes that she had killed people, but it was more like a front: an image she had cultivated over time, rather than her true self. Now and again, Deirdre's eyes held a depth that betrayed the presence of a kinder, more compassionate individual underneath. This girl, she seemed more like the real deal.

"Beatrice is with the Resistance. She and her troops were being held in the cells at the Security HQ, the old Palace, but two old women freed her, and everyone else. The whole place is now under joint control of the Resistance and Grongolian Underground forces."

"Sweet. You people done real good," said Big Merv clapping the Lieutenant on the back and making her cough. He stopped them all a few feet short of the High Priest's house and they waited. Two of Major Pylup's troops were standing guard at the door. It was only a few seconds before three other Grongle troops rushed out into the street and were stunned unconscious, with swift efficiency, by the Major's troops. Then the Major himself opened the door.

"Come," he said.

"You need to tie them up," said Lieutenant Wright.

"Already taken care of, ma'am," said one of the Major's troops, removing a pair of handcuffs from his belt.

"Nice. Alright Major, lead on," said Big Merv and, with the rest of them, Lucy followed.

When they arrived at the back door of the house they waited, in case Captain Snow had posted troops above. It appeared he hadn't.

"The Captain believes his own troops are guarding this area. If we are lucky, he will assume his back is covered and deploy his forces towards the enemy below. However, he will keep five guards on the stairs and he may have a sentry on the doorway from the roof and on the exit from the maintenance ducts in the organ."

"Any on the fireplaces?"

"Doubtful, they are not classified as a threat."

"Then we're gonna go past that door and them guards, up the buttress to the roof and down the chimneys. Beatrice, you look handy, you and your people are with me. Lieutenant, you too, an' Dave, d'you reckon you can shin up a building?"

"Course," said Dave.

"Sorted. Where's Alan?"

"On his way with reinforcements."

"Good—" Big Merv began, just as Alan arrived.

"I've got thirty Imperial Guards out there and a handful of your ex-staff."

"Nice. Then go get anyone they got what can climb. They're with Lieutenant Wright and me. The rest are gonna go through that doorway with you and Luce. She'll tell you what to do."

A few moments later, Big Merv and his group moved swiftly across the lawn and hid from sight in the lee of the buttress. From where she was, Lucy couldn't see them start climbing. She was painfully aware that she'd no clue how to fight. On the other hand, she did have a plan. She split her forces into groups of five. One of Major Pylup's troops stood by the back door scanning for any activity from Captain Snow's guards, but they weren't watching the garden. Even so, she made him monitor the windows of the gallery above and sent each small group over the lawn one by one. They went in through the door which the other of the Major's guards had opened.

Chapter 89

As the smoke cleared, the dignitaries in the pews surrounding the altar scattered as swiftly as decorum would allow, withdrawing to the side walls. The main body of the congregation started to get to their feet, not out-and-out panicking yet, but close. More of Lord Vernon's troops appeared at the back and lined up in front of the Great Doors, five rows of them, rapid-repeat laser rifles at the ready and currently trained on the beings inside the High Temple. Above the rising noise of voices came a loud electronic pinging sound as Lord Vernon fired his laser rifle into the air bringing silence instantly. Rather more discreetly now, crouching beside pews, hunkered down beside pillars and huddled by the side of the organ, GNN and the other film crew continued to film.

"Calm yourselves," Lord Vernon's voice cut through the silence. "There is nothing to fear. Please take your seats. The Hamgeean rebel has kindly brought me the correct artefacts, and in a few short moments I shall be installed again."

An eerie silence descended as the whole temple waited. Lord Vernon tutted and strolled over to where General Moteurs stood. He looked down, prodding at the stone by the General's feet, which was still bubbling, with the toe of his immaculate black suede boot.

Lord Vernon took the laser pistol from the General's hand. "Corporal." He tossed it, dismissively, at one of the troops who caught it and stuck it in his own belt. "As you see my forces are a little more," he raised his eyebrows, "loyal than you think."

Another group of troops in the black and red uniform of the army arrived with some prisoners: Deirdre, Snoofle and their deputation of Resistance Agents, including Forrest, and some members of the Imperial Guard, one of whom The Pan recognised; Corporal Jones. Struggling and kicking, they were dragged to the front of the altar and thrown at Lord Vernon's feet. There was a roar from outside and the distant pinging of laser guns being fired. The roar faded into silence. Lord Vernon stood for a moment, as if listening.

"It's lucky you Imperial Guards have such a high opinion of yourselves; if you didn't there'd be a lot more of you to round up, and as for *these* vermin," he aimed a savage kick at Forrest, "you didn't seriously expect to overcome me with this rabble did you?"

General Moteurs did not speak but calmly stood his ground.

"It seems your plan has failed," Lord Vernon chuckled nastily.

"No, Lord Vernon, you're the one who's failed," said The Pan, his mouth going into action, as usual, well before his brain. "All I had to do was show the people you're a fake. Job done, I'd say."

Slowly Lord Vernon turned to face The Pan.

"Oh you think so do you?"

"I know so. There'll be another Candidate, a better one, and he will defeat you."

"Really? I think I see a flaw in your strategy. If there is going to be another Candidate, you have to be dead don't you? I had planned to use your people as slaves but you have shown me how unwise that would be. So, over the next …" he waved his hand and the rings flashed against the suede as he thought, "four months? I don't think it'll take longer than that, I'm going to wipe every last pestilential K'Barthan leech from the surface of this planet. And all I have to do to foil your cunning plan is keep you alive until I'm done."

Smeck. The Pan could feel the colour draining from his face.

"They're not going to take this lying down, they'll fight," said The Pan.

"Yes they will, and they will die. Such a shame."

The Pan glanced helplessly at Sir Robin but said nothing.

"Checkmate," sneered Lord Vernon. He swung round and returned his attention to General Moteurs, who stood straight and dignified. If the General felt any fear, he did not show it. Lord Vernon summoned one of his guards who came and stood beside him, laser rifle covering the General.

"Your weapons, if you please," said Lord Vernon. Still holding his own laser pistol he moved closer and held out his other hand. The General unsheathed his knife and put it into his master's hand, Lord Vernon held it out and the guard nearest him lowered his laser rifle, stepped up and took it.

"And now, your sword, General," sneered Lord Vernon.

"Sir."

In a blur of swift movement, General Moteurs drew his sword and lunged at Lord Vernon, knocking the pistol from his hand and thrusting the sword towards his throat. Lord Vernon ducked, parrying the

General's second blow with his own half-drawn weapon before unsheathing it fully and counter-attacking. The two of them crashed together and fought, rushing each other. The deadly blades of their swords flashed in the light as they swung them. Wooden chips and shards of stone flew as they hacked chunks from the pews and pillars in the process of trying to hack them from each other. Finally, they broke apart and the guards around them primed their rifles with a click.

"No," Lord Vernon snarled as he and the General circled each other, "leave this to me."

"Do not force me to kill you," said General Moteurs to Lord Vernon.

"Oh *I* will be slaying *you*, General. Unless I get bored, in which case they will do it," he gestured to his troops.

"No. This ends now," said General Moteurs and he attacked. As they ducked and dived, lunged and parried, all flashing, whirling, razor-sharp steel, Lord Vernon's troops watched, distracted. Deirdre caught The Pan's eye and he understood her intent at once. She, Snoofle and the other prisoners counter-attacked. Within seconds the fighting had spread to the congregation. The black and red dignitaries who were members of Lord Vernon's forces swiftly turned on the grey Imperial Guards protecting the Grongolian ministers, but The Pan was surprised to see that some of the army Grongles had donned light blue armbands and joined the Guards. He looked up, there was no sign of Captain Snow and his troops and no firing from the gallery. Indeed, most of the fighting seemed to be in the main body of the temple, at close quarters, hand to hand.

The Pan noticed one of Lord Vernon's troops heading towards Ruth, clearly intent on removing her from the melee.

"No!" he shouted and he ran towards her, dodging through the fighting beings, intent only on her. The trooper held her round the waist, trying to drag her away but Ruth was holding onto the lectern. The Pan seized the ancient Book of Sayings lying open on top of it and brought it round in a swinging arc against the guard's head; he dropped like a stone, out cold.

Result!

"Defreville!"

"Quick!" he grabbed her hand and they ran to the safest place he could think of, underneath the High Altar.

"We have to get you out of here," she said.

"No, not yet. I have to stop this, or it's going to be a bloodbath."

The Architraves were angry, his temples burned and his ears thrummed with the power of it. He tried to use it, begging them for their help to turn the battle against Lord Vernon. He slid out from the safety of the huge lump of stone. Above the din of the fight and the Architraves in his head there was a new sound, the crowd outside was beating against the doors, which Lord Vernon's troops had barred closed.

"They're trying to get in!" shouted Ruth, beside him.

The doors creaked and groaned and the business of holding them, might, possibly have diverted a few more of the black and red army Grongles from the fight at the High Temple's altar end. But not enough.

"It's the others. I've got to help them."

Lord Vernon and General Moteurs were still at the centre of the fight, concentrating on one another but slowly and surely Lord Vernon's forces were closing in. The Pan had to do something. Now. He cast about him, taking in the melee of fighting bodies between him and the end of the aisle in a brief second. Beyond it lay the Gathering Area, where the Great Doors were situated. It was full of black and red uniforms. How was he going to get there, let alone open them?

Not like that, yer daft bugger, wi' us.

"Five?"

Lerrus show thee.

A picture appeared in The Pan's head of the heavy tree trunk barring the doors closed. He could see nothing else. He realised it came from them and understood what he must do.

"Stay here," he told Ruth and he took a step away from the safety of the altar, praying, hoping that he was capable of achieving the task before him. He half expected to get shot but the battle raged on and nobody seemed to notice him. The pain in his head intensified and blinding lights obscured his vision, but he concentrated on the picture of the wood in his mind's eye. It wasn't shifting.

"More."

Tha's had enough.

"No. More," he told them.

He felt their fear as they overloaded his system. He hadn't believed he could endure so much pain, a lancing agony pierced his chest and brought him to his knees. The pressure in his head was so acute that it felt as if it was crushing his skull. But his fingertips were beginning to tingle. He knew it was working.

"Need more," he forced the words through a jaw tightly clenched with the pain and then the voice of Five clearly and surprisingly quietly.

Tha's got ter point t' power lad with thine hand.

And suddenly The Pan understood, and he held his arm out in front of him, with his hand up, his fingers and thumb splayed. He felt the energy of the others flowing through him and focussing in his palm, he let it build, and tried to forget about the pain so he could concentrate his mind on the wood, on the molecules, on the atoms and the forces that bound them. He pictured them cleaving, becoming lighter than air, as dust and floating upwards. He went with them, rising higher and higher into the sky, looking down at the High Temple below as the doors swung open and the crowds surged in. He was blowing free in the breeze. Everything was calm and peaceful and he was drifting away.

Whump!

Or not.

Chapter 90

Lucy led her team into the anteroom. Lord Vernon's troops were now all in the nave, fighting. She took them through the side door, leaving a group in each of the other chambers. In the third, a couple of Lord Vernon's troops were using the doorway as cover, picking off Imperial Guards from the fighting masses in the temple. Major Pylup vaporised them with two swift rounds before they were aware of the danger. Suppressing the urge to gag, Lucy ran and retrieved their laser pistols. Then she closed the door and continued with her troops, distributing them evenly among the five anterooms. Now came the hardest bit. Until Captain Snow was neutralised, they could do nothing. They were eager to join the fray, to equalise the numbers but she ordered them to hold back. They must wait for word from Big Merv. Alan's volunteers kept coming and Lucy kept distributing them evenly through the rooms. Waiting.

****

Captain Snow had cut the rope Deirdre's team had used to scale the temple but thanks to Lieutenant Wright, it was soon reattached and Big Merv and his band of volunteers – agents, burglars and Grongle troops – made swift progress to the roof. He was glad of the hours he had spent going over the plans General Moteurs had given him when he located the chimney in moments. He glanced down the roof and spied the chimney from the fireplace at the other end of the gallery. Quickly, he divided his team into two groups and nodded at Lieutenant Wright who had a coil of rope slung over one shoulder, bandolier style.

"Alright, girl, you're in charge of them lot." He gestured to one of the two groups. "You're gonna take out any Grongles guarding the ducts in the organ. You gotta go down that chimney over there. You get me?"

"Yes, sir," she said.

"Sweet. The rest, you're with me. We're gonna take out Captain Snow and his goons from the other side. We gotta go in stealthy like. We ain't got much clue what's goin' down in there, so we gotta be subtle. I reckon most of 'em are gonna be watching the action below 'cept a couple of sentries but they got rapid-repeat laser rifles. They got us outgunned any way you cut it. We gotta take em by surprise, fast and silent. There's a lotta cover down there so I reckon we can. No lasers," he nodded at the Grongles with him, "we ain't got enough of them. This is gonna be up close and personal, you get me?"

"Yes, sir," said all the troops.

"Good. It's a great big effin' inglenook down there. That should give us a bit of cover an' all. Each team moves out in two waves, three and then two. Everyone clear?"

"Yes, sir."

"Smooth." He winked at Lieutenant Wright. "On you go girl. Gimme a signal when you're ready."

She and her team moved off.

Meanwhile, Beatrice who was on Big Merv's team and also carrying a rope, had already slipped it off her shoulders and was making one end fast to a nearby balustrade.

He watched until Lieutenant Wright gave him the signal and then, stealthily, silently, the two teams began their journey down the chimneys.

Chapter 91

The Pan found himself face down on the hard stone floor of the High Temple. For a moment he was motionless, then came the agony. He twitched and writhed as it all but consumed him. The Architraves in his head knew he was dying. Through the fog of pain he heard the voices from the people around him.

"He's fitting."

"No, it's the pain."

"Hold on, Defreville."

Aye, listen to 'em lad. Tha can't let go. Tha's not done wi' it yet, said Five. His voice was calm but The Pan could tell he was frightened.

Cluck, said Eight.

They don't know how to stop and I can't control them, he thought and then, he felt someone put their hands under his arms and drag him backwards.

"He must stand. Help me get him upright," said a voice, one The Pan had heard before, one he knew and trusted but, which, in his confusion, he took a split second to place.

"Sir Robin?" he mumbled.

"Yes."

His eyes were open but he couldn't see so he shut them. A part of him was detached and calm, almost standing outside the shuddering failing thing that was his body. He felt himself being lifted up, felt the stone altar against his back.

Did I … open the doors? he thought.

No lad, said Five gently.

But I thought—

Tha made a grand go of it.

Cluck, said Eight.

Smeck, thought The Pan. His left knee gave way and he felt himself sliding sideways, felt hands stopping him, grabbing him, pushing him back upright and holding him still. Then there was a new voice, Ruth's, crying.

"Defreville," she said, "can you hear me? You have to wake up and stand up on your own."

"Can't."

"Yes you can. We're this close. I'll never forgive you if you die on me now."

Her words brought him back from the nothingness he was in and somehow, he convinced his trembling muscles to function, locking his knees and leaning back against the reassuring stony solidity of the altar behind him.

"Splendid, my boy," said Sir Robin, or was it one of the Architraves in his head? Difficult to tell, "Can you hear me?"

"Uh ..." The Pan tried to nod.

"You have to take the ring from my hand and put it on, then the box which you must open."

The Pan's throat was dry and his tongue felt like feathers in his mouth.

"Can't see," he croaked.

"Open your eyes."

"No point. Blind."

"Quickly, Ruth, guide his arm," he could hear the urgency in Sir Robin's voice.

"Defreville, it's alright, I'm going to help you," Ruth again. She sounded frightened, but stoic. Even worried, her voice comforted him, held him fast to the world, to his purpose and the love of his friends. He smiled, in his head at least, although he doubted it got to his face. Then he felt someone gently take his hand, guiding it forward. His fingers touched something cold and metallic: a ring. The ring. There was a pause.

"He must do it himself."

"Stick your finger out."

Slowly, painfully, he concentrated and did as he was told. He felt the cool metal against his finger tip and moved his hand upwards. He felt it rattle to the bottom of his finger, then it tightened, cold for a moment until his flesh warmed it up. The agony he felt in his chest abated a tiny bit and his thoughts seemed to clarify. Perhaps he was getting used to the pain, or perhaps, putting the ring on had helped.

"Wonderful, my boy, now you must do that again, if you can, with the box. Pick it up and open it."

Once more he felt someone take his hand but the box was red-hot and burned him.

"No ..." he felt as if his fingertips were bubbling where he had touched it. "Please."

"My boy," Sir Robin's voice was quiet and sad but it carried through the turmoil around him as if it were inside his head with his predecessors, "you must open the box."

"Too painful."

"Defreville," said Ruth, "you have to or you'll die."

Stark. But probably true.

"And so will we," said Sir Robin.

"Please, Defreville, please. Don't give up now." The tears were still there in Ruth's voice when she spoke.

Slowly, painfully, he moved his hand, and felt again the blistering heat. Arnold.

None so stout as them that's already aching, said Five, paraphrasing the Prophet. The Pan wasn't sure which book but he took the point, and since he was already in more pain than he'd ever have believed he could bear, how much worse could a few burns be than the pressure in his skull or the agony of taking a breath.

One, two, three. He cried out in pain but he managed to fumble the box into his hand and flick at the lid with his thumb. The pain escalated, to a world of screaming, searing awfulness running through his entire body.

You were wrong, Five, he thought. The box opened and then he dropped to his knees and fell forward. The sensory overload he was undergoing was so intense that he didn't even notice the impact as his chin hit the stone. For a moment it felt as if there was something heavy on top of him. Then it was gone and there was nothing but the bone-melting agony. "I'm going to die."

He writhed and rolled over. He was on fire, burning up from the inside, his eyes stung and through his semi-consciousness he heard a sound. A wordless animal roar growing in volume and depth. It was the sound of the hills and the rain, of volcanoes and earthquakes; a sound of immense power; of hurricanes, of hail, of stones and earth, of a world screaming. And he realised it came from him.

He convulsed as, with one final sickening burst, the pain left him. He had dropped the box and from somewhere on the ground beside him he heard its lid close with a crack. Then he was lying still. He felt the cold floor against his skin and the sweat cool on his face. He took a deep breath and opened his eyes. Thank The Prophet, he could see. In the centre of his vision was the vaulted ceiling of the High Temple, smoke drifting across it. He realised he was lying behind the High Altar. Then the sound hit him.

He sat up, remembering to put the box in his pocket. Sir Robin and Ruth were beside him.

"Hurry," said Ruth, taking his hand to help him up.

"No," said Sir Robin, putting his hand on her wrist, "this one time it must be me."

The Pan took Sir Robin's arm.

"You are now the Seventy Eighth Great High Architrave of Grandy Martocks, ruler of K'Barth," said Sir Robin as The Pan stood up and immediately, four armed Grongles appeared, laser rifles primed and ready.

"Freeze, rebel trash," said one of them.

Chapter 92

Hiding in the inglenook fireplace, Big Merv realised that Captain Snow had placed his troops exactly as Major Pylup had predicted. Clearly someone was still fighting but it sounded as if the greater part of the battle had already been won, or lost. He caught sight of Lieutenant Wright in the fireplace opposite and signalled her to start the attack. There was plenty of cover, hundreds of copies of the K'Barthan Chantinal, old service sheets and religious books were piled on pallets, stacks of chairs, benches and religious ornaments all with white dust sheets thrown over them.

Captain Snow and most of his troops were watching events in the aisle below, pistols and rapid-repeat laser rifles trained on the action.

Big Merv took the first sentry, clamping one hand over his mouth, dragging him back into the inglenook and punching him unconscious. He left him there and moved on, with his team, to a spot where the sentries on the stairs couldn't see him. They had moved forward, the better to see the action unfolding below them. Lieutenant Wright's team took two and Beatrice one with a throwing knife; timing it so the noise as they fell was mostly hidden by the clash of swords on the ground below.

Big Merv waited, tense and alert but the Captain and the rest of the Grongles hadn't noticed. They were still caught up in events below them. Swiftly, Beatrice and one of the Grongles on Lieutenant Wright's team moved the bodies so they were hidden from view. Then, slowly, carefully, Big Merv and his assault team crept forward. Big Merv waited until they were close, so close he could feel the body heat of his intended victim. There was one more Grongle than there were members of Big Merv's force. He was going to have to take down two of them. He glanced to his left and right, checking his troops were ready, and signalled the attack.

Big Merv grabbed Captain Snow's collar in one hand and that of the next Grongle in line with the other, bringing their heads together with a crack. The unknown Grongle went down like a sack of potatoes but Captain Snow reeled to the left and regrouped. Big Merv went for him, hands locked round his wrists as the two of them fell to the floor. He smashed the Captain's hand against the stone flags until he dropped his weapon. Then they were rolling over and over until Captain Snow kicked him over his head, leapt to his feet and drew a knife. He lunged and Big Merv dodged sideways but the knife went into his chest, the Grongle's strength, coupled with the momentum of the lunge, forcing it through the body armour as the two of them crashed to the ground again. Big Merv grunted as the Captain put all his weight and power behind the knife.

"You thought you could kill me, mutant?" he snarled, jerking the knife. Big Merv felt the damp blood welling up and gritted his teeth as the blade cut deeper. Wait for it, wait. He would only have one chance at this. He had to be sure, and accurate.

Captain Snow was beginning to enjoy himself putting both hands on the knife. He leaned down, pressing to gloat in Big Merv's face.

"It's time to die, trash."

"Not for me, pal."

Big Merv jabbed two fingers hard at the bottom of Captain Snow's neck. The Grongle's body arched backwards as the blow made contact and Big Merv felt the soft skin give as his jabbing fingers hit their target: the v-shape between the ends of the Grongle's collarbone. He heard the crunch of cartilage as the force of the jab crushed the Captain's windpipe. Captain Snow fell sideways but he wasn't giving up. He got onto all fours, head down, desperately trying to breathe. Big Merv moved swiftly over to him and, taking a handful of his hair, slammed his head downwards. Captain Snow's forehead hit the stone floor with a brutal crunch. He rolled over and lay still.

Big Merv stood up, wincing at the pain from his stab wound. Beatrice was standing next to him and Big Merv put one hand on her shoulder.

"Alright lass?"

"Yeh, I am now."

Big Merv was out of breath but the fight was over. Captain Snow and his Grongle troops lay dead.

Lieutenant Wright approached. He noticed her look down at Captain Snow.

"He ain't gonna wake up."

"You need a medic?"

"Nah. 'S just a flesh wound. Later. First we gotta get them guns and turn things around down there. Then we wanna get some reinforcements up here pronto."

He left her, picked up Captain Snow's laser pistol from the floor where it had fallen, and walked to the edge of the gallery.

Chapter 93

Arnold's socks, what was going on? How long have I been out, The Pan wondered. Thirty seconds, a minute, no more, he was sure. The battle seemed to have ended, the only two fighting were Lord Vernon and General Moteurs.

The General was clearly accomplished with a sword; he fought with an intelligence and precision honed in battle rather than fencing classes. And he fought for survival, his mouth set in a grim determined line, adding kicks and punches whenever he could. But Lord Vernon, all fencing-school panache, maintained an impenetrable guard. Nothing the General did could break it. Lord Vernon fought as if he was playing a game, which The Pan knew it was, to him.

He drove the General backwards and lunged, for a moment the two of them were locked together, the General forced against a pillar, their swords crossed against each other, grinding and scraping in a contest of strength that General Moteurs could not possibly hope to win. Lord Vernon forced his blade closer and closer to the General's neck. Then General Moteurs delivered two swift jabs just below his opponent's ribs. Lord Vernon breathed out with a hiss as some of the wind was knocked out of him and with a last almighty effort the General pushed him away, moving swiftly back to the open floor in front of the altar as with a glare of murderous intent, Lord Vernon came after him again.

"STOP!" shouted The Pan. He put his hand into his pocket and flicked open the box.

"Shut up, freak," snarled the Grongle nearest him. General Moteurs hesitated and Lord Vernon seized the moment and lunged. The General parried but the weight of the thrust sent him backwards. Lord Vernon used his forward momentum, bringing his elbow up towards his opponent's face. General Moteurs dodged but Lord Vernon's elbow caught his shoulder, knocking him down. As the General landed on his back, Lord Vernon brought down his sword. General Moteurs managed to keep hold of his own and half parried, half rolled. Lord Vernon's blow hit the floor, but the General's guard faltered, and Lord Vernon struck again.

The world slowed down, General Moteur's expression of surprise turned to resignation as Lord Vernon's blade flicked past his effort to block it.

No.

The Pan concentrated on his wish to keep General Moteurs from harm, begging his predecessors to help him rearrange the quantum minutiae of the universe, rewrite this scene, so that the blade would turn or stop. But neither he nor they had the strength. Not yet. It drove on, straight and true. Smecking Arnold no. He put his thumb against the ring, gathered everything he had and concentrated, but he, and they, were still too weak. At the last moment, he managed to make Lord Vernon's arm jink, so the tip of the sword glanced off the shiny buckle of General Moteur's belt. The blade slid sideways off the polished metal and The Pan heard the material rip as it cut through the General's uniform, saw the first splash of blood as it sliced into the flesh beneath. It was a deep cut but it was a glancing blow and not the mortal wound it should have been. The momentum of the sword kept it moving sideways until the tip of the blade struck the floor and it stuck in the crack between two of the stone bricks. It bent with the force of the thrust and snapped.

Despite being injured, General Moteurs was quick to take advantage, grabbing his sword, leaping up and attacking before Lord Vernon had recovered his balance. Lord Vernon parried with his broken weapon but in an instant General Moteurs attacked again, whipping the blade from his hand with the tip of his own sword. There was a gasp from the congregation as it arced into the air and landed several yards away, with a clatter.

Lord Vernon drew his knife but General Moteurs extended his sword and put the blade at his throat.

"It is over, Lord Vernon," he said. He was pale and both Grongles were breathing heavily.

"Bravo, General," snarled Lord Vernon. "You can handle a sword, but it won't save you."

"Do not try anything. My reach is longer, I'll kill you before you touch me."

"And my guards?"

"I'll cut you down before they fire the first shot."

"You're bleeding, and outnumbered and you won't last long. We can wait."

"Enough," said a voice of such ringing authority that even Lord Vernon was forced to obey. It took The Pan a moment to realise it was his. Indeed, he nearly spoiled the effect completely by looking round to see where it had come from. Lord Vernon stood, eyes blazing, glaring at The Pan, while General Moteurs, tense, vigilant, kept the sword pointing at his throat.

"I said shut up, freak," said the Grongle guarding The Pan and he felt the cold metal as the trooper put the muzzle of the pistol against his head.

"Or what?" asked The Pan, the power of his predecessors might have been weak but they were able to provide liberal quantities of The Voice. His eyes met the gun-toting Grongle's, he put his thumb against the metal band of the K'Barthan Ring of State and glared at him; one man's authority and intent, plus seventy-six. The trooper's red eyes widened, as The Pan put his hand up to the gun and slowly, without breaking eye contact, pushed it away. "You shut up, and watch this, you might learn something," he said and, as he moved forward the trooper took a couple of paces backwards.

The Pan walked slowly out from behind the altar, Ruth and Sir Robin following, and the troops guarding them let them go.

"This is over," he told Lord Vernon, "I am the Architrave of K'Barth and you have no business here," he could feel the power of his predecessors' anger vibrating through him as he raised his arm and pointed. "I'm giving you one last chance, and you," the ruby on the K'Barthan Ring of State flashed, blood red in the bright light as he pointed at Lord Vernon's troops, "you can walk, all of you, even Captain Snow, if you drop your weapons now and if you, Lord Vernon, promise to abandon politics for ever, leave K'Barth and never come back."

"You are in no position to issue an ultimatum," snarled Lord Vernon.

"Aren't we?" asked a voice from somewhere, a voice that The Pan would have known anywhere; Big Merv.

"I tire of this. Captain. Kill them all," ordered Lord Vernon.

"Captain Snow ain't gonna be killing no-one no more," shouted Big Merv, "and you ain't neither. You're gonna go back to Grongolia, sunshine, and you're gonna stand trial, for what you done."

Lord Vernon glared over at The Pan, he seemed coiled, tense, ready to spring. Even if he attacked, Big Merv would shoot him before he got close. All the same, Lord Vernon still appeared to be thinking about it.

"I wouldn't," The Pan warned him. "My friend up there isn't as diplomatic as I am."

"It ain't just me," Big Merv shouted down to them.

From high above, in the gallery, came the sound of several hundred pairs of feet snapping together with a loud crack. The Pan glanced up. Lined along the edge, laser rifles trained on the aisle below was what he supposed was his army. Resistance agents, punters from the Parrot and Grongles from both the army and the Imperial Guard stood together, shoulder to shoulder, weapons at the ready. Each one was wearing a strip of light blue fabric round their arm. Meanwhile the doors to the anterooms along the north side of the High Temple opened and more forces with light blue armbands poured in, led by Lucy, a Grongle army officer and Pub Quiz Alan.

"Captain Snow's dead," shouted Big Merv, "and unless you wanna join him, I'd give it up, pal. Now."

The Pan looked over at Lord Vernon and raised an eyebrow.

"Your call."

"No," snarled Lord Vernon.

"Perhaps I should count," said The Pan. "One."

"It seems we have reached an impasse," said Lord Vernon.

"No we haven't," said The Pan.

He put his hand in the pocket, felt the reassuring presence of the box, the lid still open. He heard and felt the presence of his predecessors.

Can we do this now? he thought.

Aye, NOW, we can, said Five.

Cluck, said Eight.

Bring it on, said Seventy-seven.

Good. He held out his hand towards the Great Doors and concentrated. Now that he was Architrave, he instinctively knew how to channel the power of his predecessors, and if he hadn't already known, the sense of relief he could feel from them would have told him he could do so safely. He felt it fizzing, building in his palm. Seventy-seven K'Barthan Architraves working together – only Arnold was missing – all of them believing. Without taking his eyes off Lord Vernon, The Pan held out his hand. His palm itched and his fingertips tingled. He pictured the atoms of the huge tree trunk barring the doors, imagined them rearranging themselves in his mind's eye. He felt a little light-headed for a second and then, with a rumble, the bar on the doors dissolved into dust. "We are done with this, Lord Vernon," he said and he saw the

Gathering Area become lighter as the doors slowly swung open.

Nice touch, said Forty-three.

Aye, everyone likes a bit o' theatre.

In his head, The Pan smiled.

Why did you guys sit on this stuff?

We didn't sit on it, said Forty-three. If you must know, we didn't all have it. You're very powerful.

But, I'm not. It isn't mine. It comes from you.

No, it's yours, nobody told you the truth so you didn't know any better. You believed in a myth, like the people, and now you are one.

Natterjack's box of frogs.

More K'Barthans and Imperial Guards started to make their way into the High Temple, weapons at the ready, but the ranks of Lord Vernon's troops there did not resist. The Pan faced Lord Vernon, trying to project a calm he didn't feel.

"Give me the knife, if you please," he said.

Lord Vernon's grey eyes met his, shocked, unbelieving and still glowing with fiery malevolence, but The Pan wasn't frightened. The moment stretched to eternity as he waited. He flinched as Lord Vernon flicked the knife round so the handle was facing towards him and held it out. Holy smecking Arnold, surely this wasn't going to be as simple as opening a door? He moved forward, reaching out to take it but General Moteurs grabbed his arm. Good point.

"Put it on the ground in front of you, Lord Vernon."

Slowly, Lord Vernon walked backwards and General Moteurs followed, sword at the ready. The dark patch of blood on his uniform was widening with alarming speed, but he stood straight and tall and held the blade steady. Lord Vernon squatted down, put the knife on the ground and then took a couple more paces back.

A collective sigh of relief went up, from everyone, and Ruth ran to The Pan's side. He put his arm around her but he kept watching Lord Vernon. He was wary. This had been far too easy. General Moteurs seemed to think so too, because he hadn't dropped his guard.

"Aren't you going to arrest me? I am unarmed," sneered Lord Vernon.

"That doesn't make you any less dangerous," said The Pan.

"No," said Lord Vernon and he made his move.

Chapter 94

Lord Vernon moved fast. Too fast for anyone, even the troops in the gallery. In a lightning swift movement he unhooked his phone from his belt and hurled it, throwing star style. General Moteurs groaned as it hit the slash in his side at high velocity, with a meaty squelch. As he doubled over and fell, a round of fire from above hit the ground where Lord Vernon had been but he had already leapt at Ruth.

"No!" There was no time to think. Instinctively, The Pan pushed her out of the way with his good arm, biting back the pain as he tried to defend himself with the other but Lord Vernon swatted it aside, clamping his hands round The Pan's neck as the momentum took them both to the ground. Lord Vernon knelt over The Pan, putting his weight on his hands.

"You will never rule K'Barth."

The Pan looked up into the slate grey eyes, so alive with hatred and bloodlust.

"Neither will you," he whispered. The blackness began to close in as his vision tunnelled. This was it. But it wasn't so bad. He had done what he must. He had given his people a future, and the Grongles too, if they wanted one. He could die in peace.

Lord Vernon tightened his grip, laughing. The rushing of The Pan's blood in his ears was almost deafening him, his vision narrowing. He could hear the shouts of the others, clearly they were afraid to fire, in case they hurt him too, but then there was a ping, and he felt Lord Vernon's body stiffen as a round hit him. It was only set to stun, they wouldn't want to take risks, and it wasn't strong enough. Lord Vernon's iron grip on The Pan's neck relaxed for a second allowing him to take a gulp of much-needed air, but it did nothing else. He felt the grip tighten again. But then, Lord Vernon's face contorted for a moment.

"No," he snarled. His back arched and his fingers on The Pan's windpipe loosened. He let out a snarling, gurgling cry of pain. "No," he hissed and The Pan began to hope.

Smecking Arnold, lad! There's summat wrong wi' 'im! Fight! said Five.

Poke him in the eyes! shouted Seventy-seven.

No! Punch him in the nuts! shouted a female voice.

The Architraves were right. Something was weakening Lord Vernon and this was no time to fight like a gentleman. Lord Vernon's expression of pain intensified as The Pan followed both pieces of advice. He heard more shots and again, he felt the grip on his neck loosen. Kicking out, struggling and punching he fought to free himself. Lord Vernon screamed, his features twisted in agonised disbelief. His grip was weakening fast but his hands were napalm on The Pan's skin, hot, boiling, burning.

Now The Pan screamed. Jabbing the heel of his hand against the base of Lord Vernon's nose and delivering a second hit to Lord Vernon's groin with a well-aimed knee he finally struggled free. As he scrambled to his feet, Lord Vernon also stood and stumbled after him like some immaculately dressed, psychotic zombie, falling on him again, pawing at his cloak and grabbing the lapels of his jacket. Lord Vernon's weight sent The Pan staggering swiftly backwards but he was able to stay on his feet. The suede-clad hands clawed their way towards his neck but the Grongle's strength was spent. With a cry he slid to his knees and slumped sideways onto the floor at The Pan's feet. Twitching and writhing.

"Somebody, do something. Stop this or put him out of his misery," shouted The Pan.

Sir Robin was beside him, "It is too late for that."

Aye. There's nowt us can do, added Five.

The Pan watched in horrified fascination as smoke began to rise from Lord Vernon's clothes. He glowed, as if illuminated from the inside and the green skin of his face began to desiccate. The venomous grey eyes held The Pan's. The hatred in them never wavered until the life left them and they decomposed, drying out, sinking into their sockets and disappearing. Dust began to pour from Lord Vernon's nose and ears and from the sightless holes where his eyes had been. The sneering mouth opened to let out one final, gurgling hissing scream and he shrank to nothing, dissolved into a fine grey powder.

The Pan took another step backwards and came up against the High Altar. He felt sick and dizzy and as he reached up to his neck, the skin was tender to the touch and blistered in places. Lord Vernon's hands hadn't only felt hot. He looked around him. Lord Vernon's remaining troops lay stunned and the various GNN crews, and the Free KBC one, were still there and filming. General Moteurs sat on the floor, deathly pale, with Lord Vernon's own laser pistol in his hand. The Pan took a deep breath to contain his nausea but the smell of burning Lord Vernon was only making it worse. Never mind. He was alive and Lord Vernon … Lord Vernon, was very definitely not.

He looked around him. Barring a few, who'd been left to keep guard, the contingent from the gallery above were starting to make their way down. Others were moving among Lord Vernon's supine troops, handcuffing them. The Pan glanced at Sir Robin, who raised his eyebrows, and then Ruth was at his side and he was holding her, hugging her against him, unbelieving, unable to let go.

Chapter 95

The Pan kissed Ruth briefly and then the two of them ran to General Moteurs' side although a ballistic Deirdre Arbuthnot beat them to it.

"Ford," she cradled him in her arms, "Ford."

"Get me a medic," The Pan shouted.

"On her way, sir," said a voice from somewhere in the aisle.

"Stop fussing over me, it is a mere scratch," said the General and everyone drew back a little, although when Deirdre made to do the same, he clamped his arm around her waist and pulled her closer again. The Pan smiled. Clearly a bit of fussing, from certain quarters, was acceptable.

Lucy arrived with three army Grongles, all wearing light blue armbands.

"Is this place secure?" asked The Pan.

"Yes." She smiled, "This is Major Pylup who was kind enough to help us get in."

"Blimey, are you telling me, this is over?"

"I reckon," said a familiar voice.

"Merv!" The Pan ran to hug his friend and stopped. He had a dagger buried in his chest. "Arnold, I see knives are being worn high this year. Seriously though, you should get that looked at."

"Nah, 's no problem. 'S stuck in the body armour, innit?"

"You're wearing body armour?"

Somehow, The Pan hadn't expected that.

"Course," Big Merv laughed, a deep rumble, "can't get the smecker out. I reckon I gotta scratch underneath but it ain't serious. 'S just a flesh wound. I work out. I got big pecs."

"You still need to see a medic, I think," said Ruth, who was back by The Pan's side. He put his arm around her waist and held on to her – he wasn't going to let go of her again.

"Nah, I told yer, 's only a scratch."

The Pan looked doubtfully at the blood stains on Big Merv's charcoal pinstriped suit.

"That's what General Moteurs said about his. Both of you are lying."

The Swamp Thing started to chuckle again.

"Talkin' about General Moteurs, where's 'e got to?"

"Over here," said The Pan as he and Ruth led Big Merv to where the General was, still sitting on the floor.

"Alright mate? Sorry we was late, we ran into a spot of bother."

The General looked up at Big Merv and raised his eyebrows.

"So I see. No matter, even the best laid plans go awry, when circumstances change. The skill lies in adapting them."

"To be honest, mine wasn't the best laid plan," said The Pan.

"Yer we got that, right General? 'S lucky we made one of our own."

"Agreed," said General Moteurs drily.

"D'you want a hand up?" asked The Pan.

"Thank you." General Moteurs took The Pan's outstretched hand and two film crews, one GNN and the one which must be KBC, filmed them. On the screen behind him the picture zoomed in to The Pan's human hand clasping General Moteurs' green-skinned Grongle one. A few seconds later, as the same picture was relayed to the screen on the front of the High Temple, a cheer rose up from the crowd in the precinct.

"Are you alright, lad?" General Moteurs asked as The Pan hauled him to his feet.

"Yeh, better than you I'd say, although …" he hiccupped as he caught another whiff of incinerated Lord Vernon. His nausea wasn't helped when he turned to see that a cleaner had appeared from somewhere and was sweeping up the mortal remains of his nemesis with a dustpan and brush, decanting them into an urn. "I'd quite like to hurl."

"It'll pass."

"Shall we go to the pew over there?" asked Ruth as The Pan put one of the General's arms over his shoulder and Deirdre took the other.

"I can walk."

"Humour us," said Deirdre.

"That's right," said The Pan. "We like to feel needed."

"Come over here and sit down," said Ruth.

"Yeh, and Merv, you too."

"If I gotta."

"Smecking Arnold," muttered The Pan, "why was it … different with Lord Vernon?" he asked General Moteurs.

"I cannot tell you. The pistol I shot him with was set to stun. I'll wager you'll find your answer if you ask the old man."

"Thank you for saving my life … again," said The Pan, "I think you should try to break the habit though." He glanced down at the rip and the dark patch of blood on the grey uniform. "It's clearly not good for your health."

"Nothing about you is good for my health," said General Moteurs with a weak laugh as The Pan and Deirdre sat him down.

"Where's the medic?" said The Pan.

"Already here," said a familiar voice.

"Doctor Dot!" and he hugged her.

"Now then, everyone, out of the way, give the patients some air. And don't you be going anywhere, young man, I'll want to give you a quick check over as well."

"Thanks. Sir Robin?"

"Your Gracious Exaltedness," said Sir Robin, dropping to one knee.

There was a rustle as everyone in the temple followed suit. The world slowed down and The Pan stood, shocked and alone, as even Ruth disentangled her arms from his and with a coquettish look from under her eyelashes, sank in a low curtsey.

"Smecking Arnold!" said The Pan, "please get u—" No. Wait. That wasn't right.

All rise, said a voice in his head, peevishly. *We really are going to have to educate you.* He'd forgotten to close the box.

I thought you'd never offer, yes I'd be very grateful, he thought and he pressed the lid of the box closed.

"All rise ... please," he said and to his relief, everyone got to their feet. "As you were," he added and the world started up again. He left Ruth and the others with General Moteurs and Big Merv, helping Doctor Dot patch the pair of them up and moved a few paces away with Sir Robin.

"Sir Robin," he said cautiously. Arnold please don't let him kneel down again.

"My boy."

Phew.

Chapter 96

The Pan wanted to talk to the old man, but didn't know where to begin. "Please tell me I didn't kill him. They wanted to and I—"

"You were not the cause."

"Then did they? The Architraves."

"No. My boy, raw energy knits some things and … unknits others, there was a lot of it about and the impetus of the laser shot was enough."

"So why didn't any of the others fry? Why didn't I?"

"Because there was not so much energy around them. Lord Vernon played a pivotal role in making you who you are, you understand that."

"Yes, I do but—"

"We cannot be certain why it happened, indeed; perhaps it's best if we can't." He put his hand on The Pan's shoulder. "There are some things that should remain a mystery."

"There's something else."

"Ask."

"They're all in my head, all of them, except one. Why no Arnold?"

"He is too powerful. It's him or them but it cannot be him and them."

"So where is he?"

"He is … elsewhere."

The Pan took in how pale Sir Robin was and the way his brow was shiny with sweat, almost as if he, too, had been wrestling to contain the Architraves …

"Elsewhere, or with someone else?" The Pan asked.

"What a very intelligent question. I'm afraid, I couldn't say but, believe me, young fellow, the division is equal. Carrying The Prophet is not easy."

"Yeh," The Pan looked into Sir Robin's eyes; greeny brown and giving very little away. "I can imagine. What would you say if I told you I think I know where he is."

"I'd say I believe you might, but even if you are right, I will never be able to confirm it, one way or the other."

The Pan nodded.

"Right," a beat, "Sir Robin, I know I should talk to my people but I also need to talk to these guys about … who's going to do what."

"Haven't you done that already?"

"Er … no." He was aware that the conversation among the others had died out and they seemed to be listening. "You see, I—"

"He thought he was gonna die, the giant nerk," said Big Merv.

"Yeh."

The Pan turned to his friends, Big Merv and General Moteurs, who, despite his injury, seemed calm and relaxed – or was it shock? He had taken off his jacket and Deirdre, pale and concerned, was holding his blood-soaked shirt out of the way for Doctor Dot as she dressed the slash in his side.

"How's it going?" asked The Pan.

"Just going to stitch him up," said Doctor Dot and suddenly everyone except Deirdre moved away.

Big Merv was also being stitched up by one of Doctor Dot's medical orderlies.

"You alright, Big Man?" asked The Pan.

"Yer, 's not like General Moteurs'." Big Merv sucked the air in through his teeth. "I reckon he lost a lotta blood. Not like you'd know. I gotta hand it to 'im, he's pukka cucumber in a tight spot. Proper nails. Diamond geezer."

"That he is."

"You reckon he's gonna stick around?"

"I hope so. Talking of nails and cool-headedness in a tight spot, you're not so bad, yourself. If there's a vacancy for chief of police, I think you'll fit the bill."

"Whoa there mate—"

"I don't know what's in store for me yet, things might get a little lumpy. I need people around me I can rely on."

"Oooo," said Lucy, "I've always wanted to date a Thing in uniform."

"You gotta cheek, sweets," he warned her, but he was beaming.

Another contingent of Imperial Guards arrived, including the General's batman, with a change of jacket and shirt, and Doctor Dot left Deirdre to help him put them on.

"Your attention everyone," said Sir Robin, with habitual natural authority, stopping everyone in their tracks. "Let's see, how long do we have? Would one hour be enough?" he asked The Pan.

"I expect so, although I haven't prepared anything."

"What an incredible surprise, Mister Pan," said Ruth.

"You ain't planned nothing?" asked Big Merv. "Straight?"

"Well, no, I didn't dare. I'd hoped and prayed that you guys might make it but I didn't think I'd be here."

"I am grateful this coup d'état hinged on our belief and not yours," said General Moteurs dourly, "otherwise it is we who would be lying dead, I think."

Everyone laughed.

"Yeh, very probably," said The Pan.

Sir Robin threw a glance at General Moteurs who was now reading the screen of his mobile phone while a batman straightened his belt over a fresh uniform, "Ford, we are ready?"

General Moteurs snapped the case of the phone closed and hung it back on his belt.

"Yes, Sir Robin," he said, as Deirdre handed him his sword and gun. Assured, dignified and impossibly pristine in a new uniform he and Deirdre walked over to join them, moving with a grace and poise that belied the blood loss and the sewn-up gash in his side. Like Big Merv's, General Moteurs' smile made a marked difference to his face. Now, he seemed relaxed and at ease in a way The Pan had never seen. It was especially striking considering he had nearly been killed a few moments before. Having endured the same experience, The Pan still felt very shaky.

"Defreville, Ruth," General Moteurs bowed. Very formal, very serious but he seemed to be bursting with pride and the red eyes were smiling, "I have received word that the last of Lord Vernon's allies are now in custody. K'Barth is yours, the only task outstanding, that you claim it."

The Pan's intestines felt as if they were tying themselves into a ball.

"Thanks," he said, "I'm guessing this is where you would have installed me," he said to Sir Robin.

"Yes."

"So I can't be installed because … I already am."

"Well you can," said Sir Robin breezily. "I think it makes things neater, if I ratify your installation instead, although no-one will be any the wiser. The ratification order of service is very similar to the installation."

"It is?"

"Yes, the only difference being that when the dignitaries gather round, I don't actually stand on you."

"Good, it hurt like smeck last time."

Sir Robin chuckled, "Then let's do that."

"There are some others who need to be here," said Sir Robin.

"Too right, Trev, Gladys and Ada, some of the regulars from the Parrot—" began The Pan.

"Indeed although I was thinking more of other dignitaries, priests in hiding, any higher ranking members of the Resistance—"

"Anyone left above the rank of Lieutenant is already here, apart from Professor N'Aversion, who is on his way," said Lieutenant Wright.

"Capital."

"And Snoofle," the Spiffle looked up, "I heard you wanted to run a museum. I think someone who knows what they're doing needs to work out what's been looted from where. So if you're the Director of Ning Dang Po Museum – or the City Art Gallery if you prefer – can you fix that?"

"I—The Museum, I think, and yes."

"Right you are, then. As the Director of Ning Dang Po Museum, Snoofle here, should be a guest of honour, too."

"Quite, quite," said Sir Robin, quickly, "of course there are also our fellow members of the Grongolian Underground, Major Pylup and others, and they will elect a new High Leader of Grongolia."

"That's going to be interesting."

"Don't worry my boy, all will be well."

Big Merv nodded at General Moteurs.

"I'm surprised you don't wanna pop at that gig, mate," he said.

"I am tainted by association with Lord Vernon. I will not be welcome in politics."

"Then your politicians are idiots."

"Most politicians are. If you will permit it, I would stay here in K'Barth. I was born here but returned to the mother country to go to the Military Academy."

"Really. Where are you from, then, originally?"

"Glardy. Like many serving under me, I grew up here, and I would stay. There are enough of us to make the beginning of an army. That is, if you will have us."

Whoa. The Pan glanced at Ruth who gave him a reassuring smile.

"I would be very grateful but are you sure you don't want to go home to Grongolia?"

"No, there is nothing back there for me now but painful memories. My work is done, my wife and daughter are avenged and my honour exonerated. I can die in peace."

"I think Deirdre might have something to say about you dying straight away," said The Pan.

General Moteurs smiled sadly.

"I have stood idle and allowed Lord Vernon to perpetrate many atrocities while I waited for this day; indirectly I have aided him. Like as not I will be recalled to stand trial. I may be executed."

"No you won't. I want that army you just offered me and it needs chiefs of staff. And Field Marshall Arbuthnot over there," Deirdre's head snapped up, her expression disbelieving, delighted, "is going to need your help. At the least, I'll need someone as smart as you on the Council of Five. If I'm really going to do this, I have to have people around me I can trust, and," he addressed the wider group, "you lot are it."

"Time is pressing," said Sir Robin. "May I suggest we begin to gather the guests. If you have one of Gladys and Ada's pirate portals …?"

"I do," said The Pan, fishing it out of his pocket, "but I can help you with that if you like."

"No, my boy," said Sir Robin and he turned to Ruth, who was still by The Pan's side. "My dear, could I borrow your fiancé for a few short moments? I promise I will bring him back."

"Of course," she said.

"Excellent," Sir Robin took The Pan by the arm and led him a few paces away. "A word if I may, Defreville?" he said, except he wasn't exactly asking.

"Sure."

Sir Robin led him further away from the others.

"May I remind you that we are also prepared for a wedding. I believe there's a wonderful cake waiting back at the Palace, too. You are going to marry her, aren't you?"

"If she'll have me, but a lot has changed. It's not a question of her liking me. She has to cope with my job. She may not want to do that, and I think-I think the installation freaked her out a bit. I must talk to her before I commit her to something she may not want."

"Then might I suggest that now is a very good time to ask her. Gladys and Ada will help me with the guests."

"Thank you, I owe you one."

"Consider it my gift to you. And take all the time you need – within reason. I will keep everyone informed of any delay."

Chapter 97

When The Pan returned to Ruth she was standing apart, with Big Merv and Lucy.

"Hello Mister Pan," Ruth said and he put his arm around her and hugged her.

"Hello Chosen One," he said. "Can I talk to you for a moment? There's something I need to check."

"Can you check it here?"

He raised an eyebrow at her.

"No."

"Alright, Mister Architrave, your wish is my command."

"Is it now?"

"Behave!" She turned to Big Merv and Lucy. "I'll be back in a while."

As The Pan took her hand to lead her away, Big Merv winked.

They found a small robing room leading off the vestry and The Pan escorted her inside, shutting the door behind him. He pulled her into his arms and hugged her tight. It took all his self-control to resist kissing her straight away.

"Well, Mister Pan, what's up?"

"Listen, Ruth, I … there's …"

"Yes?"

"There's something I have to talk to you about."

"Yes?"

"It's very, very serious."

She giggled.

"Is it?"

"Yes. Last night, I asked you if you'd marry me."

"Yes and if you remember, I said I would."

Arnold yes.

"I still have the ring."

Tantalisingly, slowly, she put one hand down her cleavage and produced the hideous plastic trinket he'd given her. Arnold's socks, he was thinking about all the wrong things now.

"Mmm …" he said as he tried to collect his wayward thoughts, "but now, I'm the Architrave and things are a bit different."

Her eyes met his, dark and twinkling with mischief. She gave him that look, the one she'd once told him her mother would disapprove of and The Pan felt his blood pressure climbing to dangerous levels. Arnold's armpits.

"Nothing's changed," she said and she put the ring onto her finger.

He sighed and held her close, very close, and tried not to think too much about the way she seemed to be melting against him.

"Are you sure?"

She bent her knee so it was tight against his leg, so her thigh was against his, so that their shins and even their ankles were touching. Arnold's snot!

"Yes, Mister Pan," she said and his heart soared like a bee freshly released from a window.

"I'm so glad," he said. "It would be a pity to waste that dress."

"You like my dress?" She smiled up at him and he felt her hands under his cloak and jacket, moving across his back.

"Arnold yes," all he could think about was peeling it off her. "You look … fantastic and there's a wedding banquet all laid out at the Palace and, apparently, the cake is very nice."

"You want to get married now?"

"Yes. But only if you want – after the installation."

"Yes, I do," she said.

"Good. That's settled then."

"Yes …" she said and everything disappeared. The noise of the crowd outside, the temple, the sunlight streaming through the small window: all of it faded out and there was nothing left but her, and him.

He wanted to say so much to her, but he didn't know where to start. Bereft of words he held her in his arms, lost in wonder at the fact she was actually, really, there. He felt the warmth of her body against his and the softness of the velvet dress under his fingers. Those mischievous brown eyes smiled into his and he was beguiled, lost, utterly.

"Oh Ruth," he murmured and he held her tighter against him and tried to put the words he couldn't find into a kiss. He wanted to lose himself, to close his eyes and surrender himself to her, to the intensity of his emotions, to the touch of her fingers, her lips on his. But he daren't close his eyes, in case he broke the spell, in case the vibrant, intensity of this moment turned out to be nothing more than a dream. Hungrily, he drank in her kisses and his heart beat the rhythm of her name.

Chapter 98

After a few heavenly minutes, The Pan broke off from kissing Ruth. "I'm afraid we must stop this now," he said.

"Do we have to, Mister Pan?"

"Unless you want me to throw you over that table there and make mad passionate love to you, yes, I think we do."

She began to giggle.

"You never know, I might quite like that."

"Ms Cochrane! I'm shocked. If you must know, so might I," he laughed, "but I don't think we have the time to do it justice. Anyway, someone would be bound to walk in on us: the GNN crew, knowing my luck."

She burst out laughing.

"You are such a spanner Mister Pan, but I do love you."

"That's a stroke of luck because I love you too. Come on then wife-elect, before you change my mind about the table and we cause a press scandal."

The two of them linked arms and walked happily out into the brightness of the main building. The congregation had gone outside and the rest of The Pan's friends had arrived, including the ones who'd been missing. Gladys and Ada, with Humbert and Trev, who had been brought along by the three Resistance walking wounded who'd been looking after him. Sir Robin was the first to notice them.

"Sir Robin, this installation, could we tack a wedding onto the end of it?"

"Yes!" squealed Lucy, jumping up and down, and then their friends were all gathering round, hugging the pair of them.

"I think I have to go and address the nation now," said The Pan, except it was more of a squeak because the very idea terrified him.

"Yes," said Sir Robin, "it's time."

Together, they walked down the aisle, to the Gathering Area where the Great Doors had been closed again and a guard of honour was ranged either side. It comprised K'Barthan Resistance agents and regulars from the Parrot and Screwdriver. It also included Grongles, some in the grey uniform of the Imperial Guard and two in the black and red of the army.

All of them were wearing light blue armbands. The Pan greeted and thanked each of them, until he reached the doorway and stopped.

"Are you ready?" asked Sir Robin.

That was probably the moment it hit the others, when they looked at him and saw him as something more than just a friend. It was probably the moment when it truly hit The Pan. His stomach churned and he could feel the colour draining from his face.

Arnold's socks.

"Yeh," he said, except it was more of a croak. Ruth slid her arm around his waist and looked into his eyes, smiling.

"Busk it. It's ninety per cent bluff. Just act as if you know what you're doing and everyone'll think you do," she said. She squeezed tighter against him.

"Mmm," he said and she flashed him an encouraging smile.

"Ain'tcha planned a speech?" asked Big Merv.

"No."

"Then, what have you two been doing? No. Don't answer that," said Alan.

"Just pretend you're talking to us," said Lucy.

"Defreville knows what to do," said Sir Robin.

"Yeh," he said. Do I? he wondered. Sir Robin leaned over and muttered in his ear.

"If you're stuck, your predecessors will help. Now you're installed, I think you know that if you want to consult them, you just open the box."

"Right," said The Pan and his stomach churned some more. "Thanks."

"Good luck boy," said General Moteurs.

"Thanks. Ruth—" he began.

"I'll be waiting."

He stepped forward, nodded at the guards and with a creak they swung the Great Doors slowly open, revealing a tall oblong of blinding white light from a bank of well-placed GNN outdoor broadcast arc lights. The world stood still as he stepped out into the glare. He waited for a moment, letting his eyes adjust and then he took in the sheer size of the crowd. Thousands of K'Barthans of every shape, size and genus filled the precinct, Grongles too. He could see them stretching away as far as his eye could see down the surrounding streets. They had climbed trees, were hanging off lamp posts and fire escapes, leaning out of windows and lining the roofs. Everywhere, the eyes of K'Barthans watching him, waiting, in total silence. Some of them were armed. A cordon of assorted personnel, all wearing light blue armbands, held them back. Mixed species. Smart move from Field Marshals Arbuthnot and Moteurs. But then, what else would he expect?

The silence hung over the precinct like a thundercloud and The Pan felt naked, vulnerable, alone.

"Well, well, well. I guess old habits die hard," he muttered quietly. The beings in earshot got what he meant – that any crowd of K'Barthans had to remain silent under the old regime – and a ripple of laughter ran through them. His nerves abated a little, they sounded as scared as he was. He turned round in time to see his friends moving out into the glare lining up behind him.

GNN had provided some hastily improvised amplification but it was a Blaggysomp in a checked shirt who stepped up and handed him a microphone. It had a badge on it which read 'KBC'. Perhaps the media had conducted a little coup of its own.

"Thanks mate," said The Pan as he took hold of it and a loud scratching and booming rang out across the precinct as he biffed the end of it against his cloak. "Oops."

In front of him and across the country on TV, thousands upon thousands of K'Barthans waited in silence.

"H-" no, too squeaky. He started again. "Hello there," he said.

Silence. Well, that went down like a lead balloon. He wondered if he should have sent Sir Robin out first, as warm-up man. It would probably have been better. Still, too late now.

"I don't know about you but I've had one hell of a week." The merest hint of a laugh. Good. He took his hat off, transferring it, and the microphone, to the hand of his bad arm so he could run his good hand through his hair. The hum of expectation in the air grew. He put his hat back on and put the mike in his good hand again. "Yeh," he said, "it's been informative. I've learned a lot of stuff." He stopped. He wanted to be honest with them but not if it sounded like moralising. "Actually, I only realised who the Candidate was about a week ago and I can tell you for nothing, it was a hell of a disappointment." He got something closer to a proper laugh, this time. "I expected him to be some handsome, brave, swashbuckling bloke – Commander Thistwith-Mee reborn only perhaps with a slightly less luxuriant beard – or some incredible ninja lady, like Field Marshal Arbuthnot over there," he waved a hand in Deirdre's direction, "someone who would stride in with a bunch of insanely clever Generals and some enormous army … I confess, I'm a bit sketchy as to where I thought the army was going to come from but hey. Next we were going to whup the Grongles' arses on the battlefield, he or she was going to defeat Lord Vernon in hand-to-hand combat and we were going to fling any of the green scourge that were left standing into the sea."

A big cheer rose up.

"Right, so I'm guessing I wasn't the only one then." The crowd cheered louder. "It's not so simple though, is it?" shouted The Pan over the noise, and gradually the cheering died away. "It would be tidy, I know, if all Grongles were bad and all K'Barthans were good but this is real life and you know how it is. There's a lot of grey. And it never turns out the way you plan. So, the good news is that K'Barth is free of Grongle rule, but if you want the honest truth, the Grongles are as responsible for it as anybody. Don't mistake a bad government with a bad species and don't confuse me with a hero. The Underground, here and in Grongolia, has been planning this day for years. All I had to do was turn up. So if you want to know who to thank for deposing Lord Vernon don't look at me, these are the ones who made it happen," he turned sideways and stepped back, out of the way, so the crowd could see his friends. "When I'm done, I, and they, will be happy to answer questions."

"Any other GBIs out there or am I the only one?" A few cautious hands went up.

"Well, I think I'm going to change that. Nobody is a GBI anymore. The blacklist is revoked, as of now. This is a new Free K'Barth. Everyone is equal and nobody is vermin."

They definitely liked that. He waited for the applause to die down.

"Wipe my conkers," shouted Humbert but it got a laugh.

"This is Humbert," The Pan added hurriedly, "but I'd also like to introduce you to Ruth Cochrane. I ruined her life by choosing her, and she returned the favour by buying mine with her own." More cheers erupted as Ruth walked out onto the stairs and stood at his side. He smiled at her and took her hand.

"Finally, I'd like to thank the other thousands and thousands who resisted day by day, and I'd like to acknowledge the thousands who gave their lives to make this day happen – K'Barthans and Grongles alike. Everyone's lost someone, some of us have lost everyone, but we have a chance to start again, a new slate.

"There are some Grongles who want to stay. If they do, they will be renouncing their Grongolian nationality and becoming K'Barthan citizens." He let go of Ruth's hand, took the box from his pocket and opened the lid. He took a deep breath and the Architraves helped him out with a dash of The Voice as he added, "I know I can rely on you to make them welcome. No-one will harm anyone. There has been enough bloodshed. The killing ends. Now. This is going to take a bit of time. There is a lot of stuff to fix: wrongs to be righted and more importantly if we're going to move on, some wrongs are going to have to be forgotten. It's going to be hard. But if we pull together and look after each other, we can rebuild K'Barth."

More cheering, so loud that The Pan's ears began to sing and one of his predecessors asked him, politely, if he minded closing the lid of the box to shut out the noise.

"I can't promise you Utopia," he told the crowd as the cheering died down, "but if you're willing to help me, I'm prepared to give it my best shot." He slipped the box back into his pocket and hugged his arm round Ruth. The tannoy system crackled as with his other hand, still clutching the microphone, he gestured for silence.

"Alright, that's the pep talk over," he told them when they were quiet again. "I have to go get installed, now, and married and then, I don't know about you lot, but what about a party? And Monday off."

More cheering, jumping up and down, throwing of hats in the air and even, in some instances, the throwing in the air of smaller K'Barthans by the larger ones. The Pan and Ruth both waved and then he turned towards her, pulling her closer, and she put her arms around his neck, and kissed him. The crowd roared but wrapped up in the moment, and each other, The Pan and Ruth hardly heard it. Unwillingly, he broke off and turned to Sir Robin.

"I—Maybe you'd like to take it from here," he said.

"Of course my boy!" The Pan handed him the microphone. Sir Robin turned to face the sea of cheering K'Barthans, and began a crowd-pleasingly meandering anecdote, of the sort that seems to come naturally to the practised public speaker. Arm in arm, The Pan and Ruth slipped gratefully away, following the rest of their friends back inside.

The End

(Or, perhaps, the beginning.)

Other Books by M T McGuire

Escape From B-Movie Hell

If you asked Andi Turbot whether she had anything in common with Flash Gordon she'd say no, emphatically. Saving the world is for dynamic, go-ahead, leaders of men and while it would be nice to see a woman getting involved for a change, she believes she could be the least well-equipped being in her galaxy for the job.

Then her best friend, Eric, reveals that he is an extraterrestrial. He's not just any ET either. He's Gamalian: seven-foot, lobster-shaped and covered in Marmite-scented goo. Just when Andi's getting used to that he tells her about the Apocalypse and really ruins her day.

The human race will perish unless Eric's Gamalian superiors step in. Abducted and trapped on an alien ship, Andi must convince the Gamalians her world is worth saving. Or escape from their clutches and save it herself.

K'Barthan Extras Series: Hamgeean Misfit

Remember how The Pan had been working for Big Merv for a year, before torching his flats in The Planes? Well, the K'Barthan Extras Series of four stories (so far) describes his adventures during that time. There will be more K'Barthan Extras, coming soon, both about The Pan and other characters.

When trouble comes knocking, be out.

Outlawed and alone, The Pan of Hamgee's only real ambition is to live a normal life, unnoticed by the authorities. With this aim in mind, he travels to the city in the hope of getting lost in the crowds.

Surviving hand-to-mouth, he meets a selection of colourful characters in his quest for quiet anonymity. But when his very existence is treason trouble is never far away. Especially when the only paid work he can find is delivering messages for Big Merv, one of the scariest gangsters around.

Author News

Never miss a new release again! Sign up for M T Mail. Just visit this link: https://www.hamgee.co.uk/freebook

You will receive a handful of introductory emails, then you can choose to hear about everything or just new releases. You can also keep up to date with all things M T McGuire by joining her K'Barthan Jolly Japery Facebook Group.

To join, go here: https://bit.ly/JollyJapes

Alternatively, you can follow M T McGuire on these social media:

Website: https://www.hamgee.co.uk
Blog: https://www.mtmcguire.co.uk
Facebook: https://www.facebook.com/HamgeeUniversityPress
Instagram: @mtmcguire
Goodreads: https://www.goodreads.com/author/show/8382246

BV - #0115 - 130524 - C0 - 210/148/24 - PB - 9781907809224 - Matt Lamination